Paul Peppergrass

Mary Lee

The Yankee In Ireland

Paul Peppergrass

Mary Lee
The Yankee In Ireland

ISBN/EAN: 9783741131417

Manufactured in Europe, USA, Canada, Australia, Japa

Cover: Foto ©Andreas Hilbeck / pixelio.de

Manufactured and distributed by brebook publishing software
(www.brebook.com)

Paul Peppergrass

Mary Lee

MARY LEE,

OR

THE YANKEE IN IRELAND.

PAUL PEPPERGRASS, Esq.,

AUTHOR OF "SHANDY M'GUIRE," ETC.

With Illustrations by Harley.

BALTIMORE:

KELLY, HEDIAN & PIET, PUBLISHERS,

174 BALTIMORE STREET.

BOSTON—P. DONAHOE.

1860.

TO THE PUBLIC.

Dear Public:

Once more come we, knocking at your door, to beg the crumbs of your charity.

Twice before, indeed, have you taken us in, and twice, going out, have our grateful tears besprinkled the flags of your threshold. But then it was our own cause we pleaded; now we plead the cause of another; we bring to your arms a desolate orphan, not three days old, and without a relative in the world. Its dying parent bequeathed it to you, in the strong hope, that slender as its claim was on your sympathy, you would not have the heart to reject it. After the many favors we ourselves have received at your hands, it would be indelicate in us to do more than submit the case without word or comment to your benevolent consideration. The following letters will best explain the melancholy circumstances which brought the little adventurer to employ so poor an advocate, and one, alas! in every respect, so unworthy the sacred trust.

Your grateful servant,

P. Peppergrass.

Dear Paul:

After many weary voyages by land and sea, here I am laid up. Here I am, stretched on a straw pallet in Gooseberry Lane, with my last dollar in my pocket, and my old leather bag under my pillow. O Paul, my faithful college chum, what a desperate effort I made to reach you! Somehow I always fancied, if I could only have another

sight of your honest, "sonsie" face, and the promise of a quiet little
corner in your family grave lot, I should die the happier. Besides, as
I never belonged to any one in particular, I felt you had a sort of
claim on my remains. But it's all over with me now, and so God's
will be done! I'm a crazy, good-for-nothing, ill-tempered creature,
any way, and the sooner I'm put out of the way of decent, useful people, the better. I suppose I needn't tell you what I'm dying of — the
rheumatism, of course: what else could it be? The villain knocked
me down twice before, you remember, and then compromised it; but
this time he has fairly got death's grip of me, and refuses, point blank,
to let me off on any terms. The priest and doctor were both here this
morning, and shook hands with me at parting. So my time, you see,
is but short. Well, at all events I'm prepared — that is, in a kind of
fashion, not so well as I ought of course, but still better than I deserve
to be, considering the Edie Ochiltree life I led since I abandoned theology and the cassock. As for the world, I forgive it for all the
shabby treatment I ever received at its hands, and upon my word,
Paul, I received my share. It's of no use, though, to carry our
grudges with us to the grave; and, indeed, even if it were, I never felt
much disposed that way. Besides, the world has sins enough to answer for, God knows, without adding the injuries it has done me to
the account. So I shake hands, and forgive it. And now, Paul,
there's one request I have to make, and for the sake of the old times,
I hope you'll not refuse it, namely: When you come here and find
me dead and gone, don't mind asking any questions, for nobody
knows me but as the lame pilgrim, who frightened the children, and
lived in a garret in Gooseberry Lane. Say nothing, but just ask the
apple woman, who lets me the room, for the black leather bag I kept
under my pillow. Put your hand down to the bottom, and draw out
"Mary Lee." It's the last of the collection, and, for aught I know to
the contrary, the best of them all. Take it home with you, brush it
up a little, and give it to some charitable publisher, if you happen to
know or hear of any such person in that part of the world. Should
the little thing bring a few dollars, buy me a modest head-stone of
gray marble and inscribe my name on the corner — Peter Pinkie —
no more. For the rest, I bequeath you all my worldly goods, to wit:
my silver snuff-box (but by the way, now that I think of it, the half of
that same belongs to you already) and my ivory-headed crab-tree staff,
both which Father Mahony (by the same token he's first cousin to
Father Prout of the Prout Papers) will deliver you on presenting this
letter. And now, dear Paul, before I bid good by, let me entreat
you to say a few prayers for me, once and again, when you have leisure — for alas! alas! I need them sadly. Say them quietly, just as

we used to say them together long ago at the Virgin altar in the college chapel, and say them away by yourself in some lonely corner of the church, where the shadow falls deepest. God be with you, Paul.

Yours as ever,   P. PINKIE.

On reaching New Orleans we hastened with all possible speed to Gooseberry Lane, hoping to find our venerable friend still alive; but alas! we came too late. Early that morning the remains of a stranger whom nobody knew, but who went by the name of Peter Pinkie, were carried out to their final resting place, and deposited in a shady little corner of the Catholic cemetery. Intending to visit the grave next day, and leave directions for the head-stone of gray marble, we took occasion in the interval to call on the Rev. Mr. Mahony, and after tendering our most grateful thanks for his kindness to our dear old friend and fellow-student, received from his venerable hands the silver snuff-box, the crab-tree staff, and the following letter of explanation, written apparently but a few hours before his death.

P. P.

DEAR PAUL:

I have some remarks to make about "Mary Lee," and can't compose myself to die happy without making them. So I just swallowed an anodyne, and had the apple woman fix up the foot-board for a writing desk.

I know well when you read the opening paragraph you'll shrug up your shoulders in the old way, and pitch the manuscript across the table to your friend Dr. Grippinlip, with a "Psaugh! nonsense! what does the silly fellow mean by such an introduction as that?" But think what you please, Paul; I can't help it. It was always my way, you know, to go straight to the point; or, as our first Latin master, Terence Hardiman, used to say, to dive *in medias res* plump as a pearl fisher! I wouldn't think of Terry now either, I suspect, only the silver snuff-box he left us is here before me on the foot-board, and the curly-headed cobbler on the lid is looking straight in my face. But independently of that, my early memories crowd on me now faster and clearer than ever. Sometimes I catch myself thinking of old Sangrado at the college, and old Etty at the infirmary coming in coughing every morning, with her pharmacopœia under her arm. And what do you think? I was dreaming all last night about the rush crosses we used

1*

to weave at Michaelmas, and the segging boats we sailed in partner-
ship on the round pond before my father's door. They looked to me
just as green and natural as the leaves I saw yesterday. I don't know
how it happens, but my thoughts are ever stumbling over old times
and old places; do what I will, I can't control them. I half suspect
it's the usual sign of death — the parting look which the spirit casts
back on the opening scenes of its young and joyous life, ere it sinks
and is swallowed up forever in the source of its being — just like the
setting sun taking his farewell look of earth — the last one, the bright-
est and fondest of all. But I fear I'm digressing.

I was going to observe that if you expected me to write a preface to
" Mary Lee " according to the ordinary standards made and provided,
you will be entirely disappointed; for I may as well tell you, first as
last, that I cherish a most inveterate horror for the whole *prologomena*
family — prefaces, prologues, introductions, and explanations; and this,
I feel in duty bound to tell you before I proceed a step farther, has
ever been my unfortunate weakness since I went to study theology,
five and twenty years ago, at Louvain, under the celebrated Father Brenengo. *He* was the most tedious man in coming to a point that ever
shaped a syllogism. He often spent two mortal hours laying down
the state of the question, and found himself then just as far from the
difficulty as ever. Every thing having the slightest fibre of connection
with the subject was drawn in to complicate it. No chancery lawyer
could hold a candle to him in that respect. Old as I am now, Paul,
and near as I creep to the grave, the sound of that man's voice rings as
distinctly in my ear as when I last sat listening to it in Louvain. I
never catch the noise of a spinning wheel, or a moth ticking in the
bed-post, but I hear Father Brenengo as plainly as ever. He never
tired; there was nothing of him to tire but bone and sinew, and very
little of that to spare either; but what did remain was brought by a
practice of forty years to work like machinery. Talking was no
trouble to him — the words rolled out from his thin lips like sounds
from an automaton mandarin. On the occasion, however, to which I
would particularly refer, the question before the class was the Sacrifice
of Abraham, and the difficulty as usual in the Thomistic distinction of
the divine wills. Never did man speak as he spoke that day, laying
down his preliminaries, and yet never venturing within sight of the
question at issue. The class fell asleep, but, *parum refert*, on he drove
through it, shrugging his shoulders till you could almost hear the fric-
tion of the bones, and rapping the desk all the while with his terrible
knuckles. For the first hour I bore it with patience; an hour and a
half passed, and still, though my nerves were considerably excited, I

managed to control them sufficiently to sit quiet. At last, however, I was overpowered by a sort of delirium; my head grew dizzy, my breath came thick and short, like one after a long race, and yelling like a maniac, I sprang at one bound across the desk, and hurled a quarto volume of Bellarmine at the lecturer's venerable head. "Hold him!" I cried; "hold him! stop him or he'll kill me, he'll murder me!" His squeaking voice acting like a rasp on my nerves, hour after hour, drove me, in fact, to desperation. Heaven forgive me, Paul, I could have cloven him that instant to the brisket. One of my classmates laid hold of my collar to drag me back, but I flung him from me as I would an infant, and rushing from the hall, fled down the corridor, my long hair floating back on my collar, and my eyes leaping from their sockets in my eagerness to escape. That act of mine, dear Paul, sealed my fate forever. In the evening the physician called at my room, and politely ordered me three tumblers of valerian to settle my nerves; next day the dean handed me forty dollars to pay my travelling expenses to Buncrana, and a letter of explanation to my worthy bishop; and in two hours after, just as the bells of the city rang out the Angelus, I bid adieu to Louvain, Father Brenengo, and theology forever. Since that unfortunate day, it's needless to tell you, I regard every thing in the shape of introductions with indescribable horror. And where's the wonder? Have they not, at one blow, annihilated all my cherished hopes, stripped me of stole and cassock, driven me out a wanderer on the face of the earth, and consigned me at last to isolation, snuff-taking, poverty, and a garret?

Here the manuscript grows so shaky, owing, no doubt, to the increasing violence of the rheumatism, as to be entirely illegible. It is generally supposed, however, by his friends in Ireland most familiar with his handwriting, that the closing sentences were meant for a humble apology to the public for having ever presumed to occupy a moment of its valuable time, and especially for the many faults and anachronisms in Mary Lee.

The following note was found, some days after the editor's departure, in a corner of the old black bag, and carefully forwarded to his address by the apple woman above mentioned. In her very remarkable epistle enclosing the relic, she candidly admits never having imagined for one moment that the "bit o' ritin" could be of any earthly use to any body, and as for his "spirit" coming back in search of it, she hadn't the least fear of that in the world; for the truth was, she didn't believe in ghosts herself, nor one belonging to her; but still every body had a right to their own, and besides, Mr. Pinkie being the strange kind of man he was, she didn't fancy much retaining any part of his property in her possession, and would just sleep as sound, perhaps, after clearing her skirts of him, bag and baggage. The note ran as follows:—

POSTSCRIPT.

As my time draws near, I begin to feel more and more uneasy about the spot where the strangers will lay my remains. Of course you'll laugh at me for this, Paul, and no wonder either, for upon my word I never once thought I should feel so particular about it. But it's only another proof, I suppose, that the poor body must always be our greatest trouble even to the very last. And so I made some inquiries about the burial ground this morning of Father Mahony's clerk. His description, I assure you, is by no means satisfactory. He tells me there's not an ivy wall, nor a mouldering ruin, nor an old hawthorn, nor in fact any other shred of Christianity, to be seen in the place — what's more, there's not a fern to shelter a grave, and even the grass of the field is as wiry and sparse as the hair on my head. By all accounts, dear Paul, it's a very uncomfortable and "unchristianable" place to be buried, and so I would take it as a great personal favor, and one I'll not forget in the land I'm going to, if you could just manage in some way to take my bones home with you to your own quiet lot, or, what would please me a thousand times better, send them back to Ireland again by the first trusty Innishowen man you hear of returning to Buncrana. But do as you will, bring them or send them; I bequeath them to you.   P. P.

CONTENTS.

CHAPTER XX.

CHAPTER XXI.

CHAPTER XXII.

CHAPTER XXIII.

CHAPTER XXIV.

CHAPTER XXV.

CHAPTER XXVI.

CHAPTER XXVII.

CHAPTER XXVIII.

CHAPTER XXIX.

MARY LEE.

CHAPTER I.

Introductory.

DEAR reader, have the goodness to run your finger down the map of Ireland to its northernmost point, or, if that be inconvenient, let your imagination run down without it to the easternmost promontory of the County Donegal; you shall then have transported yourself without trouble or expense, and in a manner suitable enough for our purpose, to the spot where our story commences.

It may happen, however, in this rambling age, that one day or other you would grow tired of travelling by the map and hand-book, and make up your mind to quit the fireside and see the world for yourself — preferring your own eyes to your neighbors' spectacles. After a long tour through Europe you may yet, some fine evening in August or September, find yourself standing on the pier of Leith or Dunbarton heights, looking across the channel, and wishing you were in Ireland. Don't resist the temptation, we pray thee, but leaving your national prejudices behind you with your Scotch landlord, book yourself for Dublin, in the first packet, and with a good conscience and an honest heart take a trip over the water, and visit, were it only for a week, the land of poverty, gallantry, and song.

If, however, you happen to be one of those very respectable young gentlemen who go over to make pictures of Irish-life, with the view of being stared at and lionized in village drawing rooms on their return — one of those extremely talented and promising young men, who voyage in crowds every year, for a supply of Irish barbarisms and Romish superstitions, — if you happen, we say, to be of that class, let us remind you, dear reader, that the Mull of Cantyre is a dangerous sea, worse by all odds than the Bay of Biscay. Don't venture through it by any means, but like a prudent young man, finish your tour with Ben-Lomond and the Trossachs, and return home to the States with as little delay as possible. As for the Irish peculiarities you would go in quest of, they are now very scarce and difficult to procure — we mean fresh ones, of course, for the old sets are bruised so much in the handling as to be entirely valueless; even the manufacturers of the article, who made so jolly a living on the simplicity of. stripling· tourists twenty years ago, are no longer in existence. They have passed away as an effete race, and are now dead, gone, and forgotten. Pictures of Irish life are indeed very difficult to dispose of, at present, either to the pulpit, the Sunday newspapers, or even the Foreign Benevolent Societies; unless they happen to be drawn by master hands. Such pictures, for instance, as the " Priest and the Bottle," the " Fiddler and the Beggars," the " Confessor and the Nun," have lost all point, since Mr. Thackeray's visit to that country, and are now grown as stale and flat as small beer drippings off a pot-house counter. Twenty years ago, however, the case was very different. An Irishman then, in certain sections of the United States, was as great a wonder as a Bengal tiger, or an Abyssinian elephant; and he felt so far below the ordinary standard of humanity in those days, as to be considered unaccountable to human laws. We have ourselves been assured on most excellent authority, that certain ladies of Maine, even within the time mentioned, actually went as a delegation to an unfortunate Irishman, who strayed into their neighborhood, and set about manipulating his head all over, in order to ascertain, by personal inspection, whether his horns grew on the fore or hind part of his cranium. The manner of their reception, by the courteous and gallant barbarian, is still related by some of the actors in the little melo-drama, and though quite characteristic of his race, would hardly be accounted edifying in this simple narrative. This much, however, we may venture to affirm, that since the event took place, there has been but one opinion on the subject in that locality — that the Irish wear no horns of any description whatever, either behind or before — are endowed with the ordinary feelings and senses peculiar to the human family — and exhibit arms and legs, hands and hair, precisely like their Norman and Anglo-Saxon neighbors.

But whilst they assimilate thus in all their physical developments, there are still certain national peculiarities, which distinguish them from the people of all other nations. In the first place, the *brogue* is very peculiar. It differs from that of the Scotch Highlander, the Vermonter, and the German in what is called intensity of accentuation — and it is very remarkable that this peculiar intensity of accentuation is most striking when they speak on subjects in any way connected with religion — the broad sound of the vowels, which they have still retained since their old classic days, exhibiting a striking contrast with the reformed method of pronunciation. The collocation of their words, too, sounding so strange to unclassic ears, (though admirable in the Italian and French,) contributes perhaps in some degree to aggravate the barbarism. But we must not venture on details, or we should never have done; suffice it to say, that according to all accounts, and particularly the accounts of American tourists, the Irish are, one and all, the strangest people on the face of the earth. They never do any thing, we are told, like other people. Whatever they put their hands to, from peeling a potato to shooting a landlord, they have their own peculiar way of doing it. Whether they eat or drink, walk or sleep, tie their shoes or pick their teeth, they are noted for their wonderful originality. And it is not the people only, but, strange to say,

2 *

the very cows and horses in that remarkable country, bellow and neigh quite differently from those of other nations — the tone and style being quite unique, or, in other words, "peculiarly Irish." It's but a few weeks ago since a certain Mr. Gustavus Theodore Simpkings, of Boston, returned from Ireland with the startling discovery that hens laid their eggs there in a manner quite different from that adopted by the hens of other countries. We may be allowed also to add, by way of appendix to the fact, that in consequence of the important nature of the discovery, a board of commissioners will shortly be sent over to investigate the matter, in order that the poultry fanciers of New England may take measures accordingly to promote the interests of their excellent associations. Whether the country at large, however, will approve this new method is still a disputed question. Our own opinion is, the New Englanders will reject it, not solely because it's Irish, though that indeed would seem reason sufficient, but rather on account of the danger of propagating Popery in that peculiar way. We have heard of "treason" eggs, (Mr. O'Connell and Marcus Costello were arrested over two pair of them in Horne's Coffee Room, Dublin, five and twenty years ago avowing their guilt,) and if treason could be propagated in that fashion, we ask, why not Popery?

Now, after all this nicety to which certain things are carried, simply because they are Irish, it is quite needless to say that the national peculiarities of that people are all but exhausted, and consequently the young tourist fresh from the counting-room can expect little there to requite him for the fatigue and expense of such a journey.

But, dear reader mine, if your heart be in the right place and above the reach of paltry prejudice, if you be man enough to think for yourself, and instead of viewing Ireland in print-shop and pantomime, look at her face to face with your own honest eyes, — if you be determined to see things in their true colors and to avoid the vulgar blunder of mistaking the

Irish *brogue* for inveterate barbarism, and gold watch chains for genuine civilization — if you be one of that stamp — then in Heaven's name step aboard as soon as possible, for a crime it would be against your conscience to turn back within sight of the green old Isle where Moore and Griffin "wept and sang."

Once there, pass not hurriedly over it, for every inch is classic ground. Not a mountain or valley from Cape Clear to the Giant's Causeway but has its old tradition. If you ever read Banim or Morgan, Callinan or Griffin, ask the guide at your elbow to point out, as you ride along, the scenes they describe and the monuments they chronicle. If you ever listened to the songs of Moore, and felt the sadness they inspire, stop for a moment and gaze on the venerable ruins to which they are consecrated, and they will seem to you more sad and plaintive than ever. You may not weep over those mouldering walls and ruined shrines, like the returning exile revisiting once more the haunts of his boyhood, but still, stranger as you are, the very sight of them will do you good; the tottering tower, and the crumbling wall, and the holy well, and the broken cross, will bring you salutary reflections — will teach you that every country, to deserve a place in the record of nations, must have a past, and that, flourishing as the republic of Washington is now, its whole history up to this hour would hardly cover a single page in the future annals of the world.

But, dear reader, whenever you ramble through the old place, forget not to visit the scene of our story. It may not be so grand as the Alleghanies, nor so picturesque as the Hudson; but it will repay you well, nevertheless, for your trouble. Moreover, it lies directly in your way from the mountains of the west to the famous Giant's Causeway — a wild, solitary spot to the east of those blue hills that shelter the fertile valleys of Donegal from the storms of the Northern Ocean.

CHAPTER II.

Is in a slight Degree illustrative of Incidents in Irish Life.

THE country between Fanit or Araheera lighthouse and
the village of Rathmullen, on the Lough Swilly, is an extremely
wild and mountainous district, being indeed little more than a
succession of hills rising one above the other, and terminating
at last in the bald and towering scalp of Benraven. Standing
on this elevated spot, the traveller has a full view of the
country for a distance of some twenty miles around. Beyond
Araheera Point appears Malin Head, the northern extremity
of the far-famed barony of Innishowen, running far out into
the ocean, and heaving back the billows in white foam, as
they break against his dark and sulky form. Westward
looms up the majestic brow of Horn Head, under whose
frown a thousand vessels have perished, and close by its side
the famous opening in the rock called McSwine's Gun, thun-
dering like the roar of a hundred cannon when the storm
comes in from the west. Between these two landmarks,
standing out there like huge sentinels guarding the coast,
stretches the long white shore called Ballyhernam Strand,
and between that and Benraven, the beautiful quiet little sea
of Mulroy, with its countless islets lying under the long, deep
shadows of the mountains. Close by the broad base of the
latter — so close indeed that you can hurl a stone from the top
into the water below — is the calm, quiet lake called Lough
Ely, so celebrated for its silvery char and golden trout. As
the traveller looks down from the summit of Benraven, there
is hardly a sign of human habitation to be seen below, if, indeed, we except the lighthouse itself, whose white tower rises
just visible over the heads of the lessening hills. But when
he begins to descend and pursue his way along the manor

road, winding as it runs through the dark and deep recesses of the mountains, many a comfortable little homestead suddenly meets his view, and many a green meadow and wavy cornfield helps to relieve the barren and desolate character of the surrounding scene.

It was a fine evening in June, 185–; the sheep after browsing all day long, were lying on the green, sunny slopes of the glens, and the hoodie crows, after their rambling flight, sat dozing here and there on huge rocks by the road side, which the winter torrents had detached from the mountains, when a man might be seen wending his way slowly down the road towards Araheera lighthouse. He wore a short jacket and trousers, somewhat sailor fashion, and kept his hands thrust into his side pockets as he jogged along, whistling and singing by turns to keep himself company. Still, though he looked at first not unlike a seafaring man, there was that in his gait and general deportment which smacked too strongly of the hill side, to mistake him for one accustomed to walk the deck of a ship, or even to ply the oar in search of a livelihood. Moreover, he wore a rabbit skin cap jantily set on the side of his head, and carried a stout blackthorn under his arm — both which indicated clearly enough, that his habits of life were more landward grown than his dress and near proximity to the sea might have at first suggested. But whatever might have been his occupation in general, he appeared to have little to engage him this evening, in particular, for he loitered long on his way, seemingly quite disposed to take the world easy, and break no bones in his hurry to accomplish his journey. More than once did he stop to clap his hands and gaze after a hare startled from her form by his noisy approach, or fling a stone at a hoodie crow dozing on the rocks. In this careless manner he jogged along whistling and singing as the humor touched him. At first the words of his song were confused by the echoes of the glens, but grew more distinct and intelligible as he descended nearer to the shore, till at length the following verse of a very popular ditty rang out clear and strong upon the ear : —

> "Och ! the Sassanach villains — de'il tare them ! —
> They stripped us as bare as the ' poles ; '
> But there's one thing we just couldn't spare them —
> The ' *Kidug* ' that covers our souls.
>> Right folderolol, la la, di di,
>> Right fala la, lee," &c., &c.

He sang this verse at least half a dozen times, at different intervals, and had just commenced to sing it once more, when all of a sudden the song and the singer came both to a full stop. Had a highwayman leaped from a hedge and held a pistol to the traveller's head, he could not have halted more abruptly. In an instant he stood still, gazing at something he saw round the angle of the road, and then buttoning his jacket and clutching his blackthorn, made a step forward in a belligerent attitude, as if an unlooked-for enemy had appeared and offered him battle. And so it was. The antagonist he so suddenly encountered had taken his' position in the very middle of the road, and by his motions seemed resolved to maintain that position at every hazard. The traveller, on the other hand, was by no means slow to commence hostilities ; for twirling his staff, without further parley he struck his adversary such a blow on the sconce as might have been heard ringing sharp and hard for half a mile and more along the echoing glen. That blow, however, was his first and last ; for the next instant he lay sprawling in the dust, struck down by the superior force of his enemy's weapon. Still, though prostrate, he parried off the blows of his assailant with remarkable adroitness, and would, in all likelihood, have soon risen and fully avenged his fall, had not a third party interfered to terminate the battle. The latter, roughly seizing the staff from behind, commanded the fallen man to forbear, and then, in a milder and more friendly voice, bade him get up on his feet, and not lie there, like a *partaun*.

CHAPTER III.

Mr. Weeks tries his Hand at Fly-fishing, but finds the Sport rather below his Expectations. — Lanty Hanlon looks on, and indulges in most indignant Criticisms on Mr. Weeks's Manner of playing the Fish.

"Get up, Lanty," said the new comer, "get up, man. Why, you must be ravin mad to strike the poor witless crathur that way. Sure, it's only ould Nannie. Get up, man!"

"Nannie, or grannie!" ejaculated Lanty, — for so it seems the traveller was named, — "Nannie or grannie," he cried, turning short and shaking himself free of the speaker, "she's an ould limb o' Satan, — 'the curse o' Cromwell on her!'"

"Pooh! nonsense man! never mind her; it's only a way she has."

"A way she has! b'edad, thin it's a very oncivil way she has; let me tell you that. The villanous ould schamer can't let any body pass without a quarrel. There's that Methody preacher, she pounded almost to death last week, — one o' the civilest sowls in the whole parish. What kind a thratement is that, I'd like to know, for any dacent man to get; or is it neighborly in you, Else Curley, to keep such a baste of a goat about yer place to murther people without rhyme or raisin?"

"Musha thin, how can I help her, Lanty?"

"Kill her if ye can't — hang her — shoot her — drown her — bad luck to her, she ought to be shot long ago."

"Och, as for that, she'll soon die, any way. It's failing fast she is, poor thing."

"Die!" repeated Lanty, brushing the dust off his clothes "die! she'll niver die, and it's a mystery to me if iver she came into the world right at all."

"Arrah, whist with yer nonsense," exclaimed Else, "and don't talk such foolishness. Come away up to the house here, and take a draw iv the pipe if you don't take any thing better."

"I'll tell you what it is, Else Curley," continued the discomfited Lanty; "there's not a man or woman in the townland of Crowres but knows that my father was chased by that same goat — that very identical ould rascal there, the year before he was married, and that's jist thirty good years ago, and more by the same token, he bears the marks of her horns on a part of his body to this day; and it's no great secret either, Else, that she was every bit as ould then as she's now. It's not even'n any thing bad to ye I am, Else, but one thing is sartin as the sun's in the sky — that goat don't belong to this world."

The old woman looked sharp at her companion, as if to read in his countenance his real thoughts on a subject that concerned her so nearly, and about which she lately heard so many unpleasant surmises, but she could gather nothing from his looks. She saw he was excited by the fall, but she knew him also to be one of the slyest rogues that ever put on a sober face — as full of deviltry as an egg was full of meat; and she doubted, therefore, whether he meant to plague or offend her.

"Lanty Hanlon," said she at last, "I don't know whether you spoke that word in joke or in earnest; if ye spoke in joke I forgive ye, knowing well what ye are, and yer father afore ye; but if ye spoke in earnest, I tell ye niver to say the word again in my hearin', for if ye do, by the blessed Cairn above there, I'll be revenged for it, dead or alive."

"Pheugh!" exclaimed Lanty, when the old woman had finished, "by the powers o' war, but you'd frighten a body out o' their wits this evening! What's the matter, woman? or are you so easy vexed as that with an ould friend?" and he shook her familiarly by the arm as he spoke, and pushed her on towards the cabin to which she had just invited him.

"If you want to quarrel with me, Else," he continued, "you must take another day for it, as at present I'm engaged on particular business. So up with you to the house there, and bring me out a coal to light my pipe."

Though Lanty spoke in banter, there was still something in the expression of his face and tone of his voice that indicated misgivings of Else Curley after such a show of indignation. Not that he suspected her, for a moment, of any secret connection with the nether world, nor of keeping "Nannie" for any unholy purpose; but nevertheless he was accustomed to hear strange reports about her, ever since he remembered to hear any thing, and was taught to regard her as a woman above the common, and one whose anger was to be propitiated at any sacrifice. Hence, if Lanty had his doubts of Else, they were doubts rather of the woman than of her acts, of her capacity to work mischief rather than of her actual guilt. In a word, he never heard or saw aught of her but what was right and proper, and yet somehow he always fancied she was "uncanny," and could be dangerous if she pleased. Perhaps the sharp, thin features and large gray eyes of the tall, shrivelled old creature, as she gazed steadily into Lanty's face, helped at that moment to aggravate his suspicions. But be that as it may, he lost no time in trying to conciliate her, and his experience had already taught him, that his usual rollicking familiarity of manner would accomplish that end more effectually than any formal apology he could offer.

The house or cabin to which Lanty and his companion now directed their steps (Nannie still following her mistress at a respectful distance) was built on the southern side of a little green hill, called the "Cairn," named after a pile of stones upon its summit, which tradition says were thrown there to mark the spot where a priest had been murdered in the troublous times of Cromwell or Elizabeth.

From the top of this hill, which rises only a few rods above

3

the roof of the cabin, a full view is had of the lighthouse, and Lough Ely from its eastern to its western extremity. The lake, in fact, at one of its bends touches the base of the hill, and thence stretches to the lighthouse, a distance of little more than half a mile.

"And now, Else, avourneen," began Lanty, taking his seat on a flag outside the cabin door, (for the evening was warm,) "now that we settled that little difference, how is Batt himself, and how does the world use him?"

"Well, indeed then, we can't complain much as times go," responded Else, drawing her stocking from her pocket, and beginning to knit in her usual slow, quiet way; for she was old, and her hands trembled as she plied the needles. "As for Batt, poor ould man, he's idle the most of his time, and barrin that he goes down to the shore there of an evenin to ketch a trout or so for the supper, it's little else he has to throuble him."

"Still he gets an odd call now and then, I'll warrant," observed Lanty, knocking the ashes from his pipe, and preparing to replenish it with fresh tobacco. "A man like Batt Curley can't want a job long if there's any goin."

"O, he gets his share, to be sure; but where's the benefit o' that, when there's nothing to be made by it?"

"Well, he makes a trifle over the price o' the tibakky and the dram any way; and what more does he want? Fiddlin's now not what it used to be in ould times, Else."

"Indeed, thin, you may well say that," she replied, "when half a crown a weddin's the highest he made this twelve-month. The Lord luck down on us, I don'na how poor people can stan it at that rate."

"It's mighty hard," assented Lanty, handing the old woman the pipe, after wiping it on the breast of his jacket. "I mind the time myself when we cudn't shake a fut at a weddin short of a shillin apiece to the fiddler. But sure the people's hearts is broke out and out, Else — why, they haven't the courage to dance, even if they had the mains."

"It's not that, Lanty, acushla! it's not that, but their hearts is gone out in thim althegither. They're not the same people they used to be at all at all. Nothin shutes thim now sure but waltzin and pokin, and sailin over the flure like so many childer playin cutche-cutchoo, and with no more spirit in thim than so many puppets at a show."

"Bedad, it's no wondher you say it, Else — it's disgraceful, so it is."

"Disgraceful! No; but it's a scandal to the country, that's what it is. There's big Jamie's daughter, of Drumfad, that was married last Thursday; and lo, and behould ye, sir, when young Tom Connolly asked her out, she cudn't venture on a reel or a country dance at all at all; O, no, no more than if she was born in the skies; let alone at the hip of Graffey Mountain."

"Musha, bad luck to her impudince," exclaimed Lanty; "isn't she cockin? and her aunt beggin her bit and sup through the parish."

"Feen a word o' lie in it thin. She turned up her nose at the Foxhunter's Jig and the Rosses Batther, just as if she niver heard iv the like in her born life — and nothin would do her, savin yer favor, but go skatin over the room like a doll on stilts. Faith, it's well come up with the pack of thim."

"And as for poor Batt," observed Lanty, "sich tunes are too new-fangled for his ould fingers. He couldn't plaze her av course; O, no, he's too ould-fashioned for that."

"Plaze her! Ay indeed; after dancing in Derry City with her grand cousins, the manti-makers. Plaze her! No, Pegeliny himself, the great Dublin fiddler, couldn't plaze her. But it's the same all over the country; a man can't show a jug and glass in his windy nowadays, but his girls take airs on thimsilves aqual to my Lady Leitrem — all merchants daughters, if you plaze;" and Else laughed a dry, hard laugh, and gave the leg of her stocking another hitch under her arm.

As she was yet speaking, a stranger passed down the road

carrying a fishing rod in his hand, and stepping over a low fence, made his way slowly to a narrow tongue of land that stretched far out into Lough Elg, a spot much frequented by anglers, and particularly at that season of the year. He was a man apparently about thirty years of age, and wore a gray sporting frock, with cap and gaiters to match.

"That's the strange gentleman," said Else, "that comes down here from Crohan to fish so often."

"I saw him before," replied Lanty; "and bedad, if he knows as little about the gentleman as he does about the fisherman he's no great affair. I came across him yesterday at Kindrum, and he cast his line, for all the world, like a smith swinging a sledge hammer. Who is he?"

"Indeed, thin, myself doesn't know, Lanty; but I'm tould he's come here from furrin parts for the good of his health, and is some far out friend to the Hardwrinkles of Crohan."

"I wouldn't doubt it in the laste, for he's thin and sneaky, like the rest of the breed. Still he may be a dacent man, after all that."

"He's a quate, easy-spoken man, any way, whativer else he is."

"And plenty o' money to spend, I'll bail ye."

"In troth has he, and not a miser about it aither, Lanty."

"Humph! I see you're acquent."

"Och! ay, he draps in here sometimes when he comes a fishin."

"And opens his purse when he goes out, eh, Else?"

"O, thin, dear knows the gentleman id be welkim if he niver had a purse," replied Else. "It's not for that, but the quate, mothcrate way he has. He comes in just like a child, and looks as modest as a lady, and sits there chattin ithout a bit pride in him more nor one of oursels."

"Now d'ye tell me so? He's fond of a *shanahas*, I see, furriner and all as he is."

"Indeed, thin he's jist that same, Lanty; he's mighty fond

intirely of say stories, and likes to hear tell of the ' Saldann,' how she was wracked here below, and the crew, how they were all buried in one grave in the ould churchyard in Ramulla, and about Captain ·Pecnam's ghost, that used to be seen on moonlight nights dressed all in white with a goolden sword by his side sittin on the Swilly Rock. And thin he'll be sure to ask me something about Mr. Lee and his niece, and who they are, and how they came here, and how long since, and so on, and so on, till I'm a most tired of him myself sometimes."

" Humph ! Tired !" repeated Lanty; " bedad, thin he must run you mighty hard, Else, for may I niver ——— "

" Hould yer whist now," interrupted the old woman; " I don't want any iv yer side wipes;" and she pushed him playfully away with her thin, skeleton hand.

" Sure I didn't mane the laste offence in life," muttered Lanty, leering round at his companion, and taking a smack from the pipe loud enough to be heard at the road below; " no, but I was only jist saying that if the gentleman tired you out talkin, why, he ought to be proud iv it, for after talkin six covenanter ministers, besides a dancin master and two tailors, out iv yer house ——— "

" Hould yer tongue now, I tell ye," exclaimed Else; " hould yer tongue, or I'll slap ye in the face. Y'er niver aisy but whin yer at some divilmint. So, as I was tellin ye, he wanted to know all about the light-keeper here and his niece, and the wrack of the Saldana, though, bedad, he seems to know himself more about it nor me. Why sure, Lanty, he tells me that Mr. Lee had a brother, or cousin, or some very near frind lost in that same ship, for he niver was heerd tell of, livin or dead, since the vessel sailed from Bristol; and more nor that, Lanty, he was a high up officer, if you plaze, and a fine darin bould gentleman to boot."

" Ha! see that now ! Bedad, and it's only what I always thought myself of the same Mr. Lee, since the first day I laid my eyes on him ; for he has the look of a gentleman in his

3 *

very face, even if he *is* only a light-keeper; and what's better nor all that, Else Curley, he has the feelins of a gentleman in his heart."

"Ha, ha — look!" exclaimed Else, laying one hand suddenly on Lanty's shoulder, and pointing with the stocking in the other to the angler below; "ha, ha — he's in a mighty pucker, poor man."

"O, the bungler, the bungler!" exclaimed Lanty; "he's got his hooks tangled in the weeds at the very first cast; look how he pulls! Why, it's a sin and a shame to let him use such beautiful tackling in that lubberly way. But whist! see! by the powers iv pewter, it's a trout he has, and a three pounder into the bargain — there he jumps like a salmon! O, meel-a-murther! did iver mortal man see the like! He'll smash every thing — bad scran to him, the omedhawn, why don't he give the fish fair play — he pulls, for all the world, as if he'd a grampus on a jack line;" and the speaker grew so indignant that he threatened to run down and snatch the rod from the stranger's hands; but Else Curley counselled him to "take it aisy, and interfere in nobody's business till he was asked; if the trout breaks the man's gear," she added, "he has money enough to buy more."

By this time the fish had run out the greater part of the line, and kept backing and tugging with all its might, like a fettered partridge making a last effort to escape on the approach of the snarer. The whole strength of the trout was made to bear on the casting line; for the rod, instead of being held in a vertical position, allowing its supple point to play up and down as the fish plunged, was, on the contrary, grasped in both hands as horizontally as if he had caught a shark with a boat hook, and was actually dragging it ashore by main strength.

"The man's castin line," cried Lanty, "if he has any on at all, must be made of fiddler's catgut, or it never could stand that usage."

The trout, after thus endeavoring to shake itself free of the hook, now dived, and making a desperate sheer, ran out the line apparently to its last turn on the wheel; and Lanty felt full sure the trout had broken loose at last, and carried flies and casting line away with him into the deep. But he was mistaken; for hardly had the exhausted fish been down a moment, when he rose again, and sputtered on the surface like a wounded water hen. At this instant an object came suddenly into view which gave an entirely new feature to the scene. A little boat, carrying a small, light sprit-sail as white as snow, shot round the point, and passed within two fathoms' length of the angler before he perceived it.

"Hilloa!" cried Lanty; "there goes Mary Lee. There she is in the stern sheets, handling her cockle shell like a water spirit. And there goes Drake, too, sittin in the bows, with his cold black nose over the gunwale."

Old Else laid by her knitting and wiped her bleared eyes to look down at the scene. "Musha, thin, may I niver do harm but that's jist the darling herself, Lanty," she muttered; "there she is in her blue jacket and white straw hat, the best and gentlest girl iver sailed on Ely water."

Hardly had Else spoken, and raised up her fleshless hands to support her pointed chin, that she might gaze down more steadily on the scene below, when Drake, mistaking the sputtering fish for a wounded bird, sprang from the bows, seized it by the back before his mistress could prevent him, and then, snapping both rod and line at a single jerk, turned away from the confounded and astonished sportsman, and swam after the boat, snuffing the air and wagging his tail in an ecstasy of delight.

"Well done, Drake," cried Lanty, starting up from his seat, and clapping his hands in such glee that the pipe fell from his mouth unobserved, and broke in pieces at his feet. "Well done, ould dog! well done, my gallant ould fellow — that's it, Drake! — that's just what he deserves, the blundering gawkie, to abuse such a fish in that way."

The light breeze from the south-east had been gaining for the last half hour or so, and now blew so fresh round the point that the little boat lay down almost gunwale under, and swept past, before her fair pilot could bring her within speaking distance of the stranger. Once she tried to jam her up to windward, probably with the intention of apologizing for Drake's uncivil behavior; but the little craft refused to obey, and then, waving her hand, she let her fall off towards the opposite shore, and was soon lost sight of behind the point.

All this took place in much less time than we have taken to describe it, the boat appearing and disappearing as suddenly as a moving picture in a panorama.

The bewildered stranger gazed after the fair occupant of the little boat as long as she remained in sight, and then, peering stealthily round to see if any one had witnessed his discomfiture, disjointed the remainder of his fishing rod, and throwing it carelessly on his shoulder, walked away slowly and sadly from the shore.

"There he goes," said Lanty, buttoning his green jacket; "there he goes, sneaking off like a fox from a hen roost. O, that he may niver come back, I pray! Begorra, it's ducked he ought to be, if iver he has the assurance to cast a line in the wather again. But I must be off myself to the lighthouse, and coax Mr. Lee for a mallard wing for Uncle Jerry."

"O, ay! to be sure, Uncle Jerry! there's no one like Uncle Jerry. E' thin may be if the gentleman you're for ducking in the lough there was as free to you with his purse as Uncle Jerry, he'd just be as great a favorite, every bit. But it's an ould sayin and a true one, Lanty — Praise the fool as you find him."

"Don't say that, Else Curley," replied Lanty, laying his hand on her shoulder, and speaking more earnestly than usual, — "don't say that, for the heavens knows I wouldn't give one kind word of Uncle Jerry's lips, or one kindly feeling of his ginerous fine ould heart, for a million like him. And listen to me, Else Curley, for I'm going to tell ye a secret. I know that man off an on for a month and more, — not that I was iver much in his company; but I watched him, and watched him too for a raisin o' my own, — and I tell you plainly, Else, if he opened his purse to me ivery day in tho year, and it full o' goold guineas, I cudn't feel it in my heart to touch one o' thim."

"Arrah, you cudn't, now!" responded Else, in a half-incredulous, half-jeering tone. "By my word, it's mighty big spoken of you, Mr. Hanlon. E' thin might a body make so bould as to ax yer raisins; faith, they must be powerful ones intirely."

"I have no particklar raisins," replied Lanty; "he niver did harm to me nor mine, that I know of. But I don't like him. There's something wrong about him, and I feel it somehow when I'm near him; there's a dark spot in him somewhere that the bright light niver reached yit, Else."

"Humph!" ejaculated the old woman, looking sharply at her companion; "you suspect him of something?"

"I do."

"And what is it, Lanty?"

"I can't tell; it's a mysthery to myself. But he has that in his eye that's not lucky. What brings him down here so often, I'd like to know?"

"Why, trout fishin, av coorse — what else?" replied his companion.

"Pshaugh! nonsense, Else Curley; you can't run ' Donal' on me that way, cute and all as ye are. That man don't care a brass farthin for the best fishin in Donegal, from Onea River to Malin Head. I see it in his very motions. There's not a dhrap o' sportman's blood in his body."

"O, no! not a dhrap, because he don't go into the doldrums, like Uncle Jerry, at every fin he sees rising above the water. Humph! pity but he wud."

" The fish he's after don't live in wather, Else Curley, and you know it," said Lanty, laying his finger on the old woman's shoulder, and whispering the words into her ear.

" Me ! "

" Ay, in troth, jist yourself, Else, and sorra much iv a parish wondher it id be aither, some o' these days, if it turned out that he was trying to buy one Else Curley o' the ' Cairn ' to bait his hook for him into the bargain."

The old woman endeavored to look astonished at the accusation, but there was a faint smile in the corner of her mouth she could not entirely suppress. A stranger would possibly have called it a contortion of the lips ; but Lanty Hanlon was an old acquaintance, and knew her better.

" You needn't try to consale it, Else," replied Lanty, " for do yer best you cudn't consale it from me. I know ye too well, ould woman. There's a sacret about that man and the Lees, and no mortal in this neighborhood knows it but yerself."

" A sacret ! tut, you're dhramin," replied Else, turning away and laying her thumb on the latch of the door; " a sacret, indeed ! arrah, what in the wide world put that in yer head ? "

" The fairies."

" Indeed, then, Mr. Hanlon, one id think ye come from that same respectable stock yerself, ye know so much more nor yer neighbors," retorted Else.

" Well, good evenin, Else Curley. I must go, for I've business to do, and I find my company's growin troublesome, besides. But take a word o' warnin before I start. If yer bent on makin money out iv this stranger, and if he's willin to spend it on you and yer sacrets, well and good; I'm content. But listen to me, Else. Make the *laste* offer to thrifle wid a sartin person you know of, — say but a wrong word, — breathe but a single bad breath, was it as low as the very weasels, — and my hand on my conscience, Else Curley, from that minute I'll forget that we were iver acquaint, and my vengeance will purshue ye till the clay covers ye."

"Why, the heavens presarve us, Lanty Hanlon; what d'ye mane? You cudn't think I'd betray——"

"Think!" repeated Lanty; "well, no matter what I think; I've said my say;" and again wishing her fair thoughts and a pleasant evening, he turned from the door.

"Ah, the ould schamer," he muttered to himself, as he jerked his blackthorn under his arm, and tossed his rabbit-skin cap on the side of his head once more, "the ould schamer, she'd betray the pope if the bribe was big enough. And still she loves her—av coorse she does—and small blame to her aither; for there's no Christian crathur iver saw God's good light that shouldn't love her; and after all, I b'lieve in my conscience she's the only livin thing, barring ould Nannie, she iver did love before, in her life. But love her or hate her, there's one small raisin she can't harm her, and that's just this—there's a sartain Misther Lanty Hanlon, iv these parts, won't let her—even set in case she'd be wicked enough to thry it. So, rattle away, Lanty; the world's big enough for ye—ay, and good enough, too, ye thief, if ye only go through it as ye ought, with a stout heart and an honest conscience. Don't fear, my boy; ye have neither house or land, cow or calf, penny or purse, and who cares!—ye have clothes on yer back, strength in yer arm, a heart without spot or flaw in it, and wid the blessin o' God to back ye, what more d'ye want? So, dance away, Lanty, and as ye hop through the figures, don't forget to keep your eye on the fiddler;" and thus the reckless, light-hearted fellow tripped along the glen, still singing the old ditty as he went:—

> "The Sassanach villains—de'il tare them!—
> They stripped us as bare as the 'poles;'
> But there's one thing we just couldn't spare them—
> The '*Kidug*' that covers our souls.
> Right fol de lol ol," &c.

CHAPTER IV.

Lanty's Propensities. — Weeks introduces himself into the Lighthouse. — Finds the Keeper engaged shooting Holland Hawks. — Takes a Crack at one himself. — Assures the Keeper Yankee Boys can hit Swallows with a Rifle Ball. — Recommends the Importation of Yankee Lecturers to smarten the Irish Nation.

IT wanted still two hours of sunset, when Lanty Hanlon left the lighthouse with the mallard wing in his pocket for Uncle Jerry. His pace was now more hurried and purpose-like than when last seen wending his way through the dark glens. His song too had entirely ceased, and he held his blackthorn staff no longer carelessly under his arm, but grasped it firmly in his hand, like a traveller resolved to let no grass grow under his feet till he had accomplished his journey.

On passing the road below Else Curley's cabin, however, he looked up to see if the old woman was in sight, that he might make her a sign of friendly recognition; or perhaps it was a wholesome dread of a second unceremonious visit from Nannie, that made him turn his eyes in that direction. Be that as it may, neither Nannie nor her mistress could be seen, but in their stead, and much to Lanty's surprise, appeared the tall figure of the stranger, issuing from the door of the little mud cabin, and making his way down the hill in the direction of the light house. Lanty stopped suddenly, not well knowing what to think of this. He had seen the stranger, a full half hour before, quitting Lough Ely, and setting off towards Crohan, and naturally concluded he was by that time far on his way home. A moment's reflection, however, convinced him that the man must have hid himself·

behind some rock or hillock, and waited there till he could venture up unobserved, to pay his usual visit to Else Curley. This manœuvring was by no means satisfactory to Lanty; on the contrary, it served greatly to confirm the bad opinion he had begun to entertain of his purpose in hovering so constantly about Araheera Point. Lanty Hanlon was not a man remarkable for an extra amount of shrewdness — it was the very reverse with him; shrewdness was not an ingredient to mix with the mercury of his nature at all. But the stranger's conduct was so palpably suspicious, that he could not for an instant resist the idea of some plot between him and Else Curley. In the first place, the man had been only two days in the country when he found the old woman out — nay, went as straight to her cabin as if he had been sent there on a message, and since that time visited her every day, remaining with her often whole hours together. As for his pretext of fishing, it was the flimsiest in the world; for no one who saw him cast a line in water could ever imagine he cared a gray groat for the pleasure it afforded. Then his close and frequent inquiries about the Lees, and his knowledge of certain private affairs of the family, already communicated to Else Curley, — these, we say, put together, were clearly suggestive of some secret purpose on his part, and quite enough to raise suspicion in minds far less constructive than Lanty Hanlon's. Besides, Mr. Lee was himself a stranger in the place, having resided but eighteen months at the lighthouse, and during that time had seen but little company. The peasantry of the neighborhood, indeed, looked upon him at first as one who disliked society, preferring a quiet life at home to making and receiving visits. Hence they seldom troubled him, except on matters of business, and then only as little as possible. To be sure, the officers of the ballast board called on him three or four times a year, but that was on their tours of inspection round the coast; and Father John was seen, too, sometimes trotting down in that direction with his saddle-bags bobbing

4

behind him; but Mr. Lee was a Catholic, and Father John was the priest of the parish. All this was very natural. But it soon began to be whispered about that Captain Petersham, of Castle Gregory, was seen occasionally stepping ashore at the point when out yachting on Lough Swilly, and, what looked stranger still, taking Miss Lee with him up the lough to visit his sister. This latter circumstance led the good people, by degrees, to regard Mr. Lee as somewhat above the rank of a common light-keeper, for Tom Petersham was the crack gentleman of the county, and (though somewhat reduced himself) always felt a peg or two above associating with the squires and newly-fledged baronets of the district. So they concluded, after various speculations and gossip on the matter, that Mr. Lee must have been once a real gentleman, whom reverse of fortune had obliged to accept his present humble situation as a last resource. And so they continued ever after to regard him, saluting him with every mark of respect when they happened to meet about the lighthouse, and never presuming to intrude on his privacy except to settle their little business transactions, or when he chose to employ their services about the lighthouse yard.

Now, Lanty Hanlon saw all this long ago, and regulated his intercourse with the family to suit the case precisely. He asked no questions, made no apologies, came and went just as he pleased; and yet, as he often was heard to say himself, knew as little about Mr. Lee, or his private affairs, as the blackest stranger in the kingdom!

Young, active, and fond of recreation, Lanty always found Araheera Head a capital spot to indulge in his favorite pastime of gunning and fishing, and shortly after Mr. Lee's arrival found that gentleman quite as fond of the sport as himself. And thus an intimacy grew up between them all at once — an intimacy, by the way, which each felt it his interest to cultivate; Lanty for the sake of the light-keeper's influence with the neighboring gentry, in whose power he often unfortunately found himself, and the light-keeper for the sake of Lanty's skill as a sportsman, in his frequent excursions on Lough Swilly. Besides, Lanty kept a pair of black greyhounds, the best ever ran on four feet, and the terror of all the game-keepers in the three baronies. These enabled him to supply his friend with "hare's ear" for his flies, and if the truth must be told, with haunches for his table too, occasionally, without troubling his conscience greatly about the infraction of the game laws. Then he was moreover an excellent shot with either rifle or birding piece, and could bag a brace of grouse or wild ducks on sea-side or mountain as prettily as the best landlord's son in the parish —always remembering to reserve the wings for Mr. Lee's and Uncle Jerry's fly hooks. Sometimes, too, the light-keeper would find a white trout for breakfast of a morning, or a salmon for dinner, without any distinct recollection of having caught them himself, or bought them from any particular fish-hawker of the neighborhood. For reasons such as these, and others quite unnecessary to mention, Lanty soon became a constant and welcome visitor at Araheera Head, and indeed finally grew to be so special a favorite with the light-keeper that he could hardly prevail on himself to take his boat or his gun without Lanty at his elbow. He even offered him a salary larger than his limited means could well afford, to live with him altogether; but, Lanty invariably refused, preferring a free foot on the hill side after his dogs, and a ramble on the sea shore with his rifle, to all the inducements he could offer. These rambles, however, often brought him into trouble; but if they did, he always depended on Mr. Lee to get him out of it. On such occasions the honest light-keeper would bluster and swear as stoutly as a Dutch burgomaster never to speak another word in the villain's behalf, should it save him from the gallows, and often even went so far as to order the members of his family never to let the scoundrel inside his doors again; but somehow or other these resolutions never held out — all his indignation seemed to vanish in his sleep; and before the sun got up on the following morning, he was sure to despatch a note to Tom Petersham, or some other gentleman of the neighborhood, to beg their interest in the unfortunate fellow's behalf. Lanty, in fact, was never out of scrapes for a week together since Mr. Lee first saw him. He had either fallen foul of a bailiff, or beaten a policeman, or cudgelled a game keeper, or spread a salmon by torchlight, or stole a game cock, or — something was always sure to be wrong, whenever he was absent three days at a time from Araheera lighthouse.

Intimate, however, as Lanty was with the family, he knew nothing of their history save what he picked up from an odd word dropped now and then between Mary Lee and the light-keeper, or between himself and old Roger O'Shaughnessy, when they went up the tower of an evening to chat and trim the lamps together. What he learned from the latter, however, was never very satisfactory, for Roger considered himself too respectable and important a personage to hold much confidential intercourse with a light-headed scatterbrain like Lanty Hanlon. But whilst Roger said little of the family connections directly, he indulged frequently in little sneers at the pretensions of the Donegal aristocracy, wondered where in the world they found the arms on their carriage panels, and if they didn't one and all inherit their gentle blood from "Shemus Sallagh" or Oliver Cromwell. This contemptuous way of speaking about his neighbors was plain enough, and Lanty understood it. The nobler families of the south was a subject on which Roger loved very much to descant in a sort of soliloquial tone, when he sat down of a summer's evening in the lantern to burnish up the reflectors with Lanty at his side. Many a long sigh would he draw, talking over the olden times, when real lords and ladies used to throng the halls of a certain castle in the south (surrounded by their servants in splendid liveries) to drink the choicest wines or dance to the music of the old family harp; and if his companion ventured to inquire the name of the castle or of its owner, little information would he get from Roger O'Shaughnessy. Still, studiously averse as Roger was to the revelation of family secrets, he could not hide from his quick-witted companion the conclusion warranted by his frequent though indirect allusions. Besides, Roger always wore a curious old-fashioned coat when serving dinner, which contributed more, perhaps, than any thing else to enlighten Lanty as to the antecedents of the family. This coat was once a bottle-green of fine texture, as might be seen by those shady little corners here and there, where the sun had not been able to peep, nor the wear and tear of half a century entirely to reach. With a few redeeming spots like these, however, excepted, the rest of the garment was faded, threadbare, and polished as the cuff of a sailor's jacket. The high, stiff collar, the buff facings, and the long tails would have plainly showed it had once been livery, even if the two lonely gilt buttons on the high waist behind, bearing the family crest, had been lost and gone with the rest of the brotherhood. Every day, before the little bell rang for dinner, did Roger divest himself of his working dress, brush over the few white hairs that still remained to cover his polished scalp, and then put on his bottle-green livery with as much care and tenderness as if it had been wove of spider's web. Poor Roger! many a scold he got from Mr. Lee for keeping up his ridiculous old notions, and many a laugh had Mr. Petersham at his profound salutations, when he came to visit the family; but laugh or scold, it was the same to Roger: on he went, practising the same old habits, despite every remonstrance.

This obscurity in which the history of the Lees was involved, coupled with the mysterious conduct of the stranger, led Lanty Hanlon to suspect some deep plotting between him and Else Curley. As for the latter, he had little fear she would take part in any thing directly tending to bring misfortune on the light-keeper or his family; but still she might meddle so far with the danger as to bring them into trouble without actually intending it, — and all for the sake of gold, to obtain which he supposed the miserly old creature was prepared to run any risk, even that of her salvation. "Hooh!" he muttered, "for that matther, she'd go to the de'il's door and singe her ould beard at the key hole to earn a sixpence; and as for you, *my augeuaugh,*" he continued, gazing after the retreating figure of the stranger, "ye've the cut of a schamer about ye, any way. Be all that's bad, I niver saw ye with a fishin rod in yer hand yet, but ye put me in mind iv one i' them big long nosed cranes down there standing up to their knees in the wather, watchin round for the little innocent shiners to make a pounce on them. F'eth, may be it's some sworn inemy i' the family ye are, keeping their thrail all the time since they left the south; or may be its a sheriff's offieer ye'd be in purshuit of an ould debt; or, by jaminy king, who knows but yer some discarded sweetheart sneakin' afther Mary Lee. If yer that, I'd advise ye lave the country or buy yer coffin. But whatsomever ye are, yer a chate any way, that's sartin; and so, may sweet bad luck attind ye, *achushla,* and that's my prayer for ye, night and mornin, sleepin and wakin;" and Lanty shook his fist at the stranger as he disappeared over the brow of the hill, "and since ould Else has tuck ye in tow," he concluded, spitting on his stick and again heading for the mountains, "I'll just stand by and look on; but one thing I'll be bould to tell ye both, cute and all as ye are, that by the powers o' pewther ye'll have to rise early and thravel fast if ye hope to get the blind side iv one Lanty Hanlon."

Leaving Lanty to pursue his journey across Benraven, we return to the stranger. After examining for some time the structure of the narrow iron bridge over the chasm called the "Devil's Gulsh," he raised the latch of the gate, and finding it unlocked, pushed it open. The light-keeper's lodge, facing him directly as he entered, was a long low cottage fronting full on the sea. The light tower rose up close by its side, with its great round lantern on top, to the height of a hundred and fifty feet from the rock, as smooth and white as marble. The doors, walls, and window sashes of the lodge were also white and clean as human hands could make them; even the black stone steps by which he ascended to the hall door shone bright and spotless as polished ebony. The place, however, notwithstanding the care and trouble it cost, looked still and deserted. For full ten minutes the stranger stood in front of the house gazing round him, and yet no one came to bid him welcome. A little white bantam on the grass plot before the door, scraping up the greensward and calling his family round him, was the only sign of life to be seen. In such a remote spot he naturally hoped the presence of a stranger in his garb would draw some one from the house; but he was mistaken. At length, tired of waiting, he advanced to the door and knocked; still there was no answer: he knocked again, and yet no one came. Then turning the handle and opening the door, he stepped over the threshold, and found himself all at once in a long passage or entrance hall. On either side of this hall hung several spears and fowling pieces, here and there, fishing rods resting in brass sockets against the wall, and suspended from the ceiling, half a dozen or more reels of jack lines, with hooks and leads attached, ready for use. It was evident from their superior quality, and the excellent condition in which they were kept, these articles were used more for amusement than profit. Beyond, however, and near the opposite extremity of the passage, hung two light oars of beautiful finish, and close beside them a small sail of Russia duck, with its little sheet coiled carefully round it, and, if one might judge from its appearance, but recently used. The stranger seemed to notice this last-mentioned article with special interest; and the cold smile that overspread his long face as he looked at it plainly showed he knew well by whose delicate fingers it was handled last. Proceeding along the hall like a connoisseur in a picture gallery, he came at last to an open door opening into a spacious parlor, and entering without further ceremony, sat down on the first chair he saw, and carelessly throwing up his feet on the seat of another, began to gaze about him, like a man quite resolved to await the coming of some one, should he wait till morning.

About this apartment, in which the stranger now found himself seated all alone, there was a general air of comfort and taste, which at once suggested the idea of a lady mistress far above what he might expect to find at a light-keeper's lodge, and especially at so remote a point as Araheera Head. Nevertheless, though the room looked comfortable, and every thing arranged in excellent taste, there was still nothing in it either new or fashionable. Massive picture frames with grim looking faces in the background hung here and there round the apartment; but their rich gilding was gone, and their edges, stripped and black, made sad contrast with the newly-painted walls. The harpsichord in the corner had lost its silver handles, by which in olden times it was so often drawn out into the merry circle, and the ancient clock opposite, now silent as a tombstone, glared over at its once light-hearted companion with a melancholy expression of countenance. They had, doubtless, been friends together for many a year, and in their early days had oft conversed pleasantly from opposite corners — each after his own fashion. But age, alas! had now left his mark on both. The clock's open good na- tured face was bleared and wrinkled, so much so indeed that its early associates could scarcely have recognized it; and the harpsichord's once burnished case had lost all its polish, and its edges were stripped and lean, like the elbows of an old coat. Still, though both were broken down and somewhat shabby, they were clean and decent, like old gentlemen who had seen better days. And there, too, near the fireplace, was the high-backed sofa with its heavily-carved feet and double rows of brass nails along the edges. But conspicuous above all appeared the old family Bible lying in state upon the centre table, under its vellum cover and iron clasps. Every thing in the room spoke eloquently of the past, for every thing looked ancient and venerable, even to the bird cage over the window, where the gray linnet sat dozing with his head under his wing.

That apartment, dear reader, was an epitome of the history of Ireland, and might have furnished materials for a finer allegorical picture than ever Claude Lorraine drew — her heroes without a name or monument save those poor rotting shreds of canvas — the fire of her music dying out day by day, nay — alas that we should say it ! — almost as cold and dead as the blackened embers on her desolate shrines — her once brave and stalwart sons now wrapping their emaciated limbs in their tattered garments and resigning themselves, without a struggle, to serfdom and the grave. Had the author of the "Giaour," who could see even in the fair but lifeless form of woman the picture of "Greece, but living Greece no more,"— had he lived to sit there and gaze around him, how much more sublime the inspiration he had drawn from those sad, crumbling relics ! Yes, the nation was still living, but all her glories, save the glory of her faith, had departed.

But the stranger's heart was not one of that mould. On the contrary, he scanned every article of furniture in the room with a cold, prying curiosity, that accorded ill with the fashionable sporting dress he wore, and having at last completed his survey, drew his chair to the centre table, and opened the sacred volume.

Had he been a lover of old books, he might have paused to examine the title page before he proceeded farther, and the curiously illuminated letters it exhibited, but especially an ancient and copious note in the margin purporting to show that the book was printed at Madrid in the year 1467, by a native of Mentz, at royal request — a fact which might have greatly surprised those French and German *littérateurs* who claim for Louis XIV. and Frederic II. the honor of having been the only patrons of the art before that period. But the gentleman was either not of that class, or ignorant of the Latin tongue, in which it was printed, for he ran his eye hastily over the page, without seeming to notice either date or language.

Without pausing a moment, he turned over leaf after leaf, glancing merely at the top and bottom of the pages, and evidently in search of something he understood was to be found there. He spent some five or six minutes in this search, and at last, having discovered what he sought, drew from his breast pocket a small book of tablets, copied what items he thought necessary, and then, hastily closing the Bible, (stealthily watching the doors of the apartment all the while,) clasped it as before.

It happened in replacing the book he dropped something on the floor, and instantly picking it up, found it to be a silver beaded rosary, with a gold crucifix attached, and of exquisite workmanship. The image was of the purest gold, the nails in the hands and feet were diamonds of great brilliancy, and the cross, on which the figure hung, ivory inlaid with some precious metal, and bordered with small but costly pearls. It was evidently the relic of some pious ancestor, for the beads were much worn, and the edges of the cross had lost their original sharpness, and grown round and smooth from the wear and tear of years. It was curious to see how the stranger smiled as he held up the sacred trinket between his finger and thumb. A child could have read in his countenance how little he respected either the image or the reality —the cross or the crucified. Whilst engaged, however, in this contemptuous inspection of the venerable and precious relic,— the sneer on his face growing deeper as he gazed,— he was startled by a shadow suddenly darkening the window, and turning to see what it was, beheld the same countenance which smiled on him from the stern of the little boat an hour

before, peeping through the glass. The face was so close to
the window that the stranger might have seen, from its peculiar expression, he had been mistaken for some familiar friend,
whose visit had been expected. The side light troubled her
so much at first that she could see nothing distinctly in the
room, and raising both hands to shade it off, happened to
throw back the broad brimmed hat she wore, and thus revealed
in full view to the stranger, now advanced within arm's length
of the window, a countenance of extraordinary beauty. But
there was little leisure left him to gaze upon it — for in
another second the laughing girl had discovered her mistake,
and startled by the close proximity of a man so utterly unknown to her, and trembling with shame and confusion at her
apparent levity, bounded back as if a spectre had confronted
her, and flew away from the window like an affrighted bird.

The stranger called to her to stop and listen to his apology;
he knocked on the glass, and even attempted to raise the sash
and follow her; but all was in vain: away she ran over the
green lawn, her tresses streaming back on the gentle breeze,
and disappeared over the edge of the precipice. For an
instant the disappointed sportsman stood spell-bound, hardly
able to tell whether the form was a vision or a reality. And
no wonder. Her figure so light and airy, her extreme grace
of motion even in the confusion and hurry of her flight, and
the exquisite beauty of her modest face, might well indeed
have raised such an illusion in minds far more philosophic
than the stranger's.

And now again all was still as before; not a sound was to
be heard but the sullen break of the sluggish wave against
the rocks, or the occasional call of the little proud bantam still
scraping on the green.

The sun had sunk by this time within an hour of his setting,
and crowned the far-off summit of Benraven with his golden
light. The sky was cloudless, and the air as balmy as the
zephyrs that play round the base of the Himalayas and fan

the banks of the ancient Hydaspes.   Stealing out from under
the shadows of the island appeared the white sails of the coast-
ing vessels, with scarce wind enough to give them motion,—
so calm had it grown for the last hour; and away beyond
them in the west rose the dark form of the Horn, round whose
top the wings of countless sea birds might be seen wheeling
and glinting in the rays of the setting sun.   The scene was as
grand and picturesque as one might care to look upon, and
yet it seemed to awaken but little interest in the stranger.
Indeed, the sullen look of disappointment on his face, as he
gazed through the window on the world without, showed but
slight relish for the poetry of nature.   At last, turning away
abruptly from the casement when he saw there was no likelihood of the young lady returning, he retraced his steps to the
hall door, and was just about to follow the visionary form to
the edge of the rock, when, to his great relief, he heard the
sharp crack of a rifle, within twenty paces of where he stood.
Looking in the direction of the sound, he saw smoke curling
slowly up from the sea; then a water spaniel sprang on the
bank, and began to shake the brine from his dripping sides;
and finally a man in a pea jacket, with his pantaloons rolled
up over the tops of his boots, and a gun in his hand, suddenly
made his appearance.   He was apparently about fifty years
of age, stout and hearty looking, and carried in his face, as he
approached the stranger, a look of welcome which it was impossible for a moment to mistake.

"Good evening, sir," said he, touching his hat to his visitor,
hardly able to utter the words, so exhausted was he in climbing up the rock.

The stranger slowly introduced his arms under his coat
tails, and made a grave and respectful inclination of his head.

"Sorry you found no one in the house to bid you welcome,"
said the stout gentleman, wiping the perspiration from his face.

"Rayther think the apology should come the other way,"
replied the stranger, drawling out his words.

"O, don't mind that, sir; when you found nobody in the house, you did perfectly right to make yourself as much at home as possible."

"Mr. Lee, I presume — the gentleman here in charge?"

"The same, sir, and quite at your service — that is, as soon as I can manage to catch breath again. Heigh-ho! By George, I haven't gone through as much these ten years before. That confounded Holland hawk has the nine lives of a cat — and — and I verily believe a few to spare besides. Pheugh! heugh!"

"Been gunning, I perceive."

"Yes; fired fourteen balls — nine of them clean into his body, and there he is, yet, sound as ever."

"Well, now, that's rayther uncommon.— ain't it?" said the stranger, without moving an inch from his position; "should think one was enough."

"The bird's not natural, sir," replied Mr. Lee; "that's the best explanation I can give."

"Just so," said the stranger, nodding a stinted assent —"not natural."

"Besides," added Mr. Lee, "though he looks large in the water, the fellow is really as light as a feather. I believe in my soul, sir, you can no more pierce that bird with a ball than you can a piece of floating corkwood."

"Can't, eh?"

"No, sir, it's impossible. I'm living here eighteen months, or thereabouts, and during that time I can safely say I wasted more powder on him than would blow up the tower."

"Well, look here, why not snare him?"

"Snare him!"

"Why, yes, trap him by night, since you can't shoot him by day."

"O, tut, tut! no, sir, the bird's game. Moreover, you might as well try to snare a fox in a market place."

"Well, take him flying, and *meet* him with the ball," said

the stranger, now thrusting his hands deep into his breeches pockets, and hitching up his cap behind with the collar of his coat; "seen swallows killed that way."

"What, swallows with a ball?"

"Yes, sir; boys can do it in the section of the country I was raised in."

The light-keeper turned a sharp, searching eye on the stranger, and scanned him from head to foot without saying a syllable in reply. The last word sounded odd to his ear. In fact, it suggested a sort of vegetable idea, and the figure of the man who uttered it helped to give that idea, ridiculous as it was, something of a specific form. Or, rather, his tall, lithe figure, freckled face, and long, straight, sandy hair, made up a parsnip kind of personality that tickled the light-keeper's fancy very much, and made him laugh.

"Well," said the stranger, mistaking the laugh, "it requires considerable experience, I allow; but still our boys can do it, and as to that creetur there, I guess I can hit him flying myself."

"Flying! ha! ha! My dear sir, the bird never flies."

"He's got wings — hain't he?"

"Can't certify as to that," responded the light-keeper; "never saw any, at least — and what's still more remarkable, he never quits this shore."

"Why, you don't mean that there particular bird, do you?"

"That identical bird, sir."

"He's got a mate, I reckon, and goes off once in a while — don't he?"

"No, sir, he has no mate — never had any."

"Excuse, me," said the stranger, attempting a smile; "I'm not long in this section of the world, I allow, but I guess I've been raised too near one Phineas Barnum, you might hear of, to believe such a story as that;" and the speaker thrust his hands down lower still into his pockets, and looked knowingly at the light-keeper.

"I know nothing of Phineas Barnum," responded Mr. Lee, grounding his rifle and resting on the muzzle, "but I repeat to you, nevertheless, that the bird you see floating on the water there before your eyes has never been out of this bay for the last eighteen months, and during that time was never seen in any other creature's company, man, bird, or beast."

"Shoh! you don't say so — summer or winter? Why, I rayther think that's impossible — ain't it?"

"Summer and winter are all the same to him," replied the light-keeper. "I have seen him in January, when the storm threatened to blow the lantern off the tower, and the sea to wash this little island and all it contains into the deep, — I have seen him at such times sitting as calm and composed on the swells of the sea as a Turk on an ottoman smoking his pipe. He's the sauciest villain that ever swam, sir — look at him now beyond the boat there — see how the rascal comes sailing up to us like a swan, with his arched neck and look of proud defiance."

"Is the piece loaded?" inquired the stranger, in a quiet, modest tone of voice.

"No, sir; load to suit yourself; there's the gun, and here's the powder and ball. By George, if you kill him, I'll say you're the best marksman in Donegal."

"My name is Weeks," said the stranger, slowly drawing the ramrod — "Mr. Ephraim Weeks."

"Weeks," repeated the light-keeper; "rather a scarce name in this part of the world."

"Well, yes; I guess so — Ephraim C. B. Weeks," he added; "Mr. Robert Hardwrinkle of Crohan's my cousin, sir. You're acquainted less or more with the family, I presume."

"Have heard of them, sir; and quite a respectable family they are, by all accounts."

"Well, yes; pretty much so, I reckon, for this part of the

country — should be happy to see you at Croban, Mr. Lee, whenever you've a leisure hour to spend. My cousins often wonder you hain't called and brought Miss Lee with you of an evening."

" Your cousins are said to be very pious, and of high literary acquirements," observed Mr. Lee, not appearing to value over-much the invitation so unexpectedly and patronizingly tendered, " and I fear quite out of Miss Lee's sphere and mine. We are plain people here, sir, unambitious of further intercourse with the world than what chance sends in our way. Are you ready, sir ? "

" All ready ; and now have the goodness to remain just where you stand, and look straight in the bird's eye, whilst I take aim." So saying, Weeks knelt down, and resting the muzzle of the rifle on a projecting rock, waited in that position for nearly five minutes, giving the bird time, as he said, to forget there was a second party in the play. " Now, then," he cried, at last, " hold your hand up, to attract his attention ; " and as Mr. Lee complied, he took deliberate aim and fired.

" Capital shot ! " exclaimed the light-keeper. " Capital shot, by George — not the first time you handled a rifle, I suspect."

" We-ell, no — not exactly the first," drawled out Mr. Weeks, with a modest complacency that well became his grave, sallow countenance ; " I've handled the article more than once, I guess."

Both now looked anxiously around, where the bird might be likely to rise ; but no bird came up to dot the smooth surface of the water.

" Down rather longer than usual," said the light-keeper, at length breaking silence, " and that's a sure sign you haven't touched a feather of him."

" Guess you're mistaken," responded Weeks ; " he's floating out there somewhere as dead as a door nail. Ah ! by cracky ! there he is, lying flat on the water: see ! " — and he pointed

with one hand while he shaded his eyes with the other —
"see, there he is !"

"Where? Ah, yes! by George! and there he is, sure
enough ; well, now, who could have thought it!" exclaimed
the light-keeper, seemingly much delighted with the discovery.

The object, however, to which the stranger pointed happened to be a little whitish colored buoy, a few fathoms beyond a boat, that lay anchored within gun-shot of the island.
As it rose and fell on the light swells of the sea, it looked by
no means unlike a dead bird floating on its back. Mr. Lee
saw the mistake in an instant, and resolved to humor it.

" Dead as a herring !" he exclaimed, taking off his hat and
rubbing up his gray hair in an ecstasy of delight. "Ha, ha!
the villain ! he's caught at last."

" He'll never trouble you again, I'll bet," continued Weeks,
coolly handing over the rifle. Then laying his hand quietly
on Mr. Lee's shoulder, he added, " I make you a present of
the bird, my friend, for I really think you deserve it richly,
after such an almighty waste of powder."

The light-keeper gravely bowed his thanks.

" Well, there's one condition I would make, Mr. Lee, and
I kinder think you'll not object to it ; namely, that you stuff
the creetur, and hang it up here in the passage among the
fishing rods and jack lines."

" Certainly, Mr. Weeks, most certainly, sir, your wishes
must be gratified."

" And look here ; you'll have the goodness to use this for a
label ; " and he drew a card from a richly chased silver case
he carried in his breast pocket, and handed it to the light-keeper; "affix this, if you please, to the upper mandible, that
your visitors may know who shot the bird — not that I care
to make a personal boast about it — for did you know me
well, you would say if ever there *was* a man who despised
boasting, that man is Ephraim C. B. Weeks. But I've a

5 *

notion, somehow, that it would be just as well for the old European countries here to know what sorter people we are in the new world beyond, and consequently think it's the duty of every free-born American, wherever he goes, to enlighten mankind as to the character, enterprise, social advancement, and universal intelligence of his countrymen. Yes, sir, it's a duty our people owe to oppressed and suffering humanity to make their habits, manners, customs, laws, government and policies known throughout universal creation. If it be our duty, as a nation, to redeem the world from ignorance and slavery, as it is, beyond all question, then I say it's the special duty of each and every citizen of that nation to contribute his portion to the advancement and final completion of the great work. We must be known, sir, in order to be imitated."

As the speaker went on to develop his views of the great scheme for promoting the moral and social welfare of the human family, the light-keeper held the card out before him, and read in bronzed copperplate the following address: Ephraim C. B. Weeks, Ducksville, Connecticut.

"Humph! By my word of honor," he muttered at last, "that's a very magnificent affair." Then running his eye over the person of his visitor, he seemed somewhat puzzled what to say. The card case protruding from his pocket, the rings on both hands, and the massive watch chain round his neck, were all apparently of the costliest description, and might well have adorned the person of the highest noble in the realm; on the other hand, however, it struck him there was quite a contrast between the gentleman's language and personal appearance. How that happened he was at a loss to think, and therefore it was he made no reply, but kept glancing from the card to the stranger, and from the stranger to the card.

"I rather think, Mr. Lee, you haven't met many of our people in your time, eh?"

The light-keeper replied in the negative.

"Well, sir, you now see before you a real American — a free-born American, sir — a citizen of the great 'Model Republic;'" and the speaker again thrust his hands into his breeches pockets as deep as they could well go, shook up the silver at the bottom, and with a self-complacent smile on his thin lips watched the light-keeper's countenance for the effect of the startling announcement.

But Mr. Lee did no more than merely compliment him on his birthplace, assuring him, at the same time, he should always feel honored, as he did then, in making the acquaintance of a citizen of the republic of Washington, the model republic of the world. "But with respect to the stuffing," he continued, endeavoring to restrain a smile, "I fear there is none to be found here who understands it."

"Well, send it up to Crohan; I shall see to it myself; guess we Yankees know a little more of those things than you do here in 'the *Green* Isle.'"

"No doubt of it, Mr. Weeks, no doubt of it. I'll send it immediately, and consider it a very special favor indeed."

"Now, then, talking of Americans," said Weeks, arresting the light-keeper by the arm, as the latter began to move towards the lodge, "why don't you bring some of our men over here to enlighten you, eh? You have natural talent enough, I guess, if you'd only proper means to develop it. Could you only get up an association with funds enough to pay Yankee lecturers, you would soon wake up to a sense of your capabilities. Employ our lecturers, sir, and send them over the country here, from town to town and village to village, and I'll bet a fourpence they'll open your eyes wider than ever they opened before."

"Don't doubt it in the least," modestly replied the light-keeper; "but won't you come in, and have some refreshment after your evening's exercise? Come in, sir, and honor my little cabin with your presence at least."

"Hold on," said the American, again detaining the light-keeper on the steps of the threshold. "Look here a minute, if you're not in a killing hurry. I should like to say a word or two about shooting that Holland hawk — it may serve to show you what kind of people we are in the States. Well, to begin with, we calculate never to miss a shot at either man, bird, or beast. You may smile, sir, but it's the fact, nevertheless. My mother had a cousin once, called Nathan Bigelow ——"

"Excuse me, Mr. Weeks — let us step into my office, if you please; I've some orders to give — allow me — just for an instant."

"Well, look here," persisted the Yankee; "it's only a word or two. I was just a going to say that my mother had a cousin once, called Nathan Bigelow, and a shrewd man Nathan was. Well, he was said to be somewhere about the · shrewdest in that section of the country. So the folks thought all round. If there happened to be town meeting, Nathan was sure to be chairman; if referees were appointed by the district judge on a heavy case of damages or the like, Nathan was certain to be one of them; or if the parson and deacon had a quarrel, Nathan was always called in to settle it. Then he was consulted by half the farmers round, coming on seed time, and by the selectmen about the taxes, and some-times by the new minister about the doctrine best suited to his congregation — though the fact is, Nathan never cared much for any particular kind of religion himself — that's a fact. So, as I was going to remark, cousin Nathan had a favorite saying of his own ——"

"Hilloa, there!" interrupted the light-keeper; "pray ex-cuse me, Mr. Weeks — hilloa, there, I say! Are you all dead? Roger, let some one see to the lantern; it's almost lighting time. Come in, Mr. Weeks, and take a seat at least."

"Wait a minute — well, as I was saying," he continued, still drawling out his words slowly, "as I was saying, cousin

Bigelow had a favorite saying of his own — 'Take good care, boy, and don't waste your powder.' It always came ready to him, somehow, and he could apply it to every which thing in creation. Many a time, in the long winter nights, when cousin Nathan used to sit by the log fire in his great rocking chair, reading Tom Paine's 'Age of Reason,' and Martha Proudfut, his wife, knitting her stocking right opposite, with the 'Pilgrim's Progress' open on the table before her, and your humble servant in the corner, studying his book-keeping, — many a time, I say, did cousin Nathan turn round to me, without the least provocation in the world, and begin to illustrate the old maxim, 'Take good aim, boy, and don't waste your powder.' He made a — well, he made it a kind of text to spin a sermon from, and a better sermon he could preach — ay, by a long chalk — than the best preacher in the district. He used to tell me, Nathan used, — and if he did once he did a thousand times, — that the old saying, simple as it sounded, had more genewine philosophy in it than Aristotle and Epictetus put together; and let me tell you, Mr. Lee, cousin Nathan had a terrible regard for these same authors — translations of course, for he was no great hand at the dead languages, coming, as he did, from the old Puritan stock — his great grandfather being a true blue May Flower. Well, Nathan, to be plain about it — was a caution, I tell *you*, in the philosophy line. He never professed much admiration for any but great men, and these were what he called *ticklers*, because, as he said himself, they were the only men who ever tickled humanity in the right place, namely, Tom Paine, Benjamin Franklin, and George Washington. George, he thought, was the greatest man ever the world produced — and I guess, Mr. Lee," said the speaker, with a knowing look, " if he didn't hit the mark, he hit somewhere within a mile of that neighborhood."

"Very true," assented the light-keeper, "he certainly did. Washington was a great and a good man; all must admit that;

and I trust your nation, in the first flush of its prosperity, will not forget his wise counsels either."

"Hope not; well, what I was coming at: Nathan's old saying, 'Take good aim, boy, and don't waste your powder,' so constantly repeated, made a lasting impression on my mind. The fact is, Mr. Lee, he had a way of saying a thing that — well, kind of burnt it into you, like. There was no forgetting it nohow; it was a sort of searing of the ———"

"O, botheration to him!" exclaimed the light-keeper, no longer able to endure the tiresome description, chained as he was to the speaker; "what matters it what he was; he's dead long ago, I suppose, and gone to his account. But, excuse me, Mr. Weeks," he added a moment after, "excuse me; I'm entirely ignorant, you know, of your national characteristics. When longer acquainted, I shall understand you better. And now, my dear friend, let us step into my room —but hold! who comes here? By George, its Tom Petersham, in the Water Hen, to pay us a visit."

CHAPTER V.

Mr. Weeks is introduced to Captain Tom Petersham, and is invited by that Gentleman to spend a Day at Castle Gregory.— He also has the good Luck to catch a Glimpse of Mary Lee.

THE little craft which so suddenly arrested the light-keeper's eye, as he turned to enter the lodge, was already within five minutes' sail of the long flight of steps leading up from the base of the rock to the lighthouse yard. She was a yacht of small tonnage, but elegantly moulded. Her white hull, sunk almost to the scuppers, and her light, raking spars, gave her a janty look, that seemed to please the Yankee exceedingly.

"Why, by cracky, that's an American boat, rig and hull!" he exclaimed. "Ha! I swonnie! — had her built at one of our ship yards, I guess."

"She was built in Cork harbor," replied the light-keeper. "Timber or plank, mast or spar, there's not an American chip in her."

"Not, eh?"

"No, sir; she's Irish, every inch of her, from the truck to the keel. Tom Petersham wouldn't own her if she was any thing else."

"He wouldn't, eh?"

The light-keeper, now seeing a boat approaching from the yacht, advanced to the head of the stairs, and raised his hat to a gentleman who sat in the stern. The latter, as soon as the boat touched, stepped ashore.

"Hilloa, there, Master Lee," he shouted as he ascended the steps; "I couldn't pass without calling to pay my respects to pretty Mary — to say nothing (O Lord! this is worse than Loughdearg for Father John — deuce take them for steps; they don't leave a breath in me) — not to speak of the numerous injunctions respecting a promised visit from the saucy baggage. Heigh-ho! I say, Lee, — this is steeper than the face of Gibraltar; and let me tell you — hugh! — you must provide falls and tackle in future, if you'd have me visit here. Forty-three steps! monstrous! But who the deuce! — eh, who *is* that?" he demanded, halting to take breath as he reached the top, and wiping the perspiration from his face. "Who, in the name of all the Malvolios, is he with all those gewgaws under his sporting jacket?"

"Hush," said the light-keeper; "he's a foreigner."

"Nonsense! He's a cockney tailor come down to rusticate — eh?"

"No, sir; he's an American, and a real Yankee into the bargain."

"A Yankee! The deuce he is!"

"A native of Ducksville, State of Connecticut."

" Ho, ho! now I understand you ; he's the Crohan man —
cousin, or nephew, or something of that kind, to the Hardwrinkles.   Very good ; he's just the man I want to see ; present me
forthwith.   Kate wishes to see him too, of all things, and swears
she'll invite him to the castle herself, if I don't.   Introduce
me instantly ; I'll see what he's like, and then ask him to
visit us."

" O, the young scamp !" exclaimed the light-keeper, laughing ; " she's got some mischief in her mad pate, I warrant you.
If the good gentleman only took a friend's advice, he would
stay at home, and keep clear of her company.   But, come ;
I'll introduce you, at all hazards."

" Captain Petersham," said he, taking off his hat, and motioning with the grace of a well-bred gentleman, " let me
present to you Mr. Weeks, of Ducksville, Connecticut, United
States.   Mr. Weeks, Captain Petersham, of Castle Gregory."

The American bowed low, but without saying a word or
changing his position in the least.   Not so Mr. Petersham,
who despised in his heart all kind of formality, save and
except the formalities of the duel ground ; and these he
understood well, and could practise to perfection.

" What the plague, man ! " he exclaimed, " don't be so stiff
with me.   Nonsense ! you're an American citizen, and that's
enough, sir ; give me your hand.   Ducksville or Drakesville
— I don't care a barley-corn what ville you are, so you're a
free American.   Come, sir, let us be friends at once, and
make no more pother about it."

" Excuse me, Captain Petersham ; you make a mistake.
My name ain't Ducksville or Drakesville ; my name is Weeks
— Ephraim C. B. Weeks."

" O, hang the difference, man ! — it's all the same — what
matters it ?   Come, let's join Lee in his office — he's gone
to order some refreshments, and I'm as dry myself as a
whistle ; " and running his arm into the astonished American's, he dragged him along, speaking all the while with his

usual rapidity. "Pshaugh! it's all balderdash — what's in a name? — why, man, it don't signify a straw what you're called."

"Well, no, not much, I reckon; but if it's just the same to you, I'd rather be called Weeks — Ephraim Weeks. Here's my card, sir, if you please ———"

"Card! psaugh — all humbug. Keep your cards, my dear sir, for those foolish enough to use the toities. But if you choose to be called Weeks, I'll call you Weeks, certainly sir; and an excellent name it is for an American."

"Well, it's sort o' handy like for a business man."

"To be sure — to be sure — there's your secretary of le gation, Mr. — Mr. — what the plague! I can never remem ber names — Mr. — Mr. — O confound it — Linkimdoodle — or something of that sort, — well, sir, he's a fine fellow, that Linkimdoodle, a right honest thorough-going republican as I ever met in my life. He has an odd name, to be sure; but what of that? — No one minds it — any thing, you know, will do in a country like yours, where you've no houses yet, or pedigrees, or things of that description to trouble you. And so you're staying at Crohan with the Hardwrinkles. Well, I can only say I'm sorry for it — they'll ruin you, that's all — ruin you, sir, body and soul."

"The Hardwrinkles are my cousins, Captain Petersham."

"Just so; I know; I understand all that — but you'll not be worth a rap farthing, sir, if you stay with them many months longer, notwithstanding."

"You don't say so!"

"I do, sir. They'll first reduce you down with psalm singing, till you're as flat as dish water and as weak as a wendle straw, and then finish you off with mock piety, private scandal, and weak tea. Take my advice, sir, and stay with them as little as possible. Come up to Castle Gregory, where there's some life to be had, and come as often as you can, too — we'll be always glad to see you. So then here we are in the light-keeper's sanctum, and here comes Drake to welcome us. Hands off! — hands off, Drake — down, down, you old rogue; you're as wet as an otter — away, and bring your mistress here; I want to see her. But what's the matter? — how now! growling at your guest? — ah! Drake, Drake, that's inhospitable — what has come over you, man? never saw you act so un-Irish before. Excuse me, sir; but take a seat, take a seat, and don't be surprised to see me make so free in another man's house — it's our custom here. Heigh-ho!" he added, flinging himself down in an easy chair and his gold-banded sea-cap over his shoulder; "it takes me a full half hour to recover breath after climbing those villa-nous steps. Heigh-ho! and so you're an American citizen."

"Well, yes; I have that honor, sir."

"Right, sir, — and it is an honor — no doubt of it. But how warm it is — eh?" and he snatched off his stock and wiped his face with his handkerchief. "It's those outrageous stairs — eh! Besides, I'm not feather weight either, I sup-pose. Humph!" he added, glancing over at his companion, "you have the advantage of me there, sir — you're thin."

"Yes, rather inclined that way," modestly replied Weeks, playing with his watch-chain.

"So much the better, sir, so much the better; you're in a more comfortable summer condition."

"Well, as to the Weeks side of the house," observed the American, by way of explanation, "they were never what you might call fleshy people; but the Bigelows were about the largest boned men in all Connecticut. There was my mother's cousin, for example, one Nathan Bigelow ——"

"By the lord Harry, he's at Nathan again!" came rum-bling along the hall, in the deep tones of the burly light-keeper, as he hurried in from the tower to welcome his guests.

Fortunately, however, Mr. Weeks was at that moment in the act of speaking, so that it was quite impossible for him to distinguish the words; otherwise he had understood better the comic smile on Captain Petersham's face, as that gentleman twirled his thumbs and gazed over at him from his easy chair.

"Let me see; you're somewhere about five feet eleven inches — ain't you?"

"Yes, thereabouts."

"Well — now, as to the weight, I reckon you're two hundred, or chock up to it."

"Very likely — I might be three, for aught I know," replied the captain, laughing.

"Well, cousin Nathan was taller by nearly two inches, and mother says before he lost his eye on muster day he weighed close on two twenty-five. Still, cousin Nathan——"

"Hilloa, there! hilloa, Roger O'Shaughnessy," broke in the light-keeper again; "are we never to see that brandy and water? Come along, man, only lift your feet, and they'll fall themselves."

"Ay, ay," muttered the old man, shambling into the room in his old bottle-green livery with the faded lace and the two solitary buttons, carrying a massive silver salver, on which appeared three tumblers and a decanter with something resembling brandy on the bottom of it. "Ay, ay," said he, "it's always the same — just for all the world as if he was at home in the ould castle. Heigh! heigh! It's nothing but Roger here and Roger there — Roger, bring the venison; Roger, where's the champagne? Roger, where's the Burgundy? Roger, order this lord's carriage, and Roger, order that lady's barouche. Heigh, heigh, heigh!" Here he was seized by a fit of coughing which had the good effect of terminating his catalogue of complaints. "Och, och!" said he at length, when he recovered a little breath, "the Lord be with the time, Captain Petersham," (bowing with great formality to that gentleman,) "when Roger had plenty of servants to assist him. But sure there's no help for it now, and as I burned the candle I must burn the inch;" and the old man turned to quit the room.

"Stop, Roger; hold on; what have you got here?" demanded the light-keeper, holding up the decanter between him and the light.

"There, sir?"

"Yes, here, sir; look at it."

"Why, it's brandy, av coorse — what else shud it be? But may be its wine yer honor wants — ugh! ugh! — what kind iv wine id you like, sir? I'll bring it immadiately."

"Wine! you old schemer, you know there's not a drop of wine in the house."

"Me!"

"Ay, *you;* you know it well — nor hasn't been these twelve months."

"Och, och, the Lord luck to us!" exclaimed Roger, raising his hands in grave astonishment; "it's wondherful — wondherful, entirely. His mimory's clane gone, sir, (turning to Captain Petersham.) It's only the matther of four weeks, or so, since we got — let me see — ahem! ahem! — two pipes iv claret — one Madeira;" and he began to count them on his fingers — "ahem! two iv claret — one Madeira — one —— "

"Don't mind him, don't mind him," said the captain, rising from his easy chair, and good naturedly laying his hand on Roger's shoulder; "he's enough to vex a saint. Well, Roger — let him do as he pleases; if he choose to refuse us a glass of wine in this beggarly way, why, we can remember it to him — that's all."

"O, my heart's broke wid him, yer honor."

"To be sure it is — you're a living martyr, Roger. I declare, I don't see how you can stand it — it's insufferable — quite insufferable."

"Och, och! I wish to patience he was back in his own ould castle again, yer honor, for since the docthors ordhered him down here for the benefit of his health, there's no comfort to be had wid him, night or day — but sure, if he didn't lose his mimory, it wouldn't be so bad, allthegither. And then I'm shamed out iv my life wid him. Why, if you'd only hear to him, Mr. Petersham — ahem! that's if you were a stranger, you know, sir, like that gentleman, — you're most obedient, sir, — and didn't know the differ, ye'd think there wasn't a screed iv dacency left about him, at all, at all;" and as he thus went on to make his private complaints to the captain, still, however, in a voice loud enough to be heard by the American, he kept ever and anon glancing at the great silver salver on the table, as if making a silent appeal to it for testimony against his master.

During this little conversation with Captain Petersham, the light-keeper called him several times, but Roger was too much engaged to attend him.

"Roger! — are you deaf? Roger!"

"Sir, sir."

"Is this all the brandy you have in the house? Answer me, yes or no."

"Ahem! Answer you yes or no; why, av coorse I'll answer you — that is, if I only knew what you mane."

"Well, look here," — and Mr. Lee stepped over to the old man, and shook the decanter within an inch of his eyes — "you call this brandy?"

"Sartinly, sir, the best cagniac; it cost just seven — "

"Never mind the cost; you have here about three thimble-fulls or thereabouts — for three gentlemen."

"No, sir, there's a good half bottle, and more — ahem! ahem! it looks little, but it's on broad bottom; hem, it's a broad bottom, sir."

"Well, now, I want to know — if you've any more of the same left? — that's plain enough, I think."

"Why, dear me, such a question! Och, och — and two casks untonched in —— "

"Hold your lying tongue and answer me, sir; have you? yes or no."

6*

" Yes, yes, puncheons of it."

" Go fetch it then, forthwith — go now instantly ; " and he pushed him gently towards the door.

" Sartinly, sir, sartinly," replied Roger, moving off as fast as his old, shaky limbs would carry him, the long skirts of his old bottle-green coat oscillating as he went.   " Most sartinly, sir; it's aisy enough to do that — why, if I only knew what in the world ye were comin at, all the time, I'd have it here now."

" He's the greatest old plague, that, in the whole universe," said the light-keeper; " not a respectable visitor ever comes to see us, but he acts just in the same way.   He would make you believe, Mr. Weeks, — Captain Petersham here knows all about him long ago, — he would make you believe his master as rich as Crœsus, and staying down here only by advice of his physician.   You observed the old bottle-green livery he wears; well, he has worn that, to my own knowledge, five and twenty years, and in all probability, his father before him, for as many more.   As for this antiquated piece of plate on the table, he brings it out on every possible occasion.   The old coat and the old salver are in fact his great stand-bys, and with these he imagines he can make a show of 'dacency,' were the house as bare and empty as the ruins of Baalbec."

" Poor Roger," said the captain; " he's a regular Caleb Balderstone."

" Precisely — the only difference, perhaps — that Caleb was a creation, and Roger a reality."

" Balderstone," said Weeks; " let me see ; Balderstone — warn't he something to the Balderstones of Skowhegan, down east ? "

" Ha, ha ! " chuckled Captain Petersham; " can't say as to that."

" Well, them Balderstones of Skowhegan were tremendous smart men, I tell you ; and cousin Nathan says they fought at Lexington like tigers and catamounts."

"No no; Caleb was of quite another character," replied the light-keeper. "He was born of a wizard, and shall live as long as the world lasts. Some, indeed, go so far as to say, that he and Campbell's last man are destined to expire together."

"Well, he's not a mortal, I reckon."

"No, sir, he's immortal as the gods."

During this latter part of the conversation, Roger O'Shaughnessy had returned as far as the room door, and remained standing on the threshold, for a minute or more, looking in. In the attitude he assumed he presented a striking appearance. His once tall and powerful frame, now bent and wasted with years, — the old laced coat hanging from his attenuated shoulders in empty folds, — the white hairs that still remained brushed up on each side, and meeting in a crest over his polished scalp, gave him the look of a fine old ruin, tottering to its fall, with all its friendly ivy dead in the dust, save a few weak but faithful tendrils clinging fast to it still.

"Excuse me, Mr. Lee, for interrupting you," said Weeks, "but the old gentleman here at the door seems to want something."

"What! Roger, — well, Roger, what's the matter?"

"Ahem!" said Roger, "ahem! about the brandy, your honor."

"Well — about the brandy — where is it? why don't you bring it in?"

"The key — ahem! the key of the cellar, sir," said Roger, without venturing to look at his master.

"What of it?"

"Ahem! It's not to be found, sir; you or Miss Mary must have it."

"Me! I never touched the key in my life."

"Dear me, then, what's to be done, your honor? The brandy's in the cellar, and there's no key to open it."

"I don't believe a word of it, but did you ask Miss Lee for the key?"

"She's not to be found, either, sir."

"Ha, ha!—I thought so. I knew all the time it would come to that at last."   •

"If you could put up for this time with some of the best old Innishowen, that ever was doubled," said Roger, "you can have a hogshead of it in a jiffey."

"Innishowen!" cried the captain; "and put up with it, too! Nonsense! nonsense! Roger, bring it in here instantly. Why, you old villain, it's worth its weight in gold. Compare French brandy with Innishowen poteen, indeed! Why, the Irishman who would do that should be sent to the stocks, and physicked with frogs and assafœtida. Begone, and fetch it instanter. Away! my time's up."

Roger soon returned with a bottle of excellent whiskey, of which we must not omit to say, Mr. Weeks declined to partake — nay, absolutely rejected in the most positive manner, as a thing entirely against his principles and habits of life. But the light-keeper and his good neighbor, the lord of Castle Gregory, made no pretensions to such principles or habits; they filled their glasses and drank to each other, and to the success of the Stars and Stripes, as a compliment to Mr. Weeks, in full bumpers of Irish grog, without fear or shame, reproach or remorse.

Captain Petersham had scarcely finished his draught, and flung the tumbler on the table, loudly protesting against all state temperance laws and teetotal societies, as being the provocation of half the drunkenness in the world, when a sailor, cap in hand, presented himself at the door.

"How now, Bradley — what's the matter?"

"Mr. Ratlin says, there's a blow coming up from the westward, sir, and in half an hour we'll have ebb tide. He waits orders."

"Well, get the boat ready. I'll be with you in a second."

He now approached the window, and glanced for an instant at the west. "There it comes, Lee," he exclaimed, "tumbling up in lumps over Tory Island; you'll have it whistling about your ears here in half an hour. I must get aboard the Water Hen, and pack on sail, or she'll not fetch Ballymastocker to-night. But look here; who's that under the rock, there, speaking to Mistress Mary? He's a devilish fine-looking young fellow, eh!"

The light-keeper hastened to the window. "Hah! by George," he exclaimed, muttering the words to himself, the instant his eye rested on the person alluded to, "he is back again."

"Who is he, Lee — eh? surely I've seen that young man before — who is he?"

Mr. Lee smiled and shook his head.

"O, hoh, that's it, is it? Very well, if there's any thing particular about him, keep it to yourself."

And having requested Mr. Lee to make his apology to Mary for running away so abruptly, and invited Weeks to visit him as soon as possible, he hurried off, without further delay, to his yacht. The moment his foot touched her deck, she was seen crowding on every stitch of canvas that would draw, and then gracefully bending under the gentle pressure of the evening breeze, the little Water Hen glided up the Swilly, and soon disappeared in the deepening shadows of Rathmullen Bluffs.

The light-keeper had accompanied his friend to the head of the steps to bid him good by and a fair voyage, and the American, taking advantage of his absence, instantly turned to the window, and there kept watching Mary Lee and her companion so intently, and with so absorbing an interest, that old Roger had picked up his silver card case which had fallen from his pocket, and laid it on his knee, without his having noticed it in the least. The spot on which the young couple stood conversing, was a small patch of greensward directly above the narrow channel called the Devil's Gulsh, and canopied over by a long, flat, projecting rock. The place was some seventy feet above the roaring water, cut, as it were, in the face of the precipice, and nearly on a level with the window at which the American sat looking at them so intently. The distance between was not more than thirty feet; yet near as it was, Weeks could have distinguished little more than their mere outlines, had not the great lantern, now lit up, shed its flood of light full on their persons, revealing every motion and feature distinctly to his gaze.

A shade of melancholy overspread the handsome face of the young man as he leaned on the boat hook, (with which he had climbed the rocks,) and conversed with his fair companion. His black, waving hair fell in profusion over his blue jacket, from the breast pockets of which the silver mountings of a brace of travelling pistols glinted in the clear lamplight. His neck was entirely bare, as if the heat of the day, or his previous exertions, had obliged him to remove his cravat, and his whole bearing that of a brave, self-reliant, fearless young fellow, of honest heart and ready hand. Mary Lee stood by his side, dressed in her blue kirtle and straw hat, the picture of angelic loveliness. Her face, always smiling before, was now pale and thoughtful, as if the melancholy which shadowed the countenance of her companion had touched her heart. Her petite figure, as she leaned lightly against the rock, her modest eyes bent on the green grass at her feet, her long auburn ringlets falling in showers over her shoulders and above all, her unaffected simplicity of manner, gave her a striking resemblance to those beautiful creatures which Raphael paints in his Espousals of the Virgin. Once or twice she raised her eyes to those of her companion; but she as often turned them away, as if the sadness of his looks gave her pain. His gestures and motions were those of entreaty; but she, on her part, appeared to make no reply — save to shake her head and look up sorrowfully in his face. At length the voice of the light-keeper was heard round the house, calling her in from the approaching storm, and she could stay no longer. As the moment of parting came, she drew from her bosom something resembling a medal or locket and chain, and pressing it devoutly to her lips, gently threw it over the young man's neck. She then gave him her hand, and bidding him farewell, sprang round the edge of the rock with the nimbleness of a fawn, and disappeared in an instant. Her companion followed her with his eyes as long as she remained in sight, and then carefully concealing the little treasure in his bosom, slowly turned and left the place.

"Well," said Mr. Weeks to himself as he moved over from the window and leaned his elbow on the table beside him, "she's a handsome gal, that — no mistake about it; and that feller looks to be a purty smart kinder chap, too, and not ill lookin either. But who in creation is he? There's some mystery about him, that's sartin. I could see that by the light-keeper, when the captain asked his name. But hold on for a bit; I'll soon learn the secret from Mother Curley. That was some sorter charm, I'll bet a fourpence, that thing she put round his neck — some papistry, I reckon. But ain't she all-fired brazen faced, to go up there right straight before the window? — By cracky, they do up that kinder business sorter strange down here in these diggins — they're ahead of New Jersey, by a long chalk. But after all, perhaps it's her favorite retreat, and the feller found her there. She expected him — sartin. I saw that by her face when she came peeking in at the window, and I rather suspect she warn't aware of Captain Petersham's arrival either, or that Ephraim Weeks was in the office with her uncle. Well, she's handsome — that's a fact — and with those hundred and fifty thousand dollars I know of to back her up, she's wife enough for any man. Ha, she little thinks what belongs to her tother side the big pond — and she won't either — till she's got her nose up to the hitchin post. She'll be skittish, I guess, at first; but I'll take the old woman's advice, and coax her to it gently.　She can only refuse, do her best; and when she does, why it's then time enough to put the screws on.　They're poor as poverty, that's clear, and it won't be very hard to corner them up in a tight place.　A month or two in limbo would settle the old chap's light-keepin, and then the girl, all-fired proud and all as she is, might be glad —— "

He was suddenly interrupted in his reflections by the entrance of the two persons in whom he seemed to be so deeply interested.

"Here's an impudent, saucy little baggage, Mr. Weeks, who desires to offer you an apology for her dog's very bad behavior to-day," said the light-keeper, leading Mary by the hand.　"Miss Lee, sir.　Mary, this gentleman is Mr. Weeks, of Drakesville, Connecticut, United States."

"Ducksville, if you please, Mr. Lee, not Drakesville," said Weeks, after one of his profound inclinations to the young lady; "the difference ain't much, but still —— "

"O, excuse me, excuse me, sir," said the light-keeper; "so it is — I made a mistake — Ducksville, my dear, State of Connecticut."

"Allow me to offer you my card," said Weeks, smiling faintly and patronizingly on the young girl, as he drew it slowly out from the silver case.

"Thank you, sir," she replied, modestly courtesying and accepting the favor, without the least sign of surprise at the strangeness of the compliment.

"I regret very much, sir, the loss of your fishing lines this evening," she said; "but if you permit me, I shall replace them."

"Pray, don't mention it," replied Weeks, interrupting her. "You're exceedingly kind, Miss Lee, but I assure you I have lots of such traps to spare."

"Drake is a very bold fellow in the water, sir, and don't mind his mistress in the least, when there's any thing like game to be seen.　But then, he's so good and faithful that we must forgive him a great many faults. Drake, Drake," she cried, "where are you?" and as the brown curly-haired old fellow came in, wagging his tail, she ordered him to kneel down before the gentleman and ask his pardon. But Drake, instead of kneeling, as, no doubt, he was taught to do on such occasions, began to growl at the stranger, and would probably have sprung at him if Mr. Lee had not promptly interposed his authority, and commanded him to leave the room.

"How very strange!" said Mary, speaking to her uncle; "I never saw him act so rudely before."

"Some kink the old fellow has got in his head. But I fear Mr. Weeks will find his first visit to us down here a very disagreeable one, so many things have conspired to make it so. The loss of his fishing tackle and his fine trout, to boot; then the absence of the inmates here, and his having to sit so long alone before any one came to bid him welcome; and finally, the unkind and ungenerous behavior of Drake; why, upon my word, Mr. Weeks, you must think Araheera light a very barbarous place."

"O, don't mind—don't mind; I can get along, I guess, most any where. We'll make it all right yet. As for the loss of the flies and casting line, I feel quite pleased about it, since it has procured me the acquaintance of so lovely and accomplished a young lady as Miss Lee."

Mary blushed, hung down her head, and tried to say something; but her confusion at so blunt and unexpected a compliment silenced her completely. The light-keeper, however, came to her assistance.

"If you talk to her in that style, Mr. Weeks," said he, "you'll play the deuce with her—see, she's all over blushes already."

"We-ell, I generally calculate to speak to the point, Mr. Lee. It was always my habit to be frank with every one, and I can safely say, I should be most willing to lose all the fishing tackle I ever owned, for the pleasure afforded me by this introduction; she's a most beautiful and amiable girl, — there's no mistake about it, — and I'm not ashamed to say so, though you are her uncle."

"Mary, the gentleman will set you crazy, if you stay here much longer — away with you," he added, patting her affectionately on the cheek; "away into some corner, and hide your blushes; Mr. Weeks will excuse your further presence;" and dropping her hand, he permitted her to shrink back and glide away like a fairy from the room.

"Well, I guess I shan't wait much longer, either," said Weeks, picking up his cap and preparing to leave. "I see the storm's coming on, and I've got somewhat of a walk before me; but I was just athinkin to come down here once in a while to have a day's fishin or so, and a talk about the United States, at our leisure."

The light-keeper smiled, and assured him he should be happy to see him at any time, and cheerfully do all in his power to make his visit to the country, and particularly to Araheera Head, as agreeable as possible.

"And look'e here," said Weeks, buttoning his coat; "if there's any thing I can do to oblige you, in the way of friendship, don't hesitate an instant, but tell me right out. It may happen you'd want a friend's advice, a — well, no matter, you understand me. I'm a single man, Mr. Lee, and have a leetle more at my banker's, I guess, than I've any particular occasion to use. Good afternoon, sir."

"Good by, and thank you for your good will," said the light-keeper, somewhat surprised at the stranger's liberality. "I shall most assuredly consult with you, Mr. Weeks, when occasion requires it."

"I say — hold on!" said Weeks, again, turning back when half way down the avenue; "that bird, you'll not forget to send it, eh? — all right; guess I can get it up for you in pretty good shape." And waving his hand, he set out on his journey to Crohan, the residence of the Hardwrinkles.

CHAPTER VI.

Uncle Jerry. — His Character. — The Shipwreck at Bally-
hernan.

"HA, ha! very well, I declare! and so there you are at last!" said Uncle Jerry, raising his spectacles to his forehead and peering at Dr. Camberwell as he entered the room, a few days after the events related in the last chapter.

"Good morning, sir; how d'ye do?" said the doctor; "any calls since I left?"

"No; none but Lanty Hanlon," replied Mr. Guirkie, pulling down his spectacles again, and resuming his employment; "and there's a mallard wing he brought me," pointing at it sideways with his eye, "not worth a brass button."

"Don't doubt it in the least; couldn't expect any thing better."

"Why — just look at it. Mrs. Motherly's blue drake out in the yard there has got better feathers for a June trout by all odds."

"It looks like the wing of a young turkey; don't it?"

"Upon my word it's a fact — the spots are as big as the point of my thumb, every one of them."

"Well, you'll find Lanty out yet, some day or other, I suspect," said the doctor, sitting down on the sofa, apparently much fatigued.

"It was about the child he came," resumed Mr. Guirkie; "I had almost forgotten it — about that widow's child down at Ballymastocker."

"What's the matter with it?"

"The measles."

"The measles!"

"Yes, and I prescribed in your absence; so I suppose you'll scold me for it, eh?"

"Scold you! no. Why should I scold you? Upon my word, you know quite enough about the profession to turn doctor yourself. And so you prescribed;—what did you give him?"

"Gin, of course—good Hollands, and to be taken freely."

"Capital; the very best medicine you could order."

"But only at a certain stage of the disease, eh?"

"O, of course, at the incipient stage!"

"Very true," said Uncle Jerry; "that's just it, precisely;" and he laid down the fly he was dressing, to wax a silk thread, whilst he still continued the subject, apparently much interested; "that's exactly the very thing; taken at the proper time, it's the very best medicine in the world. It saved my life once, in Trinidad, when attacked by the small pox."

"Possible?"

"Yes, sir, and I have invariably recommended it in similar cases ever since."

"No other calls?"

"None to speak of. That Mr. Weeks was here about his headache, or faceache, or whatever ache you please to call it."

"Neuralgia, I rather think; and a pretty troublesome acquaintance it is to get rid of."

"I declare," said Uncle Jerry, snapping the thread which he should have had the patience to cut with the scissors, "I declare and vow, it matters very little whether he ever gets rid of it. He's but a very poor concern, that same Mr. Weeks."

"O, I see you have been disputing again—ha! ha!"

"Very well, it's not my fault if we have. I'm sure I never dispute with any one, if I can help it."

"No; but still you manage to do it, notwithstanding."

"Never, upon my word and honor," replied Mr. Guirkie.

"except when it's forced on me. — There now, that hook's as blunt as the very beetle;" and he flung it pettishly into the grate. — "I can't sit patiently by, and hear the man still contending that a red hackle is the best in May and June. You wouldn't expect that, I suppose, eh?"

"He must be very unreasonable," yawned the doctor, his eyes half closed from fatigue and want of sleep, for he had been up all night. "Yes, very unreasonable."

"It was actually presumptuous, considering all my experience to the contrary."

The doctor made an effort to open his eyes and nod in reply.

"I tried to reason him out of it. Upon my word, I reasoned with him as mildly as I would with a child; but you might as well reason with a madman. Why, sir, he's as wrong-headed as a mule, that man, humble and all as he seems. He's a cheat, doctor — that's the whole sum and substance of it."

"O, well," said the doctor, rousing himself a little, and speaking in a half irritable, half conciliatory tone, " let him have his own way; the point, after all, is not of vital interest to any body, I suppose."

"No, it's of no great consequence, I allow," said Uncle Jerry, raising his spectacles a second time to his forehead, and looking across the table at his companion in a manner more impressive than usual. "No, sir, I admit that freely, but the man is exceedingly presumptuous, — remarkably so, for a stranger, — and I'm much mistaken, doctor, if you yourself, with all your stoicism, would surrender to such a person without protest. Moreover, sir, the gentleman, if he be a gentleman, should avoid provoking me to argument in my own house, where he knows he has me at a disadvantage. I say, doctor, it was very indelicate of him, think what you please about it."

"And why do you let the man trouble you at all, if you think so poorly of him?"

"Trouble me?   O, I declare," exclaimed Uncle Jerry, taking off his spectacles at last and pitching them on the table with a very dissatisfied air, for he was evidently disappointed in the little interest his friend seemed to take in the subject.   "Trouble me — why, I vow to goodness, he may go to Halifax and fish for sculpins if he like, for aught I care one way or other.   But am I bound to adopt his blunders against both reason and conscience? am I?"

"By no means; why should you?"

"Very well, then," replied Mr. Guirkie, "that's all I want to know;" and as if there was no more to be said on the subject, he reached over again for the spectacles; "I know very well," he added, as he looked through them before he put them on, "I know it's quite right that every man should choose whatever side of a question pleases him best; it's republican, and has always been my way, and ever shall be as long as I live; but still I have no hesitation in saying this much, doctor, that it's morally impossible for the man who never ties a horn on a hare's ear, because the natural fly don't wear horns except in July and August; — I say that the man who maintains that doctrine, never caught better than graws or shiners in his life.   That's precisely what I think of it, and I shall take occasion to tell the gentleman so at our next meeting."

"Shall I bring in the breakfast?" said the housekeeper, opening the door softly, and waiting till Uncle Jerry had finished before she interrupted the conversation.

"The breakfast!" repeated the latter, checking at once the current of his thoughts and looking across at the doctor, now fairly a-doze on the sofa.   "The breakfast! I declare, that's a fact: well, now, upon my word, I'm the most selfish, thoughtless man in the world.   There he has been out at sick calls all night, and hasn't had a morsel yet to break his fast. Certainly," he replied, nodding at the housekeeper, "certainly, ma'am, send it in by all means."

When the door closed, Mr. Guirkie again resumed his employment, making occasional remarks, now and then, on the quality of the crottel, hare's ear, tinsel catgut, and the other various requisites for fly-dressing; and, at length, having finished his task, and put up the materials in their usual place, he came round and touched the sleeper gently on the shoulder.

"Wake up," said he, "and prepare for breakfast; it's just coming in. But how is this, doctor? Why, dear me! now that I'm near you, one would think you were after a week's march in the Indies. I declare, a Sepoy, after a three days' drill, couldn't look worse. A tedious case, I suppose."

"Very," muttered the doctor; " very bad, indeed."

" Don't doubt it in the least; you look like it."

" Shocking."

"I declare! and it detained you since midnight?"

" Yes, I left here a few minutes after twelve, with Father John," he replied, yawning and rubbing his eyes. "You heard the dog bark at the time under your chamber window, I suppose — I was afraid he might have disturbed you."

" Heard him! why, he set all the dogs in the parish a-barking, and they didn't stop for an hour after. I declare he's the most unreasonable animal in that respect I ever heard, at home or abroad. Still, it's a conscientious matter with him, I suppose, and we shouldn't blame him. Hah, indeed! and so it was a *very* shocking case."

" Fourteen of a crew cast ashore on Ballyhernan Beach," said Dr. Camberwell, raising up his sleepy eyes sympathetically to those of his venerable companion.

" Fourteen of a crew! O, may the Lord have mercy on them!" exclaimed Uncle Jerry, in pious astonishment. " That's awful."

" A schooner from New York, bound for Dublin," continued the doctor. " She foundered off Tory Island four days ago. The crew, with the exception of the first mate, who went down with the vessel, took to the long boat, and after .

drifting about all that time were at length driven ashore last night on Ballyhernan Strand."

"May the Lord protect us!" exclaimed Uncle Jerry again, slapping his knees with the palms of his hands, and looking terrified at the doctor — "all dead?"

"No, no, not *all.* Six of them are still living; the rest were dead before we reached the shore."

"The Lord have mercy on them."

"Were it not for the unwearied attention and devoted charity of Miss Lee, the light-keeper's daughter, I verily believe every soul of them had perished."

"Perished! — after reaching the shore — that's terrible to think of."

"Well, under God, she was the principal means of saving their lives."

"The angel!"

"Upon my word, I believe she's more of an angel than any thing else."

"She *is* one, I tell you — there's no doubt of it whatever — you can see it in her face."

"So you have seen her, then. I thought you had never called at the lighthouse since this new keeper came."

"Neither have I. 'Twas at the chapel I saw her — and that only for a second or two. She was kneeling before the picture of the Virgin, and I declare, glancing from one to the other, I could hardly tell which was the lovelier. I have never forgotten that face since for a single day — it haunts me sleeping and waking; every feature of it seems as familiar as my own."

"It was really one of the most beautiful sights I ever saw, continued the doctor, "her kneeling there on the cabin floor, administering relief to the poor sufferers. She looked to me the very image of a young Sister of Mercy I used to see long ago, gliding round the sick beds in the Dublin Hospital."

"So full of piety, and so gentle!" said Uncle Jerry.

"Yes, once, as she touched the parched lips of the little cabin boy with a spoonful of wine and water, her tears fell on his face, and it was impossible —— "

"I know it," said Uncle Jerry; "it was impossible to look at her, without — hem — without feeling — hem — that is, I mean it was very affecting."

"The warm drops as they fell made him raise his eyes to her face, and then such a look of love and gratitude as he gave her I never saw on human face before."

"It's the goodness of God, doctor, that sends us such creatures, now and again, to reconcile us to our miserable humanity."

"Certainly."

"We should otherwise forget our destiny altogether."

"No doubt of it."

"He scatters them over the dark world, here and there, to brighten and beautify it, as he scatters the stars over the clouded heavens."

"But to return to the sufferers," said the doctor, afraid Mr. Guirkie should fly off into one of his rhapsodies; "one poor fellow, a negro, was all but dead when I left."

"Dear me! all but dead!"

"Yes, and had seven of his toes broken besides."

"Lord save us! — seven toes broken! — that's frightful — seven toes!"

"Four on one foot and three on the other."

"Most shocking! — and what makes it still worse, he's of the despised race; but the rest — where are they?"

"In the cabin."

"What! — all huddled up together, the living with the dead?"

"Why, there was no other place to put them — no house, you know, within a mile of the strand."

"O, no! of course not; why should there?" exclaimed Uncle Jerry, not a little irritated at the disappointment.

" Why should there ?   No, no, there's never any thing where
it ought to be, sir.   I believe in my soul, sir, if there had
been a house there, not a shipwreck would have happened
within leagues of it."

" Don't doubt it in the least," assented the doctor.

" Cross purposes, sir; that's it, cross purposes — every
thing in creation pulling against every other thing.   It's outrageous, sir — no house there, where of all places in the
world it ought to be — I declare to my conscience it's insufferable."

" I know it," said the doctor ; " it's too bad, to be sure, but
so it chances to be."

" Chances ! nonsense ! — there's no such thing as chance —
don't believe in that."   And, clasping his hands round his
knee, he lifted up his little leg, and commenced rocking away
in his chair — a habit he had when any thing troubled him.
He asked no more questions either; what he heard already
supplied him with materials enough for a picture — and he
drew it, and gazed at it, till the tears fell in big drops on the
carpet.   He saw the poor wrecked sailors, stretched on the
damp floor of the warren-keeper's hut, as plainly as if he had
been there in person standing over them.

" Well, there's no use in fretting about it," he said, at
length, letting his leg fall, and looking out at the rain patter-
ing against the window panes; " it can't be helped, I suppose.
They'll die, every soul of them, for want of good fresh air
and kindly treatment.   I know they will.   Can nothing be
done ?   I wish to Heaven I was there myself; but where's
the use of wishing?   The doctor would never consent to it in
such a storm as this.   So here, then, I must wait patiently,
and make the best of it.   As for that negro, he'll die; there's
no doubt of it in the world : he'll die, just because he is
a negro, and no one to care for him.   As for Mary Lee,
she may be a tender-hearted, gentle creature as ever lived,
and no one who ever saw her once could think otherwise;

but she's a timid, fawny thing, and won't venture near enough to wet his lips with a spoonful of sangaree, or whisper a kind word in his ear, to keep his heart from sinking. Ay, that's the effect of a black skin — always, always. It was just so in St. Domingo and Alabama, and all over the world. But never mind, never mind; there's a good time coming. It won't be so in heaven;" and Mr. Guirkie rubbed his hands smartly together, and chuckled at the thought; "no, no; that's one comfort, at least; it won't be so in heaven."

"Why, dear me! there's the doctor fast asleep!" exclaimed the housekeeper, laying down the tray with the breakfast on the table. "Please wake him up, Mr. Guirkie; he needs some refreshment, and should take it hot."

"Never mind him," replied Uncle Jerry, "never mind him. Go away, Mrs. Motherly, if you please, and don't jar the door. I'll wake him the next time he turns over;" and, wiping his spectacles with the tail of his morning gown, he commenced reading a newspaper that lay on the table.

Now, it happened the paper was a week old or more, and Mr. Guirkie had read it over, advertisements and all, a good half dozen times already. For being the only paper taken at the cottage, he always tried, as he said himself, to make the most of it. It was not, therefore, with a view either to entertainment or information that he snapped it up so suddenly as he did, but merely to divert his mind from thinking of the wrecked sailors, and particularly the negro with the broken toes. Mr. Guirkie, as the reader may have suspected, was gentle and full of tender sympathies, and when a case with any thing peculiarly melancholy in it, like the one in question, chanced to get hold of his heart, he never could manage very well to shake it out of it. It was only then, with the desperate hope of excluding from his imagination the picture he had drawn so vividly but a few minutes before, that he clutched the paper so vigorously between his hands and ran his eye so rapidly over the print. It happened, however, notwithstanding the effort he made, that his success was by no means complete, for he soon began a sort of low, dry whistle, without tune or music in it, and evidently intended to help the newspaper. When he had read down half a column or more with this accompaniment, he found it, as he always found it before, to be a total failure, and that, do what he would, the picture kept always breaking in upon him. At last, unable to resist any longer, he flung the newspaper on the floor, and starting up in a sort of desperation, paced up and down the room, his slippers clattering the while against his heels, and his hands as usual clasped behind his back.

"Mr. Guirkie," said the housekeeper, opening the door gently.

"What," said Mr. Guirkie, turning on his step, and throwing up his spectacles from his forehead till they were lost in his bushy, gray hair; "what's the matter?"

"Lanty Hanlon's come for more of that medicine, sir, and says the child's doin bravely; and, sir, he brought ye the other wing of the wild duck."

"Mrs. Motherly," said Uncle Jerry, approaching the door, and drawing himself primly up, "I'm engaged, ma'am."

"Yes, sir, but —— "

"Well, but, ma'am, I'll have no buts; I'm not to be imposed on. That fellow has had more gin already than would cure half the parish; quit the room, if you please, and tell that scoundrel to quit the house."

Again Mr. Guirkie turned to the window, and looked out on the stormy sky, muttering to himself all the while in short, ejaculatory sentences. At first they were low and hollow, but grew more audible in proportion as the picture before his mind's eye grew darker.

"O, nonsense!" said he at last, "Nonsense! nonsense! there's no use whatever in attempting it. And what's more, there never was any use. It was just so always, just the same old story over and over again; and I verily believe I'm a greater fool now than I was twenty years ago. Last week I couldn't rest till I saw that distressed widow, just as if it were my business to console widows — just as if it ought to concern me a copper whether her landlord ejected her or not. But the explanation of it all is, Mr. Jeremiah Guirkie, — since that's the name you like to go by, — the explanation of it all is, that you're an incorrigible simpleton. Yes, sir, that's the short and long of it. And I saw that very word, last Friday, on the doctor's lips, when I gave Lanty the half crown for the hackle, as plain as the light there, only he didn't let it drop. Well, he thought so, of course; why shouldn't he? Forever meddling with other people's business, and neglecting my own. And now, here comes this shipwreck just at the heels of the Weeks affair to worry me again. Well, all we can say about it is, let the negro die — why not? he's not the first that died neglected. And why should it concern you?" he continued, stopping short and looking at himself in the mirror above the mantel; "why should it concern you, sir, one way or other? Psaugh! You're mighty charitable, ar'n't you? Take a friend's advice, sir, and mind your own business: you'll have plenty to do; ay, and if the truth were told, more than ever you did do in your life, sir. Of all the people in the world, sir, you're not the very man expected to keep life in these sailors, or solder new toes on that unfortunate negro."

Here the soliloquy was interrupted by the doctor speaking in his sleep. Mr. Guirkie turned his head slowly around, and stood in a twisted position for a second or two, looking at the dreamer, and waiting to catch the next words. There was a wonderful deal of benevolence in his face as it thus appeared in profile. The little round blue eyes, so full of soft and gentle expression — an expression which his recent effort to steel his heart against the influence of pity had not abated in the least; the small mouth, with the corners turned slightly up, like Uncle Toby's when listening to Corporal Trim; the smooth, unwrinkled, rosy cheeks; and stiff gray hair standing on end, — all tended to convince the beholder of Mr. Guirkie's eccentric habits and kindly nature.

Again the doctor muttered something, and then Mr. Guirkie moved gently over, and bent his head down to catch the words.

"The negro! the negro!" said the sleeper.

"That's it — the negro, of course," repeated Uncle Jerry. "He must die — that's what you mean."

"Mary Lee," continued the dreamer, "warm blankets! — the decoction!" and abruptly turning on his side, he concluded with a groan that told how fatigued he was after the labors of the previous night.

"Very well," said Mr. Guirkie, kicking off his slippers, "that puts an end to it. I have no longer a shadow of doubt about my obligations. It's evidently my duty to go down and visit them. That's as plain as the sun, and the doctor's dream is clearly providential;" and so, sitting down on the chair, he put on his shoes, and then drew over his leggings from the footstool. "As for the rain," he continued, looking out of the window, "I don't care a farthing about it, one way or other. Neither the heat of the Indies nor the cold of the Canadas has taken a feather out of me yet. I'm just as good for all practical purposes as I ever was. To be sure it rains and blows hard and fast; but I am no sugar loaf to melt in the rain, nor a jack straw to be blown away with the wind."

Talking in this strain, he put on his leggings. But he put them on, as he always did, in a very careless, slovenly sort of way — omitting a button here and a button there on his way up to the knees. This time especially he was in somewhat of a hurry, and his thoughts had nothing whatever to do with the buttons. Next he opened his desk as silently as possible, and took out what seemed to be a pocket book, looking round stealthily at the doctor as he secured it under his vest, and finally retired to his chamber to don his seal skin cap and drab surtout with the double cape, a riding dress he never laid aside summer or winter, and from which no one in the neighborhood ever thought of dissociating the idea of Uncle Jerry Guirkie. These hasty preparations concluded, he stepped on tiptoe from the parlor, and closed the door noiselessly behind him, leaving the doctor sleeping soundly on the sofa, and the breakfast cooling beside him on the table.

On reaching the housekeeper's door, however, great as his hurry was, he paused and seemed to deliberate. He was thinking whether he should apprise her of his intended journey, or steal out unobserved. There was danger both ways. If he told her, she might wake up the doctor and detain him; if he did not, his absence in such stormy weather might occasion alarm for his safety. Three or four times he coughed and hemmed slightly at the threshold, bringing his knuckle each time within an inch of the door, but as often drawing it back. At length, however, the fear of giving alarm predominated, and summoning courage, he knocked — but it was a knock in which there was no sign of authority — or rather it was the gentle tap of a child coming to beg alms at a gentleman's back door.

"Mrs. Motherly!" said he, putting his lips to the key-hole and speaking under his breath, "Mrs. Motherly! I'm going out a little; but you needn't disturb yourself. I don't require your services in the least — not in any possible way whatever."

But Mrs. Motherly knew better. She had lived now nearly five years in the family, and understood Mr. Guirkie well, and all about him. Her long residence and her well-known fidelity gave her a respectable claim on his consideration, which indeed, however inconvenient he often found it, he never failed to acknowledge. For a long time after she came into the family, Mrs. Motherly kept continually remonstrating

with Mr. Guirkie on his foolish ways, as she loved to call
them, and frequently, when provoked, would venture even to
scold him sharply, but still in a respectful and affectionate
manner—sometimes for his reckless neglect of his health,
sometimes for spending his money on objects undeserving of
charity, (for Uncle Jerry had the habit of slipping a sixpence
now and again to the beggars whom Mrs. Motherly thought it
her duty to drive from the door,) but most of all for his inveterate disregard of his dress and personal appearance. Of
late years, however, she had given him up in despair, re-
linquishing all hopes of ever being able to correct him, and
came at last to the wise conclusion that destined as she was
to remain a fixture in the place, why, like a prudent woman,
she would let him have his own way, and try to do the best
she could for him. Still there was one little peculiarity in
Mr. Guirkie's conduct, especially for the last year or so,
which Mrs. Motherly sometimes found it rather hard to put
up with; and that was, his want of regard for her feelings in
presence of third parties—the doctor of course excepted:
this was particularly the case when company happened to be
at the house, or when he chanced to come across her any
where beyond the walls of the cottage. Alone with her at
home, he was as tractable as a child; for the fact was,—and it
may as well be told now as again,—the fact was, he feared Mrs.
Motherly. It's no doubt a lamentable admission, but not the
less true for all that. And the reason was clear: Mrs. Motherly was a woman of such excellent qualities in her way, that
Uncle Jerry could not help entertaining a great respect for
her; then she took such a lively interest in his affairs that he
felt she had a good right to his confidence, and he yielded it
accordingly; and last of all, with all her humility she had
such force of character, that he generally found it easier to
submit than quarrel with her. Whether our readers of the
sterner sex—and we write down the word *sex* in order to
save it from growing entirely obsolete—whether they shall

ever agree to adopt Mr. Guirkie's rule of conduct in this respect as the safest and the wisest is more than we dare predict; still, we might venture to say, judging from the present aspect of things, and making all necessary allowance for the progressive spirit of the age, that such a revolution in the ordinary relations of life would not, after all, be so very extraordinary an event.

In the house and alone with Mrs. Motherly, Uncle Jerry, as we have said already, was generally as tractable as a child. He would turn back at her bidding, were his very foot in the stirrup, and sit down to let her sew a button on his shirt or tie a more becoming knot on his cravat — nay, sometimes, when hard pressed, would hand her his purse for safe keeping — a precaution, by the way, she generally took when she suspected him of going up to the Blind Fiddler's in the Cairn, or down to the widow with the three twins at Ballymastocker. From home, however, or in presence of strangers, he was quite another man. On such occasions, his whole bearing towards her underwent a change. He would draw himself up to the very highest stretch of his dignity, address her in a dictatorial tone, and otherwise deport himself towards her as if he regarded her in no other light than that of an ordinary waiting woman. When any one about the table chanced to make honorable mention of Mrs. Motherly, — which indeed those who were aware of Uncle Jerry's little weakness often did to plague him, — it was amusing to see how the old man would pout his lips, throw himself back, and admit, with a patronizing air, that she was — really was an honest, trustworthy servant — had her little whims, to be sure, as every one had — but, nevertheless, was a right trusty and obedient housekeeper.

This change in Mr. Guirkie's conduct towards her, Mrs. Motherly was for a long time unable to account for, and the anxiety she felt about the cause of it was far more painful to her than the thing itself. The secret of all was, however, — and

8*

the reader must be told it by all means, — the secret was, that Uncle Jerry's friends were in the habit of plaguing him about Mrs. Motherly; that is to say, about certain little leanings in that direction.   They made no direct, specific charges — not one — but kept forever indulging in sly winks and innuendoes, which mortified the poor man much more than plain, down-right accusations.   Amongst these friends, Mr. Thomas Petersham, or Captain Tom Petersham, as he was generally called, held a conspicuous place.   The captain, as the reader may have seen already, was a good natured, jolly sort of a man as one might care to meet with any where.   He cracked a good joke, rode a good horse, kept a good table, sang a good song, sailed the fastest yacht between Fanit Point and the Skerries, and never looked or felt happier in his life than when he had Uncle Jerry at his elbow to hob-nob with him after dinner.   This gentleman had so often plagued Mr. Guirkie, — and he did it in a quiet, provoking way too, his eyes sparkling the while with the spirit of the grape and mischief together, — that the good little man at last thought it prudent to assume a cold and distant reserve towards his respectable housekeeper in the presence of strangers, in order, we suppose, to offset disagreeable suspicions.   Now, of all men in the world, Mr. Guirkie would be the last to think of such an attachment. The thing was entirely out of the course of his thoughts; or if the idea ever could by any chance cross his mind, he would, very probably, walk up to the looking glass, and laugh himself out of countenance for entertaining it for an instant.   He was now sixty years of age, but as hale and hearty as he was at twenty-five — a wealthy, happy old bachelor, who had travelled half the world over — been in all sorts of society — studied men and books till he grew tired of both, and at last settled down quietly at Greenmount, resolved to spend the remainder of his days and his money as far away from city life as possible, without the remotest idea of ever changing his condition of life.

As for Mrs. Motherly, poor soul! if the thought of a nearer
or holier relation between them than that of an honest, faithful
servant to a kind, indulgent master, ever did enter her mind,
why, it wasn't so much to be wondered at, after all. She never
looked on herself as an ordinary house servant. She was
above that, both by early education and household accomplishments, and she knew it; and every one else knew it just
as well, the moment she made her appearance. It was as
plain as the alphabet. Her clean white apron, her neat, well
plaited cap, her bunch of polished keys at her girdle, and
above all, her intelligent, respectable countenance, bespoke at
once her authority and the right she had to exercise it. And
so Uncle Jerry and Mrs. Motherly lived very happily together, each well satisfied with the other, the latter yielding a
reasonable obedience, and the former exercising a reasonable
authority. If any thing ever did happen, once in a long time,
to create a little dryness between them, it was sure to be that
unfortunate habit he had of treating her unkindly before company. In vain did she try to shame him out of it, when she
had him to herself all alone of a quiet evening after tea — he
with his flies and she with her stocking sitting cosily together;
in vain did she draw on his nice sense of propriety to rebuke
him, — nay, sometimes, when more than commonly provoked,
actually charge him to his face with having taken an ungentlemanly advantage of her position to mortify her. All was
in vain. To every complaint she made on that head, Uncle
Jerry, turning away his face to hide his confusion, and making
many a *hem* and *hah*, to clear his throat, would invariably
acknowledge that it might appear strange, but he had his own
reasons for it. This, indeed, was all the explanation he ever
gave, and do what she would, all Mrs. Motherly could ever get
out of him. But to return.

"Mrs. Motherly," whispered Uncle Jerry through the key-
hole; "Mrs. Motherly," he repeated in a hard under-breath.
"I'm going out a little, but you needn't trouble yourself in

the least about it; and please tell the doctor, when he wakes, that I'll return presently."

But the good woman turned the key in the lock before he had quite done speaking, and presented herself before him, her left hand pressed against her plump side, and a look of astonishment, half affected, half real, pictured in her face.

Uncle Jerry raised himself suddenly up from his stooping posture, and gazed at Mrs. Motherly without saying a word,

"Well," at length said the latter, breaking silence, "what's the matter?"

"Why!" responded Mr. Guirkie, "what *is* the matter. It's no harm to go out, I suppose."

"No, but what does it *mean?*" inquired the matron, surveying the diminutive figure of Mr. Guirkie from head to foot; "what does it mean, in such weather as this?"

"Well, that's it; it may look a little odd, to be sure, but I can't help it."

"Why, good gracious, look at the rain streaming down the window. Is it crazy ye are, to venture out in such a hurricane?"

"O, it's not so bad as that, Mrs. Motherly."

"Bad! — it's a downright waterspout."

"Well, never mind — it won't signify. I'll return as soon as possible."

"And where, may I ask, sir, do you propose to go?"

"Go?"

"Yes, it can't surely be any thing less than life and death that'd bring you out such a day as this, after the racking cough you had yesterday."

"Well, that's just it," replied Uncle Jerry — "it's a very serious affair; but you need feel no concern about my catching cold. I'm now very prudent, I assure you, in that respect;" and he buttoned another button in the breast of his coat.

"Prudent! the Lord be about us, and save us; just listen

to that! Well, may I never do harm, if that don't beat Banagher out and out. Prudent, humph! were you prudent when you gave your new under coat to the Blind Fiddler last week, and came home to me shivering, like an old pensioner in an ague fit — were you?"

"Hush! hush!—you needn't speak so loud, Mrs. Motherly," he replied, glancing at the parlor door; "I acknowledge I was wrong in that instance."

"And were you prudent when you gave the five shilling piece to that villain of an old soldier, Manus McGillaway, till he got drunk and stole six of my geese, that the like of them weren't to be seen in the parish."

"And how could I foresee ——"

"Yes, sir, but you did, though; you knew in your heart and soul he was a thief, and especially when he got drunk, that nothing was too hot or heavy for him. You knew that well, sir. And what's more, Mr. Guirkie, you encourage the villain in his thievery, to my own knowledge."

"I encourage him?"

"Yes, sir, *you*. When Captain Petersham sent him that wet day last week for his coat to Castle Gregory, with a token to his sister, it was six bottles of brandy he asked for, instead of the coat, and you gave him a shilling out of your own very fingers, for playing the trick."

"I declare!" exclaimed Uncle Jerry again, after a moment's reflection; "I believe I must admit ——"

"O, admit — you're very good at admissions; but where's the use of them? Ar'n't you just as bad as ever, after all your promises and admissions? God help me, any way; my heart's broke with you; so it is."

"Indeed," replied Uncle Jerry, tapping his lips with the but of his riding whip, and looking as crest-fallen as a boy caught stealing apples, "indeed, it's nothing but the truth; I'm very troublesome, I suppose, to every body I have any dealings with. But you'll excuse me, Mrs. Motherly; it's time I was gone, if I mean to go at all;" and he began to sidle off towards the hall door.

"Stop," cried Mrs. Motherly, as he lifted the latch; "you're not going out that way, are you?"

"What way?"

"Why, look at your leggings."

"My leggings!"

"Yes, don't you see you've buttoned them on the wrong legs."

"That's nonsense!—the wrong legs!"

"Nonsense or not, it's the fact, nevertheless; the tongues are both on the inside, and the buttons too."

"Well, I declare," said Uncle Jerry, turning his little leg round and round, as if seeking for some pretext on which to justify the blunder; "I declare," he repeated, "I declare upon my word and honor, it's very strange, but surely I must have been asleep, when I put them on."

"O, you needn't be trying to make any excuses about it — it's just of a piece with all the rest," said Mrs. Motherly, handing him a chair to sit on, while she knelt down to adjust the difficulty; "that's the first time you buttoned your own leggings these five years," she continued, "and you buttoned them wrong. It ought to be a lesson to you, Mr. Guirkie; it ought to teach you that you can do nothing right."

"Well," replied Mr. Guirkie, with a little more irritation in the tone of his voice than usual, "I'm not so particular about the buttons, perhaps, as I ought to be; but it's only a small matter after all — make your best of it."

"Small matter, indeed! I would like to know what part of your dress you're particular about, large or small."

"Hush, Mrs. Motherly, hush, I say, or you'll wake the doctor."

"I'll not hush, sir; I can't hush; I'm responsible for you, and I must speak."

" And can't you speak without raising the town ? " said Mr. Guirkie, slapping his sealskin cap down on his knees, and scratching his gray head in utter perplexity; " can't you speak with some sort of moderation, ma'am ? "

" No, I can't, for you won't let me — but no matter ; you may go — you may go, sir," she continued, rising from her kneeling posture, and shaking both hands at him, as if she would shake herself clean and clear of him forevermore. " You may go — I'll not be accountable for you any longer — not another hour, sir ; and if you come back dead to us, don't blame any one for it but yourself."

Mr. Guirkie lost not a moment in quitting the house, as soon as Mrs. Motherly withdrew her opposition, but rushed out through the rain, ambling his way, as fast as his legs would carry him, to the stable, and mounted Scotchy, already saddled and bridled for a journey.

Hardly, however, had he got his foot in the stirrup, when Mrs. Motherly, accompanied by Dr. Camberwell, whom she had just waked up, came running out to detain him.

But it was too late ; Uncle Jerry was already in the saddle, and in the act of gathering up the reins.

" Let him go," he cried, as he saw the doctor approaching under an umbrella, bare-headed, and blear-eyed for want of sleep; " let the horse go, you scoundrel, let him go ; " and giving Scotchy a cut on the flank, off he trotted down the avenue towards Ballyhernan Beach, the rain pouring on him in torrents, and the cape of his drab surtout flapping about his ears.

" May the Lord pity you, poor man," exclaimed Mrs. Motherly, gazing after him till he turned the corner; " may the Lord pity you."

" Amen," said the doctor, closing his umbrella at the door, and retreating backwards into the house ; " he's an extraordinary individual."

CHAPTER VII.

Mr. Weeks begins to think Ireland not so very green a Country after all, and rather unsafe for Matrimonial Speculations.

QUITTING the lighthouse, apparently well pleased with his visit, Mr. Weeks threw his broken fishing rod on his shoulder, and set out for Crohan with as much speed as his long, shambling limbs and slow habits would admit of. It being already dark, and the distance he had to walk some four good Irish miles, and that over rough, mountainous roads, he resolved to travel somewhat faster than usual, in order to reach Crohan before the family retired to rest.

And here it should be remarked, that the Hardwrinkle family was a very grave and orderly family; a family, in fact, guided by rule in every thing. They never sat up later than nine o'clock on any occasion whatever. Even the night of Mr. Weeks's arrival, as soon as the deep-toned clock in the great hall struck the appointed hour, the seven sisters, in the order of seniority, rose up each in their turn, and approaching their American cousin, bade him good night with a gravity of deportment that well became the high reputation they had long acquired throughout the parish for unostentatious piety and evangelical perfection.

This strict mode of living was by no means new to Mr. Weeks, for he was bred and born in the land of steady habits himself, and therefore could well understand the value his cousins set upon that particular family regulation. This consideration, added to the danger of being caught in the approaching storm amongst the wild gorges of Benraven, prompted him to tax his physical energies a little more freely than usual.

He had not proceeded very far, however, on his journey, when he found his rapid pace suddenly checked by a tall, muffled figure, that rose up before him on the road, and commanded him to stop.

"Who's there?" demanded Weeks, coming to a dead halt.

"A friend."

"What friend — Else Curley?"

"Ay," said the old woman, wrapping her gray cloak round her head and shoulders, and advancing from the rock where she had been sitting to the middle of the road. "Ay, it's me. I stepped down to meet ye at yer up comin, to hear the news. Hem! what's the good word, sir?"

"Why, all's about right there, I guess," responded Weeks, grounding his fishing rod, and resting his hands on the end of it.

"Plazed with yer visit, I hope."

"Well, yes — got along pretty slick."

"Ye seen her?"

"Well, can't say I saw much of her to speak of."

"But ye think she'll suit ye, any way?"

"Yes, reckon so; she's handsome enough, but kinder skittish, I guess."

"O, av coorse; what else could ye expect at the first goin off?"

"No, that's all right. Irish girls are generally somewhat shy at the beginning. But I've no fear we'll bring her up to the hitchin post yet."

"Humph!" ejaculated Else, "don't be too sure o' that. Remember she has the ould blood in her veins."

"Psaugh! humbug! old blood!"

"Ye don't believe in that."

"Not I; it's all sheer gammon."

"Humph! see that now! E'then, sure we poor crathurs down there always heerd it said that the blood of the Talbots was as hard to tame as the blood of the aigles."

" The Talbots ? "

" Ay."

" And who are they ? " demanded Weeks, looking sharply in the old woman's face.

" The Talbots — why, musha, thin, did ye niver hear tell i' the Talbots ? " said Else, eyeing him with a very equivocal expression of countenance.

" No — don't remember exactly."

" Hoot ! jog yer mimery a bit — the name's not so mighty scarce that ye niver heerd it afore. But no matter ; time enough to speak o' thim things whin we're betther acquint."

" Them things," repeated Weeks ; " what things ? By golly, you're quite mysterious this evening, old lady ; say, what am I to understand by *them* things ? "

" O, nothin, nothin, worth a-talkin of," replied Else ; " you're in a hurry now, ye know ; and besides, there's McSwine's gun tearing away like fury. Ye'd betther make haste, sir, or the storm 'ill be on afore ye get home."

As Else spoke, a thudding sound broke like a peal of distant thunder on the still air, and echoed heavily and slowly along the shore, and then away among the deep ravines of the mountains. A little, fleecy cloud, too, which but half an hour gone, had been hardly perceptible on the western horizon, had now rolled up in piles dark and dense to the eastward, and passing the lighthouse, spread far and wide over the clear sky.

" What's that ? " demanded Weeks, turning to look in the direction of the sound. " It's like a heavy broadside at sea, ain't it ? "

" Ay," responded Else, " it's not unlike it ; but the reports of all the guns on the say, and the channel batteries to boot, never carried fear to as many hearts as that. God look to the poor vessels out there the night ; they'll need good gear and stout arms to win through Tory Island Gut, if this storm catches them within thirty leagues of the coast."

"And what means that bright light out there? It looks like the flame of a burning ship reflected against the heavens."

"O, that's only from the lantern of Tory light," said Else; "McSwine's gun is just beyond it to the west;" and the old woman, in reply to her companion's inquiry, explained the cause of its loud report, assigning it, of course, as all such things are popularly assigned, to a supernatural agency. "It's said," she added, "by the ould people, that it niver was heerd afore the Parliament was taken away from us, and niver will stop firing the death gun of the nation till it comes back."

"Psaugh!" ejaculated Weeks; "what a notion! That's some of your old priests' stories, I guess. But, see here, — about that Talbot——"

"And there goes the Devil's Gulsh too," interrupted Else; "look at the spindrifts as they begin to fly across the iron bridge. Take a friend's advice, Mr. Weeks, and hurry home as fast as ye can; for my word on it, if ye don't, ye'll find a wet jacket afore ye reach Crohan. Good night, sir, good night; and Else made another motion to leave.

"Say, hold on," cried Weeks, detaining her by the skirt of her cloak; "hold on; I can wait long enough to hear what you've got to say about the Talbots. How can they concern me — eh?"

"O, not the laste in the world; how could they, since ye niver heerd tell o' them afore?"

"Well, but still I may have been connected with them somehow unknown to me."

"Ha, ha!" laughed the old woman, gathering the scanty cloak still closer round her emaciated shoulders, as she felt the first breath of the coming storm, and chuckling within its folds, like one of Macbeth's witches gloating over her boiling caldron. "Ha, ha! unbeknown to ye, indeed."

"Come, come," said Weeks; "I want no more fooling just now. You kinder insinewate I had some connection I hadn't ought to with folks name of Talbot."

"Hush! don't spake so loud."

"Nonsense! loud! I'm an American born, and ain't afraid to speak out before any human in creation."

"That's mighty bould," said Else; " but cowards sometimes spake the loudest."

"Well, that's *my* way of doing things, nevertheless."

" And a brave way it is too, sir, for them that can carry it through; but sacrets, ye know, shud be spoke in whispers, and above all, *deep, dark* sacrets;" and the old crone fixed her gray weasel eyes on the face of the Yankee, and then added, " Don't mention that name again above yer breath, for somebody might be listenin."

" What name — Talbot?"

"Whist! I say, the night's dark."

"Dark! I don't care a brass cent, woman; nonsense! Well, I swonnie, if this ain't the greatest attempt at humbug I met since I left ——"

"Ducksville," subjoined Else, in a low, stealthy tone, leering at him the while from under her hood. "And so ye'd like to hear the sacret?"

"Yes, out with it," said Weeks, confidently; " I ain't afraid. If you've got a secret regarding me, tell it. For my part I know of no secret, and I dread none either."

" And might I make bould to ask ye what brought ye here then, if ye haven't?"

" Why, I came to visit my cousins."

"Humph! and are the Hardwrinkles yer cousins?" demanded Else; " eh! surely yer cousins?"

" Well, mother says so; she ought to know something about it, I guess, being the only surviving sister of the late Mr. Hardwrinkle; and so, feeling rather disposed to marry, I took a fancy to offer my hand and fortune to Mary Lee."

" And what wud ye marry her for, if it's a fair question?"

" Her beauty, of course; she has nothing else to recommend her, I reckon."

" Ha, ha, ha!" laughed Else, in hoarse, hollow tones, which

sounded like the voice of the dead from the depths of a charnel vault, her toothless gums mumbling the words as she uttered them; "ha, ha! her beauty, indeed — the beauty of William Talbot's gold 'd be nearer the truth, I'm thinkin."

Weeks heard the name distinctly, and the hearing of it seemed to paralyze him, for the fishing rod fell from his hands without his seeming to notice it.

"What!" said Else, pursuing her advantage, "marry Mary Lee for her beauty — a girl ye niver set eyes on, till ye seen her, not three hours ago, on Lough Ely. Hoot, toot, sir; don't be foolish; yer a quate aisy spoken man, to be snre, and might pass for what ye plaze with the simple counthry gawkies here on the wild mountains; but as for me, I'm a little too ould in the horn to be blindfolded in that way."

"You misunderstand me, old lady," said Weeks, picking up his fishing rod, and endeavoring to compose himself.

"Well, listen to me for a minute, and ye'll hear my raisons. Didn't ye bargain with me for my good word with Mary Lee?"

"Yes; guess so."

"And didn't ye bargain with me moreover if my good word 'd fail to delud-her her with spells and charms, an that afore iver ye seen a faiture of her face?"

"No, that's a mistake," responded Weeks; "I saw her at the Catholic Chapel before I saw you, and determined to have her at any sacrifice."

"Saw her! may be so, but ye didn't see her face; she was veiled."

"Can't say as to that; saw enough at least to know she was a handsome gal. Why should she be veiled — eh?"

"Niver mind; she has her own raisons, I suppose; but this much I can tell ye, that many's the little up settin squireen and purse proud *budagh* threw themselves in her way the last twel'month and more, as she went in and out of Massmount Chapel of a Sunday mornin, lanin on her uncle's arm, to stale a glimpse at her 'bonny een,' and got little for their pains when all was done.   No, no, sir; ye seen that bright, sunny face this blissed day for the first time in yer life, or I'm far out i' my recknin."

"Well, saw enough to know she's a handsome gal," stammered out Weeks, hardly knowing what to say in the face of Else's positive assertion.

"And listen to me again," continued the latter, still following up her advantage; "why didn't ye thry the girl yerself afore ye came my length?   Yer not so handsome that she'd be lakely to fall plump in love with ye, to be sure; but still yer not so ill-lookin aither for a foreigner; and then to the back i' that, ye've as many goold rings, chains, and gaglygaws about ye as might set any young crather's heart a flutterin. Why, in the name i' wondher, I say, didn't ye thry what ye cud do yerself afore ye'd go to the expense of engagin me?"

"Why, I wanted to be spry about it," responded Weeks. "Time's money to me; I count hours dollars, and minutes cents.   I couldn't afford to wait, no how.   But pray, how does it concern you what my views and motives are, if I pay your price when the job's done?"

"Ay, ay," muttered Else; "that's it — that's it.   Ye thought ye'd make short work of it, for fear the sacret 'd lake out.   Humph! I see; and yer cousins, as ye call them, the Hardwinkles, made ye believe I was a witch, I'll warrint, and could do more with spells and charms than you with all yer fine airs and boasted riches.   Ay, ay, ye thought I was an ould hell-born divil 'ithout sowl or conscience, ready to do yer dirty work, an ask no questions aither.   But yer mistaken, Mr. Weeks; cute as ye are, ye'll find me just as canny; and I tell ye what it is, may I niver see the sun again, if all the dollars in America cud buy me over to move one hair's breath in this dark plot, if it wasn't for the sake of Mary Lee herself."

Weeks paused for an instant before he spoke.   The solemn declaration he had just heard, and made with so much apparent sincerity, completely puzzled him. It was a phase in the old woman's character he had never noticed before. Already, indeed, he had penetration enough to see that she was by no means the kind of person common report represented her, nor such as he took her for himself on his first visit to the Cairn. Since that time, her character, it's true, had been slowly and gradually developing itself, but still in such a manner as neither to surprise nor startle him. Now he hardly knew what to make of her. Every mark, every characteristic, of the original woman seemed to have gradually vanished one by one. Her decrepitude, her stupidity, her peevishness, her deafness, her blindness, had all disappeared day after day, and so completely, that at last he could hardly believe in her very identity. The wretched being he found, but a month gone, sitting over her peat fire, with her goat by her side, and looking as stolid as if all her mental faculties had fled, now stood before him, an active, shrewd, energetic woman. All about her was changed — all save the furrows of her brown skin, and the gray elf locks which still stole out from under the band of her ruffled cap. After such a metamorphosis, what wonder if Weeks began to suspect (and especially after so solemn a declaration as he had just heard) that her reputed lust of gold was false, like all the other charges made against her! And how could he tell now, but it was her love of Mary Lee, rather than her love of gold, that led her to take so lively an interest in his affairs? Be that as it might, Weeks felt confused and puzzled to his wit's end, and finally resolved to let Else have her own way, believe what she pleased of him, and carry out her own views to benefit her *protégée* after her own fashion.

"So it's entirely for the girl's sake," he at length replied, "that you consent to aid me in the matter of this marriage."

"Humph! I love gold," responded Else, "but I love Mary Lee better."

"Then you should relinquish your claim on the remaining

three of the four hundred dollars I promised you, since you serve her interests, not mine."

"Not a brass copper of it," replied Else; "not a copper. No, no; so far from that, I'll be expectin another hundred by this time next Thursday."

"Another! whew! Well, well, you shall have it," said Weeks, promptly; "for after all, it don't matter a punkin seed to me what your motives are, if you only secure the girl."

"Nor the girl's love or beauty a punkin seed aither, if ye can only make her yer wife."

"Well — don't know about that."

"Hoot! sir, ye know, as well as the sowl's in yer body, that ye don't care a chaw i' tabacky for her beauty. Yer afther somethin ye value more nor beauty, or I'm not Else Curley o' the Cairn."

"You're not what I once took you for, that's certain," replied Weeks. "You may be the d—l for what I know — and just as like as any thing else, for all I can see to the contrary."

"Ha, ha! I'm not the dotin ould crone yer friends 'd make me out, that 'd sell her sowl to fill her pockets."

"I required no such sacrifice," responded Weeks. "I employed you to serve me in a perfectly lawful transaction, from which no injury could possibly result to either party."

"Humph! and suppose the girl was left a fortin by a friend in furrin parts," said Else, "what then? Who'd be the gainer?"

"Gainer? Why, I guess I'm good enough for her — any way you can fix it, fortune or no fortune," said Weeks, thrusting his hands into his breeches pockets, and hitching up his cap behind with the collar of his coat. "Yes, old lady, good enough if she had fifty fortunes."

"Good enough for her!" repeated Else, looking into his face — her thin, wrinkled lips turning up in scorn as she spoke. "You good enough for Mary Lee!"

"Ay, or for any other Irish girl, by crackie, ever stepped in shoe leather," cried the Yankee, jingling up the silver change in his pockets.

"Ha, ha!" laughed Else; "that's mighty modest."

"Well, them's my sentiments."

"Yer wakeness, ye mane."

"No, ma'am, my solemn conviction. The son of an American revolutionist is good enough, I take it, for the biggest — darndest old aristocrat's daughter in the land, all-fired proud as they feel."

"May be so, may be so," quietly replied Else. "But if that's yer way o' thinkin, I'd advise ye keep it to yerself. Such talk as that may sound big in America, but it won't go down here."

"Here — and what the tarnation are ye, that an American born can't speak his sentiments right out, just as he pleases?"

"O, then indeed it's true for ye; bad scran to the much we are. But still ye know we have our feelins as well as other people. And, between ourselves, Mr. Weeks, it's not very seemly to hear a man like you, without a dhrop o' dacent blood in his veins, comin over here and settin himself up as an aiqual for the best in the land. Wow! wow! sir, it's mighty provokin to see a stranger takin sich airs on himself afore he's a month in the country."

"My dear woman, you're behind the age, I guess, two three centuries down here in this section. If you only kept run of the times, you'd soon come to find, that an American always makes himself at home wherever he goes — that his very name's a passport to every which country in creation."

"Bedad, thin, if ye thry that same passport here, I'm afeerd it won't take, barrin ye spake a little modester nor ye do now. Little as ye think of the Irish abroad, faith, there's some o' them at home here 'd make ye keep a civil distance, if ye don't keep a civil tongue in yer head. Mind that, sir, and don't forget it, aither, as long as yer in the country."

"Well," said Weeks, somewhat taken aback by Else's contemptuous disregard of a claim which he thought irresistible all over the world, and especially in poverty-stricken Ireland, "well, I was always taught to reckon a free-born American good enough for any woman in creation; and I rather think, old lady, you'll have to try hard before you unsettle that opinion. Cousin Nathan — I mentioned his name once before, I guess — Cousin Nathan was considerable of a shrewd man in his way — as shrewd, I presume, as most men in that section of the country — well, he was a man that was always posted up in every thing relating to Europe and European aristocracy, and he told me, often and often, that a free-born American was good enough —— "

"Paugh! free-born fiddlesticks!" exclaimed Else. "What the plague do we care about yer free-born Americans or yer Cousin Nathans aither. We're abliged to ye, to be sure, for sendin us over what ye did in our time of need, an ill it 'd be *our common* to forget it, or indeed our childher after us, for that matter, but in the name o' patience have sense, and don't take the good out of all ye do by boastin and puffin yer Americanism that way, like an auctioneer sellin caligoes at a fair."

"Boasting!" repeated Weeks; "well there! Boasting! why, if there's any thing in this world I hate more than another, it's boasting. I never boast — never. The people of these old reduced nations here may boast, and the poorer they happen to be, the greater braggarts they are. But our nation is too dignified, too intelligent, for that; she's too great to stoop to such trifles. No, no; I merely stated a fact, and I repeat it again, that a free American, a son of the immortal Washington, is good enough for the best and highest blood in creation."

"Very good," said Else; "every body has a right to his own opinion, I suppose. But don't talk that way to Edward Lee, if you don't want to pick a quarrel with him. For never was flint fuller of fire than ye'll find him, if ye touch his family pride, by such talk as that."

"Well, hold on a bit. I've got an all-fired sure way of bringing down that same family pride a peg or two, and without a quarrel either. See if I hain't."

"Why, in deed an word," said Else, suddenly changing her tone to a confidential whisper, "and to tell ye truth, may be that itself wudn't be the worst thing ye cud do, after all, for I'm thinkin they'll have to be beggared before they're bet-thered, the crathurs.

"What does that mean?" demanded Weeks.

"Why, that afther all our schamin, Mary Lee won't have ye till she finds there's no other way to save herself and her uncle from the poorhouse or the jail."

Whilst Else was yet speaking, the crack of a pistol made Weeks turn his eyes quickly in the direction of the little cabin on the Cairn. The night, however, was so pitchy dark, he could see nothing beyond the edge of the road; but judging from the sharpness of the report, he thought the weapon must have been discharged within a dozen paces of where he stood. Wondering what this could mean in a spot so remote and a night so dark and threatening — for the evening breeze had now changed into occasional gusts, and big drops of rain began to fall so heavily as to disturb the dust under his feet, — wondering, and still keeping his eyes turned towards the Cairn, he was again startled by a shrill whistle twice repeated, and seemingly as close to him as if it had come from himself. Turning short to demand from his companion what this signal meant, and why she replied to it, he found, much to his surprise and vexation, that he stood alone — Else was gone. The moment after, however, an answer came to his question, but in a form somewhat different from what the astonished American expected; for hardly had he called the old woman a second time to come back and explain the mystery, when a flash of lightning, instantly followed by a clap of thunder, shot across the road and revealed for a second the form and face of the handsome young sailor, whom he had seen conversing with Mary Lee but an hour before, on the edge of the precipice. It was but a single flash, and lasted no longer than the twinkling of an eye ; and yet he saw the young man distinctly — standing on a little knoll within a short call of him, and resting on the boat-hook in the very position he had seen him last.

Weeks's first impulse was to follow Else and demand an explanation. The presence of the stranger, at such a time and place, appeared to him rather suspicious ; and being inquisitive by nature, as well as somewhat apprehensive of Else's fidelity, he resolved to have the mystery cleared up at once, let the storm rage as it might.

With this magnanimous intention, he strode over the low fence on the road side, and boldly advanced up the hill towards the Cairn. Breathless, as much from agitation of mind as of body, he made his way within fifty paces of Else's cabin, fully determined to have his mind satisfied at all hazards — when, alas for human hopes! he was again destined to meet with disappointment ; for just as he had gained the top of the first slope, Nannie presented herself before him, right in the middle of his path.

" Well, there ! " he exclaimed, gazing at the old white goat standing before him as stiff and resolute as a sentry on guard — " there ! you're ready for mischief again, I see ; but go ahead, old Beelzebub ; I'll be darned if you stop me this time ; " and clutching his fishing rod Celtic fashon, he straightway put himself on his defence.

Nannie, true to the well-known habits and instincts of her species, backed slowly away, till she had receded some ten or twelve paces, and then rearing on her hind feet, made a rush full against the intruder, and would probably have upset him, but Weeks, who had had some experience of the animal already, evaded the blow by stepping aside at the critical moment, and as she passed struck her on the horns. The goat, how-ever, seemed not to notice it in the least; for immediately turning and running up the hill to intercept him, she again drew herself up in a position to renew the encounter. It should here be said, perhaps, that Nannie had somewhat the advantage of Mr. Weeks, inasmuch as the latter was a stran-ger in the country, and had but a very indifferent knowledge of the use of his weapon; whereas Nannie, according to common report, was already the "hero of a hundred battles." Besides, she knew her ground better and could see more dis-tinctly in the darkness. With such odds against him, how-ever, Mr. Weeks did his devoir bravely, and showed no lack of courage in addressing himself to so strange a combat. At length Nannie again rose up, and plunged forward as before, with a furious rush, and again missing her aim, received a second blow on the horns as violent as the first.

"Come, old she-devil, — half catamount, half Lucifer, — fire up again; I'll teach you a Yankee trick or two; come on, old rattlesnake." But Nannie, it seemed, was not disposed to renew the encounter so readily as he expected. Taking it for granted, nevertheless, she would a third time repeat her manœuvre of running on before him and heading him off, he resolved to benefit by her loss of time, and have the start of her for the Cairn. With this object in view, he made all possible haste up the hill, and had gained on her a considera-ble distance, when all of a sudden, and without the slightest anticipation of it on his part, something struck him from be-hind, and threw him back head foremost, down the hill. A statue of marble thrust back from its pedestal down an in-clined plain could not have fallen more helplessly than did Ephraim Weeks. The thud of his body on the beaten foot path might have been heard distinctly at the cabin. He was now completely at the mercy of his enemy. Twice he es-sayed to regain his feet, and twice did Nannie lay him flat on his back. At length, however, he succeeded so far as to scramble up on his knees, and — as the goat, now in the heat of encounter, closed in upon him, no longer retreating and advancing, as before — he finally seized her by the horns, and speechless, breathless, furious, there he held her. But what was he to do now? He could not remain kneeling, in that attitude, looking in his enemy's face, all night, amid the rain and lightning. He was sorely perplexed, for never was he between two such horns of a dilemma before. To let go his hold, and strike with the but of his fishing rod, would only enrage her the more, without in the least extricating him from his embarrassment; and to hold her with one hand, whilst he drew out his pocket pistol (a weapon he always carried about him) with the other, was more than he could accomplish. In either case, he was likely to find himself as helpless and prostrate as ever before he could strike a blow or draw a trigger.

"Tarnation seize ye," he cried, looking into the animal's face, and shaking her by the horns; "are you man, or beast, or devil, or what are ye?"

Nannie bleated a reply. It was her defiance *a l'outrance*.

"O, good heavens!" cried Weeks, in accents of despair, "is there such another country as this in all almighty creation? Here I am on my knees, pelted with rain, half singed with lightning, and nearly beaten to a mummy by a goat, the very first day I entered on my plans and speculations."

But this condition of things could not long endure; and so Mr. Weeks, at last, prudently determined to run for it, since he could see no other way of terminating the fight. It was the resource of the coward, to be sure, but what else could be done? Making a desperate effort, therefore, he threw the goat on her side by a sudden wrench of the horns, and then, jumping on his feet, fled down the hill, over the fence, and along the road, as fast as his long legs could carry him, cursing lustily, as he ran, the unlucky day he ever had the misfortune to meet Else Curley of the Cairn. And here we must leave him to pursue his dreary journey, and return to other actors in the play.

CHAPTER VIII.

Lanty acknowledges his Weakness for Fishing and Field Sports, but thinks Father Brennan's Table nothing the worse for that. Dr. Henshaw is suddenly presented to the Reader, and Uncle Jerry discovered in the Bottom of a Boat, supporting the Negro with the broken Toes.

CASTLE GREGORY, the family seat of the Petershams, on the banks of Lough Swilly, was an odd-fashioned place as could be seen any where in Ireland or out of it. Standing all alone, cold and bare, against the side of a mountain, it looked more like a Rhenish fortress, or soldier's barrack, than a gentleman's residence. To the traveller, whether he approached it by sea or land, it presented a bleak and desolate appearance. There was neither tree to shelter it from the storm, nor portico to break the blast from the hall door. It consisted of several piles of buildings, erected at different periods, and jumbled together without the least ornament or the slightest regard to congruity of outline. High dormer-windows and tall brick chimneys rose up in remarkable confusion, and so closely packed together that all the swallows and jackdaws of the parish seemed to gather there in the season to build their nests. As to the pleasure grounds, if indeed they should be so called, they had neither gate nor stone wall to enclose them. All round about the place was open and bare ; indeed, save a few acres of green lawn before the hall door, where the old sun dial stood between the two lions *couchant,* there was nothing to be seen any where but *bent* and sand hills. In front of the castle, Ballymastocker strand and rabbit warren stretched away to Rathmullen Head, from the brow of which Dunree battery pointed its guns across the narrows of the frith, and behind it

Sugar Loaf Hill rose up like a pyramid with its little coast-guard station and flagstaff on top.

Approaching Castle Gregory by water, from the direction of Araheera Point, the immense precipices, which line the southern shore, completely hide it from the traveller's view, till he comes within an oar's length or two of the usual landing place. It was on this account, probably, that the occupants of a small sailing boat, which glided up the channel the evening after the painful events related in the preceding chapter, seemed quite unconscious of their near proximity to the place, for the steersman put up his helm, and sent the boat sheering away in an opposite direction, just as she had almost touched the nose of the quay.

"Hilloa, there!" exclaimed one of the passengers. "Where away, now? You're taking us over to Innishowen instead of Ballymastocker. Put her about, man; put her about directly."

"Why, sir, you must be mistaken," said the man at the rudder.

"Not very likely. After boating about here nearly every week of my life for the last fifteen years, I should know the lay of the land at least."

"Well, there's Doughmore, where you see the smoke; and there's Buncrana ——"

"Nonsense, sir; don't you see the spars of the Water Hen here over the rocks behind us? Round with her, sir, and let us ashore."

"Begorra, I believe you're right," muttered the skipper, giving the helm a jerk when he saw his mistake. "You're parfectly right, Father John — what in the world could I be thinkin of!"

"Some deviltry, I suppose — what you're always thinking of."

"O, don't be so hard on me, yer riverince; you can't expect every one to know the place as well as yourself, after cruisin about here on sick calls so many years."

"Hut, tut, sir; you're a pretty pilot, to carry us through these rocks and currents," continued the priest, in a half-bantering, half-serious tone. "If you knew only half as much about piloting as you do about poaching, you wouldn't be amiss. There now — take care of the shoals here — steady that, steady; and the tide will set us into the basin."

When the boat touched the ground, the steersman stepped ashore, and drew up her bows as far as he was able on the hard beach, (for it seemed the regular landing place at that time of tide was rather inconvenient for his purpose,) and then prepared to land his passengers.

"Lane on me, yer riverince," said he, as the priest stood with his foot on the gunwale, ready to jump; "lane on me; the shore's rough."

"Yes; lean on you, till you break my neck, as you came within an inch of doing last week. Away — I'll never trust you again."

"But you'll hurt yer feet, Father John," persisted the skipper, with more concern for the clergyman's safety than the danger seemed to warrant.

"Never mind my feet — stand off — I'll none of your help."

"Why, these hard, rough paving stones — they're terrible on the g— on tinder feet, I mane; plaze your riverince, just lane on me once more."

The priest, as he stood there with his foot on the gunwale, appeared to be a man of middle age and stature, and active enough, one would suppose, to jump twice the distance; but the skipper, who was evidently a humorous fellow in his way, had probably discovered his weak point, and seemed disposed to tease him about it in requital for the rebuke he gave him in the presence of strangers.

"You may take my word for it, I'll lean upon you some of these days, my good fellow," said the priest, pushing the skipper aside, and stepping ashore with the greatest ease imaginable; "I'll lean upon you the right way, too."

10 *

"But sure, yer riverince, accordin to yer own words, we're all bound to forgive one another."

"Never mind, sir; I have a crow to pluck with you, notwithstanding."

"A crow!" retorted the skipper; "bedad, sir, that's tough pickin.   But sure if ye'd accept of a brace of grouse or wild duck, I'd bring them up —— "

"Hold your peace, Lanty Hanlon," exclaimed the priest, —for the skipper was no other than our quondam friend,— "hold your peace; you're growing quite too malapert of late. Perhaps if you thought I heard all about your treatment of Mr. Johnston's gamekeeper, last Monday night, you would hardly be so bold."

"Me! sir."

"Ay, you, sir."

"Why, now just listen to that, gentlemen.   May I niver do harm, if it don't beat Banagher out and out.   Upon my conscience it's the most astonishin —— "

"O, you needn't affect all that innocent surprise," said the priest, interrupting him.   "I know you too well to be hoodwinked in that way, Mr. Hanlon.   So not another word now, but make haste to land your passengers."

"O, to be sure — af coorse — that's always the way with ye," muttered Lanty, making a show of hauling up the boat's side to the beach.   "O, no, why shud I be allowed to clear myself.   Av coorse nobody in the whole parish does the laste harm in life, from Monday mornin till Saturday night, but Lanty Hanlon.   But isn't it mighty odd," he continued, winking slyly at one of the occupants of the boat, "how bad entirely he feels about the gamekeeper, when, if report be true, he was himself, once in his days, the terror of all the gamekeepers in the barony!   But it's not that ails him — there's somethin else in the win.   I'll wager he's angry about that salmon I sent him last week;" and closing one eye hard, he looked with the other at a little man seated in the bottom of the boat. "Sure if I cud only be sartint it was that, I'd ask his pardon and promise niver to do the lake again."

"Ha! ha! Capital! capital! Lanty," ejaculated the little man from under the thwarts — "promise never to send him a salmon again if he only forgives you; he! he! excellent, I declare!"

"Salmon! What salmon, sir, do you mean?" demanded the priest.

"O, nothin worth speakin of, yer riverince," replied Lanty, pushing up his rabbit-skin cap from his eyes, and giving the boat another pull; "nothin but a small twenty poundher I speared under Mr. Watts's milldam, and sent up to the house-keeper for your last Friday's dinner; but af coorse yer riverince niver suspected how it came, or ye wudn't taste a morsel of it for the world."

"Ha! ha!" laughed the same voice; "that's it; give it to him, Lanty — that's just his deserving."

"Lanty Hanlon," exclaimed the priest, laughing at the joke himself — for he saw in an instant he had been made un-wittingly to entertain those very friends now sitting in the boat to a stolen salmon, last Friday at dinner, despite all his public threats and denunciations against so unjust and mis-chievous a practice, — "Lanty Hanlon," he repeated, "should you attempt such a trick again, you may depend on it I shall report you to the constabulary."

"Ha! Lanty, listen to that — eh, how very big spoken he is! why, I vow and declare, Lanty, I haven't seen a bit of game at his table these five years but he threatened to throw out of the window."

"O, it's wondherful, yer honor, how mighty tender his conscience is in regard of game! But isn't it quare, sir, this weakness niver comes over his riverince while there's a bone of it to be seen on the table afore him?"

"Hold your scandalous tongue," cried the good-natured priest, raising his cane, at last, over Lanty's head; "hold your impudent tongue, I say, or I'll be tempted to make this acquainted with your ears;" and shaking the weapon at the provoking fellow, he moved away from the shore, out of hearing of his voice.

"Mr. Henshaw," said Lanty, (now that Father John had gone off beyond earshot,) and changing his voice from the long drawl of the dry humorist to a more business-like tone, — "Mr. Henshaw, be plazed, sir, to step ashore, till we thry and lift that crathur of a blackamoor out; he looks like a mummy, poor sowl, he's so quate and peaceable."

The individual named Henshaw had been attentively reading a book, through a pair of gold spectacles, all the time since the boat came in sight. So absorbed indeed was he in the subject, that he never raised his eyes even for an instant, during all the previous conversation, not even when the boat first struck the beach and shook him in his seat.

"Come, sir," repeated Lanty, touching him on the shoulder, "step out, if ye plaze; we must hurry, or we'll be late."

"What's the matter now?" demanded the individual in question, in a deep, gruff voice, raising his eyes, and looking about him, as he spoke.

Lanty again repeated his request.

"Humph!" ejaculated the other, growling out his dissatisfaction at being disturbed; and limiting his reply to the monosyllable, he rose slowly up from his seat, and stalked over the boat's side, with the book under his arm.

It may be as well to say a word or two here respecting this gentleman, since he happens to be somewhat concerned, — though it be indirectly, — in the moral of our story.

He was now a man about forty-five years of age, a Scotchman by birth, and an old college chum of Father John's. They had passed several years together at Oxford, where they lived on the most intimate terms of friendship, till the latter relinquished his studies for the bar, and returned home to prepare himself for the priesthood.   Since that time, Father Brennan had entirely lost sight of his fellow-student, and probably never should have thought of renewing their former intimacy, had he not chanced to see, one day, in an English newspaper, a notice of the conversion to the Catholic church of David Henshaw, Esq., L.L. D., Barrister at Law, and a distinguished contributor to the Edinburgh Review.   This led to the formation of a close and intimate correspondence between them, which, after a continuance of two or three years, at length resulted in the doctor's present visit to his old college friend and classmate.   But the good priest was both disappointed and shocked at the first interview; for he found his old acquaintance not only a "stronger and sterner" Catholic after three years' matriculation, than he was himself, though brought up almost within the sanctuary, but so ultra in all his views of religion, that he began seriously to doubt whether the church had lost or gained by the conversion.   Henshaw was yet but a novice in the church, and only saw her doctrine under its severest aspect.   Her dogmas and anathemas were the only signs of her divine power he could discover, whilst the more gentle and delicate operations of her spirit on the hearts of men were entirely hidden from his view.   The consequence was, that he regarded her only in her coercive capacity, and entirely overlooked the charity with which she exercised it.   Hence Dr. Henshaw became a very despot in religion.   Without the least pity for those who had grown up in the midst of hereditary prejudices against Catholicity, or compassion for those who would willingly have embraced it, if they could only be made to see their error, he consigned all beyond the pale of the church — all, without exception — to unutterable destruction.   Such was Dr. Henshaw.   His head was Catholic, but his heart was that of a pagan philosopher — as cold and unfeeling as a stone.

After gazing about him for a minute or two, he walked slowly up to where the priest was standing, and folding his arms on his breast, turned his face again to the beach, and began to converse with his reverend companion. The attitude he assumed, and the air of self-complacency with which he pursed out his lips when he spoke, could hardly fail to impress the most careless observer with the conviction that he was a man quite conscious of his mental powers, and fully alive to a sense of his personal importance. But we must leave him, for the present, with the priest, and return to the remaining occupants of the boat.

"It's a bad case," said the little man under the thwarts; "a very bad case. I'm afraid one great toe and two little ones are gone entirely."

"O, well, sure, if they're gone atself, your honor, he can do very well without them," replied Lanty; "two or three toes is neither here nor there."

"No; certainly not, in one respect, I admit — but this is an extraordinary case, Lanty — you can't deny that. It's a a very deplorable case, and calls for a world of sympathy;" and as the speaker raised his eyes up to Lanty's face, now bent over him, there could be no mistaking the mild, benevolent countenance of Uncle Jerrie Guirkie."

Lanty looked kindly down for an instant on Uncle Jerry's upturned face. Not a word he said, for there was no need of saying any thing; but the smile on his honest countenance was more eloquent than words. It seemed to say, as plainly as looks could say it, "God Almighty bless you for your kind heart — you're the best sowl in the whole world."

"I hope," said Uncle Jerry, endeavoring to draw up his little gaitered legs from their painful posture, stretched out as they had been so long in the bottom of the boat, — "I hope the poor fellow may be nothing the worse for the long voyage."

"O, begorra, there's not a bit fear of him," replied Lanty; ·

"the crathur's as strong as a bullock. But isn't it mighty strange, sir, ye tuck such a liking to him all at once; why, one'd think you had Christians enough down there at the wreck to take your pick and choice iv, instead of carrying away a blackamoor like that."

"Why, the difference is only in the skin, Lanty."

"The skin!   Bedad, sir, and that atself's no thrifle."

"Well, but he's a Christian."

"That fellow?"

"Yes, indeed, that very negro; and perhaps a better Christion. too, than a great many of us."

"Ha, ha, ha!" laughed Lanty, in spite of his stoic gravity, —for he had never seen a negro before in his life, — "ha, ha! Mr. Guirkie, I see you can joke as well as another.   But come, sir, there's no time to lose now; we must thry to lift him out any way, whatever he is."

"I don't joke, upon my honor, Lanty.   He's really a Christian."

"O, it's no matter; sure I don't care a pin about it; he's good enough in his own way, I'll warrant.   Let me help you out first, sir."

"Nonsense, Lanty; you don't seem to believe me; I tell you again he's a Christian, like yourself; and perhaps, if the truth were known, a much better one too," repeated Uncle Jerry, slightly vexed at Lanty's incredulity.

"Well, bedad, yer honor," replied the incredulous Lanty, scratching his head, "I can't say the compliment's very flattherrin, any way.   Feth, maybe it's in regard of his strength of religion you like him so much, sir."

"No, not for that, either.   It's because one of his race saved my life once in Alabama, at the imminent risk of his own; and I made a vow then never to forget it to the poor fellows wherever I met them.   There's another reason, besides.   I know their natures better than most of my neighbors here, and think I can nurse him with greater comfort to himself and pleasure to me."

The unfortunate African, of whom Dr. Camberwell had told so pitiful a story, was there indeed in *proprio colore*, sitting down low in the boat, and resting his back against Uncle Jerry's breast, while the kind-hearted little man's arms encircled the sufferer's breast with as much tenderness as if it were his own son he had rescued from the jaws of death, and was now bringing back in triumph to his paternal home. In this affectionate manner he supported the poor invalid all the way round Araheera Point from Balleyhernan to Castle Gregory, a distance of nearly ten miles. Often did he speak to him during the voyage in the kindest and most soothing tones. Carefully did he wrap the blankets closer and closer round his all but naked shoulders and stiffened limbs, and pour into his parched lips a mouthful of cordial from his leathern pocket flask. Once only did the party stop on their way, and that was at the lighthouse, to exchange courtesies with Mr. Lee and his fair niece, and inquire after the little cabin boy, whom the latter had carried home with her that morning in her cockle shell over Lough Ely. At the priest's signal, Mary came running down the steps to greet him, and receive his blessing, — which indeed the good man seemed to give with all the fervor of his heart, — whilst Uncle Jerry looked lovingly up in her face, stole her hand back, and kissed it with a tender respect that was in admirable keeping with his own modest character and the maiden's gentle nature. When the boat shoved off, the fair girl ran up the steps again, and stood for a while on the edge of the precipice, under which the boat passed, her face radiant with smiles, and her uplifted hand waving an adieu like a spirit about to ascend into the regions of air.

During the remainder of the voyage hardly a word was spoken. The priest and Henshaw had been discussing literary subjects, all the way from Ballyhernan to the lighthouse, and now, on resuming their journey, seemed to think they had said enough for the present, and turned to occupy the remaining time each after his own fashion. Father John opened his breviary and began to read his office. Dr. Henshaw drew out a number of the "Edinburgh Review," and pulled down his gold spectacles from the top of his head, where he had put them out of his way. Uncle Jerry gave the negro a mouthful of wine, and gathered the blankets closer round him, and Lanty Hanlon took another hitch on the running sheet, and laid himself over quietly in the stern. In this way the little party composed themselves to rest after the fatigues of the morning, while the boat glided slowly up the lough. As they rounded Rathmullen Head, however, an accident occurred which might have proved of serious consequence to the whole party.

At this point Rathmullen Mountain runs out into the frith till it almost butts against Dundrem Bluff, on the opposite shore. On each of these headlands a battery of some ten or twelve guns protects the narrow channel, and so strong is the current here, particularly at half tide, that it is quite impossible for a sail boat to stem it, except under a strong breeze from the mouth of the lough. Lanty saw the ebb tide was beginning to tell upon him as he reached this spot, and making the helm and sheet fast, he stepped forward and shipped the bow oars to help him against the stream; but hardly had he pulled half a dozen strokes, when a large boat, rowed by four stout men and steered by a tall old woman, wrapped in a gray cloak, shot out from one of the dark corners under the headland, and passing the jutting rock, round which he was endeavoring to make his way, struck his little craft so violently as almost to jerk his unsuspecting passengers into the sea. As it was, he lost one of his oars, which, breaking the thowl pins, came within an inch of breaking his own head, as it swept round and fell overboard.

11

"Hah!" cried Lanty, when the boat righted again after the stem of the other had shaved its way down her side, and fell off across her stern into the stream,—"that was near nickin."

"Who are they?" demanded the priest, turning suddenly to look after the boat.

"If she's living, that's Else Curley, of the Cairn, in the stern sheets," replied Lanty.

"What, is it possible?"

"The very woman, sir; and that's young Barry, the rebel, beside her."

"He is a very foolish young man, I fear," said the priest; "he must certainly be caught if he stay here."

After some little exertion, Mr. Guirkie succeeded in extricating his limbs from their disagreeable position, and, with Lanty's help, found himself safe at last on *terra firma*. The three gentlemen then came together, to consult about transporting the negro to Greenmount. Uncle Jerry was for sending immediately to the next village for a horse and cart, and stretching him on a mattress laid on the bottom of it. Dr. Henshaw, on the other hand, thought he might do very well in the boat house, for the night, with some clean straw, and Lanty to watch with him; more especially as the boat house was close at hand, and the night pleasant and warm; while they could return home themselves, and send over an easy conveyance next morning. But the priest was of a different opinion from both, and thought it much better for all parties to sleep at Castle Gregory. "The night would be very dark," he said, "the roads both deep and rutty after the late rains, and, besides, 'twould take two hours, at least, to procure a suitable conveyance for the negro if they carried him home, or for themselves if they left him behind." As to accommodations for the invalid, he had no doubt Captain Petersham would cheerfully order him a comfortable berth, and send his servants to carry him up to the castle. After some objections, on the part of Uncle Jerry, on the score of delay and the immediate necessity for medical attendance, — objections which we fear very much were a little aggravated by the dread of Mrs. Motherly's grave displeasure at his long absence, — and on the part of Dr. Henshaw, against what he called an unpardonable intrusion into a gentleman's family, particularly at so late an hour, and accompanied, as they were, by a notorious poacher and a half-dead negro, " hawking the latter aboot all day," he added, gruffly, " in a most absurd and redeeculous manner, from house to house and rock to rock, till he expected the whole country round should ring with it for the next twelve-month to come"—after these objections, we say, were made and disposed of, the party, at last, concluded to leave the negro with Lanty, in the boat house, and put up at Castle Gregory for the night. Accordingly, they advanced to the house, and Father John, raising the knocker, knocked loudly on the door.

CHAPTER IX.

Being the shortest Chapter in the Book, is devoted exclusively to Mr. Weeks.

MR. EPHRAIM WEEKS, as the reader may have already suspected, came to Ireland to speculate in matrimony. He left home with a cigar in his mouth, and stepped aboard the packet as she moved past the wharf, with as careless and indifferent an air as if he were dropping down to Sandy Hook to visit a friend. As to meeting with any serious obstacle, in a country whose inhabitants, to take them in the lump, were no better than South Sea Islanders, he never dreamed of it for a moment: why should he? He knew what the Irish were,

every soul of them, and could read them through as he could
the alphabet.   He met them on the wharves, on the railroads,
on the steamboats, in the police offices, saw them dramatized
on the stage, tried at the bar, and dissected in the pulpit.   In
a word, he knew what they were at home in Ireland, just as
well as if he had been living with them there all his lifetime.
What had he to fear?   He had succeeded so far in various
speculations in New England, and how could he possibly fail
in a land of such ignorance and beggary as Ireland?   To be
sure, there must necessarily be some intelligent men in the
country — it could not well be otherwise — but what of that?
there were no smart men amongst them.   *Smartness* to him
was every thing.   It was the embodiment of all the virtues,
moral and intellectual — the only quality for which man deserved admiration or respect.   The estimate he formed of his
neighbor's moral worth was not in proportion to his integrity
of character, but to his ability for speculating and driving
hard bargains.   The man who contented himself with a com-
petence and a quiet life at home he despised; but the jobber
in stocks, who was smart enough to make a lucky hit on
'change, though he risked half a dozen men's fortunes on the
chance, was the man after his heart.   Such were Mr. Weeks's
sentiments.   Nor was he much to blame for them either; for
he was bred and born in the midst of speculators.   Every
man he met in the street, from the newsboy to the judge,
from the policeman to the governor, was a speculator in something.   He began himself, in his very infancy, to speculate in
marbles and hobby-horses; and if he made but a cent a
week, his father patted him on the head, and prophesied his
future greatness.   When arrived at man's estate, he found
himself in the company of young men, whose sole study was
to make money in the easiest manner and shortest time.   He
saw them every where engaged in some kind of traffic, — no
matter what, if it only happened to be profitable.   Whilst in
other countries each grade in the community had its own

legitimate trades and occupations, it was the very reverse in the States. There it was a universal scramble, in which every body snatched at what came handiest. The tailor dropped his needle and mounted the stump; the lawyer burned his briefs to trade in molasses; the shoemaker stuck his awl in the bench and ascended the pulpit; and the shopboy flung his yardstick on the counter and went off to edit a Sunday newspaper. Surrounded on all sides by such influences, what could Mr. Weeks have possibly been but what he was — a speculator in chances — a man of one idea — one object — one aspiration — money? Learning was nothing in his estimation, if it failed to realize money; nay, the highest mental accomplishment was not only valueless, but contemptible without money. In this respect Mr. Weeks represented a large class of his countrymen of New England; — we say a class, for it would be unjust to say more. He was not an American gentleman, by any means, either in habits or education. That was plain the instant he spoke a word or moved a muscle, and those of his fellow-citizens who could rightfully claim that distinction would never have recognized him as one of their number. He was, in short, a Yankee, — a man to be met with every day and every where — on the sidewalks — at the banks — in the theatre — in the cars — standing at hotel doors picking his teeth — selling soap at cattle shows — or lobbying for a patent right behind his agent's back in the Senate House. But to return.

With such views and sentiments as we have here ascribed to Mr. Weeks, it may be easily conceived with what assurance of success he landed in Ireland, and with what confidence he entered on his plans and speculations. The possession of Mary Lee as his lawful wedded wife was the great secret of his journey. Why it was so the sequel must tell. It appears, however, he had but a limited time to accomplish his designs; for hardly had he reached Crohan, when he called to see Else Curley. The reputation she had acquired, all the country

11 *

round, and the wonderful stories told of her power over the spirits of the nether world, led him to think he could win her to his interest by tempting her cupidity, and that she, as a secret agent, might do what it would otherwise require a long courtship to effect. How his expectations were met, in this respect, will be seen in due course of the story. For the present, we must leave him to battle with the storm as best he may, after his desperate but disastrous rencontre with "Nannie," and follow Else and the stranger to the "Cairn."

CHAPTER X.

The Outlaw's Interview with Else Curley. — Her Hatred of the Hardwrinkles, and its Cause. — Barry evades the detective Officers.

WHEN Else had placed a rush light in the wooden candle-stick affixed to her spinning wheel, and thrown off her gray cloak, she drew a small silver-mounted pistol from her bosom, and laying it on the table, motioned the young man to a seat.

"How come ye here, Master Randall, at this hour?" she demanded.

"The fates drove me, I suppose," replied her guest, smiling.

"Psaugh! — this is no time to play the fool; — why are ye here, I say?" drawing down her shaggy eyebrows, and looking sternly at him as she spoke.

"Why, how now!" exclaimed the stranger; "is Nannie sick, or old Bat's fiddle broke, that you're so much out of sorts?"

"Master Randall, look at that weapon," said Else. "I risked my life for yer sake and hers within this very hour, and carried that with me to defend it. I made this Yankee feel he was in my power, and for that raison didn't know the minute he'd silence my tongue forever with a pistol ball or a dirk knife. Now, I ask ye, is it manly in ye, after this, to come back here again to idle away yer time, tryin to get a word or a look at this silly girl, when it's in Dublin or Cork ye'd ought to be strivin to keep her and her uncle out iv the walls of a jail. Hoot, toot, sir, I thought there was more i' the man in ye."

" Well, of that," replied Randall, (for we must call him so in future,) "of that I can say little ; but be assured, Else, no trifling obstacle could balk me on such an errand. Nothing but absolute necessity compelled me to return."

" Necessity ! "

" Yes. The police headed me off below Burnfoot, after landing from the ferry, at Rathmullan, and chased me through Buncrana to Lambert's Point, where you brought the boat to my relief."

" So ye escaped in the skiff, yesterday, I suppose, from Dunree."

" Yes ; just had time to jump in, cut the painter, and shove off, when three of my pursuers sprang down after me on the beach."

" And fired ? "

" One of them, only. The ball hit me on the head, but did no harm."

" Humph ! " said Else, sitting down slowly on her low " creepie stool," " and so the bloodhounds got on yer trail, after all."

" Yes, fairly started me," responded Randall ; " when they'll run me down, however, remains yet to be seen."

" It looks strange," said Else, half speaking to herself.

" What ? "

" How they knew ye in that disguise."

"It does look a little strange, I must confess," replied Randall; "for I thought it impenetrable to every eye but those of Else Curley and Mary Lee. Judge of my astonishment, then, when I beheld straight before me, on the first public house door I passed, a full length figure of myself in this very dress."

"Tell me," said Else, after a moment's reflection, "didn't ye wear that dress ornst at Father John's?"

"I did; but it was night then, and no one saw me except the priest and his housekeeper."

"Don't be too sure i' that, Master Randall."

"Quite sure."

"Humph! didn't ye tell me about passin somebody that night, on the road near Crohan gate house, that seemed to look sharp at ye?"

"Crohan gate house—let me see. Yes, I remember now. O, that was some traveller—I suspect."

"Was he a tall, thin, dark lookin man?

"Yes, rather."

"Wore crape on his hat?"

"Yes."

"I thought so."

"Who was he?"

"Robert Hardwrinkle, of Crohan."

"What! your great enemy—this Yankee's cousin?"

"That very Yankee's cousin. He's the man that be thrayed ye."

"No, no, Else, you must be mistaken. Mr. Hardwrinkle's a gentleman, and could never be guilty of so treacherous an act."

"Cudn't he?"

"No, Else, it's nothing but your inveterate hatred of the man makes you suspect him."

"Hoot, toot, Master Randall; don't be foolish," replied Else.

"I know what he is, kith and kin, for threescore years an more. Ay, ay, to my own grief I know him. But let him look to himself, for the time's not far away when the long recknin atween him and me must be settled — let him look to himself."

" Do the man no harm on my account," said Randall : "if he has really sent these officers on my track, it's only what a thousand others had done with as little shame or scruple. For my part, I forgive him, nor would I hurt a hair of his head this moment if he lay at my feet."

. " O, forgive him, an welcome," said Else, "since yer so good a Christian ; forgive him, by all manes. I'm sure it's none o' my business if ye forgive him, and marry his lean sister Rebecca, the psalm-singer, too, into the bargain. All I say is, let him be ready ; for there's an account atween him and me that nothing but his cowardly blood can settle."

"Why, Else, this is sheer madness," said Randall, reprovingly. "How is it the very thought of this man inflames your resentment so much ? "

"So well it might," responded Else, raising her head and folding her arms on her hard, weather-beaten breast, as she looked across the table at her companion. " So well it might. Listen to me, Randall Barry. If this man's father first brought your only sister to sin an shame, and then sent yer brother to die with irons on his limbs in a strange land, for no other earthly raison than because he demanded satisfaction for the injury done his own flesh an blood — if he turned out yer mother, ould and helpless, from the homestead she was born in, and her people afore her, for three generations — when the father died, if the son sent yerself to jail twist in five years on false charges — when ye came out and built with yer own hands a sheelin to shelter ye from the storms on these blake mountains, if he burnt it over yer head — ay, and if he driv ye at last, Randall Barry, as he druv me, to

burrow here lake the 'brock' on the crags of Benraven, —
I ask ye, would ye forgive him, if he did that to you an yours?
An ye felt his neck undher yer heel, wudn't ye crush it
down — down in the dust with as little pity as ye'd feel for
the wasp that stung ye?"

"Not I," replied Randall, "not I. To kill even an enemy,
whom you happen to find in your power, is an act of cowardly murder. And, believe me, Else, your own sleep would be
none the sounder in the grave for having this man's blood
upon your hands."

"And yet," retorted Else, "you and yer companions id stain
yer hands with the blood iv thousands, that did ye far less
wrong than he did me."

"Perhaps so ; but in broad daylight, at least ; not assassin-
like, in the dark."

"I see no difference," replied Else, "night or day — it's
only death."

"Ay, but surely it's a less crime to put the enemies of
your country and of human liberty to death in a fair field
and open fight, than to commit a midnight murder like a cutthroat or incendiary, with the dirk or the brand."

"Who spoke of dirk or brand?" demanded Else.

"You did," replied Randall, promptly. "You did a dozen
times within the month. And now my fear is, your new
charge against this man will bring down your long-threatened
vengeance on his head sooner than I anticipated. But hear
me, Else Curley, —— "

"Hould yer tongue, Randall Barry," interrupted the old
woman, "hould yer tongue ; yer but a silly boy. Pshaugh !
it's little ye know iv Else Curley 'i the 'Cairn.' What! ye
think after waitin and watchin for my hour of revenge so many
long years, I'd bungle it now for your sake? Ha ! ha ! poor
foolish boy ! D'ye think a woman like me, that fursaked God
an salvation thirty odd years ago, for fear they'd come atween
her and her dark thoughts — a woman whose hopes iv ven-

geance, day after day, were like draps iv new life blood to her withered heart — d'ye think an outcast like me, a bein that men dread to look on, an women spake of undher their breath, wud drag out life as I did, for no other raison or motive, but waitin patiently for my hour to come? D'ye think, I say, Randall Barry, I'd let the paltry matter of his bethrayin you to the spies of the Castle bring down the blow one minute sooner than it ought to fall? Pshaugh! man, ye don't know me yet."

"I know you to be a dangerous woman," responded Randall, rising from his chair, and buckling his belt tighter round his waist, as if preparing to leave. "But I warn you," he continued, "I warn you I shall be no party to this contemplated murder; and, much as you have befriended me, Else Curley, I shall, nevertheless, do all in my power to thwart your wicked designs. Rebel and felon as I am, I shall never abet or connive at murder, notwithstanding."

"And what then?" again demanded Else — "wud ye turn informer?"

"Assuredly — the instant you attempt to execute your hellish purpose."

"Then," cried Else, snatching the pistol from the table, and raising up her tall form from the low stool on which she sat, till she stood erect as a statue before the young outlaw, her gray eyes flashing fire and the muscles of her face qnivering with emotion as she spoke, "I swear to ye," she cried, holding up the weapon in her fleshless hand, "I swear by them heavens I niver expect to enther, if ye were my own born son, Randall Barry, an attempt to save that man from the clutches i' my vengeance, ye'll die the death."

"Tigress," muttered Randall between his teeth, as he threw on his sea cap and turned to quit the cabin. "Tigress, I despise your threats."

"Stop," said Else, stepping back and leaning against the door; "stop, young man, and listen to me. It's now fifty long years since yer grandfather, Lieutenant Dick Barry, saved my life at the risk of his own. It was the day Colonel Clinton took Madeira. He carried me in his own arms from the spot where my husband fell. I made a vow then on my knees afore God, if iver it come in my way to befriend him or his, I'd do it."

"I release you from your vow," said Randall; "let me pass."

"Be silent, boy, and listen to me again," cried Else. "You'll not pass here till I spake. Listen to me. I love Mary Lee more nor iver I loved woman afore, barin the sister that died from me, in shame an a broken heart. Ay, she died in these withered arms; she died laughin, Randall Barry, for she died mad — mad — mad; she died with the bloom of seventeen still on her cheeks. Listen to me. I love Mary Lee more nor iver I loved woman but her; and well I might too, for it was these hands saved her from the wrack of the Saldana; it was these hands untwisted her arms from her dead mother's neck, among the rocks of Araheera; and it was these hands nursed her on Nannie's milk for eighteen months, till them came to claim her that had the right to claim her. O, no wondher she's dear t' me; no wondher I'd watch her an guard her like the apple of my eye. But still, much as I love her, an much as I love yerself, Randall Barry, for yer granfather's sake, still, I say, as there's a heaven above me, I'd rather see ye both dead at my feet this minute, than part with the hope of payin back the Hardwrinkles, mother an son, for the wrongs they did to me an mine. Ha, ha!" laughed the old woman bitterly, as she grew more and more excited; "ha! ha! they burned my cabin twiste to the groun, and driv me out to sleep at night with the black cock an the plover, an to wandher by day over the dreary mountains, hungry and barefoot; but their hour'll soon come. Ay, ay, I'll be even with them yit. Ha! ha! let them look to themselves; the blind fiddler's wife, the worker of spells and charms, the woman that'd sell her soul for money, ould Else Curley i' the 'Cairn,' has strength an courage enough left yit to handle a dirk or fire a fagot."

Randall gazed at her with astonishment as she spoke. Her person seemed to dilate and grow younger as her face swelled with passion. She had broken, with a sudden snap, the string that confined her cap, to relieve her throat from a sense of suffocation; and now, as her short gray hair fell in tufts over her forehead and cheeks, she looked like a pythoness, breathless under the frenzy of inspiration.

"My God," said Randall, still gazing at her as she stood before him, "is it possible that so much gratitude and love can exist in the same breast with such demoniac hatred for a fellow-creature? Here is a woman — ay, a very woman — who has lived since before I was born on the bare hope of being one day able to revenge her wrongs. That hope was the only ray of consolation that ever fell on her desolate heart. How great must have been her injuries to have earned so terrible a resentment! And yet this creature loves Mary Lee like a mother, and already has risked her life, more than once, to save mine."

"Else," said he, at length, laying his hand kindly on her shoulder, "I pity you from my heart. Sit down and compose yourself. I would speak with you more reasonably on this subject."

She obeyed him instantly, for the touch of his friendly hand softened her more than words could have done.

"Tell me," said Randall, "is this Yankee, this cousin of the Hardwrinkles, to be included in the catastrophe?"

"No," replied Else.

"What business have you with him, then?"

"I make use iv him to sarve my own ends — nothin more."

"And these are ——"

12

"First, that he'd supply me with money for thravelin expenses; an, secondly, that he'd be an excuse for drawin me about Crohan, to watch my chances."

"Ha! I understand you. But the travelling expenses — where —— ?"

"Connecticut, or wheriver else he came from. We must send a thrusty messenger to make out where he lives, and ye may be sure Edward Talbot's not far from that."

"So you'll employ his own money to defeat him?"

"Of coorse," replied Else.

"And why, then, did you acquaint him with your knowledge of the secret?"

"That he'd pay me the betther for keepin it."

"Good; but are you sure he'll not feel apprehensive of your disclosing it to Mary or her uncle?"

"Not the laste in the worl," replied Else.

"Still, the whole affair is but mere suspicion, after all."

"What? about Mr. Talbot bein alive?"

"Yes."

"Well, call it whatsomiver name ye plaze, it's sartinty enough for me. I niver thought any thing else but that he was livin somewhere in furrin parts."

"And how will you account for this Yankee's correspondent speaking of the dying man as Lambton in that letter of his you picked up after he left the cabin here? How can you account for that, if he be really Edward Talbot?"

"Quite easy," responded Else. "It was the name he went by in America."

"Nonsense, woman! you make the most absurd and ridiculous suppositions; would you have him change his name with his country?"

"Feth wud I, an good reason he had to do that same, let me tell you. Didn't he fire a pistol bullet at his wife in her own room, with the child in her arms, the very same evenin he come home after killing Captain Blenherhasset in a dewel that his own infarnal jealousy driv him to fight for her sake; an was there a corner in London nixt day that hadn't a bill posted up on it, offerin a reward of a thousand pound to the first man 'id take him? Humph! raison indeed; bedad, I think that 'id surely be raison enough for any man to change his name wheriver he went. No, no, Masther Randall, Edward Talbot's livin jist as sure as you're livin, if he didn't die since the first iv May last; an that very Lambton he writes about is the man. Whether he gives himself that name for fear the letter might fall into other hands, or whether Mr. Talbot took the name himself, I can't tell — but ye may depind on it Lambton's the man."

" Perhaps so."

" O, feen a doubt of it; and ye'll see that too, when Lanty comes back."

" What, Lanty Hanlon?"

" Ay, Lanty Hanlon; ye heard of him, I suppose."

" And saw him, too. Don't you remember to have recommended him to me two or three weeks ago, as a trusty messenger to send on a certain important business to Derry?"

" And ye sent him?"

" Certainly."

" Well?"

" Well, he broke trust at the very outset."

" Lanty Hanlon!"

" Ay, Lanty Hanlon. Instead of crossing the lough at Doughbeg, he strolled down the shore to Ballymastocker, to see a cockfight, and missed the tide."

" O, feth, as to that," said Else, " I wudn't put it past him. He's the very ould lad himself in regard to cockfighting."

" Yes; but he was made well aware of the urgency of the message, and should have postponed his personal gratification till his return."

"Postpone, indeed! In troth, Master Randall, he'd post-pone goin to heaven, if there wus a cockfight 'ithin five miles of him; that an huntin's his wakeness, poor fellow. An what excuse did he make when he came back?"

"He never came back to make any. Instead of that, he sent me word he was in the hands of the police for beating a gamekeeper, and would see me as soon as he got clear."

"Humph!" said Else, "that's another of his wakenesses."

"It's rather an odd kind of weakness," said Randall, laughing.

"Well, its natural for him, poor fellow, any way; the whole breed of him hated gamekeepers for five generations back. And so the man was too many for him?"

"No, he made his escape then, but the police caught him next day. It appears on his return he crossed the mountain with his dogs, and met Lord Leitrim's gamekeepers, who gave him chase. Two of them he distanced, and the third he led into some lonely spot, beat him there soundly, and then left him gagged with his own handkerchief, and tied neck and heels to an old hawthorn tree beside a well, where he was found next morning, half dead from cold and hunger."

"It's jist like him," said Else, "for the villain's niver out of mischief. But still he's as true as steel when ye keep him away from timptation."

"And how is that to be done, pray? Will he not meet with as much temptation on his way to the United States and back, as he does here in the parish of Clondavadoc?"

"Not he," replied Else; "I'll trust him for that. The minute he finds it's on Mary Lee's affairs he's goin, the sarpint himself wudn't timpt him. But," she added, correcting her-self, "I'm not sure yit whither he'll have to go at all or not; may be somethin might turn up to save the journey and the expinse too. It's well to be prepared, any way, you know."

"Certainly. But is Lanty so devoted to Mary as you say?"

"He'd lay down his life for her every day i' the year. There's not a livin thing he loves like her in the whole worl."

"Possible?"

"Didn't ye know it? He cud sit lookin at her from mornin to night, an niver be dry or hungry. And it's a mighty queer notion, too, he has about her."

"What's that?"

"Why, he thinks it 'id be a sin to love her as he'd love any other girl."

"How so?"

"Bekase she's so good, he says. And it's all come of a drame he had onst about the Blissed Virgin. — Och, och," said Else, suddenly interrupting herself, "an many a purty drame I had of her myself in my young days, when I ust to wear her scappler, an gather the May flowers for her alther; but them things is all over now. I can niver drame or pray to her again, for the black thoughts druv her image out iv my heart fer ivermore. And Mary Lee, too, the poor child, whin she spakes to me sometimes of an evenin, sittin out here on the hill side, about the marcy of Christ, an the bright heavens above, an the goodness of God to them that repent, her words and looks make me tremble all over like a windle straw. — But, as I was sayin," she continued, wiping her face with her apron, as if to brush away every thing that could blunt in the slightest degree her keen and long-cherished resentment, — "as I was tellin ye about Lanty; he had a drame one night, when he thought the Blissed Virgin come to him houldin Mary Lee by the hand, and tould him to watch her an take care of her as long as he lived, on *her* account."

"A delightful illusion, I must confess," said Randall.

12 *

"I'm not a Catholic, you know, Else, but there is a poetry in the Catholic conception of the attributes of the Virgin which always had an inexpressible charm for me. I once saw a beautiful little beggar girl at Florence, kneeling before one of her shrines, her hands and eyes raised in mute supplication for the crippled mother who sat by her side, and I thought I had never seen a finer picture of religion in my life."

"Well, well, dear," ejaculated Else; "I don't know any thing about such picthers now; I ust once, but that time's gone. But, as I was sayin, since he dramed that drame of the Blissed Virgin (God forgive me for mintionin her name) and Mary Lee, he can't think of one without the ither, an ivery wish of Mary's is like a command to him from heaven."

"How very extraordinary!" said Randall.

"The drame?"

"No, but that every one's so peculiarly affected by the words and looks of this girl."

"Well, it's jist the same with the children she taches the Christen docthrin to down there in her little chapel undher the rock; they'd pit their very heads undher her feet; an what's quarest of all, there's a dog in the town there below that tears ivery body he can get a hoult of—the crossest animal iver run on four feet; well, that dog, the first minute he seen her, crooched at her feet, and kissed her hand, jist as if she fed him with it all his lifetime; and iver since, as soon as he sees her, he runs away whinin afther her, and niver quits her company till he leaves her at the lighthouse gate."

"And old Drake, too, is very fond of her," observed Randall.

"Hoot! as for Drake," replied Else, "Drake can read her countenance betther nor you or I can. He knows who she likes an disn't like the minute he sees them. Sure, when she lay sick last Haliday, he niver left her room night or day, nor niver as much as tasted mate kind for a whole week, till Roger had to lift him on a chair by her bedside and let her feed him with her own hands. Roger swears he saw the tears fallin down the dog's cheeks, when he looked up in her face, and tuk the food from her fingers."

"She's too good and too pure for me, Else," said Randall, thoughtfully; "and I fear such a creature could never be happy with the heretic and revolutionist I am."

"You'll not be either long, if she marries ye," said Else; "take my word for it."

"And why not?"

"O, the Lord luck t'ye, Master Randall; she'd make a Catholic iv ye in three weeks 'ithout one word's spakin."

"Indeed! by what means, pray?"

"Why, she'd make her religion look so good an holy in yer eyes, jist by her ivery day ways, that ye cudn't help lovin it yerself. An as for the rest, she loves her ould country as well as you, Randall Barry, woman an all as she is, an wud suffer as willingly too, may be, if all came to all. But hush! didn't I hear some noise outside?"

"No — it's only the storm whistling in the thatch."

"Well, it's time, any way, ye'd have somethin to ate afther yer long race;" and rising from the 'creepie,' she produced a cold fowl from the recesses of a little cupboard concealed in the thickness of the cabin wall, and laid it on the table. Then stooping, she raised up the hearth-stone, and disappeared in the dark opening beneath with surprising agility for a woman of her years. The action, strange as it was, did not appear to excite the young man's curiosity in the least; he glanced merely at Else as she descended, and then leaning his head on his hand, composed himself to wait patiently for her return.

As he sat there by the table in the dim light of the rush candle, there was nothing about his person worthy of special notice. His figure was light and graceful, his limbs well moulded and muscular, and his height, if we could judge fairly in the posture he had taken, a little above the middle

size. His long black hair fell in disorder over the low collar
of his blue jacket, from the breast pockets of which the buts
of a pair of travelling pistols still peeped out. His cravat,
as we have said already, was knotted loosely in front, sailor
fashion, and revealed a neck by far too fair for a seafaring
man, and one it would have puzzled a detective officer to
reconcile with his general appearance. But if there was
nothing striking in his person, there was that in his handsome
face which gave character and interest to the whole man — a
shade of quiet melancholy, which at once impressed the beholder with the conviction that the young outlaw was no
lover of war or bloodshed for the gratification they afforded
him, but reluctantly adopted as a last and desperate resource
for retrieving the fallen fortunes of his country. His countenance was calm and composed, without a trace of the social-
ist or the red republican to vulgarize its fine expression.

  " Ay, ay," said he at length, his voice barely audible as he
murmured out the words; " let my father disinherit me if he
will, and the spies of the government dog me step by step,
till they drive me at last to bay; still I shall neither sue for
pardon, nor fly from the land of my birth and my affection
to beg a home on a foreign shore. To abandon Mary Lee
would now be impossible, were she as indifferent to me
as the meanest peasant girl in the kingdom; but were she
even dead to-morrow, and all my hopes buried with her
in the grave, I should wait and watch, and bide my time
to renew the contest; I should still cling to the hope that
God, in his own good time, would inspire the young men
of the land to rise once more — not as wranglers and
brawlers — not as mercenary anarchists and sordid dem-
agogues, but like Spartan brothers, to do, and dare, and die
for their country's weal. To see that blessed day, I could
eke out life in the lowest caverns of my native hills. To
behold the sunburst, as of old, *waving once more before an
army of gallant young Irishmen* — true to the sacred cause

and to each other — true to right, to justice, and to honor !
O, to see such an army in battle array on the sunny slopes
of old Clontarf, marching down, with fife and drum, and
colors flying, to drive the Saxon dogs from their long-lost
homes and pleasant firesides, and to be allowed to strike one
good blow myself for the sake of old times and old memories
— O, Mary Lee, Mary Lee, much as I love you, I could
abandon you for this ! But alas, alas ! years must elapse ere
it can happen; meanwhile I wander among the hills a rebel
and an outlaw, hunted and proscribed like the vilest mal-
efactor. Be it so; I have risked my all on a single cast,
and lost it. Well, I shall try to abide the consequence as
best I may. Let them hunt me, and catch me, if they
can. I'll disappoint them so long as I'm able to fly or defend myself. When I can no longer do either, I needs must
submit."

"There," said Else, emerging from the dark opening, and
laying a bottle on the table, from which she had already
drawn the cork, "there's a bottle of ould Port that lay down
there below these twenty years and more; take a drink of it
with that could widgeon Roger left me yesterday; it'll do ye
good afther yer day's fatague."

Randall had just emptied the first glass, laid it on the table
again, and was about to address himself to the cold widgeon,
when Else pressed his arm, and looked significantly towards
the door.

"What's the matter ? "

"Whisht ! that's Nannie's blate — there's somebody comin."

"O, no, it's the poor beast asking shelter from the storm."

"Hush ! I know Nannie better — there it's again."

Randall rose quickly, threw on his sea cap, and buttoned
his jacket.

"If they want me," he said, "they must follow me to
Aranmore. Good night, Else."

"To Aranmore ? "

"Yes — no possibility now of reaching Dublin by any other route. I hope to find a fishing smack there from the Skerries, to take me off."

"Take another glass, Master Randall."

"No more — good night, Else;" and jumping into the mysterious opening, he disappeared, leaving Else to replace the covering, remove the viands, and receive the new comers, whose footfalls she could now hear distinctly at the door.

———◆———

CHAPTER XI.

Weeks thinks himself very ill treated, and the Irish, the most savage, beggarly "Varmint in all Creation."— He is conducted to a Wedding, and having taken a Glass or two, under protest, dances an Irish Jig, to the great delight of the Company.

IT was now within a short hour of midnight, and Weeks, drenched and weary, still plodded his lonely way over the hills of Benraven. The night was very stormy, and Mr. Weeks very much out of sorts. In truth, he was troubled exceedingly, both in mind and body — especially in the latter, for he had unfortunately lost his cap in his rencontre with Nannie, and was obliged to use his pocket handkerchief instead. It was a poor substitute to be sure; but what else could he do? He had already drawn his coat tails over his head, but found it impossible to keep them down on account of the violence of the wind. Still, the wind and the rain together, though bad enough, were not the worst he had to contend with; the darkness was the great difficulty, for he could hardly "see his finger before him," nor tell whether he was going to Crohan, or back again by some circuitous route to Araheera Head.

Twice, indeed, he had the good fortune to meet with benighted travellers like himself, who seemed to know all about the roads, and took, as he fancied, very great pains to set him right. They kindly informed him he had lost his way, and gave him strict caution to take the left hand road, which, curious enough, was the very thing he intended not to do. But he was a stranger in the country, and of course should take the directions of those better acquainted with it than himself. Yet it was now nearly two hours since he met the latter of the two parties, and still, strange to say, he was as far from Crohan, for aught he knew, as ever. On he went, notwithstanding — on he drove through the pitchy darkness, butting his bare head against the pitiless storm, and seeing nothing but the lightning flash as it shot across his face. Many a lusty malediction did he vent, that night, on Ireland, and the unlucky day he first took it into his head to speculate in matrimony on her barbarous shore. At last, he topped the summit of a hill, which must surely, he thought, be Benraven Scalp, and had begun to descend the opposite side, when, much to his relief, he heard a voice shouting through the storm, —

"Hoagh!"

"Hilloa! who's that?" he cried, turning round; "who goes there?"

"Hoagh!" was again repeated.

"Come nearer," bawled Weeks, "come nearer; can't hear you with this infernal whistling." And no wonder, for in turning, the wind blew the skirts of his sporting frock about his ears, which kept flapping so rapidly that he could hear nothing at all. "Come nearer," he repeated, "come nearer; I'm here on the middle of the road."

"Hoagh! hoagh!"

"Tarnation to your 'Hoagh!' Hain't ye got English enough to tell what's the matter."

"Hoagh!"

"O, darn your gibberish — you're the most confounded barb——"

" Hoagh ! hoagh !"

" That's it ; go it again.　By thunder, he bellows like an ox."

" Mhoagh !"

" Well, there !　By crackie, if you're sick, it's not with the lung complaint, I reckon, any how.　But hold on — you may have got into some fix — hold on.　I'll find you out, I guess."

Weeks, actuated by compassion for the sufferer, as well as by the hope of gaining some information respecting his whereabouts, began to grope his way towards his companion in distress.　He felt quite sure the unfortunate man could not be far away, for it was impossible for human lungs to make the voice tell at more than a few yards, in the teeth of such a furious gale.　With this notion in his head, he commenced his search along the road side, floundering, as he went along, through the water tables, and tripping occasionally over the slippery rocks which had fallen from the banks into the ditches.　As it was impossible to see any thing in the darkness, his only alternative was to keep sweeping both hands out before him in semicircles, like a swimmer, with the expectation of at length touching something with life in it. In this manner, he searched up and down, both sides of the road, for a considerable time, calling loudly to the man in distress, but receiving no reply, and was at last on the point of abandoning the poor wretch to his fate, when he fancied he heard a heavy groan, as of some one in his last agony, and stretching out both hands again, to feel in the direction of the sound, stumbled once more and fell forward.

Just as he had expected, Weeks felt something warm and hairy under his open palms.

" Well, there !" he exclaimed ; "the fellow's got corned and fell in the drain.　I swow he has, and lost his hat too, for his hair's as wet as the very grass.　Say ! what's the matter ?"

he continued, shaking him. "Say! wake up, if you don't want to die here right off."

No answer came.

"Look here!" and he pulled him by the hair of the head, to make him speak. "Look here! you've got drunk—hain't you?"

At this moment, and just as he had inserted his right arm under the helpless creature's head, to raise him up, a flash of lightning illumed for an instant the person of the prostrate sufferer, and revealed to the astonished eyes of Mr. Weeks the face and form of a young steer, quietly chewing his cud under the shelter of a projecting rock.

"Heavens and earth, what's this!" he exclaimed, snatching his arm from under the animal's neck, and jumping on the bank at a single bound. "Well, there! if that ain't the darndest sniggle—I swonnie, if I didn't take the critter for a drunken Irishman, shouting for help all the time. O, Ireland, Ireland; if there's such another country in all universal space—well—if there be, I'd like to see it—that's all."

"Not so fast, my fine fellow, not so fast," shouted somebody in his ear; "you've driven that baste far enough. I'll take charge of him now, if ye plaze, and yerself too, into the bargain."

"Me?"

"Ay, in troth, honey, just your very self. You're the queen's prisoner."

"The queen's humbug—for what, I should like to know?"

"Stealing that yearling."

"Stealing! You don't say! ha, ha!"

"I do say."

"You're mistaken, ain't you?"

"Not in the laste, my good man."

"Well, I kinder think you be."

"Kinder think. Exactly—that's one of the tokens; you're a Yankee, it seems."

13

" Well, I always reckoned so — happened to be born in New England, any how."

" Just so — in Ducksville."

" In Ducksville ! — why, how the thunder came you to know that — eh ? "

" Niver mind — I know more than all that, my fine fellow. I know you've stolen three more of this same stock from Benraven Mountain, within the last fortnight, and this one makes the fourth."

" My dear man," said Weeks, " let me tell you again, this is a great mistake — I'm a private gentleman."

" Feth, may be so.   Hilloa ! come on here, Tom Henley — come on with the lantern;" and as the latter came up, the speaker raised the light to the face of his prisoner, and deliberately scanned his person from head to foot. " Let me see — *six feet in height, slender figure, knock-kneed, long sandy hair, gray frock and trousers, several gilt chains, rings, brooches, &c.*   Very good — you're just the person I've been searching for these three nights past.   Come, my lad, you must trot to Mr. Johnston's."

" Well, I'd rather not ; " coolly replied Weeks.   " I sorter think I'll sleep to-night at my cousin's, Mr. Robert Hardwrinkle's."

" Not till you see Mr. Johnston, first.   I'm his bailiff, and must do my duty.   Come, sir, no more palaverin about it."

" Look here ! " exclaimed Weeks, as the bailiff laid his hand roughly on his shoulder ; " look here — hold on a minute — don't you think you're carrying this joke a leetle too far ?   I told you already I was Mr. Hardwrinkle's cousin-german."

" What, of Crohan ? "

" Ye-e-s."

" Just so — precisely — that's another token.   You've been trying hard to pass for the foreigner visiting there."

" Trying to pass !   My dear man, I'm that very individual

himself, and was on my way to Crohan, from Araheera light-house, when I heard that animal —— "

"Ha, ha! a likely story, indeed — on your way to Crohan — here, on the very top of Cairncrit — three miles farther from Crohan than when you left the lighthouse, and the very animal we're lookin for, too, in your custody."

"Well, I reckon I must have been directed the wrong way."

"And how did you happen to get in company with the stirk?"

"Why, I heard the critter bellow, and seemed to think it might be an Irishman shouting for help."

"Ha, ha! upon my conscience, now, that's mighty flat-terin; heard a stirk routin under the rain, and took it for an Irishman in distress."

"Isn't he mighty cute, intirely?" said Henley.

"Wonderful — but tell me, Tom, didn't Lanty say the fellow generally carried a fishing rod with him?"

"Ay, did he; but who the deuce cud carry a fishin rod with him such a night as this, when the strongest of us can scarcely carry ourselves against the storm? O, as for that, you needn't be the laste afeerd in life; he's the very man yer lookin for, as sure as your name's Ned Griffin."

"Say, what Lanty d'ye mean," inquired Weeks; "Lanty Hanlon — eh?"

"Niver mind, it makes no difference to you who he is."

"Well, not much, I guess, but if I could see him just as well as not, I might save you further trouble on my account. Let me see — he lives in this here neighborhood, somewhere — don't he?"

"Come, come, my good fellow, this hoodwinking won't take just at present. You may be very smart, and cunning, and all that, but I have had some twenty years' experience of gentlemen of your profession. So, come on; we'll take you down here to one of these houses in Ballymagahey for the night, and carry you before Mr. Johnston to-morrow. You can then call on Lanty Hanlon to give you a character, and as many more as you plaze. Lift your feet and they'll fall themselves," he added, grasping the unfortunate Weeks by the collar. "Come away out of this rain; come, trot, my customer, trot — you've legs enough if you only use them."

"Trot h—ll!" vociferated Weeks at last, losing patience; "if you don't let go my collar this instant, I'll blow your brains out. Away, you ignorant, beggarly savages — darn you, to take me for a cow thief. Away — make tracks this minute or by —— "

" Be aisy, my valiant fellow, be aisy," said the bailiff, still gripping him by the collar.

"No, I shan't — let me go — I'll not put up with this, no how."

" Don't fret — we'll put you up, and in lavender, too; never fear."

"I tell you once more, I'm Ephraim C. B. Weeks, cousin-german to the Hardwrinkles of Crohan."

"O, thin, bad scran to the much ye need boast of the connection," replied Henley, helping the bailiff to drag him down the hill.

" Unhand me, villains, unhand me; I'm a stranger here — I'm a foreigner."

" An sure we're only helpin to send you to foreign parts again. O, faith, honey, we'll accommodate ye that way, and welcome."

" Look here — hold on," vociferated Weeks, as they ran him down the hill; " I want you to understand who I am — I'm a citizen — a free-born citizen of the United States, under the protection of the stars and stripes, and I protest against this violence — I command you in the name of my country to let me go."

" Bedad, that's very alarmin, Ned — isn't it ?"

" Ha, ha! mighty alarmin, intirely," responded the bailiff.

" He speaks like that Yankee fellow, in Dublin, last week, who threatened the magistrate with the stars and stripes, because he fined him five shillings for spitting tobacco juice on a lady's dress."

In this way the bailiff, assisted by Tom Henley, continued to drag the unhappy Weeks down the south side of Benraven Mountain, despite his solemn protest against the outrage, and his frequent assurances of his innocence, and finally succeeded in conveying him to a house in the little village of Bally-magahey, where, late as the hour was, a light was still burning.

As the party approached the house, several voices were heard within, some speaking loud, some laughing, others sing-ing, and now and then the squeak of a fiddle breaking out at intervals.

Without pausing an instant, the bailiff knocked loudly on the door, and the next moment pushed in before him Ephraim Weeks, haggard and torn, and dripping like a water god.

The fiddle stopped short in the middle of Miss McCloud's reel, and the affrighted dancers fell back, and left the floor clear to the new comers.

" O, *hierna!* " cried some one in a stage whisper; " he's mad — see how his eyes rowl in his head — he'll tear us in pieces."

The young females, hearing this, took alarm, and ran out of doors, screaming for protection; the elder ones ran after to bring them back; the men shouted to the runaways to stop in twenty different voices, till in a shorter time than we have taken to describe it, the place was a scene of unutterable con-fusion. Nearly all the females had disappeared one after another. The hunchback fiddler jumped through the win-dow with his instrument under his arm; and to make the din still more intolerable, the house dog set up such a howling outside as if the world had actually come to an end, when the bailiff, seeing how matters stood, stepped on a chair and

13 *

began to address the company, assuring them the man was
not mad by any means, but a notorious cow thief he had
arrested in the act of stealing Mr. Johnston's cattle from the
mountain, and then proceeded to give the details of the
capture.

Whilst the bailiff thus endeavored to quiet the apprehen-
sions of the females, Weeks stood stock still in the centre of
a curious and wondering group — his hands thrust down as
low as he could drive them into his breeches pockets, and his
eyes wandering round and round in search of some one to
recognize him — but alas! the faces he saw there were all
strange faces to him.

It was some time before the bailiff's repeated guarantee of
his prisoner's sanity of mind and peaceable disposition could
induce the females to return to the dancing room; and when
they did, each fair one, as she entered, was seen to cast a fearful glance at the tall stranger, and press closely by the side of
her partner.   Last came the little fiddler, looking twice as big
as when he fled through the window but a moment before,
and swearing all kinds of anathemas against the bailiff and
his prisoner for exposing his instrument to the rain.

Still, amid all the noise and bustle, Weeks stood there as calm
and solemn as an undertaker.   He was no longer excited —
that state of feeling had given way to a calm, contemptuous,
silent indignation.   He felt precisely as an unfortunate Irish
Catholic feels in New England, when arrested for robbery,
and happens to reflect he is the only stranger in the township,
and without a friend to say a word in his favor.   But we must
not stop to moralize ; we can only say, — to borrow a line
from the poet, —

> " We have seen such sights, but must not call to mind."

Suddenly, however, Mr. Weeks's attention seemed to be attracted by the entrance of an active, curly-headed, humorous-
looking fellow, wearing a rabbit-skin cap jantily set on the

side of his head, and supporting a laughing, dark-haired girl on his arm.

"Say, hold on there, you," cried Weeks, at length breaking silence, and motioning to the new comer.

The individual made no reply, but hastened to escape further observation by ensconcing himself behind a door in a remote corner of the room.

"Look here!" persisted Weeks, breaking through the group, and holding out his hand in token of recognition; "look here! —how do, old feller; got into a sorter snarl here, and glad you turned up to see me out."

"Me!"

"Why, yes — you're Lanty Hanlon — ain't you?"

"Ay, that's my name."

"All right; I knew you by your cap as soon as you entered. Well — I want you to clear up a mistake. This here bailiff, or constable, or whatever darned thing you call him, has arrested me for stealing a steer, up thereaway — ha, ha! —and won't believe I'm Mr. Ephraim Weeks, no how you can fix it."

"Mr. Ephraim Weeks!" muttered our friend Lanty, slowly repeating the words, and looking up in affected wonder in the man's face; "Mr. Ephraim Weeks — you're a stranger in these parts."

"Why, what d'ye mean?"

"No offence in the world, only you've the 'vantage of me."

"Advantage! How's that!"

"Why, I don't remimber iver to see you afore."

"You don't, eh? Look at me again."

"I do."

"Why, darn ye, hain't ye seen me every day this month past?"

"Me! bedad, may be so. Whereabouts, if it's a fair question?"

"Now, you go to grass," cried Weeks; "you know me as well as I know myself."

"Faith, and that same mightn't be much to brag of aither."

"Why, tarnation t'ye, hain't you sold me two dozen flies, last Thursday, at Kindrum Pond?"

"I sell you flies? Ha, ha, ha! Why, upon my conscience, my good fellow, you must be ravin."

"Well, there!" exclaimed Weeks, looking at the imperturbable Lanty as if he could run him through; then drawing a fly-book hastily from his pocket, he pulled it open, and holding the flies before Lanty's face, demanded to know if they were of his dressing or not.

" Mine — begorra, it wudn't be aisy to tell that in the state they're in now, any way,"

"Ladies and gents," said Weeks, appealing to the bystanders, "I vow I bought these flies from this here fellow last Thursday. And, what's more, he stuck me in them too, to the tune of twenty-five cents apiece."

"Why, don't they ketch?" inquired some one in the crowd.

"Ketch — no, guess they don't ketch — they're the darndest things ever fell in water. Why, I never could turn a tail with them, if I fished till doomsday."

"I admit," said Lanty, "I sold flies to a gentleman of the name of Weeks; the gentleman that's on a visit to the Hard-wrinkles, of Crohan."

"And thunderation to ye! ain't I that same Weeks?"

"You! ha, ha, ha! Begorra, that's capital — you Mr. Weeks."

"What! will you dare deny me to my face, you scoundrel?"

"Deny you? O, holy patience, did man or mortal iver hear the like?"

"Shut up, you lying rascal," shouted Weeks, gesticulating at his innocent-looking tormentor; "shut up, you unprincipled scamp; you know in your soul who I am — if you have a soul — but you hain't, — dang the one you have!"

"O, my poor man," responded Lanty, looking at his victim with all the gravity of a judge about to pronounce sentence, and shaking his head sorrowfully as he spoke, — "my poor man, how hardened a sinner you must be, to pass yourself off for the good, innocent, modest gentleman that's now lyin sound asleep in his vartuous bed."

"Well, if there be a devil on earth," exclaimed Weeks, "you're that individual, or his nearest relation, that's sartin. You stepped out from the lower regions to-night to get a cooling, and met me some two hours ago on the mountain. You're the person planned and played this here trick — no mistake about it."

"Isn't he bowld spoken to be a thief?" said one of the by-standers, nudging his neighbor's elbow.

"Ay, and purshuin to him, see how innocent he tries to look," replied the other.

"O, the dear be about ye, man; one i' them fellows that's used to it 'd chate St. Pether."

"Whist! whist! boys," remonstrated Lanty, waving his hand for silence. "Let him alone, let him alone; we shud niver rejoice, ye know, in another's misfortune. May be, if you wur like him yerselves, ye wudn't care to be laughed at."

"Come, come, my good fellow," interposed the bailiff, "you're only making matters worse. Go somewhere and get rid of them wet clothes."

"Ay, do, Mr. Stranger; take a friend's advice," said Lanty, "and don't expose your precious health. The truth will all come out th' morrow. If yer innicint, so much the betther; an if yer not, why, ye'll only be thransported two or three months afore yer time; so take courage, and don't be unaisy."

Lanty's cool impudence at last so provoked the Yankee that he could hardly restrain himself. Once or twice, indeed, he hitched up his shoulders and showed symptoms of battle; but his resentment as often cooled down again without further mischief.   Like poor Bob Acres, Mr. Weeks could never get his courage up to the fighting point ; some how or other, it always escaped through his fingers' ends, like that of his illustrious prototype.

" Well, ladies and gents," said he at length, falling back, as a last resource, on his soft sawder, " well, I must confess I feel a kinder disappointed.   Now I do ; that's a fact.   Why, it's just like this — I always heard the Irish cracked up all over creation for their hospitality to strangers.   At hum, in New England, they're tip top in that line.   Well, they're about as hospitable folks I guess as you can scare up any where between Maine and Georgia.   We get along with them slick, I tell you.   And as for extending them the right hand of fellowship, why, golly, we love them like brothers —— "

" Phew ! " cried Lanty ; " just listen to that.   He's puttin his foot in it deeper and deeper.   O, faith, my fine fellow, it's aisy seen ye niver was much in New England, or ye'd know a little betther how the Irish are thrated there."

Weeks suddenly drew in his horns — to use a homely expression.   He saw, in an instant, he had touched a delicate subject, and the sooner he dropped it the better.   Like many of his countrymen, he fancied the Irish he saw about him never could have an idea in their heads above the pick or the spade ; a ragged coat and an Irish *brogue*, being in his mind synonymous with consummate ignorance and absolute barbarism. He now felt he had gone a little too far, and that any attempt to deceive his tormentors by such barefaced humbug as he was then attempting, would only make matters worse, since, to all appearances, they knew as much about the persecution their countrymen suffered in New England as he did himself.   The broad grin that overspread every face as he went on to speak of the love which the citizens of New England cherished for their Celtic brethren assured him of this, even before Lanty could say a word in reply.   Affecting, therefore, to disdain further conversation on the subject, after hearing the laugh with which Lanty's humorous but cutting rebuke was received, he turned to the bailiff, and demanded to be taken forthwith to some resting place for the night.

"You'll get comfortable quarters," said Lanty; "never fear; but av coorse you'll take *dhoch in dhorris** with us, afore ye go, to the health of the new-married couple."

"What's that?"

"Why, something to warm ye, after the could rain."

"Don't drink," said Weeks.

"Nonsense."

"No, sir, I'm a Washingtonian."

"A what?"

"A Son of Temperance."

"Pshaugh—son of botheration. I'm ashamed of ye. Hilloa there! Hudy Branagan, bring in the bottle."

"You may bring in a hogshead," said Weeks; "I shan't taste it."

"And you in that condition! Why, the heavens be about us; d'ye mane to put a hand in yer own life."

"None of your confounded business. I shan't drink your darned liquor — that's all."

"Well, ye'll die if ye don't — and that'd be a burnin disgrace to the counthry, if ye were even as great a thief as James Freny himself. Hoot, man, what'd yer people say of us if we let ye die here in ould Ireland for want of a glass of stout potheen. Here, take this, and swallow it, like a sensible man."

"Away with it," cried Weeks.

"Be aisy, avourneen, be aisy."

"Take it away, or by thunder I'll break your bottle and glass in pieces," and making a plunge, he attempted to force a passage through the crowd, but was again driven back into the centre of the group.

* Stirrup-cup

"Let me out," he shouted, now completely excited; "let me out, ye beggarly Irish vermin. I despise your liquor, and your country to boot. I spit upon you and your nation, for you're both as mean as dirt."

"Ha, ha! there now," cried Lanty, laughing, with the bottle and glass in his hand — "there now, that's more of yer New England friendship. But niver mind; if ye were a Yankee fifty times over, we won't thrate ye the worse for that. Come, take this drop — you'll be the betther of it."

"Let me out."

"Whisht, man; sure it's all for yer own good. Arrah, don't refuse to drink to the bride and groom. It's as much as yer life's worth to refuse it. Take it; it'll warm ye — taste it, any way — it's the deuce i' the barley — it's the rale ould Innishowen," broke out from several voices, each rising higher than the other, till poor Weeks knew not what to say, nor what side to turn to. Still he obstinately refused to touch the beverage.

"Well, boys," said Lanty, at last, "take hould of him, and lay him down, since nothin else will save him. Whatsomiver the craythur is, we're Christians sure, any way, and can't let him die fur want of a thrifle i' medicine. It's a liberty we take, my good man, to be sure, but still it's betther do that, than have yer death on our sowls, the lor between us an harm."

"The sorrah take him, the spalpeen," said one of the bystanders; "isn't he nice about it; feth, ye'd think it was a physic he was goin to swallow."

"Begorra, I niver heerd the like of it."

"It's a bad sign to see him refuse the liquor, any way."

"Indeed, then, Andy, it's the truth ye're tellin; so it is; for in troth it's not much depindince iver I had in the man 'd refuse a glass in dacency."

"O, there's a bad dhrop in him; ye may take yer oath iv that; but look at Lanty, Ned, just luck at his face — as sober as if it was cut on a tombstone. Did ye iver see such a born devil in all yer life ? "

"Well, Lanty had it in for him, any way. And, begorra, he desarves all he'll get and more, for he's niver aisy, they say, but when he's running down the Irish."

"So I'm tould. He thinks no one in the whole country fit to spake to him. As for the Doghertys, and Currans, and Johnstons here, why, they're not fit to tie his shoes."

"Ladies and gentlemen," exclaimed Lanty, stepping up on a bench, and still holding the bottle and glass in his hands, " I'm goin to give ye a toast, and may the man's heart niver again warm to good nature, that does'n't drink it."

" Silence, there, silence — till we hear the toast."

" Stop that fiddle there, and listen to the spaker."

"Here's then to the honest man," cried Lanty, raising his glass, — " here's to the honest man all over the world, and confusion to the narrow-minded knave who'd make religion or birthplace a test of friendship;" and tossing off the bumper, he ordered the company to pass the bottle.

Round went the toast, and off went the glass with many a loud hip, hip, hurrah. There was shaking of hands, and touching of cans, accompanied by snatches of songs suitable to the toast, and pledges of friendship to one another, not forgetting long life and happiness to the bride and groom; all seemed joyous and happy as they could wish to be, Weeks alone excepted, who still stood in the centre of the crowd, looking silently on the noisy enjoyments of the company, and obstinately refusing all participation in the hilarity of the occasion.

"Where, in the name of patience, were you born at all," demanded the bailiff, " that you won't drink at a weddin ? "

" He's an unnatural-looking thief, any way," exclaimed another.

" Stand aside, boys," commanded Lanty, waving his hand from his elevated position, " and let us give the stranger fair

14

play.　He's all alone here amongst us, and we mustn't be hard on him.　Jemmy Bragan, fill that glass, and offer it to him again.　And now, my good man," he continued, addressing Weeks, "you heerd the toast, 'the honest man all over the world, and bad luck to the knave who'd make religion or birthplace a test of friendship'—will you drink it?"

"No," replied Weeks, "darn me if I do."

"Then, gintlemen, lay him down and administher the midicine."

Four or five stout fellows now laid hold of the unfortunate Weeks, and were deliberately proceeding to execute Lanty's orders, when a new actor suddenly appeared on the scene, and commanded them to desist.　It was the handsome, dark-haired girl whom the reader saw a few minutes before entering the room, leaning on Lanty's arm.

"Shame! shame!" she cried; "are ye men, to treat a stranger in this way?"

"Don't be onaisy, Mary," replied Lanty; "we don't intend him the laste harm in life."

"Well, you've carried the joke too far already, Lanty Hanlon; let him come with me—I'll take care of him."

"Why, Mary, it's only a bit of a frolic he brought on himself.　He tould me a dozen times the Irish were no betther nor savages, and we jist want to show him how much he's mistaken."

"And you do this to a furriner, not a month in the country; paugh! pretty hospitality that!"

"He's green, you know, Mary, and we want to saison him."

"Tut, tut! shame, shame!"

"It's for his own good—saisonin in time will make a dacent man iv him."

"Hould yer tongue, now, Lanty; ye'd provoke a saint, hould your tongue, and let us out.　I must go and find some dry clothes for him, or he'll die in this condition.　Stand back, gintlemen, if ye plaze, and give us room to pass."

"Bedad, Mary, I'm afraid to trust ye with him ; feth, may be he'd take a fancy to ye, and cut me out."

"Whisht, now, and let me go. That tongue of yours 'll hang ye up on the gallows yet, some day ; " and taking Weeks familiarly by the arm, in she led him unresistingly from the crowd, and disappeared through one of the inner doors of the apartment.

The dance was now resumed, and mirth and music made the time pass quickly and merrily for the next hour. Lanty danced with every girl in the room, and when he could no longer find a partner, danced a hornpipe himself on a door, amid the shouts and cheers of the party. Every one seemed to share in the general joy. Even the grandparents of the happy couple, old as they were, took each other's hands, and went through some ancient saltations to the great amusement of the younger spectators.

On went the mirth and up rose the song, and the little hunchbacked fiddler had just tuned his instrument once more, and commenced to rattle away at a country dance with re-newed ardor, when, all of a sudden, a shout was heard at the door, followed instantly by bravos, bravos, echoed and re-peated, till at last, in the midst of a wild hurrah, in drove Ephraim C. B. Weeks, dressed in an old blue swallow-tailed coat, and pantaloons that descended but an inch or two below the knees, dragging in the young lady who had so kindly rescued him from his late tormentors, and in rather unsteady accents, commanded the fiddler to "fire up, and let him have something to dance to." Every body now crushed and crowded round to welcome him back. Those who but a short time before were disposed to mortify him to the very utmost, in revenge for his insolent abuse of their religion and their country, were the first to call for three cheers for the "bou'd American ; " and foremost among the first was Lanty Hanlon, who clapped him lustily on the back, and ordered the fiddler to strike up something with a "sowl in it, to shuit the taste of the jolly Yankee."

It is needless, dear reader, to describe what followed. Weeks seemed to have abandoned himself entirely to the excitement of the moment. How that excitement was brought about, however, no one could tell. He drank, and drank freely, — as was evident the moment he made his appearance at the door, — but whether at the solicitation of his fair friend, or merely to preserve his health after so long an exposure to the storm, was never discovered; certain it is he was completely fascinated by his lovely partner, and danced with her as long as he was able to move a foot — swearing all the while by his " crackie " she was the finest gal in all creation, and went through her figures like a real thorough-bred Yankee, " no mistake about it."

Here, dear reader, we must stop, leaving the finale of this scene to your own charitable imagination; for a description of our friend Weeks's position on the stage, as the curtain fell, is more than we should dare attempt. One thing, however, we ought to mention, just to relieve your anxiety; he was conveyed safely home that same night, and awoke in his own comfortable bed next morning in Crohan house.

CHAPTER XII.

Kate Petersham at Castle Gregory. — Dr. Henshaw's Catholicity proves rather strong both for Kate and the Priest. — The Doctor, like Mr. Weeks, forms a very bad Opinion of Ireland and its Inhabitants. — Lanty plays an Irish Trick. — Its Consequences.

" Is Miss Petersham engaged, please?" said a servant, opening the parlor door.

" No: what's the matter?"

"Father John sends in his compliments."

"Father John!—Is it possible!" exclaimed Kate Petersham, wheeling round on the piano stool, and running to the door to receive him. "Ho, ho! indeed, so there you come at last, and Uncle Jerry too; surely something extraordinary must have happened to bring you all the way to Castle Gregory. Have you had a conflagration or an earthquake in your neighborhood?"

"Hold your saucy tongue," said the priest, slapping her affectionately on the cheek; "you're never done scolding; 'pon my word, I had better come here, bag and baggage, and live at Castle Gregory altogether."

"You'll do no such thing, sir—I hate you. You're a barbarous man. You're the most unsocial, ill-natured, hard-hearted creature in the whole world."

"O, to be sure, because I don't spend all my time playing chess with the greatest mad-pate in Christendom."

"Do you hear that, Uncle Jerry?" exclaimed Kate, turning to Mr. Guirkie; "and the man hasn't been here to see us once in a month."

"Never mind; we'll have our revenge of him yet, depend upon it. His neglect of you is absolutely unpardonable, after all your professions of regard for him."

"Pshaugh! he's not worth my revenge. I renounce him; I shall take you for my confidant in future, and leave him to his beads and breviary. So come over here, to your old easy chair, and let us have a quiet chat together;" and running her arm into his, she was hurrying him away to a corner of the room, when the priest laid his hand on her shoulder.

"Not so fast, Kate; not so fast. You've forgotten there's a stranger in the room. Miss Petersham, let me present to you Dr. Henshaw, of Edinburgh,—Dr. Henshaw, Miss Petersham, of Castle Gregory, one of the most mischievous and ungovernable of her sex."

14 *

"Don't believe him, Dr. Henshaw.   I'm no such thing.
Welcome, sir, to Castle Gregory."

"How d' ye do, my dear? glad to see you," said the latter,
bowing stiffly, and raising his gold spectacles to look at her
in detail.   "Don't trouble yourself aboot what Father John
says.   It's not all gospel, I suspect."

"Nor his preaching either, if what his bishop says be true."

"Ha, ha!   A very serious charge, indeed," laughed Uncle
Jerry; "and no doubt reason enough for it too."

"I see you've been reading Swift, Miss Petersham," said
Henshaw, taking a volume from the table.   "Do you admire him?"

"Swift — certainly.   Did you ever see an Irish woman
who didn't?"

"Well, I don't remember, parteecularly, as to that.   But
his moral sentiments are —— "

"Swift was an elegant writer, full of wit and humor — and,
best of all, he loved his country, and never was ashamed to
own it."

"Ah! and you think he deserves credit for that?"

"To be sure I do — why not?   He lived in times when
devotion to his country and her cause was a disqualification
for office both in church and state; besides, Dean Swift was
a near relation of ours by the Willoughbys, as my venerable
aunt would tell you."

"Ah! — that indeed!"

"But don't you like him, doctor?"

"No," replied the doctor, gruffly.

"You don't! is it possible? Why, I thought Swift was a
favorite every where."

"In Ireland — yes."

"You must admit he's witty and humorous, doctor."

"Not very — but that, and a keen sense o' the rideeculous,
is about all that's in him."

"O, no, no, doctor, I won't agree to that at all; you quite

underrate Swift. For my part, I think there's more sound philosophy in Swift than in any other work I ever read."

"Humph! have you read much?"

"No; sometimes, when the fit takes me, I pick up a book and read a page or two here and there."

"But do you study what you read!"

"No; I'm too great a madcap for that. I can ride a horse, though, or sail a boat, as well as any Irish girl you'll find; and these are the only accomplishments I pretend to lay claim to."

"Not very feminine, I should think," ejaculated Henshaw, pursing out his lips, and looking over at the priest, with his eyes dilated into what he intended for a smile.

"No, sir; but they suit my turn of mind. And yet Mr. Guirkie here will tell you I've got some philosophy in me, too."

"I'll have nothing to do with your philosophy," said Uncle Jerry, pacing up and down the room, and bobbing the skirts of his coat on his hands behind him. "I wish to the Lord the captain was at home; that's all I wish."

"Father John, go to the sideboard there, and find some refreshments," said Kate. "Come, doctor, you must pledge me in good stout Burgundy, and I'll forgive what you said of Swift."

"I shall wait for the captain," replied Father John, looking up from the newspaper; "the doctor there will oblige you at present."

"You shall not, sir; he may not return for an hour yet. Wait for the captain, indeed! Ain't I as good company as the captain? O, Dr. Henshaw, these Catholic priests are the most ungallant people imaginable."

Dr. Henshaw emptied the glass which Kate filled for him, adding, as he laid it on the sideboard, "you're not so mawkish, I perceive, as our young ladies generally are."

"O, I'm only an Irish girl, you know; I do what I please —

no one minds me; Father John there once thought he could manage me, but it failed him."

"Not I," replied the priest; "I never was so silly as to think any such thing."

"You did indeed, sir — you needn't deny it; you had me in leading strings for a whole week or more."

"How was that?" said Henshaw.

"He tried to convert me — ha, ha! Kept me reading night and day ——"

"Convert you? — what, from sin?"

"No, from Protestantism. Sin indeed! why, doctor, I'm ashamed of you."

"Well, Protestanteesm is sin — and a most grievous sin, my good girl."

"There, now you're at it again," muttered Uncle Jerry, still pacing the room in his usual way. "You're at it again; I vow and protest it's outrageous."

"You frighten me, doctor," said Kate; "upon my word I'll run away and leave you."

"But don't you know that if you die out o' the Kaatholic church you'll be lost?"

"Listen to that," exclaimed Kate.

"I hear him," said the priest; "the doctor's very strong on that point."

"Well, doctor, I'm not prepared to dispute with you about the matter at present," said Kate, "but I'm pretty sure of one thing — you could never make a Catholic of me in that way."

"He's got himself into trouble again," said Uncle Jerry, sitting down on a chair beside the priest.

"He deserves it," responded the latter, in a tone of displeasure.

"I declare I never saw a man in my life so fond of differing with every body as he is. Why, I vow to goodness, I thought he was going to swallow me neck and heels this morning in the boat, when I attempted to defend Tillotson and Burnet."

"That's his greatest fault; he can never dispute five minutes without losing his temper."

"And does he suppose people must put up with his temper when he chooses to lose it? I declare that's very fine."

"It's a great weakness in him, and I'm sorry, for he's a man of great mental ability."

"O, who cares for his mental ability? I wouldn't give a brass button for a man who can't talk with you on any thing but great heavy subjects. And then he goes at them in such a way too, with all his might, like a dray horse starting a load."

"Heavy subjects are his speciality," observed Father John; "he don't pretend to handle any thing else. And indeed, as a polemic and logician, he has very few equals."

"But he *does* pretend to handle *every thing* else. Why, he reviews every book he can lay his hands on — stories, novels, poetry, every thing — from a primer to a course of theology. Speciality indeed!"

"You're right; he has been doing something that way of late, now that I remember. But the truth is, I think so little of his literary criticisms I don't care to read them. He never should attempt to criticise such books at all. They are entirely out of the sphere of his taste and acquirements."

"To be sure."

"And then he goes about them so awkwardly."

"He, he, he!" chuckled Uncle Jerry; "that reminds me of his last number. Did you see his criticism on Cameron's Poems?"

"No — what does he do with it? Strangles it, I suppose."

"Not at all; he makes an exception to his rule. He praises it hugely. Cameron's a Catholic, you know, besides being a Scotchman."

"Ah, yes, there's something in that."

" In speaking of some of the fine passages he tries to be exceedingly nice in his appreciation of the beauties."

" Nice ! " laughed Father John ; " that's good ; I must read the criticism."

" Do.　It's worth the reading, I assure you."

" But he must have gone about it very awkwardly."

" Awkwardly !　He remined me of an elephant I once saw picking up a bouquet with his trunk.　He first made a —— "

" Hush ! here he comes, full of indignation at Kate's presumptuous boldness.　See how he runs his thumbs into his waistcoat pockets — that's a sure sign he's ruffled.　Kate," he added, as an offset to further controversy, " can't we have some music ? "

" Certainly — what shall it be ? "

" O'er the water to Charlie."

" Excellent — just the very thing," she cried, opening the piano and rattling away.　" How do you like it, doctor ? "

" Well, so, so.　Associations make it pleasant just now."

" Makes you think of home ? "

" Yes."

" What think you, though, of our Irish music ? "

" Very fair ; but it always gives me the blues."

" The blues ! "

" Yes.　It's so melancholy."

" Moore's songs are, indeed, rather melancholy, but exquisite of their kind, nevertheless."

" Yes — he's a vary decent lyric poet — is Moore ; and still there's nothing in him after all but sentiment and fancy — he's greatly wanting in force and power of thought."

" That is to say, he's neither Byron nor Milton."

" No, I don't mean that, either.　But he tires you with the incessant play of his fancy.　He is forever hopping from flower to flower, like a butterfly."

" Ah, then you adopt the criticisms of the Edinburgh Review."

"I adopt no creeticism. I make my own," replied Hen-shaw, gruffly.

"Well, you think with the Scotch Reviewers, that his poetry is too full of beauties, and hampered too much with imagery."

"I think simply this: he was a vary respectable songster in his way, but an immoral man and a bad Kaatholic."

"O, doctor, that's not fair. I must protest against your bringing up our poet's private character. It's not magnanimous of you at all."

"His poetry, take it all through," persisted Henshaw, "has done more to enervate and corrupt the minds of the young, than any other I am acquainted wi'; and do you know the reason, Miss Petersham?"

"No."

"Well, it was simply because in losing his faith he lost his morality also."

"My dear sir, we have nothing to do with his faith," replied Kate. "Why, you drag faith into every thing. Can't we admire a man's writings without first inquiring about his faith?"

"Yes, that's vary true; but it strikes me you value faith too little, and for that reason you cannot properly estimate a man's writings. We Kaatholics deesapprove of all books and writings injurious to faith or morals. You Protestants have no faith at all, and you let your morals take care o' themselves."

"Highty tighty," muttered Uncle Jerry, running his hands again under his coat tails, and pacing the room as before; "he's at it again."

Father John rose also, and turning Kate round on the piano stool, commanded her, under pain of his sovereign displeasure, to play "The last rose of summer," with Henry Herz's variations first, and then sing it.

"Now, she exclaimed, when she finished the song, — "now, Dr. Henshaw, I put it to you as an honorable man; did you, or did you not, ever hear so exquisite a song as that?"

"The words or the music?"

"Both together, when played and sung as they ought to be."

"Y-e-e-s, it's light, and pretty, and fanciful, and ——"

"No, no, sir. I shall not be put off with that; but tell me what poet ever wrote a song of its kind equal to that? I give you the whole world to find him; not even excepting your own Burns, Scott, Tannahill, and all the rest."

"I never trouble myself much aboot such trifles," responded Henshaw. "I leave them to the boys and girls."

"I wish to goodness you would," muttered Uncle Jerry, looking at the priest.

"Just so," replied the latter; "and if he only knew himself well enough, he would. *Ne sutor ultra crepidam.*"

"Hillo! what are you doing there, Mr. Guirkie?" exclaimed Kate; "chatting away with Father John, and I all alone here with this great reviewer, trying to preserve my countrymen from utter annihilation; come to the rescue, or he'll not leave us one of them; all, forsooth, because they happened to be Protestants."

"What's the matter?" inquired the priest, looking over his shoulder.

"Why, he's actually making mince meat of all our celebrities. He has come down now as far as Burke, and is cutting him up at such a rate that nothing will be left of him, by and by, but the bones."

The priest threw his legs across, and pulled down his waistcoat with a jerk, but said nothing in reply.

"You're growing angry," said Uncle Jerry.

"No, I'm not angry; I'm too well accustomed to him for that."

"Poor Kate's as mad as a hatter; look, how she shakes her curls at him! The man might try to be a little more courteous, I think."

"Were he in any other place but Castle Gregory, he wouldn't come off so easily, I assure you," responded the priest.

"There now," cried Kate, running away from her antagonist, and flinging herself down beside Uncle Jerry on the sofa; "I shan't dispute another syllable with him — he has no mercy at all. He opens his great broadsides on every thing indiscriminately, and goes firing away at you, all the time, his ponderous logic. I never met so tremendous a Catholic as Dr. Henshaw. He has murdered me out and out."

"And why did you continue at it so long?"

"What could I do? Am I to be challenged at my own fireside, and by a stranger, too, and not fight? O, could I only get him once aboard the Water IIen, with a stiff breeze from the southard, or on 'Moll Pitcher's Back' for a morning's heathing, if I wouldn't have my revenge, no matter."

"So you've surrendered at last, Kate," said the priest, walking over leisurely to the sofa, and tapping his snuff-box on the lid.

"Of course I have; how could I understand all the theories, and philosophies, and systems into which he dragged me? If he only could talk as other men do, and on subjects that girls like me are generally acquainted with, I might do well enough; but not a thing you can say but he reduces to logic in a minute, and measures it by some one of his new theories, as a haberdasher measures his tape."

"He don't give you latitude enough, Kate," said the priest, taking a pinch.

"No, he holds you like a vice, and then so bewilders you with his newly-imported principles and methods, and so on, that you don't know what you're saying. But, Father John, could you guess how he tries to account for the decay of nations?"

"O, ho! the decay of nations, no less."

"Yes, indeed — a subject I know as much about as old Thomas there. Thomas, tell Aunt Willoughby Father John wants to see her."

"Well, let us hear how he accounts for it."

" Why, sir, he accounts for the decay of nations generally, and of the Irish nation in particular, by the laws that regulate the circulation of matter."

" Ha, ha ! Go, you mad creature," said the priest, again slapping her on the cheek ; " you're making him worse than he is."

" It's a positive fact, sir," persisted Kate. " He says, as the world is developed, the attractive power of new countries becomes greater than those of the old, and carry away from their weaker neighbors, through the atmosphere, more than their share of animal and vegetable life."

" Ha, ha, ha !" laughed Uncle Jerry, quitting the sofa, and bobbing his skirts up and down the room. " Ha, ha! the man's fit for the madhouse. I declare! account for the decay of nations by laws regulating the circulation of matter. O, the Lord be about us — what's the world coming to ?"

" That reminds me of an article I read in some magazine last week, where the writer discovers the antipathy of the Irish to the English people to have originated in the difference between the Roman and the Celtic civilizations."

" He went far back to find it — didn't he ?" said Uncle Jerry, bobbing away as he spoke.

" He was right, neevertheless," said Henshaw, who had been listening. " I agree with him."

" Right or wrong," said the priest, " of what earthly advantage is it to us to discover the cause — is not the fact enough ?"

" No, sir, it is not enough; as a priest and a Chreestian, you should feel happy to be able to ascribe this national anteepathy to a more creditable cause than the memory of past eenjuries."

" That rebuke is unmerited by me, Dr. Henshaw," responded the priest, kindling up a little. " I deplore those unhappy differences between the two countries as much, as any man."

" And still you're never done dinning in our ears how

you've suffered and bled, and all that, under the lash of the Saxon — in Scotland we are sick of it."

"Humph! don't doubt it in the least. There has been, I must confess, rather too much of this clamor about our rights and wrongs. But, my dear doctor, delicacy, I think, should restrain you from expressing your opinions so freely on this exciting subject. Miss Petersham, you must be already aware, loves her country very much, and cannot but feel hurt to hear you speak of it so disparagingly."

"Sir, I have never withheld my opeenions any where. When I form opeenions I am not ashamed to avow them."

"But I tell you, doctor, you ought to be ashamed to avow such opinions as you have just expressed here. I have listened to you in my own house, speaking in the most contemptuous manner of our Irish writers and statesmen, and borne with you patiently, for I was then your host; but I cannot sit patiently here and hear you outrage the feelings of a young and gentle girl at her own fireside, and on your very first introduction, because she happens to be a Protestant, and is national enough to feel proud of her countrymen."

Henshaw was about to reply, when the door opened, and Mrs. Willoughby entered, carrying a letter in her hand. She was evidently beyond threescore and ten, to judge from the deep furrows of her cheeks and thin white hair; and yet she walked as sprightly and upright as a girl of sixteen. Approaching Father John and Mr. Guirkie with a smile of welcome, she extended a hand to each, and expressed the pleasure she felt in seeing them at Castle Gregory.

"Kate," she added; "where are you, Kate?"

"Quarrelling with Dr. Henshaw," replied the priest.

"O, the wild creature! She's always at some mischief. Kate, here's a note from Mary Lee."

In a moment the delighted girl was at her aunt's side, and kissing her hand fervently for having carried the precious billet, bounded off again to read it.

"News for you, Uncle Jerry," she exclaimed, as she ran her eye rapidly over the contents: "Mary Lee comes to-morrow, and you must stay to see her. You can't refuse, for you know how anxious you've been to converse with her."

"Come over," said Uncle Jerry, "and sit beside me here on the sofa; we must talk a little of your friend. Do you really know who this girl is, or whence she came, or what's to become of her?"

"Not I," replied Kate. "All I know is, I love her dearly, and that's all I want to know."

"But of her father?"

"She never speaks of him; I never even heard her mention his name."

"I declare!—isn't that strange, and you so intimate?"

"Very—she told me all about her uncle's embarrassment, though. She fears he can't hold out much longer. His creditors in Dublin and Cork are pressing him very hard, and he has no means left to meet their demands."

"God help him, poor fellow, God help him; if he didn't happen to be a gentleman, it hadn't been half so bad."

"Have you called to see him yet, as you promised?"

"No, I thought better of it."

"How so?"

"My visit might be disagreeable, perhaps."

"Disagreeable?"

"Yes—he might feel embarrassed."

"What! ashamed of his poverty?"

"No; but if he happened to find out that I was the purchaser of Mary's pictures, what should I do? Roger would never sell me a picture again."

"He knows nothing about it," said Kate. "Roger would die sooner than tell him; even Mary herself don't know who buys her pictures. She thinks Roger sells them in Derry to a picture dealer. All she don't understand about the matter is the high price she gets for them."

"Nonsense!" ejaculated Uncle Jerry; "she receives the value of them, and not one stiver more or less. I'm not such a fool as to throw my hard-earned money away for nothing."

"Fool!" repeated Kate, looking at Uncle Jerry till the tears came to her eyes; "I wish to God we had more fools like you, then."

"There it's again," said Uncle Jerry, turning away pettishly from his fair companion, for nothing irritated him more than to charge him with the crime of benevolence; "there it's again; always harping on the same string. I'll stay at home, in future," he continued, "for I shan't be plagued in this way any longer. I'll not let a beggar — I'll not let a man with a torn coat, nor a woman with a child in her arms — within a league of my house; as I live I shan't."

"Don't grow angry with me, Uncle Jerry," pleaded Kate, taking his hand.

"I shall grow angry; I can't help it; a saint couldn't stand it. I'll turn off Mrs. Motherly too, for she's the cause of all this. I can't fling a copper to a beggar, but she reports it a pound. Upon my word it's a pretty thing to be taken for a simpleton at the age of sixty years; humph! a mighty pretty thing, indeed."

"I only hinted at your generosity — I mean your goodness — in — a — in — why, in giving fair prices for Mary's pictures, that's all."

"Fair prices ——"

"Yes; and I thought you wouldn't be angry with me for saying *that*."

"Of course I wouldn't; but you said nothing of the kind — not a syllable," replied Uncle Jerry, softening down a little, notwithstanding.

"Because you wouldn't wait to hear me," said Kate; "I certainly think it's very good and kind in you to buy these pictures from the poor girl when you don't want them yourself. I say *that*, Mr. Guirkie, and I shall always say so."

15 *

"But I *do* want them — I want all she can paint for a twelvemonth to come; and I wouldn't give one of them for twice the price they cost me. Do you hear that, now, Miss Petersham? Not for twice the price."

"O, well," said Kate, humoring the whim, "that accounts for it, then."

"Certainly. You thought all the time, I suppose, I bought these pictures as an act of charity. He, he!" he chuckled, endeavoring all the while to belie his own heart; "when I buy, Kate, I have an eye to business."

Kate raised up hers in appeal against the sacrilege, but dared not venture a word.

"And that's the real reason, Kate, I don't visit at the light-house," said Uncle Jerry, holding his head down, for his conscience smote him for bearing false witness against himself; "that's the reason, precisely."

"O, very well," said Kate; "I'm satisfied if you are."

"I must acknowledge it's a selfish motive," continued Uncle Jerry; "but I have been a man of the world, and doubtless my feelings are hardened by long intercourse with it."

"Hardened! And so you won't visit at the lighthouse, lest Roger should never come with his pictures again?"

"Precisely. If the old man saw me once there, he should never come knocking at my door again. He's a wonderful man, that Roger, and I think I should miss him very much."

"He's a faithful creature," replied Kate; "like the ivy, he clings on to the last; when the old house falls into ruins, he falls with it."

"He is very obliging to me, at all events," said Uncle Jerry, "to make me the first offer. But keep the secret to yourself, Kate," (and he whispered the words in her ear,) "don't breathe it to a soul for your life."

"Never fear; I'll not discover."

"And now, can you tell me, has Mary Lee any friends or relatives in or about Rathmullen?"

"No, not that I know of."

"You're not certain?"

"Well, as certain as I can be, without actually hearing her say so."

"Then I must have seen her *ghost*."

"Her ghost, forsooth! where?"

"In Rathmullen graveyard."

"O, some one like her you saw. She has no relatives interred there. The Lees, you know, are absolute strangers in this part of the country."

"So I understood; and yet, upon my word, I saw her there, at two different times, as plainly as I see you now. On both occasions, it was late in the evening, and she passed within a few yards of me, apparently on her way to the shore."

"You must have been mistaken. Mary never goes there; I should hear of it, if she did. Sometimes, in calm evenings, she and Lanty Hanlon take a run up the lough together in the jolly-boat, but I never heard of her visiting the graveyard."

During this little conversation between Uncle Jerry and Kate, Dr. Henshaw and Mrs. Willoughby were busily engaged talking on various subjects, and particularly those relating to Scotch and English society. Being of an old aristocratic family herself, the good lady was very fond of speaking of her ancestors, dating them back as far as the Conquest, and of the various noble houses all over England and Scotland, with which she had become connected during a long succession of years. Dr. Henshaw, on the other hand, coming as he did from an old Puritan stock, and still proud of his grim old warrior fathers, was not inclined to set much value on his venerable companion's reminiscences of the past, and indeed went so far in his rough, brusque manner of speaking of the English nobility, as to shock the old lady's prepossessions very much, and finally to consign his own, as well as her ancestors, to perdition, as enemies of the Catholic church.

Fortunately, however, a circumstance of rather a ludicrous character occurred just then to prevent an open rupture.

Lanty Hanlon, as the reader may remember, was appointed to take charge of the negro in the boat house, and keep him as comfortable as possible under hay and blankets, till a carriage could be sent next morning to convey him to Greenmount, if it should so happen that no accommodation could be had for him at Castle Gregory. Lanty waited patiently till the half hour was up, expecting by that time to see some of the castle servants coming down to relieve him. But when the half hour passed, and no one came, he began to feel somewhat uneasy at the prospect of being obliged to sit up all night with so unsociable a companion. The next half hour passed away also, and no one came. Lanty went to the door to listen — but all in vain — not a sound could he hear, but the occasional screech of the peacock perched on the old sun dial.

" Begorra," he muttered to himself, at last, scratching his head and returning to his weary post, " begorra, it's a mighty agreeable okkipation, sittin here all alone nurse-tendin a blackamoor, an not a sowl within call of me. I'd like to know what Mary Kelly will say when I'm not there to take her up to Ned Callahan's christenin. I'm sayin, Mr. Blackamoor," he continued, turning to the negro, who now lay motionless on the flat of his back, " I'm sayin, ye'd do me a mighty great favor if ye'd let me off till daybreak. I've some weighty business on my hands."

" Berry sick, massa," responded the negro.

"O, I don't dispute that in the laste. But there's no fear of you dyin till mornin, any how.",

" Berry bad, massa; berry sick; no tink me live."

" O, musha, bad luck to the fear of ye, my *augenach*; yer more frightened than hurt."

" Me no feel toes — none at all."

"O, botheration to yer toes — I'm not goin to stay here all night nursin them, without as much as a drop i' drink, or even a draw of the pipe to warm me. So start, my darlin; I'll carry ye to the castle."

"You kill me, massa."

"Dang the fear of ye — come, now, get up, my fine fellow — ye'll ride on a Christian's back, any way, and that's an honor ye little expected."

The poor negro begged hard to be left where he was for the night, but Lanty was inexorable; the dance at Ned Callahan's christening, with Mary Kelly for a partner, was too strong a temptation. After various twistings and turnings, he succeeded at length in seating the invalid on the top of an empty barrel, and then backing in, wound the creature's arms round his neck, and tied them there with his handkerchief, lest he might happen to grow faint, and fall on the road. In this fashion Lanty started off with his burden, intending to leave him in one of the out-houses till morning. When he reached the castle, however, he found them all locked. The only door, in fact, he saw open, after hawking his load all over the place, was the great hall door of the castle itself. So, after some hesitation, he took courage, and in he went. Looking round the spacious hall, and seeing no one coming, he determined to deposit the negro on a door mat, and then, having rung the bell, disappear as fast as possible. Unfortunately, however, he selected the wrong place, and worse still, in turning round to drop the negro behind him, he stumbled backwards, burst open the parlor door, where the company we have just left were quietly seated, and rolled into the middle of the room, with the negro's arms clasped around his neck as tight as a vice.

The uproar was awful. Mrs. Willoughby screamed; Mr. Guirkie shouted thieves and murder; Dr. Henshaw upset the table and lights, in his effort to catch his aristocratic

antagonist, as she fell fainting from her chair. Kate ran
to one door, and the priest groped his way to another, calling on the servants. Within the room all was darkness and
confusion. Uncle Jerry, in his attempts to escape, capsized
chairs, tables, tumblers, decanters, dumb waiters, and every
thing else that came in his way. Mrs. Willoughby, in a fit
of hysterics, wriggled furiously in the arms of the tall
reviewer, whilst Lanty kicked and swore lustily at the
" blackguard blackamoor " to let him go.

At length the servants came running in with lights, one
after another, all out of breath, and all inquiring what had
happened. The shouts and screams of the party had attracted to the spot every domestic in the house, from the boot
boy to the steward. But their stay was short, for the instant
their eyes fell on the negro's black face, they mistook him for
a certain gentleman of the same color, and fled away, tread-
ing on each other's heels, and screeching like very demons,
till the din grew ten times greater than before.

"What's all this clamor about?" demanded the priest,
motioning back the affrighted servants. "Brave fellows you
are, to be scared in this way by the black face of a poor
African. But where's Lanty Hanlon?" he inquired, suddenly
recollecting himself; "eh! where's Lanty Hanlon? away,
and bring the villain here forthwith; he's the cause of all
this trouble. Bring him here instantly."

" Lanty Hanlon, where are you?" shouted one.

" Lanty Hanlon, the priest wants you!" cried another.

But no answer came. Lanty Hanlon was gone.

CHAPTER XIII.

Dr. Henshaw's Pride is deeply wounded. To be taken for a Burglar, and treated as a Burglar, is more than he felt prepared to put up with. Captain Petersham apologizes for his Blunder, but to no purpose.

CAPTAIN PETERSHAM, booted and spurred, and accompanied by an officer in undress constabulary uniform, entered the parlor the moment the servants rushed in with the lights, and there beheld, to his utter amazement, the insensible form of his venerable aunt, in the arms of a tall, red-bearded stranger. The groans of the unfortunate African on the floor, and the cries of Uncle Jerry, mingling with the screams and confusion of the affrighted servants, left him no room to doubt the man was a burglar; and fired with indignation at the outrage thus offered his relative, he snatched a pistol from the mantel-piece, and bounding over chairs, tables, broken glasses, and every thing else that lay in his way, presented the weapon at his head.

"Villain, desist," he cried, "or I blow your brains out."

"Hold on, sir," ejaculated Henshaw; "remove your weapon."

"Lay down the lady on the sofa, sirrah — lay her down instantly!"

"Are you mad, sir? — I have no — no —— "

"Down with her, or by —— "

The doctor, feeling the cold muzzle of the pistol touch his forehead, dropped his burden as suddenly as if she had been a bar of hot iron, and then drawing himself up, and pursing out his lips, demanded to know who dared assault him thus.

"Silence, villain," again thundered the captain, "silence."

"Sir, I'm no villain, and I demand ——"

"Another word!" and the excited captain again raised his weapon.

But the police officer, fearing his fiery temper might drive him to extremities, arrested his arm, and begged him to see to the lady, while he took charge of the prisoner.

"Hold him fast, then," he cried. "Let him escape at your peril. Ho! there," he continued, shouting to the servants — "ho! there, rascals; let two or three of you remove Mrs. Willoughby to her room, and the others start off and scour the country for the rest of the gang; five pounds for the first capture; come now, my lads, lose no time; tumble out and be active."

As the excited captain rushed from the parlor, after issuing his orders, he came full tilt against Uncle Jerry, and laid him sprawling on his back.

"Thank you," said the latter; "I'm exceedingly obliged, upon my word. Well, I vow and declare," he added, as he kicked up his little gaitered legs, and wriggled like a capsized crab — "I vow and declare there's not such another place as Castle Gregory in the whole world."

"Kate Petersham! Kate Petersham! Hilloa, Kate, where are you?" cried the captain, leaving Mr. Guirkie to his own resources.

"Here," said a voice behind him.

The captain turned, and to his surprise beheld his sister in an arm chair, her head thrown back, her hair all down over her shoulders, and her whole frame convulsed with laughter.

"What in the name of all the Furies does this mean?" he demanded, beginning to suspect some mistake.

But Kate, to save her life, could not articulate a syllable; all she could do was to point to Uncle Jerry, on the floor.

"Who is he?" said the captain; and turning to the prostrate man, he seized him by his arm, and raised him on his feet.

" Why, how now ! is it possible ? — good Heavens ! — how came you here, Mr. Guirkie ? "

" That's not the thing, captain ; no, sir, that's not the thing; the question is, how I'm to get away, for the devil's in the house."

" Where is Dr. Henshaw ? " inquired the priest, stopping a servant running across the hall.

" Who the deuce is Dr. Henshaw ?   What — and Father John here too ?   Can you explain this uproar, Father Brennan ? " demanded the captain.

" Lanty Hanlon's the cause of the whole of it — at least I suspect as much — but I must leave you with Mr. Guirkie — he can enlighten you on the. subject, whilst I go in quest of the doctor."

" Lanty Hanlon ! he's the very devil, that fellow.   Why, here's an officer of police in the house this moment, in search of him."

" For what ? "

" For an aggravated assault on a foreigner of the name of Weeks."

" The Yankee ? "

" Very likely."

" Well, upon my credit," said Uncle Jerry, " I'm quite sure he deserved all he got, for he's a very presumptuous fellow.   What d'ye think, captain ?   He had the impudence to tell me that a horn on a hare's ear for a June fly was all a humbug.   Just imagine a stranger tell me that, after fishing over five years in these waters."

" Can no one say where Dr. Henshaw is ? " inquired the priest, accosting Mr. Guirkie and the captain.

" Dr. Henshaw again !   Who the mischief is Dr. Henshaw ? "

" A friend of mine I brought with me to see Castle Gregory."

" He's an awful man," said Uncle Jerry.

"Awful man?"

"Yes, he wields theology like a sledge hammer, and sends all Protestants to misery everlasting."

"Hold," exclaimed the captain; "I fear I've made a confounded blunder.   Good Heavens! what have I done!   That must be the very man I left just now in the breakfast parlor, in custody of the officer."

"Ha, ha! he, he!" chuckled Uncle Jerry again; "that's glorious!"

"Why, I took him for a robber in the act of carrying off my aunt."

"Excellent! he, he! excellent!   Capital idea, such a man as Dr. Henshaw carry away your aunt.   Ha, ha!"

"Are you ready?" cried Kate, marching up to the captain with a cutting whip in her hand, and the strap of her riding cap under her chin.

"Don't provoke me, Kate.   Go away now."

"What, sir, turned coward? and your whole retinue in the field."

"Begone, I say."

"And your venerable relative wrested from the arms of one of the gang!"

The captain retreated into the parlor, but Kate followed him.

"Shall I have the five pounds if I succeed?—five pounds, you know, for the first capture."

"Begone this minute," ejaculated the mortified captain, turning short and pursuing her; but the mirth-loving, provoking girl was too swift for him, and fled from the room laughing till the spacious hall rang again.

But to return to the prisoner in the breakfast parlor.

The wrath of the distinguished reviewer, on finding himself shut up in custody of a police officer, knew no bounds. "Open that door, sir," he exclaimed, violently, pointing at it with his finger—"open that door eenstantly, and give me free egress from this infernal house."

"Keep quiet, my good man," coolly replied the officer — "keep quiet."

"Stand from the door," vociferated Henshaw, raising his clinched fist, " or I'll fell you to the earth."

"If you don't keep your temper, I'll handcuff you," replied the officer, with as much coolness as before.

"Handcuff me! Sirrah," cried Henshaw, running his thumbs into his waistcoat, and swelling up till he looked like a Jupiter Tonans. "Handcuff me — caitiff, cuif!"

"I have shackled as strong men in my time."

"You preesumptuous pygmy," growled the doctor; and he shot at his keeper a look of withering scorn like Glenalvon when he said to the young Douglas, —

> "Knowest thou not Glenalvon, born to command
> Ten thousand slaves like thee?"

"Pray, fellow, what do you take me for?" at length he added, a little cooled down under the officer's imperturbability of look and tone.

"A robber — caught in the very act of abducting one of the ladies of the house."

"A robber! Look at me again, sir! Am I like a robber?"

"Can't say as to that. I've seen robbers as good-looking in my time."

"You're an eensolent scoundrel; but go on, play oot the play. This is my first Irish lesson, I presume."

"And you'll find it a sharp one, too, I suspect, before it's over."

"Humph! you're an Irishman, I take it."

"I am — what of that?"

"Why, I suspected as much, by your insufferable eensolence."

"See here, my good man; that's a reflection on my country," said the officer, "and I don't like it. Say what you please of myself, as long as you're in my custody — but if you value your health, let my country alone; for my knuckles itch when I hear it lightly spoken of, especially by a foreigner."

At this moment a knock was heard at the door, and presently Captain Petersham entered.

" I hasten," said the portly captain, with a smile on his honest, jolly face — " I hasten, Dr. Henshaw, to offer you an apology for this —— "

" Sir, I shall accept no apology," growled the doctor. " All I require is permeession to quit this house — instantly."

" But, my dear sir, will you —— ? "

" No, sir; you've offered me an unpardonable insult."

" Will you not listen to an explanation ? "

" No, sir — I'll listen to no explanation."

" Pshaugh ! nonsense, my dear friend — don't take it so ill. Why, I've been making and apologizing for blunders all my lifetime. Father John here will tell you the little boys on the streets call me nothing but blundering Tom Petersham."

" That's a positive fact, and good reason for it, too," muttered Uncle Jerry, ambling about the room, and bobbing his skirts up and down as usual.

" Come, come, doctor," persisted the captain, again offering his hand, " let us forget this foolish mistake, and drink success to Bonnie Scotland over a good stout bottle of old Port — supper awaits us in the next room."

" You must excuse me, sir; I can't partake of your hospeetality," said the doctor gruffly, turning away and moving to and fro like a caged lion.

" Don't you remember Eolus ? " said Uncle Jerry, whispering in the priest's ear — " *Vadit per claustram magno cum murmure rauco.* He, he ! he's the very man."

" Is there no way to conciliate him ? " inquired the captain, turning to the priest.

" None that I know of."

" Let us start Kate at him," said the captain; " if the man has a soft spot in his heart, she'll find it."

And Kate did beg and entreat him to stay for the night, and begged and begged again, but all to no purpose — the doctor was inflexible. Nay, he went even so far at last as to rebuke her harshly for her familiarity; and Kate, the poor kind-hearted girl, unaccustomed to such language, blushed like a child under the reproof, and stole away, mortified, from the room.

"Now, then, in the name of all the gods in Olympus," exclaimed the captain, who had been watching Kate, and witnessed her repulse, "that makes an end of it. An apology is as much as one gentleman can require of another, and I've already satisfied my conscience on that point. Ho, there! who waits — Thomas?"

"Here, sir."

"Let the coachman drive up instantly, and take this gentleman home. Confound such stubborn — sulky — mawworms," he added, turning again to the priest. "I'm sorry, sir, for this ridiculous blunder on your account; but hang me if I can play the supplicant any longer."

"Of course not."

"Should he happen to be a gentleman, and desire satisfaction of another kind, I shall be most happy to accommodate him. He can have Johnson of Birchfield, you know, in a moment's warning."

"No, no, captain," replied the priest, smiling; "he must dispense with such favors for the present. For myself, I exceedingly regret having brought him with me to Castle Gregory. But there was no help for it. The night was dark, and Mr. Guirkie absolutely refused to part with the negro till he had seen you, and placed him under your special protection. I'm sorry also I must accompany the doctor; for I had promised myself a long chat with Kate on a certain interesting subject which ——"

"Which is neither more nor less than the comparative merits of the Anglican and Catholic churches. I suspected

all along, my dear fellow, what you and Kate were about;
but it's no concern of mine — let her please herself. If she
wishes to adopt a new form of religion, I'm satisfied — only
let it be a decent one; for by all the saints in the calendar, if
she dared look even sideways at any of those tinkering
religions they manufacture nowadays, I'd hang her up for
the crows to pick."

"Ha, ha! you don't like these new-fangled systems, I
perceive."

"Like them! why, they're the most damnable nuisances in
the country. One of those canting fellows who peddle them
round here, called on me last week, and after disgusting me
with his hypocritical twaddle, had the impudence to invite me
to what he called a prayer meeting. Ha, ha! By George,
I had a good mind to fling the fellow, neck and heels, out of
the window. No, sir; I was bred a Protestant myself, and
intend to live and die one; but Kate is old enough now to
know what she's about, and may, for aught it concerns me,
turn Catholic, if her taste lie that way — but let her keep
clear of these pettifoggers; that's all the stipulation I make."

"Well, but suppose," observed the priest, smiling — "suppose her taste led her to adopt the Methodist ——— "

"O, hang the Methodist. I'd rather see her peddle eggs
with a basket on her arm."

"You don't apprehend much danger of that, I suppose?
Kate's not exactly of that turn of mind."

"No; but you can't tell, sir, what may happen — you can't
tell. These Hardwrinkles are here night and day since she
stopped going to church on Sundays."

"Humph, and these visits are intended to counteract the
influence of Mary Lee, I suspect."

"Poor Mary! Is she not a most fascinating creature?"
said the captain, earnestly. "I tell you what, sir, I believe
in my soul I'm in love with that girl."

The priest looked at the burly captain and smiled.

"Well, hang me if I know what to make of it; but I feel sometimes as if I could propose for her myself. Ha, ha! what think you of that, sir, from a bachelor of forty-five?" and the captain laughed till his fat sides shook again at the idea of such a match.

"You would have but little chance against Randall Barry, I fear," replied the priest.

"The young outlaw?"

"Yes; and the foolish boy is now somewhere in the neighborhood, I understand."

"Saw him myself, and a devilish fine-looking fellow he is —saw him at the lighthouse yesterday."

"Is it possible! and you didn't arrest him as in duty bound? You're a very pretty magistrate, indeed. Why, captain, I must report you to the government as an abettor of treason."

"Nonsense— I'm not a policeman, to carry handcuffs in my pocket."

"But you might have ordered his arrest."

"Humph! when I order the arrest of a fine young fellow like that, whose only crime is to love his country, I shall be no longer Tom Petersham. Still, if he happen to be brought before me, you know, as a justice of the peace, and fully identified, I must commit him."

"Of course you must. The boy is acting very rashly in coming here at all, after all the warnings he has had."

"He must be a bold fellow, knowing there's a reward of three hundred pounds offered for his capture."

"I wish to mercy he could be induced to quit the country for a time, for if he happen to be taken, Mary will break her heart."

"Well, he shall be arrested, you may depend on it, sooner or later. Three hundred pounds, these hard times, is a strong temptation. Why, this very officer, in the house now, chased him two days ago from Buncrana to Lambert's Point."

"Carriage at the door," cried a servant.

"And what of supper?"

"On the table, sir."

"Come then, my dear friend," said the captain, taking the priest familiarly by the arm; "let us pick a bone together before you leave. Kate, go ask Dr. Henshaw to join us. Where's Mr. Guirkie?— Mr. Guirkie, come forth — come forth, thou man of indescribable sensibilities."

But Mr. Guirkie had left the parlor a few minutes before, and was now making arrangements with the steward for the safe conveyance of the African to Greenmount next morning. He soon made his appearance, however, and joined the captain and the priest in a glass of wine. It was all the refreshment they ventured to accept, as Henshaw still doggedly rejected every attempt at conciliation.

"Well, good by, doctor," said the good natured captain, accompanying the party to the steps of the hall door; "I'm sorry you leave us in anger — but I know you'll think better of it to-morrow. Good by, sir."

The distinguished reviewer growled something in reply.

"Kate," said the priest, "don't neglect to cultivate the acquaintance of Mary Lee, nor forget to read that book I lent you on the beauties of the Catholic religion."

"Never fear," replied Kate; and then having promised Uncle Jerry to see particular care taken of his poor African, she waved her hand in adieu, and the carriage drove off at a gallop down the avenue.

CHAPTER XIV.

Kate and Else at the Bedside of the Cabin Boy. — Else begins to suspect the little Fellow will yet unravel a Mystery. — A Visit from Kate Petersham, who receives a Letter from Lanty Hanlon, announcing Randall Barry's Arrest.

A SEVERE attack of fever, resulting from the hardships he endured in the life boat, had now confined the little cabin boy to his room at the lighthouse for several days, during which Mary Lee was his constant attendant, hardly ever leaving him, day or night.

Doctor Camberwell had called to see the patient several times, and as often found Mary patiently watching by his bedside, with the fidelity and affection of a sister. Strongly did he remonstrate with her (as did her uncle also) on the imprudence of shutting herself up so constantly in the sick room, especially when Else Curley and Roger O'Shaughnessy were there to attend him. But all in vain. Nothing could prevail on her to quit her post. She only smiled, and assured them she apprehended no danger whatever.

The room in which the boy lay was a small apartment on the north side of the lodge, directly over the Devil's Gulch, and looking out on the far-famed Swilly Rock, which lay in the very mouth of the lough, about half a mile distant, showing its long black back now and then, as the swells of the sea broke over and seethed down its sides. Beyond it, in the distance, appeared the rugged outline of Malin Head, casting its deep shadow far out into the sea, and frowning a sulky defiance at each passing ship as she rounded the dangerous bluff. It was to avoid that headland the ill-fated "Saldana" ran for a harbor, and struck on Swilly Rock. On that rock she lost her helm and masts, and then, broken up by the fury of the ocean, drifted in fragments to the shore.

Every soul on board perished, that night, but one little infant; and that infant, now a lovely girl of eighteen, her eyes turned to the fatal spot, was praying for the little wrecked cabin boy, laying beside her. She was kneeling before a crucifix, with a rosary in her hand, and old Drake, resting his nose on his shaggy paws, was peering up in her face.

Suddenly she turned, and looked towards the bed.

"Sambo — Sambo," muttered the boy; "where are you, Sambo?"

Mary rose, and advancing to the bedside, laid her hand gently on the forehead of the little sufferer — it was burning hot.

"Sambo, dear Sambo," he again repeated, "let us return home. Mother calls me."

"It's the crisis," murmured Mary; "six hours more will terminate the contest between life and death. O Mother of God, Mother of our Redeemer," she added, "save this wandering boy." And slowly sinking on her knees again, she prayed and wept over him, till the tears rolled down her cheeks, and dropped unheeded on the bed.

"What's that you're doing, Sambo?" muttered the boy; "you scald me with drops of lead."

"Hush, hush," whispered Mary in his ear. "Keep quiet; I'm with you."

"Take me home, Sambo, take me home."

"Where?"

"Where! to Old Virginny. There it is, right before you; don't you see the old Potomac? Massa shan't blame you a mite — it was all my fault, and I'll tell him so. Won't you take me back, Sambo?"

"Yes, to-morrow — to-morrow; but keep still now, or I must leave you."

The threat of desertion seemed to silence the little fellow completely. Mary then applied a napkin steeped in vinegar and water to his burning temples, and after smoothing his pillow, was returning to her seat near the window, when all of a sudden she found herself clasped in the arms of Kate Petersham.

"Kate!" she exclaimed; "is it possible?"

"Yes — your own Kate — and I love you now a thousand times better than ever."

"You won't scold me, will you?"

"Scold you! for what?"

"Not going to see you, according to promise."

"And abandon your little charge there. No, no, Mary, I know your heart too well for that. But I must scold you for something else, Mary. I must scold you for staying here so constantly in the sick room."

"There's no danger in the world, Kate."

"Danger! Why, Dr. Camberwell says it's typhus fever, and of the most malignant kind, too."

"Well, but, dear Kate, you need not feel the least concern about that, for I'm not afraid of it; and you know where there's no fear there's no danger."

"I don't know any such thing. On the contrary, I'm sure you're running a great risk."

"Not the slightest. The Mother of God will protect me."

"Ah, you can't be certain of that."

"Quite certain. She never forsook me yet."

"But if you've acted imprudently and rashly, why should she protect you?"

"Listen to me, Kate, and when I tell you how all this happened, you'll say there's something mysterious in it. It was just eighteen years, to the hour, since the wreck of the Saldana, the night this poor boy was cast ashore on Ballyhernan Strand. The circumstance struck me as something strange when I heard it mentioned by the warren-keeper in the cabin, and pondering over it as I wet the lips of the little mariner with a spoonful of wine and water, the idea occurred to me that the Blessed Virgin had committed him to my special care. You may smile, Kate, but the providence of

God has its own ways and means of accomplishing its ends.
' How very like my own fate is this little wanderer's !' said I ;
' perhaps he, too, has neither father nor mother left to watch
over him.'   Just as I muttered these words to myself, he
raised his eyes to mine, and seemed to make such an appeal
to my heart that I couldn't, for the life of me, say a syllable in
reply.   So I only nodded a promise.   He understood it
though, perfectly, and smiled his thanks as I gave it."

"And you feel bound by that promise," said Kate, "though
not a word was exchanged between you."

"O, indeed, as for that, Kate, I believe I had made the
promise to the Blessed Virgin before he looked at me at all.
For why should he have been cast ashore that night, of all
the nights in the year, and consigned to my care too, by the
doctor, if there hadn't been something mysterious in it ?"

"And now, you're prepared to risk your life to save his ?"

"No, no," replied Mary, throwing her arm round her companion's neck, and leaning her head gently on her bosom —
"no, no, dear Kate, there's no risk for me, since the Queen
of Virgins has promised to save me."

"But may not this be superstition ?"

"Superstition !   O Kate, Kate, if you only felt for one
short hour the blessed hopes which the Mother of God
inspires in the hearts of her suffering children, you would
speak less coldly of our beautiful religion.   Indeed, Kate,
only for the consolations I have drawn for the last six years
from that pure fountain of pity and love, I should long since
have sunk under the weight of my sorrows."

"Ah," responded Kate, compassionately; "you've had
sorrows enough, poor child."

"And yet, strange as it may seem, it's the cheerfulness
with which he bears his misfortunes that wounds me the
most."

"His misfortunes !   Whom do you mean ?"

"My uncle."

"O, I thought you were speaking of your own griefs."

"No; I never had any thing to grieve for but him — he is all the world, though, to me; for, indeed, I think, Kate, he loves me more than his life."

"Don't wonder much at that, Mary."

"To see him falling, step by step, from the proud position he once occupied among the best and noblest of the land; to see his friends — alas! they were sorry friends — deserting him day after day; to see his creditors, who were wont to come to him bowing in lowly reverence, now insolently rebuking him for his reckless extravagance; to see his stables empty, his hounds all dead and gone, his servants forsaking him one by one; and to see himself smiling and happy-looking as a bridegroom in the midst of all that desolation, — O, Kate, it was that which almost broke my heart."

"On the contrary, Mary, I think it should have consoled you to see him bear his misfortunes so bravely."

"Ah, yes; but it's all deception — an outward show. He only affects to be happy on my account."

"You may be mistaken, Mary; it's his natural disposition, perhaps."

"O, no," replied the gentle girl; "I can tell his very thoughts, though he fancies them hidden from all the world. Often have I watched his countenance as he read over those insulting letters of his creditors, and seen how he struggled to hide his indignation under a smile. And now, Kate, they have found us out at last."

"What — discovered your retreat?"

"Yes; and threaten Mr. Lee with arrest, if their demands are not immediately satisfied. One man has bought up several of his bonds, and demands payment before the first of next month."

"And what's to be done? Can my brother do any thing to avert the blow? Shall I speak to him on the subject?"

"Not for the world, Kate."

17

"And why so? you know he loves your uncle."

"Yes, but for that very reason he would be the last man of whom he should ask a favor."

"To whom, then, will you apply for help?"

"I have applied already, Kate, to a dear friend."

"You have?"

"Yes; to one who never refused me in my need."

"Ah! I understand you.   Indeed! And you expect succor from her.   But why not apply to the Redeemer himself — the fountain of all goodness?"

"Because, dear Kate, I fear I'm not worthy to approach him; and I know, besides, he will hear the prayer of the Mother who bore him sooner than mine."

"Then you apply to her merely as an intercessor? Why, I always thought you expected aid directly from herself."

"Kate, Kate, how often have I told you the contrary!"

"Yes; but I have heard it preached about so often in our pulpits."

"Hush! some one knocks.   Come in."

The door opened, and Else Curley, wrapped in her old gray cloak, entered the room.

Without uttering a word of recognition or apology, she advanced to the bed, and laid her withered hand on the temples of the patient.   Then, having satisfied herself as to the progress of the disease, she turned slowly round, and throwing back her hood, addressed Miss Petersham in her usual hoarse, hollow tones : —

"Young woman, why are you here?" she demanded.

"That's my own affair," replied Kate.   "By what right do you ask?"

"The right which the age and experience of eighty years give me.   I seen many a faver, girl, in my time, but niver yet so dangerous a faver as this.   Away from the room — it's no place for idle visitors."

"And pray, old woman, what reason have you to feel so much concern for my safety?"

"The raison's too ould," replied Else, "to spake of now. Yer grandfather, if he lived, cud hardly remimber it. But here," she continued, drawing a piece of folded paper from her bosom; "read this, and judge for yourself, if it's at Araheera Head ye ought to be."

Kate took the paper from her hand, and accompanied Mary to the parlor.

"Ha!" said Else, now that she found herself alone with the sick boy; "if he hasn't lost his senses, I'll try what can be done to clear up this mystery. If the nigger started back frightened, as Lanty says, when he first seen Weeks at Mr. Guirkie's, he must know something about him ; and accordin to all accounts, the nigger and the boy come from the same plantation. Ay, ay, there's a hole in that wall somewhere worth the ferretin.   Look up," she continued, touching the lad on the arm with her fore-finger — "look up an spake to me."

"Who's that?" murmured the boy, turning on his side, and gazing at the old woman; "are you Sambo?"

"Ay, I'm Sambo."

"You're not Sambo — nigger Sambo."

"Don't you know me?"

"Yes, but you sure you're Sambo — very sure you're Sambo Nelson?"

"Quite sure — and what's *your* name?"

"My name — my name's Natty."

"Natty what?"

"Natty Nelson."

"And where's your father?"

"My father — my father — well, let me see, my father — where's my father."

"Where does he live?"

"Who?"

"Your father."

"Sambo, Sambo, whisper; don't be afraid; he shan't flog you."

" Who shan't flog me ? "

" Father — old Danger, you know. So take me back to old Virginny — take me back, mother calls me. Listen, ain't that the wash of old Potomac against the ship's side ? "

" Hush ! don't speak so much, Natty — tell me, Natty."

" Ay, ay, sir, by the mark — seven — send all hands aloft — take in sail."

Else, finding it now impossible to draw any further information from the boy, took a small vial from her pocket, and pouring a few drops of the contents into a spoon, gave it to her patient.

" There," she muttered, " that'll make you sleep for the nixt hour; and when ye waken, if yer senses haven't come back, I'll try some other manes to rache the sacret." Then drawing out her stocking, she sat down on a low stool by the bedside, and commenced her knitting.

" This is a very pretty piece of paper indeed," said Kate, looking at the address as she entered the parlor.

" To her ladyship, Miss Petersham."

" Good, so far; now for the inside. Eh ! what in the name of all the fairies is this? ' Lanty Hanlon is my name, and Ireland is my nashin, Donegal is my dwilin. plas, an heven is my xpectashin.' His expectation, the villain ! Ha, ha! if heaven were full of angels like him, I u rather be excused from joining the company. It must be the fly leaf of the fellow's prayer-book. But hold, here's something on the other side."

" This is to let you no, that " — here Kate suddenly dropped her voice, and read over the remainder in silence : " Randall Barry lies woondid and a prisner in Tamny Barrics, i'll meet yer ladyship this evenin at the castil about dusk, behint the ould boat-house, no more at presint

　　　　but remanes your abaident to command
　　　　　　　　　　　　LANTY HANLON."

"Any thing amiss?" inquired Mary, as Kate finished the reading of the precious document — "you look alarmed."

"Alarmed! do I? O, no, it's nothing particular."

"Lanty's full of mischief — been playing you some trick, perhaps."

"Lanty! no, no — it's a mere trifle; I must get home, however, as soon as possible. Please ring for Roger — I want him to call the cockswain."

As Mary turned to ring the bell, Roger made his appearance at the door, carrying the old silver salver, and awaiting the command of his young mistress to enter.

"Come in, Roger; what have you got there?" said Kate.

"A little refreshment, please, madam. Mr. Lee sends his compliments to Miss Petersham."

"Is he at home?"

"No, madam; he went out in the direction of Araheera a few minutes ago, and gave orders to have cake and wine sent in afore he left."

"What kind of wine is it, Roger?" inquired Kate, smiling over at Mary as she put the question.

"Ahem! what kind, madam why, it's a — it's — a very delaceous currant wine — very pure and delicate."

"Indeed!"

"And just twenty-five years old next Christmas. No, I make a mistake there — hem! — twenty-four years next Christmas — ahem! just twenty-four years — exactly."

"O, it don't matter," said Kate laughing; "a year, you know, is nothing."

"It's the wine Lady Templeton ust to like so much when she visited the castle, if you remember," observed Roger, bowing to his mistress.

"Currant wine's but a sorry beverage at best, Roger," said Kate, mischievously.

"Well, perhaps, ladies, you would prefer Champagne or Sherry?"

"O, no; no, Roger, don't trouble yourself."

"No trouble in life, ma'am ; only just say so, and I'll be happy to serve them.   But if you try this here, you'll find it delaceous."

"Very well; we must taste it on your reccommendation : and now, Roger, send my men aboard — we must leave instantly."

When the old servant left the room, Mary laid her hand on Kate's shoulder, and looking at her affectionately, again expressed her fears that something was wrong at Castle Gregory.

"Nothing, Mary — nothing, whatever."

"And yet you look deeply concerned.   Has Captain Petersham or Mrs. Willoughby been sick ? "

"No, no, dear ·child they're both quite well.   It's something I must attend to before to-morrow, having no immediate relation to any of the family."

As Mary stood there, leaning her arm on her companion's shoulder, and looking wistfully in her face, she exhibited a form and features of exquisite beauty.   The rays of the declining sun had just then entered the window, and for a second or two bathed her whole person in golden light, illumining her countenance with that celestial glow which holy men say overspreads the features of the seraphim.   Never breathed a fairer form than hers — never shone a fairer face ; and yet the beauty of her soul transcended far the loveliness of her person.   O, when loveliness of body and soul unite in woman, how truly does she then reflect the image of her Creator — the great source of purity, beauty, and love !

"Kate, dear Kate," murmured Mary, "when shall we kneel together before the same altar?   When shall we become sisters in faith, as we are now in affection ? "

"Sooner, perhaps, than you anticipate," replied Kate, kissing the forehead of the lovely girl.

"You've read the little books I gave you ? "

"Yes, and liked them too; but I've been reading another book, which speaks more eloquently of your faith, and draws me nearer to the threshold of your church, than all the controversial works ever written."

"O, I'm so delighted, dear Kate! What is it?"

"I can't tell you that."

"Why so?"

"You would blush all over, and run away."

"Did I ever read it?"

"Never, I believe, though it belongs to you, and to you alone; for there's not another like it in the whole world."

"Belongs to me?"

"Yes, to your very self, and yet you're quite unconscious of its possession; but come with me to the steps — I must not delay another minute."

The two young friends now walked hand in hand across the green lawn, and stood at the head of the long flight of steps, looking down at the boatmen preparing to leave.

"Randall's coming here to-night," said Mary.

"Poor fellow! I wish he were safe off to the south; for, indeed, he must soon be caught if he stay here much longer. Do you remember him in your prayers, Mary?"

"Sometimes," murmured the blushing girl, looking down on the grass at her feet.

"Then pray for him earnestly *to-night*," whispered Kate; and tenderly embracing her dear young friend, she ran down the steps before the latter had time to ask a single word of explanation.

"Now, my lads," she cried, jumping into the stern sheets, and taking the tiller in her own hands, "now for it — out with every oar in the boat, and stretch to them with a will; we must make Castle Gregory in an hour and twenty minutes, if it can be done with oar and sail."

"Can't, Miss Kate! impossible!" said the cockswain, tautening the foresheet; "the ebb tide will meet us at Dunree."

"Not if this breeze freshens a little," responded Kate, looking over her shoulder; "and it shall — for there it comes dancing in to us from the mouth of the lough." As she spoke, the little boat, impelled by four stout oarsmen, shot out from under the shadow of the rocks, and began to cut her way through the waters. Mary stood for a moment looking down at the receding form of her reckless, light-hearted companion, as she sat in the stern with her hand on the rudder; and then, waving a last adieu, returned to resume her charge of the cabin boy.

———•———

CHAPTER XV.

Weeks begins to develop himself. — The Hardwrinkles. — Robert Hardwrinkle's ultimate Designs on Mary Lee. — Visit from Constabulary Officer.

"COME in," said Weeks, glancing over his shoulder at the tall, dark form of his cousin, Robert Hardwrinkle, standing in the doorway. "Come in; I'm not engaged."

"Thank you," said his host, creeping softly in, and closing the door noiselessly behind him. "I thank you; I merely called, at my good mother's request, to inquire for your health. She always fears, poor creature, you're not well when you don't come down to join us in family prayer."

"Well, can't say I'm sick, exactly," responded Weeks, throwing up his feet on the back of a chair, and offering his companion a cigar, which the latter modestly declined. "Can't say I'm sick, though I hain't got quite clear of that confounded wedding scrape yet. But the fact is, my dear fellow, I dread these almighty long prayers of yours — I do, really."

"Is it possible ?"

"A fact; I feel a sorter out of place like, sitting down there in the family circle — well, kinder green, you know. Why, it's just like this — I ain't accustomed to it exactly; business men in the States hain't got time to pray, as you do here in the country."

"Ah, but, my dear Ephraim, you should make time, for prayer is indispensable to salvation. You cannot please God without it."

"O, prayer is a very good thing, I allow," said Weeks, slowly puffing his cigar, and beating off the smoke with his hand. "It's an excellent thing for those who can attend to it; but it don't suit men in trade to spend whole hours at prayer, and neglect their business."

"Ah, but you can attend to both, if you only try."

"Why, we do try. We read the Bible, and go to meeting three times on the Sabbath; that's about as much, I reckon, as could reasonably be expected."

"Perhaps so. The people of New England, I'm informed, have acquired a great reputation for sanctity."

"Certain, and deserve it too, take the hull of them on an average. There's the women, for instance, and the farmers, and the country folks all round — they're all church-going people, and do most of the praying, while the merchants and traders are busy at their commercial pursuits. Well, it's just like this: one class of our people does the praying, and the other does the trading — kind of makes it easy, you know, on both; so that, take them on the hull, they're a very religious people."

"Ah, but, my dear Ephraim, that thing of halving the worship of God is forbidden by the rules of the holy gospel. Every creature is bound to worship God, and pray to him always — in season and out of season."

"What! and have their notes protested at the bank? My dear fellow, business is a sacred thing, and must be attended to."

"Ah, but you forget, my good cousin, that the great, and, indeed, the only business of life is salvation."

"Well, supposing it is, (I always thought, myself, salvation was a pretty good kinder doctrine in a general way, and I rather guess too the world should hardly get along so well without it,) still you know it won't cancel a note, Cousin Robert."

"Ephraim! Ephraim!" said Hardwrinkle, his cold, stern, sallow countenance exhibiting an expression of saintly sorrow as he spoke, — "Ephraim, where did you learn to speak of religion with such contemptuous indifference? Have you so soon forgotten the lessons of your pious mother? She, indeed, was a devoted servant of the Lord. O, *she* was a holy soul — praying in season and out of —— "

"Precisely," interrupted Weeks, taking the cigar from his mouth, and knocking the ashes off with his finger, "precisely — that's just it. She was forever running off to contribution parties and prayer meetings, and neglecting her business at home. By gracious, when father died he war'n't worth a five dollar bill in the world, and I had to slink off to the south to earn my bread, 'mong niggers and cotton bales. It's all very well to pray, and I don't object to it no how — but I don't see either the darned use in praying all day and neglecting the main point."

"The main point? and what's that, cousin?"

"What's that! why, it's money, ain't it?"

"Money! — you call money the main point?"

"Yes, *sir*," responded Weeks, emphatically; "I call it nothing else. Should admire to know what you call it."

"You shock me, Ephraim. Really you shock me."

"You don't say!"

"Why, you must be a downright infidel, to speak in that irreverent manner."

"Don't know about that. But I've got my own notions about religion, and ain't agoin to change them for any man's way of thinking. Guess I'm old enough now to judge for myself. And as for nine tenths of the religions going, I believe they're danged humbugs."

"Which of the different Christian denominations do you belong to, may I ask?" inquired Hardwrinkle.

"Well, can't say I belong to any in particular. I rather think, though, I like the Unitarians better than most of them. Their ministers are pretty smart sorter men, as a general thing, and preach first-rate sermons once in a while. No, I never seemed to have any choice in that way. The fact is, I always calilated to do about right with every man, and I kinder thought that was religion enough for me."

"Cousin," said Hardwrinkle, after a little reflection; "will you permit me to ask you one question?"

"Certainly, my dear fellow; why not? Ask as many as you please. Ain't you my cousin?"

"I hope you won't be offended, or think me impertinent, Ephraim. You're my mother's sister's child, you know, and it's but natural I should feel a lively interest in your welfare, spiritual and temporal."

"Of course, I'm your mother's sister's child — well!"

"Well, it's merely this. Do you really believe in the existence of God? Now, answer me candidly. It's rather a strange question, but no matter. Do you believe in that dogma?"

"Yes, *sir*," replied Weeks, thrusting his hands into his pockets, and shaking up the silver. "Yes, *sir*, I believe that — no mistake about it."

"The Lord be praised!" exclaimed his pious cousin, turning up his eyes. "I'm thankful you have not fallen yet into the lowest depth of the abyss. I really feared, Ephraim, from your manner of speaking, you were an atheist."

"No, sir; I believe in two things firmly, and no living man can make me change that belief. I believe in the existence of a first cause, and the perfectibility of man."

" And is that all ? "

" That's all, sir — that's the length and breadth of my creed."

" And how, think you, is man to be perfected ? "

" Why, by reason, science, and experience. That's about all he needs — ain't it ? "

" And what of religion ? — shall it take no part in his perfection ? "

" Well — yes, guess it might help some ; that is, if he'd only keep clear of these darned *isms*, and adopt some sensible kind of religion for himself. The worst thing in the world, cousin, for a business man, is to have any thing to do with the details of religion. They sorter cramp him, you know. Let him lay down a broad platform like mine, and stand upon it flat-footed — that's the way to get along in trade."

" And you're quite serious, Ephraim, in avowing those shocking sentiments."

" Shocking or not, they're mine ; that's a fact. Why, look here, my good friend ; I have seen too much of your hair-splitting religions in New England not to know what they are by this time. Those deacons, and class leaders, and old maids, and methodistical-looking crowds we see going to church every Sabbath, with their Bibles under their arms, are, in my humble opinion, a darned set of dupes and impostors, the whole concern of them. There's neither honor nor honesty amongst them. By crackie, they'd cut your throat with one hand and carry the Bible in the other. No, sir, a first cause, and the perfectibility of man, or, in other words, the irresistibility of human progress, is about as much as any business man can profess to believe with safety to himself or the interests of trade."

" But is that belief sufficient to save your soul ? "

" Save my soul? O, that's quite another affair. If there be such things as souls, (which is now rather a disputed point,) why, the Creator, who made them, knows best how to take care of them, I presume."

Hardwrinkle had never heard such language before on the
subject of religion. Bred in the country, and little acquainted
with the world, he supposed that however abandoned men
might be, or whatever infidel sentiments they might really
entertain, the respect in which religion was held by the great
majority of mankind would naturally repress their inclination
to avow them. Brought up as he was, a strict Presbyterian,
and accustomed from his childhood to hear religion spoken
of with the utmost reverence, he now appeared both astonished
and hurt to hear his cousin talk of it with such cold, reckless
contempt. For himself, he was the very impersonation of a
hypocrite. Mean, sordid, and cunning as a Jew, he had the
bland smile and the saintly look forever at his command, and
could play the Christian or the demon, as it suited his purpose, with equal adroitness. All his religion was external.
It consisted of long prayers, demure looks, pious conversation,
black garments, and an ascetic aspect. At church he was
never missing on the Sabbath; hail, rain, or snow, he was
there, sitting upright in his pew, motionless and impassible as
a statue. And there, too, sat his seven black sisters beside
him, tall, thin and lank, like himself; not a white spot to
be seen about them but their pocket handkerchiefs; even
their very fans were as black as ebony. In the whole world
round never was seen so solemn, staid, and church-loving a
family, from Robert, the heir and master, down to Deborah, —
or, as she was commonly called by her elder sisters, Baby
Deb, — now a young lady of seven and twenty. It happened,
however, that religion, by some misfortune or other, instead
of softening and expanding their hearts by its divine influence,
had withered them up. Its gladdening and exhilarating
touch seemed only to have chilled them like an icicle. The
bright look and the pleasant smile, which denote the presence
of religion in the soul, were never once seen to light up their
features. Like melancholy spectres, dark and stern, they
passed through the busy streets, or stole silently away in the

shadows of the houses — no one caring to look after them, or bid God bless them for their charity. O thou cold, stern monk of Geneva, thou whose heart never thrilled with a generous emotion, whose pulse never throbbed with sympathy for thy kind, this death-like picture of religion is thy handi-work. Thou subtle betrayer of the human conscience, thou dark plotter of treason against the sovereignty of the human soul, how could you look up at the bright heavens above, and see the blessed sun gladdening the earth with his beams, or behold the stars dancing in their orbits to the music of the spheres, and yet be demon enough to curse humanity with such a lifeless religion as this?

But of all the members of the Hardwrinkle family, Robert was the most heartless; or if, indeed, he had a heart at all, it was as callous as a stone. When the stranger beggar came to his door, (for those of the parish knew him too well to enter his gates,) he neither ordered him from his presence nor hunted his dogs on him. No, he kindly admonished the sufferer to guard against the many dangers and temptations that beset him in his mode of life, counselled him gently to beware of evil company, and then gave the shivering supplicant a religious tract to teach him resignation to the will of Heaven, or a Dispensary ticket to procure ointment for his sores. Money was his god, and he adored it. To part with a shilling, save in usury, was like rending his heart-strings. He loved it, not for the use he could make of it in giving employment to others, or in serving the interests of the parish, without loss to himself, but for the mere pleasure of seeing and feeling it with his hands.. In this respect his cousin Ephraim was an entirely different man. He, like a true Yankee, was fond of money too; nay, ready to go through fire and water to obtain it; but yet he was just as ready, on the other hand, to lend it to a neighbor in a pinch, and think it no great obligation either. He valued money only as a circu-lating medium — as an agent to carry on trade, or acquire a position for himself in society. He was forever talking, to be sure, of dollars and cents; but still it was evident to those who happened to be at all acquainted with his disposition and habits of life, that he was by no means a mercenary man. Nor was he, like most lovers of money, envious of his neighbors' prosperity — not he; on the contrary, he was pleased to see every one thrive and do well, and ready to bid them God speed into the bargain. There was one peculiarity in him, however, which at first sight looked rather damaging to the character of an honorable man. He never scrupled taking advantage of his neighbor in speculations; because every man, he contended, should have his "eye peeled," and deserved to suffer if he hadn't. It was by sharp bargains men were made smart, and by smart men trade was made to flourish; and if it happened now and then that a few fell short of their expectations, why, the country at large eventually became the gainer. On the other hand, if his neighbor happened to "come the Yankee over *him*," to use a favorite expression, it was all fair in war — he neither grudged nor grumbled, but "peeled his own eye" a little closer, and went off to speculate on something else. Such were the two cousins. Both were fond of money — the one to gloat over and adore it, the other to use it as an agent to attain the objects of his pride or his ambition. But to proceed with our story.

"Merciful Heavens!" exclaimed Hardwrinkle, after a long pause, during which he seemed to have lost his speech, for he uttered not a syllable, but kept looking intently at his cousin; "merciful Heavens! such an expression from the mouth of a Christian man — '*if there be such things as souls.*' Ephraim, Ephraim! I fear you're irretrievably lost. O, let me entreat you to pray for light and grace to dispel this darkness of unbelief. O, if you only read the word of God, join our family prayer every night and morning, and come with me thrice on the Sabbath to hear the outpourings of that faithful servant of the Lord, our dear and reverend brother, Mr. Rattletext,

be assured your eyes would be opened to the light of glory
shining through at a distance ———"

"Say," interrupted Weeks.

"The light of glory shining out to ———"

"Say, hold on; I've heard all that before — could repeat
it myself as slick as a deacon. There's no use in thinking to
come it over me with that kinder talk. What I believe, I
believe, and I ain't agoin to believe nothing else, no how you
can fix it. A first cause, and the perfectibility of man, is my
platform."

"Ah, too broad, my dear friend —'narrow is the way,'
you know."

"Broad — that's just precisely what we want. We want
a platform broad enough to cover the hull ground. We are
a young nation, sir, strong, active, and ambitious, and must
have room to stretch our arms east, west, north, and south.
Our resources are immense — inexhaustible, and we want a
wide field to develop them — and that field, I take it, sir, is
the liberty of conscience."

"You mean liberty to cheat and take advantage of your
neighbor if you happen to be clever enough to accomplish it
with impunity?"

"Why not? That's the life of trade, my dear fellow —
that's what makes smart men. Hence it is the Yankees are
the smartest business men in all creation. Your evangelical
rules would ruin us in twelve months."

"The laws of God ruin you? Do you really mean what
you say?"

"Well, look here; I speak only of our merchant and
trading classes; with respect to farmers, laborers, mechanics,
women, and all that kinder folks, they can adopt as many
rules and regulations as they please, in the religious line. It
don't make any material difference, I presume, one way or
other, since they hain't got no business to transact; but
you might as well think of corking up the Atlantic in a

champagne bottle, as expect the commerce of the States to thrive under the old, stiff, evangelical rules of our grandfathers."

"Ah, Ephraim, Ephraim, speak with respect of those holy men," said Hardwrinkle. "O, I hope and pray," he continued, again raising up his hands and eyes in pious supplication, "I hope and pray we may stand as well before the judgment seat as they did."

"Cousin Robert," said Weeks, looking sideways for a moment at the upturned face of his companion, and twirling his watch key as he spoke, — "Cousin Robert, you're a very godly, pious man, I reckon, and an honest man too; no mistake about that. But pious people, let me tell you, *ain't always* to be trusted; hold on now a minute; hold on; I'll just give you an instance in point. I knew a man once in our section of the country, named Pratt — Zeb Pratt, they called him. Zeb was deacon of the Methodist church in Ducksville, for nearly ten years in my own time, and a real out and out Christian of the first brand. Well, he was cracked up so for his sanctity, that he went by the name of Pious Zeb, of Scrabble Hollow. Now Zeb never was known to be absent from meetin, morning, noon, or night — he was punctual as the town clock. Every Sabbath morning, as the bell rang, there was Zeb crossing the Commons, with his old faded crape on his hat, and his Bible under his arm. He was president of all the charitable societies, too, in the district, attended all the prayer meetings, carried his contributions of eggs and chickens every year to the minister, distributed religious tracts to the poor —— "

"O, what a treasure!" exclaimed Hardwrinkle, unconsciously interrupting the panegyric. "What a treasure!"

"Treasure! What, Zeb Pratt! By gracious, he was the darnedest old villain in all creation — he a treasure! — the old cheat, he'd swindle you out of your eye teeth. Why, the old hypocrite cleared out one morning with all the funds of the Christian Benevolent —— "

18*

" Letters for Mr. Weeks," said a servant, knocking at the door.

" Hand them here," cried the latter, promptly, throwing the stump of his cigar into the grate, and snatching his feet off the back of the chair. " Ha, just what I've been expecting this whole week past — they're from that lawyer of yours, Robert."

" Of mine ? "

" Why, yes, of your choosing.   Rather slow though, for my money."

" And, please, sir, Miss Rebecca wishes to know," said the servant, " what tracts to distribute this morning, sir ? "

" Tell her it don't matter a great deal which ; but she might as well, perhaps, try that last package from the Home Missionary Society."

" Yes, sir."

" And William —— "

" Yes, sir."

" She had better take Deborah with her, and leave Judith, Miriam, and Rachael to meet Mr. Sweetsoul, the colporteur, and make arrangements with him about that Sabbath school at Ballymagahey."

" Yes, sir ; and please your honor, sir, that woman is here with the three orphans from Ballymastocker."

" What woman ? "

" McGluinchy's wife, sir.   Her husband died, if you remember, sir, last winter, of the black fever."

" And what does she want with me ? "

" Why, sir, she can't pay the rent, she says, till the new crop comes, and she wants your honor to grant her spareance. The bailiff gave her notice to quit yesterday."

" Well, you must tell her, William, I pity her very much. I do, indeed, for hers is a very bad case. · But I have always made it a rule never to interfere with the law ; it must take its course."

"Yes, sir; very well, sir;" and the servant bowed and quitted the room.

"So you've heard from your lawyer at last, Ephraim," said Hardwrinkle, turning to his cousin, who had just finished reading his letter.

"Y–e–e–s," replied Weeks, "after waiting a whole week for it. These Irish lawyers of yours are rather slow coaches, I expect."

"Fast enough, Ephraim, fast enough for the poor man, when he has their claims to satisfy — ay, ay, Heaven look to the poor when they happen to fall into their hands."

"Listen to his letter."

"DEAR SIR: Agreeably to your instructions of June ——, I wrote yesterday to Mr. Edward Lee, notifying him of the purchase of his notes of hand for one hundred pounds, by Ephraim C. B. Weeks, Ducksville, Connecticut, United States, now staying at Crohan House, county Donegal, and of his (Mr. Weeks's) anxiety to have the debt cancelled by the first of next month, or secured by responsible indorsers, as it is his (Mr. Weeks's) intention to return home as soon as possible. Shall be happy to receive further commands, and have the honor to be   Your very obedient servant,

"JEREMIAH DIDDLEWELL.

"Dublin, 26 Great James street, June ——."

"Humph!" said Hardwrinkle, after Weeks had read the letter over; "so you've made a beginning."

"Certainly. I've got to; the girl won't look at me otherwise. I have now called on her a dozen times, and wrote her as many letters, and yet she treats me as coldly as if I'd been an absolute stranger. We'll see, however, what the screws can do."

"You say Lee himself never gave you any encouragement."

"Why, no; he only kinder laughs when I allude to it. I swonnie, I don't know what to make of the man. His con-

duct's most unaccountable. Why he must either take me for
a fool or a madman."

"You are mistaken, Ephraim; he takes you for neither.
He merely laughs at your presumption in aspiring to the
hand of such a high-blooded girl as Mary Lee."

"High-blooded humbug — hang your high-bloods!"

"Don't feel offended, my dear Ephraim — I had no intention —— "

"No, but that darned old witch, Else Curley, keeps talking
to me just in the same style about her aristocracy, so that I'm
sometimes most tempted to cowhide her for her impudence.
When I inquire how she gets along in bringing things round,
the only answer I can get from the old rascal is, 'Wait a
while, wait a while, till her pride comes down another peg or
two.' Yes, by crackie," he continued, rising and pacing the
room, with his hands stuck down in his pockets jingling the
silver; "yes, wait a while, till her pride comes down; just
as if the grandson of an old revolutionist of seventy-six warn't
good enough for the best blood in the land."

"My dear Ephraim, you don't understand the Irish people,
or you wouldn't talk so. They're an old people, you must
remember, and like all old people, proud of their ancestors.
You, on the other hand, being a new people, measure the
respectability of men and families by the amount of money
or property they're possessed of, simply because you have no
ancestors yourselves."

"Well, look here, cousin; be that as it may, I'm not agoin
to stay here much longer, any how. This affair must soon be
fixed one way or other. When you wrote me, to say this
girl was the daughter and heir of old Talbot, I gave up my
business and came over here, without waiting even to bid my
friends good by. Well, after three weeks' search and inquiry in Cork and all round for the old woman said to have
nursed her, and as long spent in Dublin hunting up the certifi-
cate of her mother's marriage, I came down here fully confident,

from your assurances of success, that the girl and her uncle were so almighty poor, they'd jump at my proposal, right straight off. Now then, here I am all of five weeks sneaking up and down to that confounded lighthouse, through thunder and lightning half the time, and groping my way through rain and darkness the other half; and by crackie, I ain't one mite nearer my object now than ever."

"I'm sorry, Ephraim, very sorry indeed," replied Hardwrinkle, looking down and sighing regretfully; "sorry you're so much disappointed; but indeed, indeed it's not my fault, for surely I've done all that could reasonably be expected to expedite the affair. As for the two thousand pounds you kindly promised in acknowledgment of the little assistance I might be in the matter, you know I should have just as cheerfully done as much, my dear Ephraim, if you never had promised a farthing. No, no; money has never influenced me, thank Heaven. No, Ephraim; I hope I have a conscience to direct me, and a heart too, to love my relatives well enough to do them a kindness without expecting a recompense."

"I know it, cousin. I know it. You have been exceedingly kind, and I ain't agoin to forget your kindness either; but just look how the case stands. Here I've spent already five hundred dollars for the note, that ain't worth a red cent. Of course, when you recommended me to buy it, you thought otherwise, and so I took your advice. Well, there's four hundred dollars and over to Else Curley; and how can I tell but the scheming old witch is 'doing' me all the while? That and my travelling expenses, and loss of time besides, will amount to a pretty considerable sum, let me tell you."

"It is a pretty round sum, I admit," muttered Hardwrinkle.

"Well, it's just such a sum," said Weeks, "that I've made up my mind I ain't agoin to lose it for nothing. I'm determined to have the girl — no mistake about that. And if she ain't willing to marry me one way, she shall another."

"Ah, indeed; what mean you by that, cousin?"

" Well, I've got my own notions about it; that's all. By jolly, I ain't agoin home to Ducksville again empty-handed — catch me at it ! "

" You wouldn't carry her off by force — would you, eh ? " said Hardwrinkle, dropping his voice to a whisper, and looking round the room to see if the doors were closed.

" The thing has been done," replied Weeks, "and pretty often too in this country of yours, if I ain't greatly mistaken."

" Yes, I admit it has occasionally been done. But in this case I can hardly see how it could be accomplished without danger."

" Why, there's such a thing as a *boat* to be had, I guess, and the distance to carry her ain't so very far that you can't find half a dozen stout fellows to do it. I shouldn't like much though to go to these extremes if there was any possibility of obtaining her consent by other means. But have her I shall — no mistake about that."

" Hush, hush ! " ejaculated Hardwrinkle ; " there's some one at the door — come in."

The door opened, and an active, muscular-looking man, of middle age, entered and advanced to the table at which Hardwrinkle was sitting. He was the officer of constabulary whom the reader has seen a few nights before at Castle Gregory, with Captain Petersham.

"Ah, it's you, is it ? " exclaimed Hardwrinkle, rising suddenly from his chair. " Well, any news of Barry ? "

" He's arrested, sir, and now a prisoner in Tamny barracks."

" What, arrested ! eh ! that's capital news. Please step to the next room — excuse me, Mr. Weeks ; I'll return presently."

" Go ahead — don't mind me," replied Weeks, drawing a cigar from his case and preparing to light it.

"Now," said Hardwrinkle, carefully closing the door, "now for the details. Mr. Weeks's notions of these young revolutionists don't exactly harmonize with ours, you know, so it's just as well he don't hear our conversation on the subject. Now for your story."

"Well, sir, we crossed the ferry, as you suggested, proceeded on to Doe Castle, and thence to Rann Point. There we met the man who gave you the information first about Barry's intention to escape — I forget his name — he's one of your tenants."

"Carson, you mean."

"No, sir; the man you sent down to spy about the lighthouse, you remember; the one who listened at Else Curley's door, and overheard the conversation between her and Barry about his going to Arranmore."

"O, yes, yes; Barker, the Bible reader."

"Barker — precisely — that's the man; a pious soul he is, too."

"Very — very, indeed. He's a most excellent man, is Barker."

"Well, sir, we met him coming up from the shore, where he had been distributing tracts among the fishermen, by way of an excuse. He told us he had just seen Barry jump from a boat in company of three or four stout fellows, and enter one of the huts. They were all strangers to him, he said, except Barry himself, and another who seemed to be the most active of the party, and whom he had seen before, but couldn't remember where."

"Stop a moment; did he describe his dress or person?"

"He did, but I paid little attention to it, not thinking it a matter of much consequence. It appears to me, though, he said something about his wearing a green jacket or a fur cap, or something to that effect."

"The very man, sir; that's Lanty Hanlon, if he's alive, and quite as dangerous a man, too, as Barry."

"Lanty Hanlon — impossible, sir. You mean the fellow against whom you issued the warrant for the assault on Mr. Weeks?"

" The identical person."

" Pardon me — that cannot be, Mr. Hardwrinkle — Hanlon
was seen at a cockfight in Kindrum not six hours ago."

" I have no doubt of that," replied Hardwrinkle. " But,
my dear sir, you little know what that villain is capable of
doing. Why, sir, it was once sworn on oath before me, that
this very Lanty Hanlon was seen at a wake in Crantin Glen,
at a wedding in Ballymagahey, and at a christening in Callen,
the self-same night, and yet these places are seven miles apart,
and nearly equidistant from each other."

" He must be an extraordinary man," said the officer,
smiling incredulously.

" He's a most dangerous man, sir, to be permitted to go free
in any community. What do you think, sir? — that fellow met
one of Mr. Johnston's gamekeepers on Benraven Mountain,
some six weeks ago, where he happened to be coursing for
hares. Well, sir, he first took the gun from the keeper, and
then left him gagged and tied to a tree for the whole night ;
and next morning, when the unfortunate man was accidentally
discovered by one of the herdsmen, he was more dead than
alive from cold and hunger."

" Was he punished for the outrage ? "

" No, sir; he managed to escape that very cleverly. The
moment he secured the keeper, he jumped on the first horse
he found on the mountain, galloped for life to Sandy Mount,
then, secreting the horse among the trees, walked into Mr.
Johnston's parlor, and having apologized to that gentleman for
having, contrary to law, shot some grouse on his preserves,
and obtained his pardon, again mounted, rode back, and left
the horse where he found him. Next morning, when the
gamekeeper returned and made his complaint against Hanlon, Mr. Johnston ordered him instantly from his presence,
called him a drunkard and a liar, and protested he had never
heard of such an attempt at imposition in his life — Hanlon
having been that very night, and at the very time the outrage

was alleged to have been perpetrated, standing before him in his own room. But with respect to Barry, how did you succeed in arresting him?"

"Simply enough, sir. We hired a boat, got our men in, and lay at anchor some five or six fathoms from the beach, knowing well Barry and his party would endeavor to escape next morning at daybreak, by rowing along the shore as far as Horn Head, and there set sail for Aranmore. It turned out just as we expected. At the first peep of day, the party got into the boat and shoved off. They were ahead of us when they started, and we let them keep ahead for two miles or more, till we had gone clear out of sight of the fishermen's huts. Then, stretching to our oars, we soon came alongside, and grappled with irons we had taken with us for the purpose."

"Hah! and so secured him at last?"

"Yes, sir, we secured him, but not without considerable difficulty."

"What! did he resist?"

"Resist! yes, as man never resisted before. It appears the crew that conveyed him to Rann Point left him there, and returned home, confident he was out of all danger, and the fresh hands appointed to convey him to Aranmore were old men, hardly able to paddle an oar or handle a sheet. He was, therefore, left to depend almost entirely upon his own resources. The instant we laid hold of the gunwale of his boat, he sprang up in the stern sheets, and demanded what we meant by stopping him. 'I'm a queen's officer,' said I, 'and hold a warrant for your arrest.'"

"'Ah, a queen's officer,' he repeated, glancing at my civilian dress. 'Indeed! Well, sir, take me if you can;' and coolly drawing a pistol from his belt, he said to his men, 'Comrades, you'll find another pair in my overcoat; use them if necessary.' Then stepping across the thwarts, and before I could rise from my seat, he snatched the anchor from the bows of his boat, and with one hand swung it as he would a walking stick

19

into the bottom of ours. The effect was instantaneous; the sharp iron cut right through the thin sheathing of the little gig, and in two minutes she filled to her water line."

" 'Now, my lads,' he cried, 'loose the grapples, and away with them.' "

" Good Heavens!" exclaimed Hardwrinkle; "his object was to sink you."

" Of course it was — and a bold attempt he made to accomplish it. When I saw how desperate the case was likely to prove, I ordered my men to jump aboard and secure him at all hazards, leaving our own boat to her fate; and setting them the example myself, I sprang into the stern, presented a pistol at his head, and commanded him to surrender, or I should instantly fire. I had hardly uttered the words, however, when the board on which I stood was struck from under me, and in another second I found myself in the water, plunging and grasping for something to lay hold of. By this time my men had succeeded in scrambling over his boat's side; so they immediately took me in, and then unhooked the grapple to relieve us of the sinking gig. But now that we did succeed in boarding him, we found ourselves in a greater difficulty than ever. Our firearms were entirely useless, — the powder being wet with the sea water, — and there stood the young outlaw, pointing a brace of pistols at our heads. 'Surrender,' said I; 'I command you, in the name of the queen, to surrender instantly.'

" 'Ha, ha!' he laughed — 'surrender to hounds like you! O for the firm earth to stand on, and a good thong to kennel such cowardly dogs. A pistol bullet is too honorable a death for such drivelling slaves.'

" This taunt stung me to the quick; and calling on my men to rush on him in a body, I sprang forward myself to seize him; but, alas, I was again unfortunate, and fell flat on my face on the bottom of the boat. In another instant his heel was on my neck.

"'Lie there, dog!' he cried, crushing me till my eyes seemed to start from their sockets; 'lie there, and die the only death you deserve.'   But the braggart, in his turn, had little time to enjoy his advantage; for my men, seeing the danger I was in, and maddened by the fellow's scornful language, closed in upon him.   As they rushed forward, he fired both pistols in their faces, and two of them fell wounded beside me."

"Dreadful!" exclaimed Hardwrinkle.

"'Now,' cried I, rising from my disgraceful position, 'now, my men, hold him; handcuff him; kill him if he attempt to escape.'   But my orders were of no avail, for he had sprung into the sea, and was making for the shore.

"'He's gone, sir,' cried one of the men.

"'Gone!'

"'Yes; there he is, with his coat off, swimming away from us like a water dog.'

"'What's to be done? what's to be done?' I cried in an agony of disappointment.   'Has no one presence of mind to think of some means to capture him?   He's within half a gunshot of the beach, and will reach it before we can get our oars into the rollocks.'

"Just then the thought of the firearms in his overcoat occurred to me, and snatching up the garment, I drew a holster pistol from its pocket, and aiming as deliberately as I could in a moment of such excitement, fired.   The ball, as good fortune would have it, struck him on the right arm, and disabled him.   'Now,' cried I, as I saw him sputter in the water like a wounded bird, 'now, my lads, to your oars, and pull for your lives — pull — pull — with all your might, or he sinks before we can reach him.'

"In another minute we had taken him aboard, exhausted and bleeding, and there he lay in the boat's bows, without word or motion of any kind, till we reached the quay under Tamny Barracks."

"Well, thank Heaven," said Hardwrinkle, "he's safe for

the present at least, and to-morrow I sign his committal to Lefford jail. As for you, Mr. C——, you have done your duty as a faithful servant of the crown, and shall not go un-rewarded. And now let us return and carry the good news to Mr. Weeks.

"My dear cousin," said Hardwrinkle, entering Weeks's room, followed by the officer of constabulary, "I have good tidings for you."

"You have — eh?"

"Yes, tidings of great import."

"Indeed — let's hear what they're like."

"Why, Randall Barry (your rival)," he said, whispering the word in his ear, "is a prisoner in Tamny Barracks."

"Pshoh — you don't say so? Is it possible?"

"A fact, sir."

"On what charge, pray?"

"Treason — treason against the state. You've heard all about him — have you not?"

"Why, yes, I've heard of his being connected with some young revolutionists — that's all."

"Humph! you speak lightly of the matter, my good cousin."

"And I think lightly of it too," replied Weeks, promptly, "so far as it may be regarded as a crime. Were I in his place, I should do precisely what he has done."

"What, revolutionize the country?"

"Yes, by crackie. It's full time, I should think, the people got rid of these old fogy monarchies of yours. These darned old tyrannical governments ought to have been sent to kingdom come long ago. As for his being a rival of mine, why, I don't think the less of him for that; and if you have busied yourself about his arrest on that account, I tell you, Robert, you make an almighty mistake if you think I'm under any obligation to you for the job."

"Why, cousin, you surprise me."

"Well, them's my sentiments, notwithstanding. He's a fine, spirited, gallant-looking young fellow, that Barry; and if he hate and despise your slow-going, drivelling old kings and queens, by thunder I like him the better for telling them so to their teeth; and if he loves Mary Lee, why shouldn't he try to catch her the best way he can? Let every man have a fair chance."

"If these be your sentiments, my dear cousin," said Hard-wrinkle, "they are very different, I must confess, from what I had expected of you."

"Well, sir, they are my sentiments precisely — real true blue Yankee sentiments, and no mistake."

"Well, well, I must acknowledge I was deceived in you, cousin, and I'm sorry for it. But we must postpone further discussion on the subject for the present. I see Rebecca and her sisters out there on their way to Ballymagahey, and must speak to them a word or two of caution before they leave. Pray excuse me, Ephraim."

"Go ahead, go ahead," replied Weeks, preparing to light another cigar — "go ahead, and don't mind me;" and the Yankee was left alone, at last, to enjoy the comfort of a quiet Havana.

CHAPTER XVI.

Reflection on an Irish-Churchyard. — Miss Rebecca and her Cousin Weeks. — Piety and Infidelity.

MR. WEEKS left his room soon after his cousin, — it being now somewhat advanced in the forenoon, — and with a cigar in his mouth, descended the steps at the hall door, and sauntered out to breathe the fresh air. It was a delightful morning. Every thing looked cheerful and pleasant. The new-mown hay lay in long swaths on the lawn, exhaling its perfume under the warm sun. The mowers, swart with toil, were slowly sweeping their scythes through the ripe grass, and moving onwards, side by side, with measured step across the broad field. Over the tops of the trees which skirted the demesne below, and through the vistas which time or the axe had made, appeared patches of Mulroy Bay, shining as calm and bright as a mirror. On its southern shore a little white-washed building, showing a gilded cross on its gable, stood facing the sea, and round about among the fern and hawthorns, with which it was surrounded, a number of white headstones peeped out here and there to mark it for a burial place of the dead. This was Massmount, where our foreign friend first saw Mary Lee, as she knelt at the altar. It was a solitary spot, and as pleasant for the dead to rest in as could be found in the whole world. No house within a mile of it, and no noise to disturb its repose but the twitter of the swallow about the eaves of the little church, or the gentle wash of the waves amongst the sea shells at its base. And if, on the Sunday morning, the silence which reigned there through the week was broken, it only seemed to make the stillness which succeeded the more solemn and profound. To the eastward of the chapel, and surrounded by a belt of trees, stood the modest residence of Mr. Guirkie — its white chimneys just visible from the windows of Crohan House; and trending away to the westward lay a long tongue of meadow land called Morass Ridge, on the tip or extreme point of which rose up the still majestic ruins of *Shannagh*, once a stronghold of the far-famed O'Dougherty of Innishowen. Midway between these two prominent features in the landscape appeared the old churchyard of Massmount, with its little white chapel facing the sea.

Mr. Weeks, touched by the simple beauty of the scene, laid himself down half unconsciously on the greensward to enjoy it at his leisure.

Dear Irish reader, let us sit down beside him for a moment, and view the picture also. There is nothing in it new to your eyes — nothing you haven't seen a thousand times before. It was only an old churchyard, and old churchyards in Ireland, you know, are always the same. The same old beaten footpaths through the rank grass — the same old hawthorn trees which in early summer shed their white blossoms on the green graves — the same old ivy walls overshadowing the moss-covered tombs of the monk and the nun. No, there was nothing strange or new in the picture — on the contrary, every thing there was as familiar to you as your own thoughts. But tell us, dear reader, — now that we can converse quietly together, — does not the sight of such a spot sometimes awaken old memories? Do you still remember the place in the old ruins where the prior's ghost was seen so often after sunset, or the fairy tree beside the holy well which no axe could cut down, nor human hand break a branch off with impunity? But, above all, do you remember the shady little corner where the dear ones lie buried — the grassy mound where you knelt to drop the last tear on bidding farewell to the land you will never see again? O, dear reader, do your thoughts ever wander back to these blessed scenes of your youth? When in the long summer evenings, after the toil of the day is over, you sit by the porch of the stranger enjoying the cool night air, and gazing up at the sparkling heavens, does your eye ever roam in search of that star you should know better than all the rest, the bright one that shines on your own "native isle of the ocean"? When your heart feels sad under a sense of its isolation, — nay, when it turns with disgust from the treacherous and the cold-hearted, who, having wiled you to their shores, now deny you even a foothold on their soil, — does memory then ever carry you back to the old homestead among the hills, where in bygone years you have met so many generous souls round the humble hearthstone? Alas, alas! when you look at those once stalwart limbs you gave your adopted country as a recompense for the freedom she promised you — now wasted away in her service — when you think of the blood you shed in her battles, the prayers you offered for her prosperity, the pride with which you heard her name spoken of in other lands, and the glorious hopes you once entertained of seeing her the greatest and the best of the nations of the earth — and yet to think, O, to think that the only return she makes for all this is to hate and spurn you, — when thoughts like these weigh down your heart, dear reader, do you not sometimes long to see the old land again, and lay your shattered frame down to rest in that shady corner you remember so well in the old churchyard?

But they tell you here you must not indulge such thoughts as these. On the contrary, you must forget the past; you must renounce your love for the country that gave you birth; you must sever every tie that knits you to her bosom; you must abjure and repudiate her forevermore: the songs you sang and the stories you told so often by the light of the peat fire, must never be sung or told again; all the associations of home and friends, all the pleasant recollections of your boyhood, all the traditions of your warriors and sainted ancestors, must be blotted from your memory, as so many treasons against the land of your adoption. Or, if you do venture to speak of old times and old places when you meet with long, absent friends round the social board, it must be in whispers and with closed doors, lest the strangers should hear you as they pass by. And behold the return they make you for these sacrifices! They give you freedom! What! freedom to live like helots in the land they promised to make your own — freedom to worship your Creator under a roof which a godless mob may, at any moment, fire with impunity — freedom to shed your blood in defence of a flag that would gladly wave in triumph over the extinction of your race. Speak, exile! are you willing to renounce your fatherland for such recompense as this? O, if you be, may no ray of sunlight ever visit your grave — no friend or relation, wife or child, ever shed a tear to hallow it. If you've fallen so low as to kiss the foot that spurns you, and grown so mean as to fawn upon a nation that flings you from her with disgust, then go and live the degraded, soulless thing thou art, fit only to batten on garbage and rot in a potter's field. Go! quit this place, for the sight of an old Irish churchyard has no charms for you.

Mr. Weeks had been sitting for half an hour or more contemplating the scene before him, when, hearing the sound of approaching footsteps, he turned to see who was coming.

It was Rebecca Hardwrinkle, accompanied by the colporteur and two of her younger sisters, on their way to Ballymagahey.

" Well, there," said Weeks, rising, and shaking off the chips he had been whittling from a withered branch that happened to lie within his reach — "there! I thought you'd gone long ago."

"My brother detained me," replied Rebecca, "to select some tracts from a parcel he had just received as I was leaving the house; and seeing you here, I passed this way to offer you one for your inspection. It's on the efficacy of prayer."

" Humph! I know what you're coming at, I guess; I haven't been at family worship this morning."

" Ah, cousin, were it only once you absented yourself, we might find some excuse, but to be absent so often — O, dear!"

" Well, now, look here; I don't profess to be much of a Christian, you know, and consequently you can't expect me to get used to your traces right straight off."

" Well, but your religious sentiments are so very shocking, Ephraim, that I tremble to think of your soul, and the end which awaits it if you turn not speedily to the Lord. Read that little book, however, attentively, and you will find it of great spiritual advantage. And then, dear cousin, I shall have you prayed for next Sabbath."

"Me prayed for?"

"Certainly."

"Guess not."

"Why, can you have any possible objection to be prayed for by the God-fearing, pious servants of the Lord?"

"Well, yes, I rather think I have — a slight one."

"How very strange! Did you only once feel the benefit a Christian derives from the prayers of the elect ——"

"Just so — but I'm kinder green, you know, in that line."

"Brother Robert, and Deborah there, and Hannah, and all of us, have been prayed for so often, and have always felt our strength renewed in so wonderful a manner!"

"All right. But you see, I feel considerable strong as it is, and ain't disposed to trouble you just at present. Say, cousin, whereabouts here is the priest's house? Ain't that it over there west of the pond? I want to call on the old feller this morning."

"Yes, that's his house; but what can your business be with *him*, Ephraim?"

"Well, not much, if any; should like to ask him a question or two — that's all."

"Are you not afraid?"

"Afraid! — afraid of what?"

"To converse with him in the weak state of your soul."

"Why, what in creation do you take me for?"

"Don't be offended, cousin. I speak to you for your own good."

"My own good! I ain't a fool — am I?"

"No, no, dear Ephraim, but you know you're weak."

"Weak! shoh! you don't say so."

"I speak the truth; you will never be able to resist him. He's a most insinuating, dangerous man."

"The old priest?"

"Yes. You've heard, I suppose, how he converted the tutor at the old parsonage?"

"No — can't say I have."

"And poor Kate Petersham, too," put in Deborah; "she's on the very verge of the gulf."

"There! by the way, I had almost forgotten it. I must call on these Petershams right off. What sorter girl, though, is this Kate you speak of? 'Kinder crazy — ain't she?"

"A little weak," responded Rebecca, "but still a good natured soul. Some of her neighbors, poor thing, have lately been telling idle stories about her; but I'm sure they're all false. For my part, I can't believe them. And I'm sure it's nothing to me if she turned Catholic to-morrow. Only people will talk, you know, Ephraim."

"Well — nothing prejudicial to her honor, I presume."

Rebecca glanced significantly at her sister and Mr. Sweetsoul, but said nothing in reply.

"Excuse me," said Weeks; "I shouldn't have put that question, perhaps, but the fact is, the young lady has invited me to Castle Gregory, and I can't very well refuse; besides, her brother, Captain Petersham, is anxious to have me call on him."

"Did the lady invite you herself?" inquired Rebecca.

"Why, certainly. I had a note from her a week ago to that effect."

"Written by herself?"

"Well, her name was signed to it — Kate Petersham."

Rebecca again glanced at her companions, and tried to blush and look mortified.

"Well, it did seem kinder strange, I allow," said Weeks; "but not being well posted up in the customs of the country, I didn't know but it was all right."

"Don't go, Ephraim," said Rebecca, laying her black-gloved hand affectionately on his arm. "Don't go; take my advice."

"She can't hurt me, I reckon — can she?"

"No, dear Ephraim; she can't hurt your body, but she might your soul. You're weak, you know — very weak indeed, and she very captivating both in person and conversation. I don't like, my dear cousin, these visits to Miss Petersham and the Catholic priest, especially without some one to protect you against the dangerous influence of their society."

"You don't, eh?"

"No, dear cousin."

"Look at me, Miss Hardwrinkle," said Weeks, thrusting his hands down into his pockets, and hitching up his shoulders.

"I see."

"Is there any thing remarkably green about me?"

"Green! no."

"Ain't I a Yankee, born and bred, eh?"

"Certainly."

"And do you really believe I don't know nothing — that I can't take care of myself among a parcel of Irish. What sorter folks d'ye think we Yankees are, any how?"

"Don't grow vexed with me, dear Ephraim; don't grow vexed. I would not offend you for the world. I only speak for your own good, dear cousin. Mr. Sweetsoul here knows how often I have wept over your weakness, and how incessantly I have prayed that the light of truth might dispel the darkness —— "

"Stop! stop! — thunder! Hain't I been listening to all that long talk till I'm enamost crazy?"

"O, dear, he has grown so nervous of late, Mr. Sweetsoul," said Rebecca, wringing her hands, and turning to the colporteur, "that he cannot bear a single word of advice."

"Nervous! and where's the wonder, with seven sisters of you talking religion at me from morning till night. Why, I can't smoke a cigar, by crackie, but I'm taken to task for it. It's too great an indulgence, or it's too worldly-looking, or it's one darned thing or other."

" But listen to me, dear Ephraim ; don't you feel that we have your spiritual welfare at heart? and don't you know, when we speak to you of religion, it is only because we love you too well to see you perish before our eyes? O, if the sweet dew of religion only once touched —— "

" The dew of religion ! there !   That's the talk — go ahead, cousin ; I shan't say another word on the subject — go ahead. I'll stand it out, I guess, if any man can ;" and he picked up the branch he had just been whittling, and set to it again, as vigorously as if he had been whittling for a wager.   Ephraim C. B. Weeks was evidently excited, but tried very hard to keep cool.

" And now, Mr. Sweetsoul, you may judge whether we have reason or not to fear for our dear cousin," said Rebecca, again turning to the colporteur.   "Just look at this trinket.   Here is a pair of popish rosary beads, which the chambermaid found on the floor of Mr. Weeks's bedroom the morning after he first entered the lighthouse lodge at Araheera ; " and the speaker held them up between her finger and thumb for inspection.

. " Dreadful ! "

" This was his first lesson from the Romish light-keeper and his pretty daughter."

" I have already explained to you how I came by these beads," said Weeks.   " I picked them up where they had fallen from an old Bible at the lighthouse, and unthinkingly put them in my pocket.   But no matter now ; fire away."

" Don't grow angry, Ephraim."

" I ain't angry."

" I merely call your attention to the beads to show you the danger you have to guard against in forming Catholic associations.   Is there any thing in that to make you angry ? "

" I ain't angry, I tell you ; not a mite."

" You are angry.   I see it in your countenance, Ephraim. O, if you only experienced religion for one little week, how

20

easily you could repress this irritability. There, now! see how you cut up that stick so pettishly. Just see how nervous you are."

"I tell you I *ain't* nervous," cried Weeks, at the top of his voice.

"Well — so excited."

"I ain't excited."

"Why, dear me, Mr. Sweetsoul, only look at him."

"There!" broke out Weeks at length, losing his temper altogether, and flinging away both knife and branch; "there! by thunder, if this ain't the most inhuman treatment ever man suffered."

"Stay, Ephraim, stay, cousin; do, for one moment," entreated Rebecca, endeavoring to lay hold of his arm.

"Not a darned second," he cried, buttoning his coat and hurrying off, full of indignation at the idea of being treated so like a child or a fool. "By gracious thunder," he added, halting for an instant on his step and looking back, "you ought to turn to at once and spoon-feed me."

———————

CHAPTER XVII.

Weeks visits Mrs. Motherly. — A Conversation on Slavery. — Weeks seems rather disagreeably surprised to meet an old Acquaintance in Uncle Jerry's Negro.

MR. WEEKS, on parting with his lady cousins, (which he did rather abruptly, as we have seen in the last chapter,) returned to Crohan House, and lighting another cigar, mounted the sober animal he generally selected for a morning's ride, and set out for Father Brennan's. When he arrived at the reverend gentleman's residence, he felt somewhat disappointed to learn from the servant that his master had gone some five or six miles on a sick call, and could not possibly return till late in the evening. , Resolving, however, to have an interview with the good priest as soon as possible, he drew a card from the richly-carved case he always had about him, and having written a request to that effect on the back of it with his pencil, handed it to the servant, and then turned his horse's head in the direction of Greenmount Cottage.

Mrs. Motherly was sitting on the steps of the hall door, knitting her stocking, and looking quite happy as she plied her needles. The good woman was dressed as usual in her large, well-frilled cap and white apron, with her bunch of keys hanging by her side, as much perhaps for show as convenience. On the, grass at her feet a gray cat lay stretched in the sun, with half a dozen kittens playing about her on the green.

"Good afternoon, Mrs. Motherly; how do?" said Weeks. "Mr. Guirkie at home?"

"Your sarvint, sir," replied the matron, rising and running her needles into the stocking, after she had waited to count the stitches. "Mr. Guirkie's not in, sir."

"Ain't?"

"No, sir; he left here about an hour ago for Rathmullen."

"Rathmullen — let me see — that's the place he visits so often?"

"Yes, sir."

"Goes there every week — don't he?"

"Every Thursday, sir."

"On business, I presume."

"No, sir."

"Got relatives there, perhaps."

"No, sir; he has no relatives living, I believe. People's plazed to say, though, he's often seen sittin on a tombstone there in the ould graveyard."

"Well, must be some friend, I guess."

"Why, if the gentleman was a native o' this part o' the country, it might," responded Mrs. Motherly, "but he's not; he was born in Cork."

"Does he never speak to you of these visits, Mrs. Motherly?"

"Niver, sir."

"You don't say so! It's odd — ain't it?"

"O, it's just of a piece with the rest of his doings," replied the good woman, opening, as usual, her budget of grievances. "He niver thinks of telling me any thing, of coorse; why should he? I'm nothing but a sarvint, ye know. I'm only here to do the work, slavin and sludgin from mornin till night, strivin to plaze him and humor him, till my heart's a'most broke, and all the thanks I get is mighty easy told, Mr. Weeks."

"Don't doubt it. He's a very odd kinder man in his ways —that's a fact."

"You may well say it, sir. He's the provokinest man ever drew breath. But won't you light and come in, sir?"

"Well, guess I shall, come to think of it. Say, can't I write a note here, and leave it for Mr. Guirkie?"

"Sartintly, sir; come in, there's paper there, and pens plenty in the parlor. As for the cratur on the sofa, he'll not disturb you in the laste."

"Hilloa! who the thunder is this?" exclaimed Weeks, as he entered the parlor, and beheld the African stretched at his full length on the sofa, apparently fast asleep. "A nigger —ain't he?"

"Yes, sir; that's our new boarder," primly replied Mrs. Motherly.

"But how in creation did he come here?"

"Mr. Guirkie, sir, carried the gentleman home with him from the wreck."

"Ah, that's it. I have heard of a wreck lately somewhere here in the neighborhood."

"He's a very respectable boarder for a lone woman — isn't he, Mr. Weeks?"

Well, don't know exactly; that's all a matter of taste. Some folks like niggers very much. There's our New England ladies, for instance; they're terrible kind to niggers. I'd venture to say, if this here chap happened to be cast ashore any where along the eastern seaboard, they'd gather round and clothe and feast him like a prince, before he got well out of water."

"You're jokin, Mr. Weeks."

"No, *mam*, I ain't jokin a mite."

"And ye tell me they're so fond of them as all that?"

"Fond? yes — guess they are fond — they're the most almighty fond creatures in that way in all creation."

"Bedad, then, Mr. Weeks, I don't envy their taste."

"Well, it ain't just that, either, for the fact is, they despise niggers as much as any people in the world. But it's a sorter philanthropy, you know, that's made up of a half sentimental, half benevolent kinder squeamishness, with a slight dash of the religious in it, by way of seasoning."

"Yes, sir, of coorse."

"You understand me?"

"O, parfectly, sir. They must be mighty charitable intirely, God bless them."

"Very charitable indeed. That is, I mean to the slave portion of the race. Sometimes their philanthropy impels them even to pawn their jewels to buy a slave from bondage —it's a fact."

"See that now! Isn't it wondherful to think of it? And still I often heard Mr. Guirkie say the craturs out there in America warn't so badly off after all."

"Well, no — guess they're pretty well off for clothes and food, and all that sorter thing. But they hain't got their liberty, you know; and no American born ought to see a human in slavery and not try to liberate him."

"True for you, Mr. Weeks; you speak like a Christian, so you do Dear knows it's a poor sight to see God's craturs bought and sould, as they say they are over there, just for all the world like a cow or a horse — it's onnatural."

"It's shocking!"

"And still," said Mrs. Motherly, "they tell us the poor Irish there isn't trated much better than slaves."

"The Irish! My dear woman, don't believe a word of it."

"Why, I have a letther in my pocket here, from a niece of mine, that's livin in a place called Boston, and she tells me it's tarrible to think of what they suffer. There it is," continued the good woman, opening it, and pointing to a particular passage, which ran as follows: 'We're thrated here like slaves, and have more to suffer from the Yankees, specially in regard to our religion, than ever we had at home from the bloody, parsecutin English.' It's a wonder they're not ashamed to purfess so much tinderness for the slaves, and trate the poor Irish so manely as that," said Mrs. Motherly.

"My dear woman, you don't understand the case. It's only the lower orders of our people do so."

"And why don't the upper orders make them behave better?"

"Can't do it. It's a free country."

"O, bad luck to such freedom as that. I wudn't give ye a brass button for it. There's my niece, as dacent a reared little girl as ever crossed the water — I'll say that much for her, though she is my niece — and her mistress, who's nothin after all but a shopkeeper's wife — may be not as decent a father and mother's child either, — and the best word she has in her cheek for the cratur is the 'Paddy girl,' and the 'Papist,' and the 'ignorant booby,' and 'go to the old priest — he'll forgive you your sins for a ninepence.' What kind of talk is that, Mr. Weeks?" continued the good woman, rolling up her arms in her apron, and looking at him.

"Well, that ain't right, I allow."

"Right — bedad, if the girls would do as I would, they'd slap them in the face. And that's what I told Bridget in my last letter. Humph! pretty thing, indeed! because they pay their girls six or seven shillings a week, they must have a right to insult and abuse them into the bargain."

"Very few think so, Mrs. Motherly, very few indeed. I know many, very many families in New England, who respect their help very much, and are as kind to them as if they were relatives of the family."

"To be sure you do, sir, and so Bridget says too, in her letter here; but they're *respectable* people. I mane yer upsettin, half and between fine ladies, that think they ought to take airs on themselves as soon as they can afford to hire a girl to do their work — that's the kind I mane."

"Just so; that's all right enough — but still, Mrs. Motherly, some of your girls are pretty spunky."

"I don't doubt it, sir, in the laste, and may be there's plenty of them desarves to be turned out of doors too for their impudence. But can't all that be done without casting up their religion and their priest to them? Ah, that's mane, sir, mane as dirt, to insult a poor girl for her religion."

"Well — as I hain't got many minutes to spare now, Mrs. Motherly, let us put off this subject till another time. So I'll just sit down here, if you hain't no objection, and write a note for Mr. Guirkie, which you'll please hand him as soon as he returns."

"Sartintly, Mr. Weeks, with the greatest pleasure in life; I hope Sambo here won't disturb you, sir."

"Not in the least. He's asleep — ain't he?"

"So it seems; and still it's quare to see him asleep at this hour. He was sittin up a minute or two before ye came. I'll see. 'Sambo! Sambo! wake up.' There's not a stir in him, sir."

"Don't mind him, Mrs. Motherly," said Weeks, dipping the pen in the ink. "Don't mind him."

"Well, I niver saw him asleep but he snored strong enough to draw the sides of the house together. And see now, he hardly seems to breathe. ' Sambo,' she repeated, shaking him by the arm, — ' Sambo, wake up; here's the gentleman you were asking about the other day.'"

" About me ? "

" Yes, sir; he started just as if he'd been shot, when he saw you pass the window last week."

" Last week — why, I don't remember to have seen or heard any thing of him. I didn't know you'd got a nigger here till this minute."

" Well, he saw *you*, sir, any way, and looked as frightened as if you came to drag him to the gallows."

" Indeed ! Wake him up, and let's see what he's like."

" Sambo ! hilloa, Sambo ! " cried Mrs. Motherly, again shaking him roughly by the arm; " look up, man, and speak to us — he won't though, not a budge he'll do. Bedad, Mr. Weeks, may be he's dyin."

" Not he — the fellow's coming possum over us, that's all ; but hold on a bit; I'll make him speak — bet a fourpence ; " and striking the African a smart rap on the shin with his knuckles, the sleeper started up in an instant to a sitting posture, and bellowed as if he had been stabbed with a bayonet.

" Shut up," said Weeks; " you ain't murdered — are you ? "

" O, Massa Charles, Massa Charles," cried the African, rubbing the wounded part with his hand, " you know him place strike poor nigger."

" You see that," observed Mrs. Motherly; " he seems to know you, sir."

" Massa Charles — why, who the thunder are you — eh ? "

" O, golly, there, Massa Charles not know Sambo ! "

" What Sambo ? "

" Why, Jubal Sambo — gosh ! that very sprizin; many time massa licked Sambo on old plantation."

" Where ? " demanded Weeks, his words growing few and faint as the negro's voice and features grew more and more familiar to him.

"Where! yah, yah! no remember Moose Creek, old Virginny? Massa Charles look him my back him; know Sambo better: ebery one knows him own marks."

"Moose Creek!—good Heavens!" there! exclaimed Weeks, "well, by crackie, if that ain't the most unexpected——"

"Yah, yah!" chuckled the African, now that his shin no longer troubled him. "Massa no spect see Sambo so far from home. Sambo no fraid massa now. Sambo free nigger—yah, yah!"

"Mrs. Motherly," said Weeks, turning to the housekeeper, who stood looking on apparently much interested in the conversation, "may I beg you to quit the room for a moment? I should like to say a few words to this poor fellow—seems to me I have seen him before."

"Indeed you have, sir, I'll warrant that," said Mrs. Motherly, looking sharply at Weeks, now as pale as a sheet of paper. "But sure if you have any thing in private to say to him, I'll not prevent you. Strange how people meets sometimes so far from home, and when they laste expect it, too. Ha, ha! isn't it quare, Mr. Weeks?"

"Very much so indeed—but you'll excuse me, Mrs. Motherly."

"Sartintly, sir; I was only just going to tell ye how Mr. Guirkie, thravellin in America, once met with an ould rival of his in the same way, that he thought was dead twenty years before. It was the oddest thing in the world. Him and Mr. Guirkie, it seems, in their young days, were both courtin the same young lady; but, lo and behold you, she went off at last with the other gentleman; and then Mr. Guirkie made a vow never to marry, seein he had no heart to give away, for he loved the girl beyond all raison; and indeed to this very day he carries her picthur about him wherever he goes. Well, he went across the seas to thravel, thinkin to forget her among the strangers; and what would ye have of it, but after leaving the West Indies, and landin in the States of America, the first face he knew was that of his ould rival.   There he was standing on the quay right before him as he stepped ashore from the vessel."

"Very strange, indeed," assented Weeks — "a very remarkable circumstance — exceedingly so.   But won't you allow me, Mrs. Motherly —— ?"

"Sartintly, Mr. Weeks — sartintly, sir."

"Gosh, dat berry queer," muttered Sambo.

"What?"

"Why, Massa Guirkie meetin him old ribal on de wharf."

"How so, Sambo?"

"Well, old Massa Talbot just say same ting.   Moder told me all about it long time ago.   Massa walk on de wharf, and dere comes him old ribal right out of de ship afore him berry eyes, de man he tink was dead and buried.   De sight almost knock him blind."

"Any thing else I can do for you, Mr. Weeks?"

"Nothing, Mrs. Motherly, nothing at present."

"Well, then, I'll leave you together, to settle your own affairs ; only I would advise you, Mr. Weeks, before I go, to caution this foolish fellow not to call you Massa Charles any more, for the people of this wicked world are always watchin and peepin into other people's business, ye know, and ten chances to one but they'd say you weren't the man you purtended to be, at all, at all."   So saying, Mrs. Motherly made her usual courtesy at the door, and closed it behind her.

CHAPTER XVIII.

*Mr. Weeks treats himself to a Ride on a Rathlin Pony. —
Its Consequences. — Kate takes him with her to Castle
Gregory.*

DURING Mr. Weeks's long and secret conference with the
negro, (for Mrs. Motherly was carefully excluded from the
room,) Hardwrinkle still remained closeted with the officer
of constabulary at Crohan House, devising plans for the immediate committal of Randall Barry to Lifford jail. A difficulty, however, presented itself, which Hardwrinkle had
entirely overlooked in his zeal for the safety of the state —
namely, the presence of Captain Petersham, of Castle Gregory, who, as senior magistrate of the barony, was very much
in the habit of taking such cases into his own hands, and dis-
posing of them according to his own peculiar views of the
law thereunto made and provided. Hardwrinkle, it appears,
in order to avoid unnecessary delay, was for having the prisoner brought before himself, and committed forthwith ; but
the officer demurred on the ground that the captain had
already, in anticipation of Barry's arrest, given strict orders
to have the young man brought before *him*, and no other.
Hardwrinkle denied Captain Petersham's right to issue such
orders, inasmuch as the crime charged against Barry was a
capital offence, requiring prompt and summary action by the
nearest of her majesty's justices of the peace, without distinction of rank. Furthermore, he contended that Captain
Petersham, from his well-known disaffection to the government, and his notorious opposition to its measures for the
"amelioration" of Ireland, was neither a fit or proper person
to try the case at all. Still more, — he assured the officer
that the captain's anxiety to take Barry into his own hands

was but the consequence of a secret determination on his part
to let the young rebel escape, if he could possibly do so; and,
therefore, to trust such a man with the case was virtually to
defeat the law, and frustrate the designs of the government.

These remonstrances, however, seemed to produce but little
effect on the police officer, who still persisted in his determination of bringing the prisoner before the senior magistrate as
in duty bound — adding, by way of makeweight, that he valued
his life too highly to risk it by an act of premeditated diso-
bedience to the orders of such a madman and fire-eater as
Captain Tom Petersham, of Castle Gregory.

At length, after various plans and schemes had been proposed and rejected, it was finally agreed that nothing could
be done for the present, but that early on the following morning Hardwrinkle should despatch his servants post-haste to
certain magistrates of the neighborhood, on whose loyalty he
could depend, requesting their presence next day on the Petit
Sessions bench, in order to neutralize any efforts that might
be made by Captain Petersham to free the prisoner. In the
mean time the barracks should be well guarded, particularly
through the night, and every possible precaution taken against
attempts at rescue by the friends and abettors of the young
outlaw. With this understanding, the two zealous defenders
of church and state separated, each congratulating the other
on having secured at last the person of so dangerous and
malignant a traitor as Randall Barry.

Whilst the above consultation was going on, Weeks had
quite recovered from his consternation on recognizing the
negro in Mr. Guirkie's parlor, and, after leaving his message with Mrs. Motherly, was now proceeding on his way to
Castle Gregory, looking as grave and composed as if nothing
had occurred to disturb his equanimity.

The animal on which he rode — we have said already —
was by no means remarkable either for his beauty of shape
or swiftness of foot, and so low withal that his rider's boots

almost touched the ground as he jogged along. Still, though a mere pony, he was remarkably thick set and stout, and looked strong enough to carry a much heavier load, if he only made up his mind to do it. We add this saving clause, because the little fellow happened to belong to the species of horse called the "Rahery or Rathlin breed," well known in the north of Ireland, and famous not only for its great strength, but its inveterate habit of resisting all attempts at coercion; so that "as wrong-headed as a Rahery" had long become a common expression throughout the province.

Mr. Weeks, when he first took a notion to try the horse for a morning's ride, was cautioned by his Crohan friends not to trust him too far. Rebecca, especially, took great pains to acquaint her good cousin with the pony's bad habits, and to put him on his guard. But Weeks, confident of his superior horsemanship, and anxious to verify the truth of his favorite saying, "that no living critter could come it over him," would listen neither to advice nor caution.

The little Rahery, as we have before observed, being neither fast nor handsome, and having little therefore to feel proud of, contented himself with trotting along in his own quiet way, without the least pretension in the world, and caring just as little for the opinions of his neighbors as he did for the spurs of his rider.

Notwithstanding all our hero's boasting, however, it was quite evident he knew little how to govern the horse he rode just then, whatever he might have been able to do at home in New England; for he kept tugging at the reins and pricking the creature's sides with a constant uniform motion, as if the double movement of hand and heel constituted an essential part of the exercise. Whether the gruff, bull-headed little brute felt he had a greenhorn on his back, or whether he resolved "to hold the even tenor of his way" despite bridle and spur, is difficult to tell. But certain it is, Mr. Weeks's efforts seemed to mend the matter but very little. In this fashion he managed to dodge along for a mile or two, his legs swinging to and fro under the horse's belly, and his left hand jerking the bridle at every step; when all of a sudden the pony come to a dead halt, and absolutely refused to proceed another inch in that direction.

Mr. Weeks, who had ridden the horse half a dozen times before, and never had any difficulty with him, felt rather surprised at his conduct, and took good care to express himself accordingly, both in word and deed. After spurring for a while without any effect, it occurred to him the saddle gear might have got out of place, and he instantly dismounted to examine. But to his great disappointment he found himself mistaken. Every thing was exactly where it ought to be. Taking the reins then, he tried to lead the pony past the spot; but the pony decidedly refused to lift a foot. It was very provoking to Mr. Weeks, to find himself there "on the public highway," beating and shouting at the perverse little animal, and every body laughing at him as they passed by. It was unpleasant, to say the least of it, and Mr. Weeks, as might be expected, felt very uncomfortable indeed. At length, when he tried and tried in vain, and saw no likelihood of succeeding by ordinary means, he drew a knife from his pocket, cut a stout ash sapling from a tree by the roadside, and then remounting, laid on the pony with might and main, determined, if he still refused to proceed, it shouldn't be for want of urging. The animal, finding matters growing serious, but resolved, notwithstanding, to have his own way, now took the bridle bit between his teeth, and poking down his head, wheeled round, and started off to Crohan House at full gallop. Weeks, unable to manage the sapling any longer, threw it from him, and seized the reins with both hands to haul him up; but alas! he might as well have seized the horns of a buffalo: on drove the headstrong little Rahery at the top of his speed, and apparently with as much ease as if he carried a child on his back.

"Hoa! hoa!" shouted Weeks; "hoa, ye darned critter."

The pony, unaccustomed to the Yankee manner of address, mistook it probably for a command to go the faster, and on he drove accordingly.

"Tarnation to ye!" cried Weeks, as his hat flew off, and his long sandy hair floated back on the breeze. "Tarnation to ye! hain't ye got no mouth on ye nor nothing? hoa, there, hoa! I say. O merciful Heavens! such a country."

At this moment, a party of ladies and gentlemen, some five or six in number, came riding up, meeting him at a smart trot, and Weeks, seeing their approach, motioned them to stop his horse. One of the riders crossed the road for that purpose, and waved his handkerchief; but the mischievous animal, on seeing his way blocked up, instead of coming to a sudden halt, wheeled off sideways, and ran, or rather tumbled, down a steep bank by the road-side, right into a farmer's kitchen, with the rider's arms clasped round his neck. The blind impetuosity with which the pony drove on, and the nearness of the house, left him no time to choose; so that rider and horse were both in the man's house before they knew it. Then came the catastrophe; for the pony, unable to stop his speed down the bank, not only passed through the door with resistless force, but came full tilt against the " dresser," which stood opposite, breaking at a single crash every article of delft on its shelves, and confounding man, horse, and dishes in one common disaster.

The confusion which followed was amusing. The man's wife ran out with a child in her arms, screaming murder and robbery — half a dozen little boys and girls ran after her, yelling and crying for help — the pony backed out after doing the mischief, and scampered off to his manger — and the owner of the house made his appearance in his shirt sleeves with a pitchfork in his hand, swearing all sorts of instant vengeance against the "murdherin" villain in the kitchen.

" Stop, stop, my good fellow," exclaimed one of the party on horseback, who, seeing how matters stood, had dismounted and arrested the weapon. " Stop — this is a mere accident, my good man."

" Away—out i' my road," shouted the farmer. " Stand
off, and let me at him this minute, or by ——— "

But here he paused and swallowed the oath, for on looking over his shoulder he found himself in the hands of Captain Petersham.

" I beg yer honor's pardon, sir, but I'll have his life."

" Silence," commanded the captain.

" I can't, sir ; look at the wrack he made, the murdherin
villain !   I'll brain him this minute.   I'll smash ——— "

" Listen to me, sir."

" Flesh and blood cudn't stan it, captain."

" Stop this instant, or I'll horsewhip you within an inch of
your life."

" The thievin vagabond ! where is he ? till I knock sauce-
pans out of him."

" Will you not listen to me, you dog ? "

" The bloody cutthroat, I'll have his life."

" Robert, ho there, Robert, hand the reins to Mr. Whately.
Quick, sir ; and you, Mr. Johnson, help him to gag this blundering fool, while I go in and see what the matter is."

" Bekase he's one i' the quality, he has lave to do what he
lakes ; but I'll tache him the difference."

" Who is he, Mr. Whately ? " inquired one of the ladies,
whose horse kept prancing in front of the door.

" Is the unfortunate man of this neighborhood ? " demanded
another.

" Is he much hurt ? " said a third, addressing the farmer's
wife, who was now making her way through the crowd of
horses, with the child still in her arms.

" How can I tell yer ladyship whether he's hurt or not.   But
the sorra's cure to him any way, the dirty gomeril — to smash
our bits o' plenishin, that I bought only last week in Francy
McGarvey's with the dribs i' money I earned hard with my
own four bones.   Bad luck to him every day he rises."

By this time Captain Petersham succeeded in making his

way through the kitchen over broken plates and dishes, and there found the hero of the tragedy with his hands thrust down into his breeches pocket, standing in the midst of the ruins he had made.

"What's the damage, major?" said the Yankee, shaking up the silver, as the captain approached him, "what's the damage? I'll foot the bill. Scissors! such a country!" he muttered to himself. "O, if I were only once — say, what's the damage?"

"Damage?"

"Yes — hold on though ; you ain't boss of the shanty, — are you?"

"I, no, sir. Why, my Heavens! is this you?"

"Well, yes, I guess I'm that particular individual."

"Mr. Weeks of Drakesville, eh?"

"No, sir, it ain't — Ducksville, if you please."

"Yes, yes, I recollect — Ducksville. I'm really very sorry, Mr. Weeks. Upon my honor, my dear fellow, I'm exceedingly sorry."

"Why, who the thunder are you? Hold on. As I live, Captain Petersham, of Castle Gregory! How do, captain? Glad to see you. Got into a kinder snarl here."

"Ha, ha! you're not accustomed to our Irish horses yet," observed the captain, laughing. "Got hurt, eh?"

"No, sir, not a mite — got my coat torn and lost my hat — that's all."

"Well, never mind — it might have been worse. Come, I've a horse at the door to carry you to Castle Gregory. You'll dine with us, of course."

"Well, the fact is, I was a-going there when this confounded accident happened."

"Thank you. Come then. I'll settle all this for you tomorrow."

Whilst the foregoing colloquy was taking place, the owner of the house had been gradually quieted down by the cap-

21 *

tain's friends outside, and the captain himself had succeeded in leading Mr. Weeks to the door, where his servant's horse awaited him to mount. As the latter, ashamed and discomfited, slowly advanced and looked up, he felt "kinder uncomfortable," to use one of his own phrases, at seeing so many eyes fixed on him. But the confusion lasted only a moment, for, like his countrymen, Mr. Weeks's recuperative powers were always at hand.

"Ladies and gentlemen," said the captain, by way of a passing introduction, "this is Mr. Drake, of Weeksville, Connecticut, United —— "

"Mr. Weeks, if you please "— and the speaker drew forth a card from his silver case, and presented it respectfully to his friend. "My name, sir, you will perceive, is Weeks — Ephraim C. B. Weeks, Ducksville, Connecticut, United States."

"Just so, Mr. Weeks. Excuse me, my dear fellow; I'm the most confounded blunderer imaginable. Hang it, I'm always blundering about that name some how, and can't tell how it happens."

"Never mind the name, Mr. Weeks," said one of the ladies on horseback; "mount this horse here, and come with us to Castle Gregory; " and the speaker, touching the spirited animal she rode on the flank with her riding whip, broke through the crowd, and prancing up to the door, stretched out her hand to the American; " come, sir; I've been long wishing to see you; and now you and I must ride together and have a chat in advance of the party."

"Who is she, captain?" whispered Weeks, after he had touched the lady's hand.

"That's my sister — Kate Petersham."

"You don't say!"

"Never saw her before, I presume?"

"No — often heard of her, though. Kinder smart, ain't she?"

"Yes, sometimes — when she takes the notion."

"She looks sorter spry — rides well, I guess."

"Yes; does pretty fair at a fox hunt. Like to cross a ditch or two with her, eh? You can have any of my horses you please."

"No, I thank you; I should rather not at present. That's a pretty piece of horse flesh she rides — ain't it?"

"Yes, sir; that's the best mare of her inches in the province of Ulster. I'll back her against any thing of her age and weight in Ireland, for a thousand."

"Should like to own the critter."

"Can't, sir; Kate would as soon part with her right hand as part with 'Moll Pitcher.' See how she dances, the wild creature — she's mad to get off."

"What detains you, Mr. Weeks?" cried Kate.

"Excuse me, madam, for a moment; I'll be with you presently."

"Make haste then," urged the captain; "the lady will feel quite offended if you keep her waiting."

"Here, my good woman," said Weeks, taking a couple of sovereigns from his purse, and handing them to the farmer's wife; "here, take these, and replenish your shelves."

"You seem to be in a great hurry to repair the damage," observed the captain.

"Well, I guess it's just as well, ain't it?"

"To-morrow had been time enough."

"To-morrow. By jingo, I shouldn't wonder if that crazy coon, her husband, had my life before half the time. These countrymen of yours, captain, ain't to be trusted."

"Ha, ha! I see you're not acquainted yet with the disposition of the Irish."

"Ain't I though? Well, I rather guess I am some. By crackie, if I ain't, for my short time amongst them, I don't know who is. Say, my good woman, hain't you got a hat I could have for a day or so? Fly round and see if you can find one."

"Mr. Weeks, Mr. Weeks," cried Kate again — "here I am waiting for you all this time, and Moll Pitcher so restive that I can hardly manage her."

"Never mind the hat," said the captain, dragging Weeks by the arm — "never mind it now; we'll pick up your own on the road."

"Hold on a second — hurry up, my good woman; let me have something to cover my head.   Hilloa! what's that?" he demanded, as she handed him a rabbit skin cap.   "What the thunder is this?   IIain't I seen that cap before?"

"No matter; put it on," entreated the captain, impatiently, "and let's be off."

"Wait a minute — what's this in the bottom of it, eh? — a letter, I swonnie it is, — and to Miss Kate Petersham, too.   Why, how's this?"

"Who owns the cap?" demanded the captain.

"I own it," said a new comer, issuing from a door of a little room behind the dresser.   "I own it, sir."

"Lanty Hanlon!"

"Let me have the cap, sir — here's one to replace it," said Lanty, handing Weeks another of nearly the same description, and taking his own without the least ceremony from the hands of the astonished Yankee.

"Well there! — say, captain, can you tell me how many duplicates of this individual are to be found in the deestrict, or, in other words, is he really the old gentleman himself?"

"Lanty Hanlon, how came you by this letter?"

"Don't trouble yourself about it, captain," replied Kate; "it's only a love letter.   Hand it here, Lanty.   I'll meet you at the *place you know*, this evening.   Be punctual now, or I'll discard you."

"Niver fear, my lady; I'll be there; but mind, if you don't be up to time yourself, we must break the engagement."   And throwing the cap carelessly on his head, he disappeared as he came.

"I see, captain, you know that fellow."

"O, yes; I have known Lanty for years."

"Well, he's a tarnation villain; let me tell you that."

"Lanty — ha ! ha ! O, no, he's not a bad fellow.   Fond of playing tricks, that's all."

"Tricks — he's the darnedest rascal unhung."

Weeks now mounted the groom's horse, which proved to be a gentle, well-disposed animal; and with the captain on one side and Kate on the other, rode in front of the procession, his rabbit-skin cap jantily set on the side of his head, and his hands and feet jerking and swinging as before, to the no small amusement of the party.

CHAPTER XIX.

Uncle Jerry and the " Three Twins." — A Surprise.

THE reader will remember that Mrs. Motherly had a strong objection to Mr. Guirkie's carrying his purse with him, whenever she suspected him of going to visit the blind fiddler at the Cairn, or the widow with the "three twins," at Ballymastocker.. She insisted it was her duty to search his pockets on such occasions, and he permitted her to do so, with all the docility of a child, save and except when a third party happened to be present; then he drew himself up, and proclaimed his independence both by word and look, but so ostentatiously withal, that any one with the slightest discrimination might have seen it was only the advantage the coward takes, when he unexpectedly finds help at his back.   Uncle Jerry was, we must admit, rather peculiar in the exercise of his benevolence, or, as Mrs. Motherly used to say, very odd in his ways.   It was not exactly because Batt Curley

of the Cairn was destitute of the ordinary means of living,
that he took such a kindly interest in him, for Batt always
earned enough to eat and drink by his fiddle, hard as the
times were; it was because he was old and blind, and only
a fiddler at that. So also with respect to the widow and the
" three twins," at Ballymastocker: there was nothing very
lamentable in her case either; but the thought of a poor lone
woman, with three children born at a birth to take care of, so
fixed itself about his heart, that he found it impossible to
banish it. And it was only because the case of the negro had
something peculiar in it, his sympathy was so suddenly excited in his favor. Had the doctor told him the negro's arms
had been broken, he would have felt for the poor sufferer, no
doubt, as he felt for every body in distress; but to have all
his *toes* broken and disjointed, was something dreadful to
think of. A poor African wounded in this manner touched
the tenderest sympathies of his generous soul.

The reader must not imagine for a moment, notwithstanding all we have said, that Uncle Jerry's fancy had more to do
with his benevolence than his heart. No such thing; fancy
was only the angel of light that stood by, while charity, the
first born of the Redeemer's love, drew the picture of human
sorrow, and held it up before him. Christian Charity, love-
liest of virtues! when the Saviour, who gave you in triumph
to the world, first presented you on Calvary, how beautiful
you were then! When, taking you by the hand, he led you
up the hill, and pointing to the Sun of Christianity just beginning to rise, bade you go forth to bless and bind all hearts
together, till the light of that Sun should again be absorbed in
the source of its life forevermore, — how modest your blushing face, and how timid your noiseless step, as you then came
out from the darkness of paganism, to weave your web of love
round the great heart of regenerated humanity! You had
worshippers in those days to fall in millions at your feet; but
where are they now? Alas, alas! like the deserted king of

Greece, looking round the Bay of Salamis for his scattered ships, —

> "You counted them at break of day,
> But when the sun set where were they?"

The goddess of Charity whom men worship now, how unlike thee she is! Bold and proud, she walks with stately step, and shuns the lowly cabin on her way to princely halls. She extends no friendly hand to the helpless and houseless in the darkness of night, but waits for the broad glare of noonday, to carry her gifts to the market place. She stalks along the public thoroughfares in wanton attire, surrounded by followers whom she attracts by the splendor of her garments and the stateliness of her mien. She sets herself up as thy rival, modest, blushing child of God. In the flaunting dress of the courtesan, she disputes thy empire over the hearts of men; and, alas, that we must confess it! she gains the victory.

But, dear reader, fallen as the world is, there are some true hearts to be found in it still; some who, like Uncle Jerry, will steal away into obscure places to comfort the poor, and blush like him to be caught in the act. So was it now.

It appears that Mr. Guirkie, instead of going directly to Rathmullen, on his weekly visit to the old churchyard, as Mrs. Motherly had supposed, fell in with the priest, on his way to visit the widow with the "three twins" at Ballymastocker, who was taken suddenly ill, and instantly resolved to accompany him to the house.

As Captain Petersham, with his party, rode along, two horses, standing at the widow's door, attracted his attention; and on coming up, he recognized them as Father John's and Mr. Guirkie's. At once he made up his mind to invite the two friends to Castle Gregory, and accordingly dismounted for that purpose.

On entering the humble dwelling of the widow, or rather as he stepped on the threshold, a sight met his view which

caused him instantly to draw back. Uncle Jerry was sitting
near the fireplace, with his back to the door, and so intent
at his occupation, that he neither heard the captain's footstep,
nor observed the shadow his person cast upon the wall as he
came in. The latter, as the reader knows already, was a blunt,
out-spoken, honest-hearted, rollicking country-gentleman of the
old school, and Kate, knowing his ways so well, had been
expecting every instant to hear his voice in high banter with
Uncle Jerry; but, instead of that, she was rather surprised to
see him steal out again on tiptoe, with his hands raised up in
wonder, as if at something he had witnessed within.

"What's the matter, captain?" she demanded; "is the
widow dead?"

"Not that I know of; but such a sight as that I haven't
seen for years — come down and behold it with your own
eyes;" and lifting her from the saddle, he escorted her to the
door of the cabin.

Mr. Weeks and the other gentlemen of the party, hearing
the captain's words, were instantly excited by a natural curiosity to see what was going on, and alighted also.

Uncle Jerry was still intent on his work. He was rocking
a cradle of more than ordinary proportions, made of coarse
wicker-work, in which the three twins were soundly sleeping. On a low stool beside him lay his pocket handkerchief,
which he had been using when the captain first saw him, and
had only laid down as the party came crowding round
the door.

"Gentlemen," said Kate, turning to her friends and whispering her words low, "I beg you'll retire. This is no fitting
scene for profane eyes like yours. Away, and leave the
captain and me to speak to him."

They did as directed; and then Kate, motioning the latter
to keep his place, stepped across the earthen floor with
the lightness of a bird, and stood behind the watcher. She
was about to touch him on the shoulder with her finger to

make him aware of her presence, but drew it suddenly back again, and waited a minute longer.

In that short minute Uncle Jerry had laid open his whole heart to her. She could read it as plainly as a book. Inserting his hand into the lining of his great seal-skin cap, he drew forth from a secret pocket, which Mrs. Motherly had failed to discover, a Bank of Ireland note, and rolling it up into convenient shape, took the hand of one of the orphans, and wove it in between its fingers. As he did so, a big tear dropped on the hand, and Uncle Jerry took up his handkerchief to wipe it off.

"Hold!" said Kate; "let it remain there, to consecrate the offering."

"God bless me!" exclaimed Mr. Guirkie, looking up with his eyes still full. "Why, I thought I was alone."

"And if you were," replied Kate, hardly able to restrain her own tears, "the lesson had been lost."

"What lesson?"

"That," said she, pointing to the child's hand holding the money, with the mercy drop glistening on it.

"Why, upon my word and honor, Kate," said Uncle Jerry, wiping his tears, "I don't know how it is, but the smoke of the peat fire affects my eyes more than ever—perhaps it's because I'm growing older."

Kate took his hand and pressed it lovingly in hers. "God bless you," she said. "I never see you but I feel my heart growing better. If charity and faith ever dwell in human bosoms, they are surely to be found in yours. But tell me, where is Father John?"

Uncle Jerry pointed to the room.

"Has he finished?"

"Yes—you may go in."

Kate opened the door gently, but seeing Father John kneeling by the bedside of his penitent, closed it again.

"Come in," said the priest, turning his head a little, and
22

seeing her form as she opened the door; "come in, Miss Petersham; and as I administer the sacrament of the body and blood of the Redeemer to this poor dying creature, beg of him, by the love he bore you in the institution of this adorable mystery of the eucharist, to convert you to the true and living faith."

Kate fell upon her knees.

"God of love," said the priest, prostrate before the open pix, "if ever I have done aught to deserve a blessing at thy hands, I now implore thee to touch the heart of this erring child. Breathe into her soul the spirit that quickeneth unto life, that she may one day feel how good thou art, and how inestimable a treasure she possesses in the sacrament of thy love. And thou, O Mary, Mother of God, pray for her, that she may soon break asunder those earthly ties that hold her back from the arms of the church of Christ stretched out to embrace her."

He then rose and administered the viaticum to the dying woman, afterwards the sacrament of extreme unction, and, kneeling once more by her bedside, recommended her soul fervently to the God who gave it.

As he turned to quit the room, Kate looked up in his face, her cheeks flushed with the emotions of her heart. "Father," she cried, still kneeling before him, "father, give me thy hand;" and kissing it, she placed it on her head, and asked his blessing.

He gave it from the depth of his heart. Then Kate rose, and silently accompanied her two friends to the door, where the party impatiently awaited their coming.

The captain, who had been a silent witness of the whole scene, touched his cap respectfully as the priest appeared, and silently mounting his horse, rode off with his friends to Castle Gregory.

CHAPTER XX.

*Mr. Weeks professes Washingtonian Principles, but is in-
duced, notwithstanding, to taste Whiskey Punch. — Its wonderful Effects.*

"MR. WEEKS," said Captain Petersham, after dinner was
over and the cloth removed, "I'm delighted to see you at
Castle Gregory; and now, as the ladies have left us, we must
drink a glass of stout Innishowen together. Mr. Johnson,
shove down the decanter to our American friend."

"Excuse me, captain," said Weeks; "I never drink."

"Nonsense! you must drink. By George, that's a pretty
thing! not drink, indeed! why, you're not a teetotaler, are you?"

"Well, pretty much. I'm a Washingtonian."

"Of course you are — I know all that. But you don't
mean to say that every Washingtonian's a temperance man?"

"You mistake, I reckon," said Weeks. "A Washingtonian don't mean an American, exactly, but a member of a
certain temperance society."

"O, I see — that's the meaning of it. So you belong to
a temperance society, then! Well, 'pon my honor, friend
Weeks, I had formed a better opinion of you."

"Don't think it wrong to take a pledge against liquor,
do you?"

"No — not perhaps for the working classes — but I think
no gentleman should take it. If a sense of his position, and
respect for his honor, don't restrain a gentleman from brutal-
izing himself, then I say he's no gentleman, and no pledge or
oath can bind him. What think you, Father John?"

"You're right, captain; except in those rare instances
when gentlemen regard excess as a sin against God: in such
cases a pledge may restrain them when their honor can't not
Perhaps Mr. Weeks is one of this class."

" How — regard intoxication as a sin against God ? "

" Yes — for which he, one day, will bring you to account."

" Well, as to that," replied Weeks, " I reckon it depends materially on the kinder notions one has formed on that ere point. Folks differ, you know, considerable about the sorter being God is ; and, as for myself, I can't say I ever got well posted up on the subject. But I always maintained that the abuse of liquor was a sin ~~against society.~~"

" Of course — there never was a second opinion about that."

" And I always set my face against it on that account."

" Precisely ; you adopted the prevailing sentiment — for I can call it by no other name — that the abuse of liquor should be discouraged, not because it's offensive to God and injurious to the soul, ~~but because it's offensive to society~~ — to modest eyes and ears polite."

" Father John, take my advice, and drop the argument," said the captain, " or you'll be head and ears into one of your long sermons directly. Mr. Weeks, don't mind him — he's forever moralizing. Come, fill your glass, like an honest man, and drink your national toast — 'Success to the stars and stripes.' "

" Don't drink, I assure you, captain. Should be most happy to oblige you, but it's against my principles."

" Against the — ! against a man's principles to drink a glass of punch at a friend's table ! "

" Don't urge the gentleman," said two or three of the company — " don't, sir ; he has scruples about it. Every man should know what suits himself best."

" Nonsense ! I can't bear to look at a guest sitting at my table as dry as a stick."

" Well, to please you, I'll taste something," said Weeks, at last ; " though it's against my principles to drink. Mr. Johnson, have the goodness to make me a spoonful or two of sangaree "

" Sangaree. Ha, ha, ha ! " laughed the captain. " Not a drop of it, Johnson — not a drop ; make him a glass of whiskey punch. Or, stop — send it up to me; I'll make it myself."

"No, no — hold on, captain; excuse me," said Weeks, intercepting the decanter on its way to the head of the table; "excuse me; I'd rather not; Mr. Johnson will make it."

"Why, it seems so strange — Whately, could you have imagined it? a freeman, a citizen of the model republic, and neither Presbyterian nor Quaker, to belong to a temperance society. Ha, ha! it's monstrous! — it shocks all my American prepossessions."

Weeks smiled in his usual cold way, and assured the captain the "Sons of Temperance" were very numerous in the States; and that, for his part, he had been strictly temperate since he was fifteen years old.   .

"And, pray, Mr. Weeks," said the captain, filling his glass from the tumbler, "what pleasure or advantage can you derive from this self-denial you practise — it's not for your sins, I suspect — eh?"

"No, sir; don't believe in that doctrine."

"And why the mischief do you abstain, then?"

"Why, because it suits my constitution best, and saves my pocket besides."

"O, that indeed; I understand you now."

"Two excellent motives — ain't they, captain?"

"You must ask Father Brennan, sir; that question involves a knowledge of morals of which I profess to be entirely ignorant. What say you, Father John? will his motives stand the test of your theology?"

Father John shook his head, but said nothing in reply.

"Well, look here," pursued Weeks, turning to the priest; "I ain't a-goin to dispute the matter now; but just multiply fourteen years (the time I've been temperate) by three hundred and sixty-five dollars saved each year, — and that's about the lowest estimate I can make, — and you have precisely five thousand one hundred and ten dollars, exclusive of

22 *

interest. Now I call that a saving. I may be mistaken, but I call it a saving."

"Not a doubt of it," replied the priest, smiling—"not a doubt of it; you calculate very closely though — don't you?"

"Well, no, sir; I merely follow Cousin Nathan's advice, and don't waste my powder. I had a cousin once called Nathan Bigelow ——"

"There!" ejaculated Uncle Jerry, laying down his glass untasted, and rising from the table; "there! he's at Nathan again. I vow and declare I can't stand it—this is the fifth time."

"What's the matter, Mr. Guirkie?" inquired the captain.

"Nothing very particular," replied Uncle Jerry, making his way out; "I'll return presently."

"Well, this cousin of mine," continued Weeks, "this cousin called Nathan ——"

"O, he's the man, used to preside at town meetings, direct the minister what to preach, and so forth. Yes, yes, you needn't mind; we have heard of him."

"Have, eh?"

"Yes; he's quite familiar to us."

"Well, I was only going to say that I merely followed his advice. And now, with regard to my second motive, I found, when about fifteen years of age, or thereaways, that liquor proved a leetle too exciting for my constitution, both mentally and physically."

"Ah, indeed," said the priest; "how so, pray?"

"Well, it softened my heart a leetle more than I found convenient."

"You drank too freely, perhaps, for a boy of your age?"

"Well, guess I did —rather; can't say I got drunk, though —got tight once in a while. But the darned thing used to draw a sorter skin over my eyes, that I couldn't see clearly what I was about."

"Hence you gave it up?"

"Yes. You'd like to know, perhaps, how it came round?"

" Certainly — let's hear it by all means."

"Well, it was kinder funny, too. Father sent me one morning, when I was about fifteen or a little over, to a place called Meriden, with chickens and squash for the market. It happened I took a young colt with me father bought short time before, and he was a smasher of his age, I *tell* you — only rising five, and as pretty a piece of horse flesh as you could scare up in the hull county. After selling the provisions and putting the proceeds in my wallet, I dropped into a bar room to have a drink before I'd start for hum. Just as I took a cigar after the brandy, a long-legged, green-looking chap — Vermonter, guess he was — comes up to the counter, and says he, ' Youngster, that horse of yourn's pretty smart horse, I reckon.' ' Well, yes,' I said, ' considerable smart for a colt.' ' What time does he make?' ' Three and a half.' Says he, ' No; can't do it.' ' Can't?' says I. Says he, ' no, hain't got the points for three and a half, nor four neither.' ' Well,' says I, quite coolly, as I lit my cigar, ' you can bet, if you've a mind to.' 'Agreed,' says he; ' what'll it be?' ' I ain't particular,' said I. ' Well,' says he, ' treat for all round, if you've got no objection?' ' None,' said I; ' I'm quite agreeable.'

" Well, having got the lend of a sulky from a doctor in the neighborhood, we marked the course, appointed a time-keeper, and off I started. Crackie, how that colt did put that day ! Well, he went it slick, I tell yer. The critter knew just's well as I did myself what he'd got to do, and he struck out like a good fellow."

" Won the bet, of course?"

" Won it ! Ye-e-s; and twenty seconds to spare besides. ' Well,' said the tall fellow, coming up to me, as I stepped from the sulky, and clapped the colt on the back, — ' well,' said he, ' he did his prettiest, I reckin?'

" Said I, ' No; not by a long chalk.' ' Darn the matter,'

said he, 'he won the bet, any way; so come in and have a drink.'   As the chap spoke, he beckoned to two or three other hard-looking customers, that seemed to be loafing about the corner, and then dove into an oyster cellar.   'Brandy smashes and cigars for five,' said he, passing the bar-keeper. 'You'll go that, youngster, won't you?'   'Well, don't care if I do,' said I, 'though I ain't much accustomed to it.'"

"So you drank too much on that occasion?" observed one of the company, interrupting the details, for he thought Mr. Weeks was growing rather tedious.

"You'd better believe it, friend.   Well, to cut the story short, before I left the cellar that afternoon, I lost the price of the squash and chickens, and swapped the colt besides for a Canadian pony, a gold watch, and thirty-seven dollars in cash.   Next morning came though, and O, scissors! if I didn't feel like suicide."

"Conscience stricken," said the priest, "for the night's debauch?"

"Conscience stricken!   Why, no; but letting that green chap come it over me so smooth.   Well, I swow, I never felt so cheap in my life — that's a fact."

"He cheated you, then?"

"Yes — guess he did cheat me.   Hold on a bit though; you'll hear.   About seven o'clock next morning, father came into the kitchen swearing like fifty.   I was lying abed at the time, just thinking of getting up."

"'Where's the young scamp?' he cried; 'by thunder, I'll cowhide him this minute within an inch of his life.'

"'Good gracious!' exclaimed mother.   'Why, Amasa Weeks!   Ain't you ashamed?'

"'No, I ain't.'

"'You oughter then.'

"'Stand aside,' shouted father, 'and let me pass.'

"'Amasa, ain't you crazy?'

"'Shut up, I say.   The young scoundrel!   I'll teach him how to trade!'

"'Poor child,' said mother, 'it was his first trade; and what could you expect of a boy of fifteen? Why, gracious, if he *was* taken in about that watch, it ain't agoin to ruin you — is it?'

"'But the horse! the horse!' shouted father.

"'The horse! why, what's the matter with the horse?'

"'The matter! — thunderation's the matter! — the critter's blind!'

"'Blind! — why, you don't say!'

"'And lame! lame! the tarnation villain!'

"'Pheugh,' said I, jumping out of bed and bolting through the open window with my jacket under my arm; 'it's time I warn't here, I reckon;' and without waiting for further information on the subject, I cleared."

After the suppressed titter, which accompanied Weeks's story all through, had at last broken out into a broad laugh, and then subsided, Father John quietly observed that the gentleman's first lesson was rather an expensive one.

"Should think so," said Weeks in reply; "it cost me, or father rather, somewhere in the neighborhood of two hundred dollars."

"And so, after that, you concluded to drink no more?"

"Gave it up, sir, right straight off; I saw it wouldn't pay."

"And that, I suppose, was your only motive for becoming temperate?"

"Why, yes — of course it was."

"Well," said the priest, "I can't admire it much. Had you only united that motive, selfish as it was, with a desire to please God and save your soul ——"

"Whew!" ejaculated Weeks, interrupting the priest; "that's quite another affair. My principle is, to leave Christianity and religion, and all that sorter thing, to those whose duty it is to look after it. I'm a business man, squire, and my object is trade, and nothing else."

" Good ! " cried the captain, returning and clapping Weeks
on the shoulder as he passed him on his way to the head of
the table.   " Good, sir ; that's honest speaking.   By George,
Weeks, you're a trump."

" Well, them's my sentiments, and I ain't afraid to avow
them either," said Weeks, taking courage from the captain
and the poteen together.   " I'm a business man, and make no
pretensions to piety, nor nothing else."

" Certainly not, sir; that's as much as you can attend to."

" Of course it is — no doubt of it."

" And see here," said Weeks, after finishing the last glass,
and making the spoon ring in the empty tumbler, — " see
here, captain ; I may as well say what I think.   I never saw
a pious business man yet worth a copper to the country.   I
swonnie I never did."

" Ha, ha ! " laughed the captain ; " listen to that, Father
John."

" And I tell you what, sir," continued Weeks, turning to
the priest, — who now kept his head down to hide a smile,
while he toyed with his watch chain for an excuse, — " I tell
you what, sir, ministers may say what they please, but they're
a darned set of humbugs ; that's the hull amount of it."

" Hah ! take that, my reverend friend," chuckled the captain again.   " The truth occasionally, you know, will do
you good."

" I'm quite surprised, Mr. Weeks," gravely observed the
priest, while the smile still kept playing about the corners of
his mouth, — " I'm really surprised to hear you speak so
irreverently."

" Well, hold on a bit — hold on — see here : I know as
many as fifty ministers in New England alone, and more too,
abandoned their pulpits last year, and went off to speculate in
this, that, and t'other thing, to make money.   Some went into
the fish business, some into the lumber trade, two on 'em from
my own town turned to the law, and the majority managed to

squeeze themselves into the legislature. Now, if these men had, what they pretended to have, a vocation to the ministry before their ordination, where in thunder did it go after? I'd like to know."

"It's no doubt a melancholy fact," said the priest, "that your Protestant clergy of New England, especially those with limited revenues, in very many instances have renounced their sacred calling for more lucrative trades and professions, thereby disgracing themselves and their religion. Such instances are very rare in this country, however."

"Are? — how's that?"

"Why, we don't love money here, perhaps, so much as you do in the States; and besides, we haven't the same opportunities to speculate."

"Well, that may be all very true; but it's my opinion ministers, in general, make a trade of religion every where, one way or other. I have had a pretty good chance myself to see how the thing works, and I reckon I can tell as much about it, too, as most folks. Been a class-leader once in my time."

"What!" exclaimed the captain, leaning his folded arms on the table, and gazing at the Yankee, bedizened all over as he was with chains and brooches. "What, a class-leader — you?"

"Yes."

"A Methodist class-leader?"

"Why, certainly."

"A canting, Methodist class-leader?"

"Of course."

"May the Lord forgive you, sir." (The reader is already aware of the captain's special contempt for that particular sect.) "Why, you must have lost your senses."

"Well, they are a kinder scraggy, I allow."

"And you made such a spooney of yourself as to snivel away with this psalm-singing set. By the Lord Harry, Weeks, I thought you were a different man altogether."

"Well, I admit it was sorter mean — that's a fact. But wait a bit; let me tell you how it happened. I had an object in view."

" O, confound your object ! "

" Wait a minute; you'll say it warn't a bad one, if the thing had been properly managed. Well, there was a gal in our neighborhood, named Brown — Zepherina Brown, or Zeph, as she was called for shortness sake."

" Pardon me, Mr. Weeks — your glass is empty," said the captain. " Whately, send up the bottle."

" You'll excuse me, captain."

" Hang your excuses; make a glass of punch, sir, like a man."

" Well, I'd rather not, just at present."

" Nonsense ! "

" I'm not used to it, you know."

" Used to it ! used to Innishowen whiskey twenty years old ? Are you used to new milk ?   'Pon my honor, sir, I'm ashamed of you. If you don't drink, by the Lord Harry I'll think you're a Methodist still."

" Well, I rather think I'll be ashamed of myself before long, if I hold on at this rate. It begins to wake me up already. I swonnie it does."

" Psaugh ! my dear sir, you might drink a puncheon of it. Irish whiskey's meat, drink, washing, and lodging for every human being under the sun. Come, send up your tumbler; I'll mix it for you. There's Madeira and Claret on the sideboard, and I wouldn't give a brass button for oceans of it, while there's a drop of this real old Irish whiskey here to soften my heart. By George, sir, if you only drank it for six months, it would make a man of you."

" Humph ! guess it would — the wrong way."

" No, sir, but the right way. It would cure you of that passion you have for speculating and money-making. It would make your heart grow twice as big as it is — ay,

big enough, by George, to take the whole human race
into it."

" Well, it's a fact," said Weeks, " it does make a feller feel
kind of good ; but guess it's not to be trusted tco far, either,
for all that."

" Never fear, Weeks, never fear ; you go on with the story,
and I'll mix the punch."

———•———

CHAPTER XXI.

*Mr. Weeks grows eloquent after the second Tumbler, and makes
a crack Speech, but declines a Duel with the Light-keeper as
not being in his Line.*

" WELL," said Weeks, making another start, " Zeph lived
at a place called Pratt's Corner, five six miles from Ducksville. She was kinder related to us somehow by the Bigelows, and mother and she terrible intimate. Zeph used to
invite mother to prayer meetings, and mother, in return, sent
Zeph presents of apple-sass twice a year regular. Well,
Zeph got to be considerable old, you know, and kinder
wrinkly about the nose, and, as a matter of course, pious
in proportion — but to balance the. wrinkles, Zeph had the
cash."

" Ho! ho!" cried the captain, " did the wind blow from
that quarter? "

" She had two sawmills of her own, and some twenty
thousand dollars in railroad stocks besides. Well, I made up
my mind one day to try if I couldn't induce Zeph to take a
partner to help her manage her business affairs, and forthwith
set about making the necessary preparations. I felt kinder
green, then, you know, in the religious line, and so thought

23

better attend two or three prayer meetings in Ducksville beforehand, to get into the way of it, like."

" Capital ! capital !" ejaculated the captain.

" When the day came for my first trial, I shaved clean as the razor would cut it, mounted a black suit and half yard crape on my hat, and then put for Pratt's Corner. As I entered the room, Deacon Lovejoy was holding forth strong against the old pope, (his favorite theme ;) so, slinking in with a face as grave as I could conveniently command, after so short a practice, I took my seat longside Zeph, without seeming to notice who was in it. After the deacon resumed his chair, Zeph turned her head a leetle mite sideways, and siz she, in a low, touching voice, ' O Mr. Weeks, how I do rejoice to see you at last among the servants of the Lord !' ' Ah !' said I, looking up in her face kinder dreamy like, — ' Ah ! how pleasant it is to dwell in the assembly of the faithful — O dear——'

" ' You've been a wanderer,' said Zeph.

" ' Alàs ! alas ! I have,' said I, looking up at her again. ' I've been a poor, sinful wanderer, seeking for the waters of life among the swamps and quagmires of a wicked world; but Heaven be praised, the blessed light hath come at last to guide me to the pure spring.' "

" Excellent ! capital !" shouted the captain, rapping the table till the tumblers rang again. " Ha, ha, ha! by Jove, Weeks, you're a clever fellow. Gentlemen, let us postpone the courtship for the present; I see the ladies coming ; and fill your glasses — fill them up ; bumpers let them be — nothing less than bumpers. I give you Mr. Weeks and the stars and stripes forever."

The company rose and drank the toast with a hip, hip, hurrah ! and nine times nine ; and Kate, no longer able to restrain her curiosity, came tripping in from the drawing room, accompanied by half a dozen ladies, declaring she could sit no longer among a parcel of silly, moping girls.

with such distinguished company in the house. "Besides," she added, glancing archly at Mr. Weeks, "I want to hear a speech. I'm actually dying to hear a speech from a citizen of the great republic."

"Gentlemen, please take your seats," said Captain Petersham, with a wave of his hand; "I see Mr. Weeks is about to speak. As for you, ladies, you're a set of saucy, impudent baggages, to intrude upon us here over our cups."

"Mr. Weeks," "Mr. Weeks," "Mr. Weeks," was now heard from all parts of the room.

"Ladies and gents," said the latter, rising slowly, and running one hand into his vest pocket, while he rested the other on the table, — "ladies and gents, I ain't a-goin to make a speech; speech-making's not in my line. But I ain't a-goin to sit silent, either, when such honor is done to the flag of my country. Ladies and gents, I'm an American born, of the true blue Puritan stock, a citizen of the model republic of the world. ["Hear, hear."] I ain't given to braggin much, I expect, and besides, it don't become a foreigner to brag of his country in a strange land; but speaking as this here gent and I were (turning to Father John) about religion, I ain't afraid to assert that you can't find, in all creation, a class of men professing more enlarged and liberal views of religion than the merchants and traders of New England.

"We are liberal in all things where conscience merely is concerned, and conservative only with a view to preserve order in society, that trade may flourish under its protection. Yes, ladies and gents, whatever tends to cripple trade or impede the progress of social advancement, whether it be a new theory or an old theory, a new creed or an old creed, we strangle it. We *strangle* it as the heathens in old times used to strangle deformed children. Business men in our country ain't so very particular as to difference in religious denomination. They don't care much whether the creed be Orthodox, Universalist, Episcopalian, or Baptist, if it only gives free scope to intellect, and a clear track for human progress. There's but one creed they object to; and that is (excuse me, friend, said the speaker, turning to the priest) — that is the Roman Catholic. ["Hear him! hear him!" cried Captain Petersham, that's the kind of talk I like." "Hear him! hear him!" echoed half a dozen others, following the lead.] Well, the fact is, ladies and gents, they can't go that kinder doctrine, *no how;* it tightens them up so they can't move one way or other. The laws and rules of the Catholic church hain't got no joints in 'em; you can't bend 'em no shape or form. Then they have what they call 'confession;' and if one of their society happens to speculate beyond his means, the priest brings him right chock up for it; so he hain't got no chance to risk any thing in the way of trade, no how he can fix it. Again, if a Catholic happens to find a pocket book, for instance, with five or six thousand dollars in it, he must restore it to the owner right straight off, when, by waiting for twelve months or so, he might make a few hundreds by the use of it to start him in business. Such a creed as that, ladies and gents, no true American can tolerate. Well — he wouldn't deserve the name of a freeman if he did. The question for Americans is, not whether any particular form of religion be young or old, true or false, divine or human, but whether it suits the genius of the country; that's the question — the only question — to decide. Our country is young, ladies and gents; she has done little more, as yet, than just begun to develop her resources — the greatest resources of any nation throughout all universal space; and we feel it's our best policy to moderate the rigors of the gospel — to temper it, as it were — well, to make it as little exacting as possible. Hence our ministers, as a general thing, especially in cities and large towns, seldom preach about sin, or hell, or the ten commandments, or that kinder subjects, because such themes are calculated to disturb and perplex business men, to the injury of trade. And we have long made up our minds that trade must be cared for, whatever else suffers. Yes, ladies and gents," continued the speaker, growing more animated as the old Innishowen began to warm up his blood, " our country is bound to go ahead of every other country in creation. Excuse me, ladies and gents, for speaking my sentiments *right out* on the subject; but they are *my* sentiments and the sentiments of every native born American."

" Bravo, bravo, Weeks ! " cried the captain ; his fat sides shaking as he clapped his hands. " Bravo — that's the talk."

" Yes," continued Weeks, I'm a Yankee, and them sentiments are true blue Yankee sentiments. We ain't a-goin to be fettered by any form of religion under the sun ; if it don't encourage trade and commerce it don't suit us — that's the hull amount of it. Had the United States hung on to the old worn-out creeds of Europe, what should our people be now ? — perhaps in no better condition than yourselves, ladies and gents, at this present moment."

" That's cool," muttered some one in an under tone.

" It's a fact, nevertheless," said Weeks, catching the words. " The antiquated religion of our grandfathers would have acted like a strait-jacket on the nation, cramping its energies and stinting its growth. Had we not shaken ourselves free from the trammels both of pilgrim and priestly rules, could we have become in so short a period so intelligent, enterprising, and powerful a nation ? Yes, ladies and gents, could we have flung our right arm across the Gulf, and laid hold of Mexico by the hair of the head, as we do now, and be ready to extend our left over your British American possessions, at any day or hour we please to take the trouble, and sweep them into our lap ? I ask, ladies and gents, could we have done *that* ? "

" Hurrah ! " shouted the captain — " capital ! glorious ! "

" I don't profess, ladies and gents," still continued Weeks, " to belong to any particular religious denominination myself.

My creed is, 'a first cause and the perfectibility of man:' that's the length, breadth, and thickness of my religious belief, and I stand on that platform firm and flat-footed. Still, I go in for three things in the religious line, as strong as any man —almshouses, observance of the Sabbath, and reading the Bible. These are excellent things in their way, and ought to be encouraged by every man who loves order and likes to see trade flourish. But I can go no further; I can never believe, sir (turning to the priest), that the Founder of Christianity intended a nation so intelligent, so intellectual, and so civilized as ours, should be bound down hand and foot by the strict rules of the gospel. No, sir; he intended we should moderate and adapt them as far as possible to the interests of the state and the requirements of society. With these ideas and these principles, ladies and gents, we are bound to go ahead — we must go ahead — we can't help it — prosperity forces itself upon us — we on our part have only 'to clear the track' for it. Nothing can bar our progress, for our destiny is universal empire. Nothing can stop our course — no obstacle, moral or physical, on earth or air, on sea or land. Yes, our energies are immense, and must be expended. Ladies and gents, were it necessary to bore the earth through, we should do it. Yes, by crackie, tunnel almighty creation to find an outlet for our resources."

"Glorious, glorious!" shouted the captain; "hurrah! for the stars and stripes! Well done, Weeks; bravo, bravo! my boy."

And "bravo, bravo!" echoed from all parts of the room; even the ladies stood up and waved their pocket handkerchiefs. In the midst of this general acclamation, however, and just as Mr. Weeks had hitched up his shoulders for another start, a loud, piercing shriek came from the entrance hall, which startled and silenced the noisy company in an instant.

"What the fury is that?" demanded the captain. "Ho, there, James, Thomas — go instantly and see what that noise means."

Kate rushed to the door, followed by the other ladies, curious to learn what had happened; and the gentlemen, fearing some serious accident, darted out pell-mell after them.

"Who the mischief are you?" growled Captain Petersham, grasping a tall, grave-looking man by the arm, as he hurried out from the parlor. "Who the mischief are you, fellow?"

"Pardon me, sir," replied the stranger in the mildest manner possible; "my name is Sweetsoul. I came with ——"

"Who! what! the colporteur! the Methodist Bible-reader!"

"The same, sir."

"And what do you want here, sir?"

"Excuse me, sir, I ——"

"I shan't excuse you, sir; you have no business in my house, you canting rascal; out of it instantly."

"But the lady there, sir."

"Lady, what lady?"

"Hush, hush! brother Tom," whispered Kate, catching him by the button-hole, and whispering in his ear, "it's Baby Deb."

"What, one of the Hardwrinkles?"

"Yes, yes," she replied, convulsed with laughter; "her sister Rebecca — ha, ha, ha! — her sister Rebecca — ha, ha!"

"Cease your folly, Kate, and tell me."

"Well, she's — ha, ha! — gone off with ——"

"Eloped?"

"Yes, fled away with —— O, dear!"

"Rebecca Hardwrinkle eloped? Nonsense, Kate, you're only fooling me."

"It's a positive fact," said the light-hearted, mischief-loving girl — "ask Baby Deb, there, if you don't believe me."

"O, dear! O, dear!" cried the latter, clapping her hands; "she's gone! she's gone!"

"Well, there," ejaculated Weeks, when he heard what had taken place, "there! eloped! if that ain't going it strong, I don't know what is. By thunder, if this ain't the most infernal country ——"

"Miss Hardwrinkle," said the captain, kindly taking the disconsolate young lady by the arm, " let me conduct you to Aunt Willoughby's room.   And tell me as we go how all this happened."

" Won't you send the police in search of her, captain ?   I came all the way with Mr. Sweetsoul to entreat you to send them."

" Certainly, certainly, my dear young lady, I shall do so forthwith ; but how did it happen ? "

" Why, a man came to the house in Ballymagahey, where we had been distributing tracts, and told Rebecca a dying wo- man wanted to see her immediately, and have some spiritual conversation with her before she departed."

" Humph ! I see; well ? "

" Well, poor Rebecca ! — you know, captain, how eagerly she thirsted for the salvation of souls —— "

" Yes, yes, I know all that — well ? "

" The instant the man delivered the message, she started off as quickly as if —— "

" Yes, of course — I understand you ; well ? "

" Her holy zeal, you know —— "

" Never mind her zeal.   What the fury have I to do with her zeal — excuse me, Miss Hardwrinkle, but can't you tell me how she was carried off at once ? "

" O, dear ! you hurry me so — and then I'm almost dead with the fright."

" Listen to me — did you see her carried off ? "

" See her ? "

" Yes, yes, did you *actually* see her ? "

" With my own eyes."

" Then *how was* she carried off ? "

" Behind a man !   O, dear ! O, dear ! "

" Behind a man ? "

" Yes; on — a — on — a — " Here ·Deborah tried to blush and cover her face.

"Confound it, on what?" roared the captain, losing patience altogether. "Can't you speak at once if you wish me to take measures for your sister's recovery. How did he carry her off?"

"On a — on a — O, dear, on a pillion! behind him."

"Phew! on a pillion! Ha, ha! By the Lord Harry, that *was* a sight."

"It was shocking — in broad daylight too; O, dear!"

"It was villanous," said the captain, endeavoring to smother a laugh — "most atrocious! to carry such a saintly young lady, and one so reserved in all her habits of life, over the open country in broad daylight, on a pillion. S'death! the scoundrel should be hung for it."

"And O, captain," said Deborah, "I can never forget the terrific shriek she gave, as she flew past me behind the inhuman wretch. It still rings in my ears — it was heart-rending."

"Who could have played this trick, Kate?" said the captain, turning to his sister; "eh — what does it mean? — I confess I don't understand it."

"And how can I?" replied Kate, covering her face with her handkerchief; "how can I, if you don't?"

"Kate!"

"What?"

"Look up."

"There — what's the matter?"

"This is some of your devilry."

"Mine!"

"Yours. Come! come! no evasion now; you're in the plot, whatever it is, as sure as your name's Kate Petersham. It's exactly like you — you needn't try to look serious."

"Why, brother Tom!"

"Psaugh — brother Tom! — that won't do, Kate. I vow to Heaven, you're the most mischievous — but stop — wait a minute," he added, as a sudden thought seemed to strike him. "Miss Hardwrinkle," said he, again approaching the afflicted young lady, "Miss Hardwrinkle, do you remember to have seen the man before?"

"What, the wretch who ——?"

"Yes — have you any recollection of seeing him before?"

"No; for I could see nothing but his form, he flew by so fast; and besides, he kept whipping the wretched animal so dreadfully all the time."

"He, he, he!" chuckled Uncle Jerry to himself all alone on the sofa; "it must have been an amusing sight."

"You're a barbarous man," said Kate, overhearing the words as she passed him by — "you're a barbarous man to say so."

"O, you young trickster," exclaimed Uncle Jerry, shaking his finger at her as she turned back her laughing eyes upon him; "the plot is of your making, as sure as the sun."

"What was the color of his clothes?" again inquired the captain; "or did you see any thing remarkable in his form or appearance?"

"Nothing — I could see nothing distinctly, except that he wore a cap."

"A cap — what kind of cap? — black or blue?"

"No. I rather think," replied Deborah, "it was a sort of fur cap; it looked rough rather, and somewhat high in the crown."

"Whitish?"

"Yes. Something like a hare or rabbit-skin cap."

"That's enough!" exclaimed the captain, "that's quite enough; I know the villain! I know him! — I suspected who he was from the beginning; he's the most daring, impudent, reckless rascal, that, in all Christendom."

"Who is he — who is he?" demanded half a dozen together.

"Lanty Hanlon, of course; who else could he be? No

man but Lanty in the three baronies would dare play such a trick."

"Lanty Hanlon," screamed Baby Deb, in semi-hysterics; "O, my gracious!"

"Don't be alarmed," said the captain; "your sister's in safe hands."

"O, no, no, captain; that man will murder her!"

"Not he; nor hurt a hair of her head, either."

"Why, you surely mistake, captain," said several of the company. "Lanty Hanlon's the most notorious robber and wrangler in the whole neighborhood."

"I can show you a wound he gave me here on the top of my head, captain," said the colporteur, sneaking into the room.

"What, you! Out of my house, you scurvy vagabond," shouted the burly captain, collaring the Bible-reader, and sending him head-foremost from the room. "Ho, there, fellows, James, Thomas, bundle out that snivelling rascal. By the Lord Harry, if he come in my sight again, I'll horsewhip him."

"Well, but, captain, you must be mistaken about this Hanlon," said one; "it was he beat my game-keeper."

"The same fellow robbed my salmon box," said another.

"And poached on my premises," said a third.

"Yes, and by crackie, it was that tarnation villain drugged me first with poteen whiskey, and then danced me to death, at the wedding," put in Weeks. "He's the most provoking rascal, too, I ever met, for he keeps as cool as a cucumber all the while."

"Gentlemen," said the captain, "you may say what you please of Lanty Hanlon, and think what you please, too, but I know him better than the whole kit of you put together; and by the Lord Harry, he's one of the best specimens of his class I ever saw. He's an honest-hearted, reckless, rollicking. light-hearted Irishman, who likes his bit of fun as well as the best of us, and will have it if he can; but tell me the man ever knew Lanty to do a mean thing.   He may have speared your salmon, and shot your game, and broke your bailiffs' heads; but where's the harm in that?   Can you call it a crime to kill the trout that swims in the mountain brooks, or the black cock that feeds on the mountain heather?   What right have you to forbid a man to catch the trout that jumps in the stream before his own door, or kill the game that feeds on his own pasture?   May the devil take such game laws, say I, and may the man that respects them never know the taste of a white trout at breakfast, or a black cock at supper.   As for you, Mr. Weeks, you must have said or done something to provoke Lanty, or he never had put you through the coarse hackle in that way.   Besides, you didn't matriculate here yet; you're green in the country."

"Gentleman wishes to see Mr. Weeks," said a servant, interrupting the speaker.

Mr. Weeks followed, and was conducted to the breakfast parlor.   As the door opened, the visitor advanced to meet him, with an open letter in his hand.

"Ha! Mr. Lee, glad to see you, sir — how d'ye do?"

"Good evening, sir," replied the light-keeper, stiffly.   "Pray, Mr. Weeks, is this your handwriting?"

"My handwriting?"

"Yes, sir; Miss Lee received that letter this morning through Tamny post office; it bears your signature."

"Why, what's the trouble?"

"Do you acknowledge it yours, sir?"

"Well, yes, I reckon so; what's the matter? you seem kinder put out about it."

"Mr. Weeks," said the light-keeper, "you have managed in some way to get hold of my note of hand; may I now ask how you came to know of the existence of such a paper — or was it through Mr. Robert Hardwrinkle you discovered it?"

Weeks bowed his assent.

"Ah, I thought so. Well, sir, having bribed an old woman to play the black-foot between you and my, and Miss Lee, and not having succeeded as soon as you anticipated, you directed your attorney to mark a writ against me for debt; and now, at the heels of the writ, Miss Lee receives that letter, making her proposals of marriage, and assuring her at the same time of an account at your banker's of a hundred thousand dollars. What does this mean, sir?"

"It ain't the first letter, I guess — is it?"

"Not the first you sent, sir, but the first came to her hands."

"Shoh! you don't say so! That infernal she devil then has played me false — well, there! Tarnation seize the whole darned pack —— "

"Hold, sir. Did you or did you not take out this writ against my body with a view to compel Miss Lee to marry you?"

"How's that?" muttered Weeks, affecting not to understand the question.

"Answer me, yes or no," said the light-keeper; "I have no time to spare."

"Look here, friend; I ain't a-goin to be catechised this fashion."

"Catechised — by all the gods in Olympus, I'll catechise you, my fine fellow, and the right way, too. Your villany's discovered at last, sir. Else Curley has revealed to me all your plots and schemes."

"Well, but you needn't get into such a fuss about it, my dear man," responded Weeks, quite coolly; "if you ain't disposed to let me have the girl, why don't, that's all; but you've got to pay the face of the notes, or go to jail —— "

"Scoundrel, let *you* have the girl!"

"Ain't I good enough for her?"

"You!"

"Why, yes. I'm an American born — good enough, I

reckon, for the best Irish girl ever stood in shoe leather — all-fired proud as they are."

"And why didn't you ask her like a man, if you thought so ? No, you hadn't the courage, sir. Your meanness of soul wouldn't let you. You preferred to scheme and plot with Else Curley, and to sneak about my house day after day like a hungry spaniel. By George, if I suspected what brought you there when you first came, I'd have flung you neck and heels into the Devil's Gulch. What! because I'm poor, you tried to compel my niece to marry you through fear of my incarceration. Begone, sir ! let me never see you within a league of the lighthouse again, or if you do, I'll horsewhip you as I would a dog."

"Say, don't get into such a fury about it."

"Fury !" repeated the light-keeper, buttoning up his coat, and darting a look at the crest-fallen Yankee so full of contempt that the latter cowered under it. "Paugh, sir," he added, "you're beneath my scorn. Had you the slightest pretension to the character of a gentleman, I should have compelled you before I left this room to apologize for the insult you offered — but coxcomb and a coward as you are, I let you pass."

"Coward ! guess you're mistaken — ain't you?" replied Weeks, shoving his hands down into his breeches pockets, and hitching up his shoulders.

"You're a disgrace, sir, to the name of America," continued the light-keeper, without noticing the reply. "Your country is a noble country, sir ; your heroes of the revolution rank among the first soldiers of the world; your orators and statesmen have already eclipsed some of the first celebrities of Europe; your people, in the main, are a high-minded, generous people ; but you, sir, and such sneaking rascals as you, with your godless liberalism, and your national vanity, are enough to bring your country into contempt wherever you go. I have loved America ever since I was able to lisp the name; but if you be a fair specimen of your countrymen, I would rather be a dog than an American. If you're a Yankee, the New Englanders must have sadly degenerated since the revolution. Go, go!"

"Well," said Weeks, "can't say as to that; but I rather guess they're a leetle ahead of the Irish yet."

"Yes; you and such as you, in vending hickory hams and wooden nutmegs, may be somewhat smarter, I suppose. But smartness, without either honor or principle, is a poor recommendation. Go home, sir, go home again, and tell your countrymen, — that class of them at least to which you belong, — that hucksters and speculators are less respected here in Europe for their smartness than despised for their love of gold. Tell them you failed in your own speculation in matrimony, because you relied too much on your low cunning, and valued too lightly the character of the people on whose simplicity you came to practise. Tell them you saw in Ireland a poor man proud — bankrupt in every thing but honor — who, reduced to beggary and a jail, would rather see his child mated with the poorest peasant on his native hills, than give her to a peddling, speculating foreigner, with a hundred thousand dollars at his banker's. There, sir," he added, flinging the letter in Weeks's face, "take back your vile proposal, and begone. I came with a brace of pistols here in my breast, to demand the satisfaction due from one gentleman to another; but you're too contemptible a scoundrel to smell an honest man's powder;" and so saying, the light-keeper flung on his slouched hat and left the room.

Weeks stood full three minutes gazing at the door through which the light-keeper passed, without moving a muscle — his hands, as usual, thrust into his pockets. He seemed completely confounded at what had taken place. "Well, there," he ejaculated at length, throwing himself down in an arm chair and taking out his penknife to whittle a small mahogany rule that lay beside him on the table, apparently without the least consciousness of what he was doing, — " there, that's the end of it, I reckon.   Humph! well, Mr. Charles B. Bigelow, or rather I should say, Mr. Ephraim C. B. Weeks — since that's the name you have chosen for the present — I think you ought to feel kinder cheap — eh! four hundred dollars lost for spells and charms — that is, considering the sort of bills they were — not to speak of what the note cost me — and fooled into the bargain.   Go it, go it, my boy, — that's the way to make a fortune out of the ignorant Irish.   Well, I'm in a fix, that's a fact — a tarnation ugly fix, too.   O Else Curley, out of h—ll there's no such woman as you.   I reckoned I was pretty smart myself, but I guess you're a leetle mite smarter. Humph! of some twenty love-letters, the girl has received but one, and that the very one I mailed myself at the post office.   And there's that darned cabin boy — only for him I might get along slick enough yet; for come to get the light-keeper into jail, Cousin Robert and I could manage to carry off the girl somehow.   But the boy, if he recover, will reveal all, and then the whole secret is blown.   Sambo says he'll go down to the lighthouse to-night and demand the young scamp — and Cousin Robert promises to send a constable with him to enforce his right of guardianship — but should he blab the secret before they reach him, I must put for Ducksville right straight off.   As it is, I'm cornered up rather close to feel comfortable.   O, Ireland, Ireland — could I once get off with this girl under my arm, I should advise every stranger that values his life to keep clear of you a day's sailing at least."

CHAPTER XXII.

Else and Mary. — The Solitary and her Foster-child.

THE reader will recollect that when Kate Petersham parted with Mary Lee at the steps, the latter looked somewhat alarmed at the serious tone in which her light-hearted friend begged her to remember Randall Barry that night in her prayers. She made an effort, in fact, to detain Kate for an explanation; but Kate eluded her grasp, and bounded down the steps, the moment she uttered the words, with the fleetness and agility of a fairy.

On her return to the sick room, the agitated girl found Else seated on a low stool beside the little cabin boy's bed, knitting her stocking.

"What ails ye, dear?" said the latter, with a tenderness of look and tone she seldom betrayed even to her favorite. "What ails ye, Mary? yer so pale."

"Pale! am I pale?"

"Yer as pale as a ghost, dear — what's the matther?"

"Nothing. But come to my room — I have something to ask you. We mustn't disturb our little patient, you know. How is he now, Else?"

"Better."

"You're sure?"

"Sure as can be, dear — he's recoverin fast. He got the cool [crisis] this morning, an his pult's quieter now."

"Thank God," exclaimed the grateful girl, with all the fervor of her pure loving heart. "O, I knew well the Blessed Virgin wouldn't forget him. Her intercession has saved him.

24 *

Poor little fellow, he'll see home and friends once more.
Won't he, Else?"

"Hope so."

"But, Else!"

"What?"

"You have a secret for me."

"A secret?"

"Yes; I saw it in Miss Petersham's face, and I see it
now in your's. You needn't try to keep it from me, Else.
Randall Barry's arrested."

"Randall Barry! Why, what in the world, dear, put that
in your head?"

"Else, you needn't try to deceive me. I know well he's
taken."

"And what if he is asthore," said Else, smoothing down
the dishevelled tresses of her lovely *protegée* with her hard
bony fingers, whilst the muscles of her own face twitched with
emotion — what if he is? sure it's only for a day or two.
He'll soon be free again."

"Had I only taken my dear uncle's advice, and told him
never to come again, this had never happened."

"And didn't ye tell him that a hundred times?"

"Yes; I told him often how my uncle loved me, and how
it would break his heart if I leave him — and how little I knew
of the world, and how poor a companion I would make for one
like him. I told him all this many and many a time, Else,
and begged him to return home to the south, and wait for
better and happier days — but he knew my heart belied
my words."

"God love yer innocent heart," exclaimed Else, while her
old eyes filled with tears; "God love ye, dear; yer too good
for this world."

"Had I only prayed fervently to God for strength," continued Mary, "I might have overcome my weakness. But

alas! Else, I'm so selfish; I was thinking only of his love for me all the time, when I should have thought of nothing but his safety. And he's now a prisoner on my account, with shackles on his limbs, and the doom of the rebel before him. O, if I had only parted with him forever the last time he clambered up these rocks to see me."

"And if ye had," said Else, "ye'd have nothin for it. Ye were both intended for one another, and for that raison ye niver cud part him. So take heart now, and all 'll be well yit."

"O Randall Barry, Randall Barry! so brave — so faithful — so true to his country and to me!" cried the distressed girl. "Else, Else, could I see him free once more, were it only for an instant, I would bid him farewell forever, should my heartstrings break in the parting."

There was a sense of desolation in the words or the tones of Mary's voice that touched the old woman deeply. But when the former spoke of her heart breaking, the very idea seemed to call back again into life the better and holier feelings of her nature, and unable to control any longer the emotion that agitated her soul, the old woman flung her arms around the neck of her foster-child, and wept over her like a mother.

"God forbid! God forbid! asthore machree," she cried, "God forbid yer heart 'd break. Darlin! darlin! why shud it ever break? for it's little this world can spare a heart like yours. O angel! ye don't know what yer heart is, or what yer pure innecint soul is worth to a sinful earth like this. It's little ye know, dear, what ye are. Modest, wee crather, yer as simple and bashful as the daizy that grows undher the green fern by the mountain strame; no one sees ye, no one knows ye, no one thinks of ye down here in the black bins of Araheera — but I know ye, *asthore*, I know what yer heart is; och, och, it's I that does, ivery pulse of it. And why shudn't I,

Mary, darlin? wasn't it these withered hands tore ye from yer dead mother's arms, here among the rocks; wasn't it me nursed ye on ould Nannie's milk, and rocked ye in yer cradle up there in my poor cabin on the Cairn. I know what the valie of your heart is, *alanna.* An to spake of it brakin for Randall Barry, or sufferin one minute's pain — niver, niver," she exclaimed, suddenly rising, "niver, Mary, while I'm livin and able to prevent it."

The change in Else's look and tone was quick as thought. For a moment her heart had softened under the mesmeric touch of the angelic being she embraced. But it was only for a moment. Again the dark shadow came rushing back upon her soul, and again the relaxed muscles of her face resumed their usual hard and stern expression.

"Let me pass, girl," she cried; "I have work to do."

"What work?"

"No matter — let me pass."

"Else, your countenance terrifies me. O, I know that dark, awful temptation is upon you again."

"Away, child; take your hands off my cloak — I must be gone."

"What's your purpose, Else?"

"Purpose! I niver had but one purpose for thirty years, and the time is come now to execute it."

"You shan't leave *me*," said Mary, kneeling; "you shan't leave *me*, Else, till you promise to do no harm to Robert Hardwrinkle or his family."

The old woman folded her arms on her brown, half-naked breast, and looked down on the face of her foster-child.

"Mary Lee," she said, — her voice husky with the passion she strove in vain to conceal, — "Mary Lee, yer tears balked me of my vengeance twiste before — take care they don't a third time, for I swear by —— "

"Hush! hush! Else," interrupted her fair *protegée*, holding up the crucifix that hung suspended from her neck, and laying her forefinger on the lips of the figure. "Hush! these lips never spoke but to bless."

"Take it away, girl; take it away," cried Else, averting her eyes from the image, as if she feared to look upon it lest her courage should fail; "take it away, and listen to me. I'm bound by a vow made at the siege of Madeira, by the side of my dead husban, niver to forget what Lieutenant Richard Barry did for me that day. Randall Barry is that man's grandson, and he now lies a prisiner in Tamny barracks through the threachery of Robert Hardwrinkle. The time is come to fulfil my promise, and I'll do it; I'll save Randall Barry, should I lose body and soul in the attempt."

"Else, Else, this is impious," said Mary; "remember there's a God above you."

"Paugh!" ejaculated the old woman; "I knew no God these thirty years;" and as she spoke she wrested Mary's hands from her cloak, and caught the handle of the door. "Let the villain luck to himself now," she cried — "let him and them that brought my only sister to shame and an early grave, — that driv my brother from his father's hearthstone to die among the strangers, — that hunted myself like the brock through the crags iv Benraven — hah — let them luck to themselves now, for as Heaven hears me, if Randall Barry's not a free man in four and twenty hours, their roof tree smokes for it."

"Else, stop for a moment."

"Away, girl!"

"Else, Else," entreated Mary, again attempting to detain her. "Would you commit murder — deliberate murder?"

"Murdher! is it murdher to burn a nest of vipers?"

"Else, think for a moment. You have an immortal soul to be saved."

"Me! I have no soul. I lost it thirty years ago — let me pass."

"Listen to me."

"No, no, no; I listened to you too long — away!"

"Grant me but one favor. It may be the last I shall ever ask — for I fear, Else, we must soon fly from this place, and then I can never hope to see you more. Grant me but one favor."

"What's that — mercy to the Hardwrinkles?"

"No, dear Else, but mercy to yourself — to your own soul, dearer to me than the wealth of worlds. Here," she continued, throwing her rosary over Else's neck, "tell these beads to-night before you sleep, and as you pray, fix your eyes on the crucifix."

"Stop, stop!" exclaimed the old woman, her face flushed with passion, while the hood of her cloak falling back on her shoulders and revealing her gray elf locks, gave her the look of a maniac. "Stop!" she ejaculated, repulsing the pious and affectionate girl — "stop! I can't touch this blissid thing. Eh, what? God of heaven! what's this?"

"The image of Christ," responded Mary, "whose life was one continuous act of love. Look at those arms extended to bless and forgive the whole world, and tell me, can you behold the image of that dying Saviour, and yet feel so hard-hearted as to take the life of your fellow-creature?"

"Whisht, girl, whisht," said Else, sinking back on a chair, as if her emotions had completely overpowered her; "whisht! and tell me whose rosary is this?"

"Father John's — he lent it to me when I lost my mother's."

"Good God!" exclaimed the afflicted woman, covering her face with her hands, "this rosary was once mine."

"Yours!"

"Ay, ay; I brought it with me from the West Indees, and giv it to ould priest Gallaher of Gortnaglen, Father John's uncle. Augh, hoch, it lucks ould and worn now like myself;" and the unfortunate woman burst into tears.

"I wish it had grown old and worn in your own hands, Else, dear," said Mary, sitting beside her, and pushing back the gray hairs from her wrinkled forehead. "I wish it had, Else, for then your long life had been better and happier."

"May be so."

"How consoling, to reflect, in your old days, you had served God faithfully!"

"It's useless to think of that now, *alanna*; I'm lost."

"Lost! O, God forbid. Only forgive your enemies, and God will forgive you. Think how he forgave the Jews who put him to death; think how he forgave Magdalen and the penitent thief."

"Child," said Else, with a smile that made Mary shudder — it expressed so plainly the depth of her despair; "child, you speak only of sinners, but I'm a devil."

"No, no, don't smile and speak to me so; you are not, you are not," cried Mary, clinging to her old nurse's neck; "you never could love as you loved me, and be so wicked. O, never speak those awful words again, Else; they terrify me. No, no, you are not so wicked. You are not lost; the friend of the poor orphan can never be lost."

As Mary was yet speaking, a knock came, and Roger O'Shaughnessy presented himself at the door. He had been engaged, it would seem, burnishing up the old silver salver, for he held the precious relic under his arm, and had pushed the chamois leather, with which he had been rubbing it, into the breast pocket of his old bottle-green coat.

"What now, Roger? Has Mr. Lee returned?"

"Not yet, plaze your ladyship," replied Roger, bowing respectfully. "O, it's only Else Curley," he added, correcting himself; "I thought you had company. No, he's not come back yet; and I wish he was, for there's strangers approachin, and not as much as a bit or a sup in the house fit to offer them. I wish to goodness they'd stay at home. I declare I don't know what they want down here, the half o' them."

"Never mind, Roger; receive them at the door, and show them in."

"Indeed, then, I won't, plaze yer ladyship," replied Roger; "they'll have to find the way themselves; and if they're any of the master's acquaintances, you know, they'll not expect any thing, 'hem! if you only hint, ahem! that the butler's not at home."

"Very well, Roger; do as you please."

"And now," said Mary, turning to Else; "you promise to tell these beads to-night under the invocation of the Blessed Virgin.   Do you promise?"

"Ay, ay, ay, I'll say them to plaze ye," replied Else; "but it's of little valie they'll be, for I haven't bent a knee to God since afore you were born."

"No matter.   God is merciful.   He has converted worse hearts than yours.   Offer your prayers to-night, Else, and who knows but the old rosary, once so familiar to your touch, with God's good grace, may awaken those better and nobler feelings which so long have lain dormant in your heart."

"God be with ye, child," said Else, tenderly kissing the forehead of the gentle girl.   "God be with you, *asthore*.   I tould ye my intintion, that ye'd know what happened me, if the worst comes to the worst."

"I have no fear of that, dear nurse; there's still a bright spot in your soul to redeem it from the sins that cloud it, were they as numerous as the sands of Araheera.   Go, and remember your promise."

"Ay, ay, I'll remember it;" and so saying, the old solitary of Benraven wrapped her gray cloak about her shoulders, and passed from the room.

After paying a visit to the little cabin boy, and finding him still asleep, but apparently much easier, Mary approached a window that looked out upon the iron bridge, and the narrow road leading to the village of Araheera.   She expected to see the strangers, whom Roger had announced, coming down the hill; but they had already passed the gate, and entered the lighthouse yard. Else Curley's tall form was the only object she could see, hurrying back to the cairn, accompanied by Nannie, who had waited for her, as usual, outside, and now went bleating and trotting after her.

CHAPTER XXIII.

Lanty takes the Loan of Miss Hardwrinkle, and carries her off on a Pillion. — Else feels certain she has discovered a Clew to the Mystery.

WHEN Else reached the Cairn, she was somewhat surprised to find the door of her cabin forced open, and the scanty furniture it contained tossed here and there, as if somebody had been searching the house. Lighting a rush candle without further delay, and inserting it in the wooden candlestick attached to her spinning wheel, she threw off her gray cloak, and took a hasty survey of the room. Her first glance was at the hearthstone under which Randall Barry had so mysteriously disappeared, when Nannie's bleat announced the presence of Hardwrinkle's detectives; the second, at the cupboard, concealed in the thickness of the wall, from which she furnished the widgeon and wine to her young friend before setting out on his perilous journey to Arranmore. Both, however, had escaped discovery; at least, there was no visible mark of their having been suspected or examined. Satisfied, apparently, with these observations, Else drew over her creepie-stool, and sat down to build a fire for the night. Hardly had she touched the tongs, however, for that purpose, when a piece of closely folded paper fell from them on the ashes.

25

" Humph!" ejaculated the old woman, picking it up; "what can this be? From Lanty, I'll warrint; it's like his contrivin, to put it in the joint o' the tongs;" and hitching over the creepie nearer to the wheel, she brought the piece *f* crumpled paper close to the dim light, and read as follows :—

" Och, thin, sweet, bad luck to ye, my ould darlint; isn't this the purty pickle ye got me into? The hole country's out afther me, and here I am waitin for ye this half hour, with Miss Hardwrinkle sighin and sobbin on the pillion at yer doore. Upon my conscience it's hung ye ought to be, to thrate me this way afther all the promises ye made to stay at home. But *naboklish*, I'll be even with ye yit, Else, if I only live to get over the amplush I'm in. Of coorse I'm expectin to be shot every other minit, for the polis is afther me in all direcshins. As for the damsel herself, O *hierna!* mortial ears niver heerd the bate of her. Her schreechin brought out ivery livin soul atween here and Ballymagahey. She'd listen naither to rime or raison. I tried to soother her, but ye might as well try to soother a weazel. Bad scran to the haporth, she did but squeel and spit at me all the time. Thin I tried to raison with her. I tould her I hadn't the laste bad intintion in life, it bein only the loan of her I was takin in a dacent way, till a friend of mine got over his throuble. That made her worse. She wudn't even stop to listen to me. Bad luck to me, Else, if iver I met so onraisonable a female since the hour I was born. Atween scripthur and schreechin, she has nearly driven me out of my senses. Hould! whisht! there, by all that's bad, she's at it again as hard as ivir. O, Heaven forgive ye, Else Curley, for the throuble I'm in on your account this blissed day. But I can't stay another minit. I'm off again over the mountain; and remimber if any thing happens me, ye'll find her ladyship at Molshin Kelly's of Carlinmore. No more at present, but remain your obedient,   LANTY HANLON.

" Note bene. As ye valie yer life, keep close to Mary."

" Hegh!" ejaculated Else, throwing the paper on the ashes again. " Hegh! but I'm sorry I didn't get a hoult of ye, ye spawn of the sarpint. Hah, I'd tache ye a lesson ye'd remimber till the clay covered ye. Little ye thought who was watchin ye this mornin, when ye went to Ballymagahey with yer tracts. Little ye thought who the ould woman was that passed for the widow with the three twins — the poor, desarted crathur, that's dyin with the curse of herself and her dead husband on yer back. Hah! hah! Randall Barry, ye'll not have so many constables to guard ye the morrow, while such a high-bred dame as Rebecca Hardwrinkle's to be sought and found. Ay, Robert, ye'll want more peelers than ye can spare, to guard your prisoner, or I'm far out of my reckonin. Devil as ye are, ye have yer match for wunst. And now do yer best, ye black-hearted villain; do yer best, and niver fear, ivery time you play the Knave I'll strike with the Five-fingers."

Else was here interrupted in her soliloquy by the approach of footsteps, and turning on her creepie, seemed somewhat surprised to see the tall but stooping form of Roger O'Shaughnessy entering the cabin.

" Humph! what now?" she demanded; " any thing wrong at the lighthouse, that yer here so soon?"

" No, nothin to speak off;" replied Roger, familiarly taking a seat, and stroking down the few gray hairs that remained, with the palms of his hands. " No, nothing in particular. Only the constables are there after Mr. Lee," responded Roger.

" Humph! so they're come at last, are they?"

" And so," continued Roger, " I thought, as they cudn't do much harm in the master's absence, I'd step up at my leisure to Mr. Guirkie's, and see if he'd buy this picthur. If it brings only a couple of pounds atself you know, we might lay in a dozen or two of chape wine — Cape Madeira or so, to keep up the credit of the place."

As the old man spoke, he drew from beneath his coat a small oil painting, and laid it on the table beside him.

"What is this?" exclaimed Else, looking at it for a moment. "Roger, it's her mother's portrait. You shan't sell it."

"I know ; but, ahem ! it's only a copy."

"Copy or not, ye can't sell it."

"We can't starve, either," said Roger, apologetically.

"Starve !"

"Of course, when there's nothing left."

"Hoot ! nonsense ! yer always complainin."

"Bedad, then, may be I've raison enough to complain, when the bacon's all gone, and not as much as the smell of wine or whiskey within the walls of the house. It's aisy for you to talk, Else ; but if ye had the credit o' the family to maintain, and nothin to maintain it with."

"Yer not so bad off as that, Roger, altogether, eh ? Have ye nothin at all left after the bacon ? "

"Nothin to speak of. There's some chickens, to be sure, but ―― "

"Some chickens. Is there no sheep ? "

"Ahem ! sheep ; well, ay, three weeny wethers, but there's not a bit on their bones. Surely three poor, weakly wethers is a small dependence through the long winter. As for the bits o' picthurs, the poor child could do nothing at them since that weary cabin boy came ; and, in troth, it went hard enough on me, Else, to see the young creature workin away, from mornin till night, unbeknown to her uncle, tryin to earn with her brush what'd buy little necessaries for the house, when she ought to be roulin in her coach, with her footman behind her. Och hoch ! Else, it's a poor day whin I'm driven to make lyin excuses to sich gentry as the Johnsons and Whatelys, in regard to the house. God be good to us, it's little I thought, forty years ago, when I ust to announce Lady Lambton, and Lord Hammersly, and Marquis ―― "

"Stop, Roger Shaughnessy ― stop yer claverin," interrupted Else, lighting her pipe ; "yer niver done braggin about yer lords and ladies."

"Ahem! braggin—bedad, it's no braggin, Else, but the truth, and not the whole o' that same aither, let me tell ye. Ahem! may be, when I ust to get seventeen pipes o' the best wine'——"

"Hoot! hould yer tongue. Here, take a draw o' this till I scrape up some supper. I have a journey afore me, and I can't delay a minute longer."

"Well, ye may think as ye plaze, Else," said Roger, taking the pipe from his venerable companion, "but they're changed times with us any way, when them that wanst thought a castle too small to resaive their company must now starve in a dissolit lighthouse. Ochone! ochone! the good ould times, when we ust to think nothin of fifty coaches of an evenin, drivin into the court-yard."

"Hoot! man, make it a hundher at wunst," said Else; "what signifies a score or two, in or over?"

"Well, may I niver do harm, Else——"

"Whist, *bedhahusht*, I say, I'm in no humor now to listen to such foolery. I ought to be on the road by this time;" and advancing to the cupboard, she drew down an oaten bannock from a shelf, and breaking it into several pieces, consigned it to her pocket. Then bringing the silver-mounted pistol she was in the habit of carrying on her journeys, close to the light, she examined the priming, and finding it satisfactory, thrust it into her bosom. "There," she ejaculated, "yer aisy carried any way; and who knows but ye may be of sarvice afore Randall Barry gets clear of his blood-hounds?"

"Where are ye bound for, Else," inquired Roger, "with that waipon about ye?"

"That's my business."

"Yer not bent on murdher, I hope."

"Not if I can help it."

"Bedad, then," said Roger, "I wudn't trust ye if ye got into one of her tantrums. Ahem! yer a dangerous woman, Else, when yer vexed, or, as the ould sayin is, yer a good

25 *

friend, but a bad inimy. But, Else, cudn't ye lend us a thrifle o' that money ye got from the Yankee? Ahem! I'd pay it back at the end o' the quarter."

"Not a farthin, Roger. I'm keepin that for another purpose."

"Well, it's not much I'm askin," said Roger; "only just the price of a dozen o' wine, and a cheese or two, for the credit o' the house."

"Let the house take care of itself," responded Else, throwing the gray cloak again upon her emaciated shoulders. "I'll have good use for the money afore long, Roger. As to buy cheese with it, or wine aither, I'm afeerd it'd be more likely to buy a rope to hang me for passin it. Ay, ay, Roger, ye'll hear news about that money yet, or I'm greatly mistaken."

"Ahem! yer in a mighty hurry, Else; wait till I get the picthur under my coat. Ahem! as for a dhrop of any thing, I suppose it's not convanient."

"Humph! a dhrop of any thing. I thought it'd come to that at last;" and again opening the cupboard, she drew forth a bottle, and held it for an instant between her and the light. "Ay, there's some left," she added, laying it on the table. "Drink it, and let me go."

Roger raised the bottle also, and seeing it nearly full, laid it down again. "Ahem! ahem!" said he, stroking down his long gray hairs, and looking wistfully at his companion. "Ahem! it's a liberty I take, Else, but if ye have no objection, I'll carry it home with me."

"Carry it home?"

"Yes. Ahem! Captain Petersham and the Johnsons 'll be down to-morrow, and there's not a dhrop to offer them."

"Take it, then — take it, and away with ye. I ought to be in Crohan by this time."

"Ye might had company," observed Roger, carefully corking the bottle and dropping it into his capacious pocket. "Ye might had company if ye only left sooner."

"I want none; the dark night's all the company I seek."

"Well, that blackamore came down with a constable, just afore I left the lighthouse, and took away the boy."

"What, took the boy away in the state he's in?"

"Troth did they, and without as much as sayin by yer lave atself. The constable had a writ with him signed by Mr. Hardwrinkle."

"Hah, the villain," exclaimed Else; "that's more of his plottin. Was the boy willin to go?"

"Willin — ye might well say that. The minute he saw the blackamore, he all but jumped out o' bed with joy, and the poor blackamore himself kissed and hugged the little fellow till I thought he'd niver let him go. Bedad, I niver thought them naigers had so much good nature in them afore."

"And so he had a writ from Robert Hardwrinkle," muttered Else, reflectively. "Ay, ay, that was the Yankee's doings, I suspect. Humph, I'm beginnin to think, from what Mrs. Motherly tould me about the nigger, when he first got a glimpse of Weeks, they must be ould acquaintances, and may be he thought the boy'd tell tales when he recovered his senses. Hah, hah, Robert! I'm on yer track again. So the boy's gone."

"Ay, i' he; and mighty well plazed I am at that same, in regard to Miss Mary, for the crathur cudn't do a hand's turn while he staid — but hould," said Roger, suddenly checking himself, "hould; I'll wager what ye plaze he tuck the rosary with him."

"What rosary?" demanded Else.

"Why, Mary's mother's — Mrs. Talbot's; and I declare I niver thought of it till this minute."

"The one with the jewels?"

"Ay. She forgot all about it, I suppose."

"Forgot what?"

"That she lent it to him."

"She never lent it; she hadn't it to lend since the day

the Yankee first came to the lighthouse. She mislaid it somewhere that day, and niver could find hilt or hare of it since. Hoot! ye're dhramin, Roger."

"Dramin — bedad, then, it was a mighty quare drame, when I saw it with my own eyes, and handled it with my own fingers."

"Her mother's rosary?"

"To be sure. How could I mistake it? Didn't I see it a hundred times, when we — ahem! when we lived at the castle? Bedad, Else, it's not a thing to be aisy mistaken about, for there's not the like of it in the whole world; but one, and that same's many a thousand mile from here — if it's in bein at all."

"Ye mane Mr. Talbot's?"

"Of coorse. They were both as like as two eggs, and presents from the Duchess of Orleans to Edward's father and mother, when they went to France long ago."

"Ay," said Else, resuming her seat, and looking up sharply in Roger's face, as if she feared his mind was wandering, — "ay, ' as like as two eggs.' And where did the boy keep the rosary? for it's strange I never could see it about him, though with him late and early."

"Well, ahem!" said Roger, "I must tell ye that, Else, since ye ask me. Ahem! one day last week, as Lanty was going to Rosnakill, I wanted him to bring me a bottle o' wine; for feen a dhrop was in the house, and we expected company that evenin. Well, it happened Mr. Lee had no money convanient; and naither had Lanty himself, nor Mary; and I didn't know what in the world to do in the amplush I was in, for as luck 'd have it, the brandy was out as well as the wine, and not a taste of any thing in the house but a thrifle o' whiskey in the bottom o' the decanter. So, thinks I to myself, since I can do no better, I'll, ahem! I'll try — may be the cabin boy might happen to have some change in his pockets, and I'll borrow it till he gets well."

"So ye searched his pockets?"

"I did," replied Roger; "ahem! It wasn't right, I suppose; but seein the pinch I was in, I couldn't very well help it."

"And found the rosary?"

"Yes; sewed in the linins of his waistcoat pocket. I thought first from the hard feel it might be gold pieces, and I ripped it open."

"Sewed in the linins of his waistcoat?" repeated Else, pronouncing the words slowly, and gazing vacantly at her companion as she spoke.

"Ay, she sewed it in herself, I suppose; thinkin the blissed crucifix might help him in his sickness."

"Roger Shaughnessy," said the old woman, suddenly rising, after a long pause, during which she kept her eyes unconsciously fixed on him, — "Roger Shaughnessy, can you swear on the holy evangelist, you seen that rosary in the boy's possession?"

"Swear! Of coorse I can. Why, is there any thing strange in that? Ye seem to be all of a flutther about it."

"No matter — I have my own manin for it. Now go you back to the lighthouse, and stay with Mary; she's all alone, and needs yer company. I must hurry as fast as I can to Castle Gregory, and then back to Crohan."

"The Lord be about us!" exclaimed Roger, as he stood looking at the receding form of the old woman descending the hill. "What does she mane now? There, she's off to Castle Gregory this hour of the night, and thinks no more of it than a girl would of sixteen. Ahem!" he added, buttoning his coat over the picture, and moving off towards the lighthouse; "she's a wondherful woman."

CHAPTER XXIV.

Uncle Jerry and Mrs. Motherly quarrel, and the Captain suggests a Means of Reconciliation.

"UPON my word, it's very strange," said Mr. Guirkie to Father Brennan, as the latter entered the breakfast parlor at Greenmount to make his usual morning visit; "I declare it is exceedingly strange."

"What's the matter now? any thing new since last night?" inquired the priest.

"No; but that abduction of Miss Hardwrinkle — Mrs. Motherly has just returned from the post office, and says there are no tidings of her yet. What in the world could the fellow mean by carrying her off?"

"You'll soon find that out, I suspect. Lanty seldom plays a trick without an object."

"You think Lanty's the man, then, without doubt?"

"Certainly — no other would attempt it;" and the priest picked up a newspaper, and familiarly took a seat at the window.

"Why, God bless me, if Robert Hardwrinkle gets hold of the unfortunate fellow, he'll transport him," said Uncle Jerry, pacing the room uneasily, and bobbing the tail of his morning gown up and down as usual. "He certainly will transport him — eh?"

"Never mind. Lanty can take care of himself. With all his recklessness he manages to keep clear of the hangman. Ten chances to one, if caught with the lady in his custody, he would make it appear he was only taking her home."

"Just so. I wouldn't doubt it in the least," assented Uncle Jerry; "the fellow's capable of doing any thing. In fact he has imposed on myself a hundred times. No later than last week the rogue sold me hare's ear and crottle, not worth a brass farthing —— "

"Ha, ha!" laughed the priest, "you're beginning to find him out at last."

"Well, but after all, the villain has something in him one can't help liking. He's full of tricks, to be sure, but still he's honest in his own way. I wish to Heaven he was out of the county for a while, at all events; for if he stay here that serpent will destroy him."

"Who? Robert Hardwrinkle?"

"Yes; he'll follow him like a blood-hound. But, by the by, I had almost forgotten. What of your young friend Barry? Will he be committed?"

"I fear it. Captain Petersham says he can't help committing him. The case is so clear there's no possibility of getting over it."

"Poor fellow! I'm sorry for him, and I'm very sorry on Mary Lee's account. Can nothing be done to save him — eh?"

"Nothing — the sergeant of police here — Mullen, who is really a very honest, decent fellow — says he must identify him."

"They say he's a fine young man, this Barry."

"Very much so, indeed. He's as handsome and high-minded a lad as ye could meet with any where. But like all young men in love, he is very imprudent. So much so indeed, that I often think he must have been crazy to act as he has. The idea of his running the gantlet through all the constables and spies between here and Cork, with a reward of five hundred pounds for his head, merely to see a foolish young girl, is so provoking to all who feel an interest in his welfare, that —— "

"Hush, hush! Father John! nonsense! say no more about that. Love's a thing you're not competent to speak of, you know. It's out of your line altogether. So far from think-

ing the less of him for his imprudence, I think the more of
him.   But apropos of the Lees," he added, throwing up his
spectacles and halting before the priest; "have you found out
who they are, or what they are?"

"No, sir; so far as regards their family connections, I know
no more about them than you know yourself."

"I declare!   It's very strange.   I can find no one to give
me the least information respecting the family. .I tried once
to draw something from Kate Petersham, she's so intimate
there; but the young baggage was as close as an oyster.   As
for Roger, I darn't venture to approach the subject, lest he
take alarm; and then he would never come to sell me a picture again.   But have you no conception of what the mystery is?   It can't be murder, I suppose."

"O, no! nothing of that nature.   It means, I suppose, that
Mr. Lee got embarrassed in his money affairs, and left home
for a time to avoid his creditors — that's all, I suspect."

"Poor fellow," said Uncle Jerry; "it's a pity of him."

"It is indeed a great pity; for he's an honorable, generous-
hearted man as I've met in many a year."

"God comfort him," ejaculated Uncle Jerry again, twirling
his thumbs as he looked through the window.   "O, dear! O,
dear — what a poor sight, to see a high-minded, well-bred
gentleman like him reduced so low — so low as to trim oil
lamps for a living!"

"It's hard."

"Hard!   Why, only think of it.   Here am I, a miserable,
good-for-nothing old imbecile, without kith or kin in the
world, and yet plenty of money in my purse, and a comfortable house to live in, whilst down there in the black binns of
Araheera there's a gentleman of birth and education, with an
angel of a child to take care of, and not a shilling in his
pocket to buy the common necessaries of life.   I declare it's
awful."

"The ways of God are wonderful."

"Wonderful? I tell you what, Father Brennan, one must be well fortified by religion to bear up against it. A beautiful girl like Mary Lee, pining away in poverty and solitude, working, working, night and day, night and day, at her easel to earn a morsel of bread, and I a worn-out old fellow, doing nothing, nay, occupying some useful body's place in the world, when I should have been kicked out of it long ago. Why, sir, it's outrageous to think of it. It's actually outrageous."

"Stop, stop — take care, Mr. Guirkie," said the priest, "you talk too fast."

"Sir, it would provoke any man. I say if Aristotle were a saint, it would provoke him;" and Uncle Jerry rose and pushed back the chair violently.

"But this is taking God Almighty to task, Mr. Guirkie. You should remember he orders every thing for the best, and that inscrutable are his judgments, and unsearchable his ways."

"I know that. I know God is good, and I know all that seems strange to us now will be fully explained hereafter, of course. Why, if I didn't believe that, I wouldn't put up with it half the time."

"Ha, ha!" laughed the priest — "put up with it? You haven't much to put up with, I should think?"

"No matter for that; I have my own feelings, and you know very well, Father John ——" Here Mr. Guirkie was interrupted by the entrance of Mrs. Motherly.

"Humph! may I beg to know, ma'am," said he, turning half round and looking angrily at his respectable house-keeper, — "may I beg to know why we are interrupted?"

"It's no offence, I hope, to come with a message," said Mrs. Motherly, deprecatingly. "I niver thought it was."

"Didn't you? It's no matter what you thought."

"Don't be unkind to the good woman," said Father John, who understood Mr. Guirkie well, and knew all his little

26

weaknesses respecting Mrs. Motherly. "Don't be unkind to her, Mr. Guirkie. She is a very excellent woman, is Mrs. Motherly."

"Humph—good enough, if she only knew her place. But I protest against her inveterate habit of interrupting me when I have company. I shan't tolerate it, sir, any longer."

"Just listen to that, Father John, when he knows in his heart and soul it's his own story he's tellin."

"My own story, woman?"

"Yes, sir; jest yer own story. For ye niver have company in the house but ye thrate me this way. There's no livin with ye, when there's any body to the fore."

"And how is it when he's alone?"

"He's as quiet as a lamb, your reverence."

"It's false," said Mr. Guirkie; "I say it's false."

"False! O, the Lord pardon ye, sir, the Lord pardon ye, for beliein yerself; for I'd take it to my death, Father Brennan, there's not a quieter nor a kinder man livin, when he's by himself."

"Indeed!" said the priest, emphasizing the word, and looking significantly at Mr. Guirkie. "Ho! ho! that's the way of it!"

"Pray what do you mean, Mr. Brennan?" demanded Uncle Jerry.

"O, nothing, nothing particular. I was merely thinking of what Captain Petersham says of you and Mrs. Motherly."

"Of me and Mrs. Motherly?" repeated Uncle Jerry.

"Of me and Mr. Guirkie?" echoed Mrs. Motherly. "What could he say of me, yer reverence? I defy him to say any thing of me but what's dacent."

"Of course you do, Mrs. Motherly. You have always been, since you came to reside in my parish, an honest, respectable woman. Captain Petersham, when he spoke of you and Mr. Guirkie, never pretended to insinuate ——"

"O, I dar him to it," exclaimed the good woman; "I dar

him to it; and he'll be here face to face afore many minutes, for the message I came with was from his groom that he'd call here on his return from the barracks. I'll dar him to say any thing against my karacter. Och, och, it'd be a poor day with me to hear my name now in the mouth of the people, after livin fourteen long years a widow, without man or mortal ever presuming to throw dirt at my door. *Hierna!* the Lord be about us — to spake of Mr. Guirkie and me in the same bieath!"

"My good woman," said the priest, rising from his chair and approaching her, "you take this quite too seriously."

"Well, listen to me, yer reverence, for a minute."

"No, no, not now — some other time — it's all a joke, you know."

"Joke! but I'll let neither man or woman joke with my karacter, Father Brennan. I'll not lie under it, sir. Mr. Guirkie's a good man, sir, and a dacent man, and has the good will of rich and poor; but may I niver cross that flure again, if he had the vartues of all the saints in the collinder, and all the gold in the Bank of England to boot, if I'd ever as much as think of him, barrin as I ought to do, and as it becomes my place to do. I know he's kind to me, sir, and very kind to me ——"

"Quit the room, ma'am," commanded Uncle Jerry; "quit the room instantly;" and snatching the spectacles from his face, he motioned with them to the door. "Kind to you, indeed! I command you to quit the room."

"And yer house, too," replied Mrs. Motherly, raising her apron to her eyes. "O, dear, O, dear! isn't it a poor thing that an ould woman like me can't button her master's leggins, or tie his cravat, but he'll suspect her of thinking of what she never dreamt of?"

"I suspect you!"

"Ay, just you, Mr. Guirkie; for I believe in my heart no one else could ever make up such a story. I don't deny that

I liked ye for a master in spite of all yer odd ways, and that I tried to take care of you, when I seen ye couldn't take care of yourself; but it's little I thought ye'd conster my kindness in the way ye did."

"Listen," said Uncle Jerry, running his hands under his skirts, and bending towards his housekeeper; "may I beg to be informed whether I am master in this house; and if so, why you don't quit the room when I command you."

"As for this cruel thratement, after so many years slavin and workin for ye, night and day," continued the weeping widow, without paying the least attention to her master's request, "I forgive ye for it. I do, indeed, forgive ye from my heart and soul."

"You're resolved, then, not to quit the room; eh, have you actually made up your mind *not* to leave?"

"Och, hoch! ye'd be dead in yer grave many a year ago, Mr. Guirkie, only for the way I watched ye; for, yer reverence, ye know yourself, the poor man has no more wit nor a child —— "

"Humph! I see *you* won't go, Mrs. Motherly. Very well, then," said Uncle Jerry; "I shall. Let me pass."

As he rushed through the entrance hall, his slippers clattering against his heels, and his spectacles swinging from his fingers, the hall door opened, and Captain Petersham entered whip in hand.

"Soh, ho! what now?"

"Good morning, sir," responded Uncle Jerry, bowing stiffly.

"You're excited, Mr. Guirkie, eh? What's the matter?"

"Excited! can't I get excited in my own house, if I please, Captain Petersham, without being obliged to account for it?"

"Undoubtedly, sir, most undoubtedly. Why not?"

"That is," said Uncle Jerry, correcting himself, "that is, if I'm *master* of the house; but it seems I am not. My housekeeper, Mrs. Motherly, there, is master;" and he glanced back at the parlor door.

"Ho, ho! it's only a lovers' quarrel, then.   Come, come, Mr. Guirkie, you musn't get angry with Mrs. Motherly; if the good woman grows jealous of you now and then, you must try to conciliate her, you know, the best way you can."

"Captain Petersham, your language is offensive," said Uncle Jerry, "and I shan't put up with it any longer."

"And, Captain Petersham, you must clear my karacter this very minute," sobbed Mrs. Motherly, coming up from the parlor with her apron to her eyes, followed by Father John. "I'm a lone woman, sir, and have nothing but my karacter to depend on."

"By the Lord Harry," exclaimed the captain, looking from one to the other, "here's a pretty piece of work.   Ho, ho! and Father Brennan, too.   By George, sir, you're the very man.   You can settle the whole affair in a jiffy."

"How so?"

"Why, marry them at once, sir.   Marry them instantly. Nothing else will ever put a stop to their love quarrels."

Mr. Guirkie, on hearing this, could contain himself no longer.   "Captain Petersham," he cried, "I shall not ask you to quit my house, for nobody ever did quit it yet at my request, and nobody ever will, I suppose; but, sir, I'll leave you and your friends to occupy the premises.   For my part, I leave this neighborhood to-morrow, and seek for some place where I can live in peace."

"Mr. Guirkie, are you mad?" said Father John, stopping him as he turned the handle of the hall door.

"Gentlemen, dear, don't let him go out without his cap," said Mrs. Motherly; "and them slippers of his, sure they're no betther than brown paper — he'll ketch his death of cold. O, *hierna! hierna!*"

"Mr. Brennan, am I to consider myself a prisoner in my own house?" demanded Mr. Guirkie.   "Say yes or no, sir, at once, and be done with it."

As the priest was about to reply, the clatter of horses' feet

26 *

was heard approaching, and next instant Kate Petersham,
mounted on "Moll Pitcher," came cantering into the court-
yard, and reining up at the door, jumped from the saddle.

"Mr. Guirkie, a word with you," she said, taking his arm,
and leading him back to the parlor; "as for you, Father John,
I must see you before the trial comes on."

* * *

CHAPTER XXV.

*Mrs. Motherly, before quitting the House forever, wishes to
leave some Directions about her Master's Flannels. — Mr.
Guirkie, in the mean time, sheds Tears over the Portrait of
Mary's Mother. — His first Love and his last.*

It was now approaching noon — the hour at which the
neighboring justices of the peace usually assembled in the
little court house at Tamney, to hold their petit session once
a fortnight. Already the courtyard was filled with men,
women, and boys, (a thing of very rare occurrence in that remote and peaceable district,) eagerly talking in groups, here
and there, about something in which they seemed to take a
more than ordinary share of interest. Two or three policemen, whom Hardwrinkle had ordered from the next town, to
take charge of the barrack in the absence of its proper occupants, now in search of his sister among the glens of Benraven,
were pacing up and down before the grated windows, anxiously awaiting the arrival of the magistrates. To judge from
the smothered imprecations of some among the crowd, and the
more significant gesticulations of others, one might easily suspect there was mischief brewing. Here and there a stalwart
fellow might be seen hitching up his pantaloons, and spitting
on his shillaleh, as he clutched it in his brawny hand; and now

and then a boy would jump to a seat on the low stone wall
that enclosed the courtyard, with pockets well stuffed, and
more than usually heavy. The fear of the law, and the presence of the police, small as the force was, had the natural
effect of preventing, for the present, actual breach of peace ;
but still it was easy to see that something serious was likely to
take place before the close of the proceedings. One individual in particular seemed very busy amongst the crowd,
apparently giving orders and directions. This was a woman
of tall stature, wearing a gray cloak, with the hood drawn
over, but behind which, notwithstanding its depth of shade,
several white elf locks were plainly visible. The reader will
at once recognize in this personage our old acquaintance, Else
Curley, of the Cairn. Still erect and lithe as a sapling, though
the snows of eighty winters had passed over her head, she
made her way through the throng of men and women, with a
step as firm as when she trod the battle field on the heights of
Madeira, forty years before. Nor had she lost entirely, either,
that imposing presence, which in her younger days must have
stamped her as a remarkable woman. Age, it is true, had
furrowed her skin, and pinched her cheeks with its iron
fingers ; but the bold forehead and the deep-set gray eye were
there yet, to tell of her resolute and indomitable will. As she
turned from side to side to deliver her commands, the women
and boys fell back and gazed at her with fear, and the strongest men there shrank from her touch, as they felt her hard,
bony hand upon their shoulders.

Suddenly a horseman appeared in sight, cantering on from
the direction of Greenmount cottage ; and instantly the cry rose
that Captain Petersham was coming. Then the crowd began
to sway to and fro, the boys to jump from their seats on the
low wall, and the policemen to shoulder their muskets. But
they were doomed to be disappointed ; for the horseman, on
nearer approach, proved to be only one of the captain's
grooms, who, riding up to the gate, beckoned to a constable,

and handing him a warrant, commanded him, in his master's name, to execute it without delay.

The man seemed to hesitate for a moment after reading the document.

"The captain's orders are, that you proceed to Crohan House instantly," said the groom, "and bring the boy into court."

"Yes; but I don't feel at liberty to quit my post," replied the constable. "Our force is small."

"As you please," said the servant; "I have delivered my orders;" and wheeling round, without further parley, he galloped back to Greenmount.

"Well, Thomas," demanded the captain, meeting the groom at the door, "you handed the warrant to one of the guard — has he gone to execute it?"

"No, sir; he seems to have scruples about quitting his post."

"Scruples! ho, ho! Is that the way of it? Scruples! Look here, sir; ride back, and tell him for me, if he don't start within sixty seconds from the time you reach him, I'll have him in irons ten minutes after. Begone now, and hurry back to report."

"The scoundrel!" he continued, plucking off his sea cap, and rubbing up his curly hair, as the servant rode off; "the sneaking scoundrel! I'll thin off his constables for him! By the Lord Harry, he'll not involve me in his villanies, if I can help it. It's most atrocious. What! send a fine, gallant young fellow like that to the hulks or the gallows, because he loves his country more than his king? I'll be hanged if I do it, so long as I can throw an obstacle in the way."

"Captain," said a voice behind him, "if it's plazin' to yer honor —— "

"Hilloa! who's here? What! Mrs. Motherly — and still in tears? Come, come, go to your room, woman, and get reconciled. Away! You're as great a fool as your master!"

"Indeed, then, that's the truest word ye said yet, captain; for if I wasn't a greater fool, I wouldn't stay with him. But there's an end to it now, any way."

"End to what?"

"I'll leave him; that's all."

"Nonsense!"

"Indeed, then, I will, sir; I'll niver sleep another night in this house. My heart's been a-breakin with him every day these five years, but it's broken now, out and out. O, *winastru, winastru!* and this is the thanks I'm gettin after workin and slavin for him early and late, night and mornin, every hour since I first darkened his doors. But sure it's all past and gone now, any way."

"Hold your peace, woman, and go to your room instantly. Mr. Guirkie is too good for you. Away, and thank God you have such a master."

"O, it's little yer honor knows about him, captain. Ay, ay, it's little you know about him, poor man. Och, hoch, dear, if ye lived in the same house with him as I did these five long years! But no matter now, sure. God forgive him as I forgive him; and that he may live long and die happy is all the harm I wish him. And now I wash my hands of him forevermore. I'll never —— "

"Mrs. Motherly!"

"O, it's no use, it's no use, captain. I can't stay, nor I won't stay. If ye went down on yer bended knees to me, I'll never close an eye under his roof. And now let him find one that'll tie his cravat, and button his leggings, and bathe his feet, as faithfully and constantly as I did for these five long, weary years; and if he does, then all I have to say is, let him forget there ever was born in this world such a woman as Nancy Motherly."

"Captain Petersham, have the goodness to step this way," said Father Brennan, opening the parlor door, and interrupting the conversation, much to the captain's relief.

The disconsolate housekeeper entreated his honor to wait and listen to her, but all in vain.

"Why, how now," exclaimed the latter, throwing his portly person on the sofa, and glancing round the room ; "all alone, eh ? — where have they gone — Kate and Mr. Guirkie ?"

"Hush! don't speak so loud. They're all three inside there."

"All three — who's the third ?"

"One you would never dream of seeing here — Roger O'Shaughnessy."

"O, it's Roger, is it ?"

"Yes; the old man, it appears, came up this morning from the lighthouse to sell a picture to Mr. Guirkie."

"A picture ?"

"Mary, you know, has quite a taste for painting, and Roger's her salesman."

"Poor thing ! "

"Only for that, the family had suffered long ago."

"You astonish me ; are they really so very destitute ? "

"So I'm informed. Indeed, from what I have seen and know myself, I believe they must be reduced as low as they can be, and live."

"God bless me ! "

"Why, I thought Kate had told you of it."

"No. She said something, I remember, of their being poor, and all that, but never hinted at any danger of their suffering. By the Lord Harry, sir, this can't be. It shan't be. The thought of Mary Lee in distress actually frightens me."

"And then, she's so patient and gentle," said Father John ; "never seen but with a smile on her face. Working at her easel through the long day, and often far into the night, with old Drake sleeping by her side as she plies her brush — working, working, without complaint or murmur, to earn the bare necessaries of life for her beloved uncle, and that good old man who has followed them so faithfully, in their fallen fortunes."

"She's a delightful creature," exclaimed the captain. "I wish to the Lord she could be induced to come and stay with Kate at Castle Gregory. I would be a brother to her as long as she lived."

"She never would consent to part with her uncle and old Roger."

"Then, by the Lord Harry, let them all three come. Castle Gregory's large enough. As for me, I suppose I must remain an old bachelor, since there's no help for it. Lee's an honest, kind-hearted, generous fellow himself, as ever broke the world's bread; and I should take it as a favor if he came and took up his quarters with me at the old castle. By George, I must call down in the Water Hen to-morrow, and see him about it."

"Don't speak too fast, captain," said the priest. "Have a little patience. There's a mystery now solving in that room, which may balk you, perhaps, of your generous purpose."

"Mystery!"

"Yes. Shall I tell you what it is? or have you time to hear it? The court sits at noon — does it not?"

"Hang the court! Go on with the mystery."

"Well, Roger has been selling pictures to our friend, Mr. Guirkie, it appears, for the last six months or more, and, queer enough, never imagined for a moment the purchaser had the least suspicion of the artist — having passed himself off as a picture dealer from Derry; while, on the other hand, Mr. Guirkie was well aware of the secret, and all the time kept buying her pieces, and indulging his good, kind heart by paying double prices."

"Ho, ho! I understand. Roger was unwilling to expose the poverty of the family, and therefore went under an assumed name."

"Precisely. Well, this morning, it seems, he started from

the lighthouse to sell a picture, as usual. When he reached here, he felt rather shy about coming in, lest he might happen to meet somebody who had seen him before, and would recognize him. So, sitting down under the window, to wait for an opportunity of seeing Mr. Guirkie alone, and feeling somewhat fatigued, perhaps, after his long journey, he fell fast asleep. In that position Mr. Guirkie discovered him, with the picture carefully concealed under the breast of his coat, just as Kate entered the parlor. You heard the shriek he gave when the portrait met his eye, I suppose."

"Shriek — no, I heard no shriek. Portrait! why, what does that mean?"

"It means that he recognized the likeness, and in so doing, almost lost his senses. But wait, you shall hear. In the first place, it happened to be a copy Mary had taken of her mother's portrait, which Roger carried off, either by mistake, or because he could find no other ready."

"Yes, very well — go on," said the captain, impatiently; "it don't matter which."

"And this very portrait now reveals the whole mystery."

"The mystery! There, you're at it again. Mystery! — Good Heavens, sir, can't you tell me what mystery you mean? Excuse me, Mr. Brennan; but you know how deeply interested I feel in every thing that regards this girl — and then you're so tedious."

"Have patience a little longer and I'll explain," said the priest, smiling. "You are already aware that Mr. Guirkie has been for the last five years in the habit of visiting, once a week, the old churchyard of Rathmullen, and that nobody could tell his reason or motive for so doing."

"Certainly, every one in the parish knows that — well?"

"And you remember to have heard Mr. Guirkie tell how he saw a young lady quitting the churchyard several times, as he entered?"

"Yes."

"And that he thought, or fancied he thought, the figure of that lady strongly resembled Mary Lee. Well, it now turns out, that our dear old friend and Mary have been all along visiting the same grave."

"Hah! the same grave!"

"Yes, the grave of her — mother!"

"You surprise me! her mother! Are not the Lees strangers here?"

"Yes. But you recollect the circumstances of the wreck of the Saldana, and how the body of a woman, wearing a gold crucifix on her neck, with the name of Harriet Talbot engraved on the back, was cast ashore, and interred in Rathmullen churchyard. That woman was Mary Lee's mother."

"Good Heavens! Mary Lee's mother?"

"Yes, sir, Mary's mother."

"Humph! and so that accounts for those strange rumors we heard of the white lady and gentleman, seen so often quitting the churchyard and sailing down the Swilly on moonlit nights. But what business had Mr. Guirkie at her mother's grave, eh?"

"That's the secret," replied the priest.

"The secret! confusion! to the — But no matter — no matter; have your own way, have your own way. I shall ask no more questions. I suppose you'll tell it some time — when it suits you. By George, sir, you're the most circum——"

"Captain, dear," said Mrs. Motherly, opening the door gently and cutting the word in two, "'I want ——'"

"Want! What the fury *do* you want?" thundered the provoked captain.

"Only one word, yer honor, afore I go. It's about the master's flannels. I'm afeerd ——"

"Confound your master's flannels! To blazes with them; what have I to do with your master's flannels?" he exclaimed furiously; "begone this instant!"

"I'll not keep ye one minute, yer honor. I'm only afraid Mr. Guirkie'll ketch his death o' cold."

"Woman, quit the room!"

"Away, away, Mrs. Motherly," said the priest, interposing good-naturedly, and closing the door; "I shall become your intercessor with Mr. Guirkie as soon as possible; but don't quit the house, by any means, till I see you again."

"What now?" cried Kate, stepping from the little room in which she had been closeted all this time with Mr. Guirkie, and laying her hand on the captain's shoulder. "What now? Brother, how is this? out of temper, eh? What's the matter?"

"The mischief's the matter. Between Father Brennan's mystery, and Mrs. Motherly's importunity, and those confounded constables, I'm almost crazy."

"Well, well, brother Tom, you're so impatient, you know, and so impetuous. Hush, now! not a word. Listen — I have something to tell you."

"What?"

"About Uncle Jerry."

"Well, what of him? Has he had a fit? is he dying? is he dead?"

"No, not exactly that — but, there's a — mystery — in it."

"Mystery! — d—n the mystery! — there it's again! Mystery, well, if this isn't enough to provoke — away! stand off! I'll be humbugged no longer. Let me pass — I must see him instantly — away! begone!"

"You shall not, captain," cried Kate, endeavoring to prevent him; "you shall not."

"By the Lord Harry, I shall, though."

"Nay, nay — it's a very delicate affair, brother; and indeed he'll never forgive you if you do — you know how bashful and sensitive he is."

"Is he still insensible?" inquired Father John.

"Quite so," responded Kate; "he has not moved a muscle since he saw the picture."

"Insensible!" repeated the captain; "then, Kate, be it delicate or indelicate, I'll see my old friend, think what you please about it;" and freeing himself from his sister's grasp, he advanced and opened the door of the adjoining room.

The first object which met his view, was Mr. Guirkie himself, seated at a table on which lay, what appeared to be, a framed picture some eight or ten inches square. His forehead rested on his hands, and his eyes seemed riveted to the canvas. Indeed, so absorbed was he, that the noise which the captain made in forcing open the door seemed not to disturb him in the least. When Kate saw her brother gazing so intently at Mr. Guirkie, she suddenly ceased speaking, and gently passing him by, took her place behind Uncle Jerry's chair. All was silence now. Old Roger stood leaning his back against the wall, looking down pensively on the floor; Kate, like a guardian angel, took her stand by the side of her unconscious friend; the priest laid his hands against the door casing and peeped in; and the boisterous, burly captain, so noisy but a moment before, remained on the threshold silent and motionless as a statue.

"Look!" said the priest, whispering over the captain's shoulder, and pointing to the picture.

"What?"

"Don't you see something drop — drop? — listen! You can almost hear them falling on the canvas."

"Tears?"

"Yes."

"God bless me! I don't like to see him weep. Shall I wake him up?"

"No, no," said Kate; "let him weep on."

"But, Kate, what portrait is that — eh?"

"The likeness of a long-lost friend — Mary Lee's mother."

"Long-lost friend — Mary Lee's mother?"

"Yes; the only woman he ever loved. Old Roger, here, will tell you all about it, some time when he has more leisure."

"It's only now I could recognize him, your honor," said Roger, "though I seen him many a time this twelvemonth past.   Years, you know, make a great change in us."

"Kate, I must try to rouse him," said the captain; "I cannot bear to see those tears falling there so silently on the canvas — it's very unpleasant."

"Not yet — not yet," remonstrated Kate, motioning back the captain with her hand; "let the faithful soul indulge his rapturous reverie.   These are not tears of anguish, brother, but of love.   O, think of the love of that heart, after an absence of twenty years.   Surely, surely such love is not of earth, but of heaven: so pure, so gentle, so enduring.   A wanderer over the wide world, seeking solace for a widowed heart, he returns to his native land, and after years of patient search, discovers her lowly tomb at last among the ruins of Rathmullen Abbey.   Week after week, for six long years, has he visited that tomb.   Every stain which the mildew had left on the humble slab that bears her name he has obliterated, and every letter the moss of years had filled up he has lovingly renewed.   O, tell me not, Father John," continued Kate, her cheeks flushed with the emotions of her heart, "tell me not, that the pure, gentle, blessed love of the olden time has all died out from the hearts of men.   No, no, no — God is love, and God never dies.   Noble, generous, faithful heart!" cried the enraptured girl, bursting herself into tears; and falling at Uncle Jerry's feet, she removed his hand from his forehead and kissed it with enthusiastic affection. "O that I had but studied this book more carefully! how much more I should have learned of the beautiful and the good.   How cold and insipid are all printed words, compared with the blessed teachings of a heart like thine.   Mary Lee, Mary Lee, angel or woman, whatever thou art, would to God he could now look on thy seraphic face, and press thee —— "

"Mary Lee," repeated Mr. Guirkie, at last breaking silence and looking on the face of the suppliant girl, while the tears still glistened on his own,—"Mary Lee! I think I have heard the name before. Poor Mary Lee! Are you Mary Lee?"

"No, no," replied Kate; "I am but a child of earth — your own poor, foolish, loving Kate Petersham." As Kate spoke, she motioned to the beholders to quit the room, for she dreaded the effect an exposure of his weakness before the bantering captain might produce on a mind so sensitive as his; and fully appreciating the delicacy of her fears, they withdrew silently from the apartment and closed the door, before Mr. Guirkie's consciousness had completely returned. And, dear reader, we must withdraw also, for the time of court-session is already past, and Mr. Robert Hardwrinkle is anxiously looking from the court house door in the direction of Greenmount, and wondering what can detain the chairman of the bench, or why he should presume to keep a gentleman of his importance waiting so long.

CHAPTER XXVI.

The Priest and Dr. Henshaw. — The Influence of Catholicity. — Its attractive and repulsive Features. — The Priest's Garden and the old Tombstone.

FATHER JOHN, having waited to see Mr. Guirkie completely restored to his usual equanimity, and Captain Petersham in the saddle ready to set off for the court house, took the near cut over the hill, and soon reached his humble home. On his arrival, the servant handed him a letter, and informed him that several persons had called, and among the rest Else Curley of the Cairn, who expressed great anxiety to see him before the court opened. Mr. Hardwrinkle also had sent his man in haste to say, that a riot was appre-

27 *

hended in the event of Barry's committal, and requesting Father Brennan's presence to maintain order and assist the magistrates in the discharge of their duty.

"A very modest request, upon my word," said the priest, opening the letter, and seating himself quietly in his easy chair to read it. "Very modest, indeed; but I have a duty of my own to discharge at present."

The letter ran as follows :—

"MY REVEREND FRIEND: The blow I have so long been evading has fallen at last. My creditors have discovered my retreat, and placed a writ for my immediate arrest in the hands of the sheriff. I leave here to-morrow, by daybreak, and cross over to Malin Head; but where, after that, fate only must determine. What is to become of poor Mary, God alone can tell. For the present, at least, you must be her protector, for I know of no other to whose care I could entrust so precious a charge. I should much rather, for my own part, go to jail and weather out the storm as best I might; but the thought of my incarceration would take the dear child's life. I must quit this place to-morrow, too, without seeing her; for I never could summon courage enough to bid her farewell. The furniture here will, of course, be sold for debt. Save the old Bible and harpsichord, if you can. They are of little value, to be sure, to any body; but still they are links — alas! the only links left us now — to connect us with the past. If you speak a kind word to the captain about old Roger, I'm sure he won't let him want. Be kind to Mary, and comfort the poor child in my absence.

"God bless you.

"Yours, faithfully,   E. LEE."

"John!" cried the priest, as he read the letter — "John!" "Sir."

"Take the horse and gig immediately, and drive as fast as

possible to the lighthouse.   Give my compliments to Mr. Lee, say I received his note, and tell him to come up without a moment's delay, and bring Miss Lee with him.   You understand?"

"Yes, sir."

"And see here — don't wait to feed the horse, but go at once."

"No, sir."

"Let Mr. Lee have the gig, since he has no conveyance of his own, and you can return on foot at your leisure."

"Certainly, sir."

When the servant closed the door, the priest leaned back in his chair and composed himself to read vespers.   And a snug, pleasant little room it was, that parlor of Father John's, to read or pray in, with its latticed windows looking down on the placid face of the beautiful Mulroy, now sleeping calmly in the bosom of the hills.   Close by the side of the humble edifice grew a long line of gooseberry and currant bushes, and up from between them, here and there, the honeysuckle stretched its long neck into the open windows.   Out before the door stood an old elm tree, majestic and lonely in the centre of the grass plot, spreading its giant branches far and wide over house and garden.   Many a name was carved on that sturdy old trunk in its day, and many a time the priest and his good old reverend uncle sat on the stone bench together, and leaned back against it in the summer evenings, to say the rosary and tell the beads.   And there, too, round about grew many a flower of native growth, fresh and fair, simple and modest, like the virgin whose altar they were intended to decorate — the mountain daisy, white as snow; the primrose, its faithful companion, at its side; the cowslip, with the dew always on its face; and the lily of the valley, hiding its head in the grass, as if it had no right to occupy a place in the world at all.   These and such as these were the only tenants of that modest garden.   O, well we remember it — that garden where none but wild flowers grew — those pretty wild flowers, nature's own spontaneous offering. And every morning would the priest pluck a bunch to scatter on the shrine of the virgin, as he ascended her altar to say the holy mass, knowing well she loved them best; for it was such as these Joseph used to gather for her, long ago, by the way-side, when his work of the day was done.

Down below the garden, and over the copse which lay be tween, appeared the whitewashed walls of Massmount Chapel, rising from the water's edge, and on either side facing the sea, the white gravestones peeping out from the long grass and tangled fern. But in that solitary spot there was one particular grave, on which the priest's eye often loved to rest, as he sat by the window gazing down on the old churchyard. It was the grave of an old and long-cherished friend — of one who found him in his early days an exile and a wanderer, and took him into his house and heart; one who paused not to ask the poor wayfarer from what nation he came or whither he went — for his big heart knew no distinction of birth or race; who lavished on him all the loving fondness of a father, and at last took him by the hand and led him within the sanctuary. On that humble slab, covering the old man's grave, the priest's eyes often rested, as he sat by the window of his little parlor; and often he sighed and longed for the day to come when he might see that stone replaced by a monument worthier the great and holy heart that slept beneath it. But, alas! he sighed in vain; for he was poor, and his love alone could never raise it.

Dear reader, many a noble heart lies mouldering in a forgotten grave; and many a grave on which gratitude should have erected a monument to virtue, lies deserted and abandoned to the nettle and the dockweed. We have seen such in our own day. Alas, alas! that the world should be so ungrateful.

Once upon a time we stood beside an open grave on a green hill side in N —— E ——. It was a grave in which the mortal remains of a great and good man were soon to be deposited — a man whose virtues were the theme of every tongue. And well they might, for never breathed a purer soul, nor throbbed a nobler heart than his. At once unaffectedly simple and unconsciously sublime, his nature was a compound of the finest qualities of the Christian and the gentleman, without a single jarring element to mar its modest grandeur.

The funeral procession at length reached the spot, and the coffin was laid beside the grave with the lid thrown open, that the mourners might look on the face of the dead for the last time. Never was seen such a crowd as that morning gathered there. Fathers and mothers leading their little children by the hand, and young men with bearded lip, and old men with hoary heads, were there, and strangers from distant cities were there, and bishops in purple cassocks, and priests in black stole and surplice. Kneeling on the greensward, the incense rose, and the psalm was sung, and the people of high and low degree mingled together, and prayed for the repose of his soul; and whilst they prayed their tears fell thick and fast. It was a sad but glorious sight to see that multitude weeping and prostrate that morning before the open coffin; and gazing on his face, they saw it still beaming with that look of love which ever marked it through life; nay, he seemed at that moment as if making them his last appeal for an affectionate remembrance. And each one answered the appeal by a silent vow — a vow to honor, to gratitude, and to God — made while they gazed on his face through their tears — made with their hands upon his coffin — a vow never to forget him.

Ten years passed away, and again, after many wanderings, we returned to that green hill side, and looked round for the monument which that crowd of loving hearts had erected to the memory of their benefactor and friend. "What seek you, stranger?" said an old man, seated on the grass, by a little mound of clay. "The monument erected to the memory of the illustrious ———" "Here it is," he replied, laying his hand on the sod beside him. "That!" "Yes, this is the monument; I have just been sowing a few flower seeds at his feet." "But his friends!" we inquired. "Friends!" repeated the old man, smiling bitterly. "Yes, that mighty multitude which ten years ago we saw weeping and wailing here before his unburied corpse — what has become of them?" "Dead." "What, all dead!" "Ay, they all died on the day of his burial — all save one and myself. That one comes often here to say a prayer and drop a tear on the grave, for living and dying he loved him best of all the world. But alas! he is poor, and those whom he trusted to for help have proved un-grateful." "Nay, say not so, old man," we replied; "may-hap he has not solicited their aid. It were sad indeed to think ———" "Solicit!" he repeated, again interrupting me; "no, he could never do that — the peculiarity of his relations with the dead forbade it. But, friend," he added, "true grat-itude never waits for time, nor place, nor man to call forth its expression."

Pardon us, dear reader, for this disgression. Perhaps it is out of place, but for the life of us we couldn't help making it.

Father Brennan had but little more than commenced to read his office, when the parlor door opened, and a servant announced a visitor. Presently our old acquaintance, Dr. Henshaw, entered, and the priest instantly laid his breviary on the table, and rose to receive him.

"Dr. Henshaw, this is very kind. I'm very much pleased to see you — pray be seated."

"Sir, you'll excuse me; I merely called to return this vol-ume of Bailly's Theology, and to thank you for your hospee-tality before I leave."

"Ah! then I see you're still angry with me, doctor; and, in-deed, not without some show of reason, for I may, in a mo-ment of irritation, have said more than was becoming in the presence of strangers. Still we must not indulge resentment, you know."

"More than was becoming. Why, sir, you said what was both offensive and unjust," replied the doctor, gruffly.

"Perhaps so. If I did, I sincerely regret it."

"But, sir, your regret is not enough. In justice to me, you are bound to retract the charges you made against me in presence of the parties before whom you made them."

"That I shall, sir, most willingly. Whatever those parties may think unjustifiable in the language I used that night, I am ready to retract and apologize for. What I said, Dr. Henshaw, merely regarded your inveterate habit of intruding your faith into every thing. Why, you had hardly been five minutes conversing with Miss Petersham,. when you told her she would certainly be damned if she didn't renounce Protestantism and join the Catholic church forthwith."

"And why not tell her so at once, sir? where's the use of dilly-dallying about it? Humph! it's charity, sir, to let them see the whole truth at a glance — I say it's charity, sir."

"And as a consequence of that charity," subjoined the priest, "they're both shocked and disgusted."

"Be it so — the sooner shocked, the better. Protestantism is a chronic disease, sir, and it's no by syllabubs and sirups you can cure it; no, sir, but by the most searching medicine, administered vary frequently and in large doses."

"Such treatment, I fear, would more likely kill than cure," said the priest.

"I maintain the contrary, sir. Error should be taken by the horns, and no by the tail. I have seen how you converse with that girl — Miss Petersham; why, you talk to her, sir, as if you were making an apology for the severity of Catholic deescipline, and the conservatism of Catholic doctrine. Hoot, sir, you can never make a Catholic of her by such a course of training as that."

"You think so?"

"Most assuredly, sir."

"And yet she is preparing to join the church in a few days."

"I can hardly believe it, Mr. Brennan."

"Why not?"

"Why, she hasn't the look of a convert."

"What, because she don't appear grave and solemn?"

"No. But her deportment is not like that of a girl desirous of saving her soul. She's cracked, sir, or, as we say in Scotland, she's 'clean daft.'"

"By no manner of means, doctor; you mistake her character altogether. Under all that apparent thoughtlessness lies concealed a fund of natural piety and love of truth, which, if you only knew her as I do, would surprise you. Kate Petersham is not a Scotch girl, you know, to look glum, and shake her head like a 'canny' Presbyterian; nor English either, to wait for the slow conviction of her intellect before she surrenders the heart; but a genuine, true-blooded Irish girl, inheriting the enthusiasm and impulsiveness of her race, whose soul feels the divine attractions of religion drawing her to its bosom, long before her mind recognizes its presence. Like all Irish girls, Kate is playful, witty, light-hearted, and tries ever to hide her piety under an affected recklessness. She will steer the Water-Hen in the teeth of a gale, or ride Moll Pitcher at a steeple chase, over break-neck walls, when the humor takes her; but see her in her closet, when she shuts the door against human eyes, and you'll find her a very different being. Yes, sir, Kate is an Irish girl in every sense of the term — generous, impulsive, way-ward, if you will — but with a heart full of true piety, and a disposition as humble and gentle as a child's."

"Humph!" ejaculated the doctor; "and may I ask, sir, after this extraordinary eulogium, how you set about her conversion?"

"Not by dosing her with dogmas, anathemas, and philosophy, I assure you," replied the priest, smiling.

"No, that's not your method, I perceive. You began, I suppose, like all others of the old school, by pushing her down gently from Protestantism into infidelity, and when she could go no farther, led her up again by the old negative process, step by step, through all the isms into the true church."

"No, sir, that course would only have confused without converting her."

"And what then?"

"I merely pointed out to her the beauties of our holy religion, and sent her down to Mary Lee to see them illustrated."

"Ah! Mary Lee — the light-keeper's daughter?"

"Yes. She converted Miss Petersham without a word of controversy — converted her by the mere example of her every-day life. It's precisely to the force of similar example we owe so many conversions, by the Sisters of Charity, for instance, and the various other religious societies."

"I admit, sir, they are useful in their way — nay, of great advantage as helps to religion, especially as regards the weaker sex; but men of intellect must be treated otherwise, sir. Intellectual men need intellectual treatment; and whilst your Sisters of Charity, and so forth, have done much, and are still doing much, in their own way, there is still need of men who, like myself, endeavor, according to our poor abeelities, to defend truth and combat error, by means of that vary pheclosophy, logic, and theology you seem to think of so lightly. Each in his own sphere, sir, is an old adage."

"Certainly, and a good one, too. But you misapprehend me, doctor, if you think I disparage one or the other as means of conversion. Not at all. I merely say *you* overrate them, and give too little credit, in your account, to the grace of God and the influence of example. In fact, sir, like the majority of converts, you make a mistake in the very beginning. You think — or seem to think, at least — that nothing has been done in the church for the conversion of heretics till you joined her, and that in the ardor and freshness of your zeal you are expected to make up for the neglect. This is a grievous error, doctor, and if allowed to go unchecked, might lead to lamentable consequences.   Take yourself, for instance. Instead of studying, like a child, the primer of the church, and learning therein the thousand helps to salvation, and the thousand beauties to be found in her ceremonies and pious observances, you leave all such little things to the ignorant, and jump at once into the higher region of dogma, without the slightest preparatory training.   The result is, that you often introduce subjects in your writings and lectures which are not only ill timed and uncalled for, but really dangerous in hands so inexperienced as yours.   I willingly admit, Dr. Henshaw, you're a very able writer.   Indeed, in that department of letters you have chosen as the field of your operations, you have, so far as I know, very few equals. But the greater your abilities, the greater the danger both to yourself and the church.   To yourself, because of the inordinate pride such talents are apt to generate, and to the church, lest your non-Catholic readers might mistake your productions for fair specimens of the true tone and spirit of Catholicity.   In that case the church would certainly suffer; for I cannot help telling you, doctor, that so far, at least, you have only presented the church in a repulsive attitude."

"That is," replied the doctor, smiling serenely, "I have not tried my hand at namby-pambyism yet."

"No.   You certainly have not, sir.   But by taking the very opposite extreme you have, in my opinion, done very little good to religion.   What pleasure or benefit can you find in the use of such language as you uttered that night at Castle Gregory — and not only there, but wherever you had occasion to speak of Protestantism?   Then your profound reasoning and subtle logic, on the other hand, may convince intellects, but, be assured of it, will rarely convert hearts.   In such an age as this, you must exhibit the church under her most alluring and attractive form, or you will make no true converts.   Men will read your elaborate articles, admire your vigorous thoughts and your cogent arguments, but their hearts will remain untouched. If ever, indeed, by such a course, you do succeed in bringing a Protestant within the vestibule of the church, he will stand there like a converted philosopher, scanning the books of the new school and examining the principles of the new philosophy, but he will hardly fall before the altar, and with heart bowed down before his God, acknowledge himself a humble and penitent child. No, sir; it's not enough to convince the intellect; you must convert the heart, also, or you will make no converts. Father F——r has done more for the conversion of souls, in the smallest and least valuable of his works, than you have ever done, or ever will do, with all your great talents. And the reason is plain. He is not ambitious — except, indeed, for the promotion of God's glory, and the happiness of his fellow-beings. His thoughts, as he writes, are never of himself. He aims not at the admiration of men, but at their salvation. It is the writings of such converts as he is we want to see, and not elaborate essays on subjects neither practical nor necessary. If you want to make your talents useful to the church, don't strain them to reach where your readers can't follow you, but write for the people — write for the millions, sir, not for theologians and philosophers. If you do that, you will save your own soul, and convert thousands of others; but, if not, I fear you will lose both."

"Humph!" ejaculated Henshaw, after the priest had concluded his somewhat long speech, and buttoning his coat, as if preparing to leave — "I was not aware that I solicited your advice in the matter; if I had, no doubt I should be prepared to defer to it; but as it is ——"

"Doctor," interrupted his friend, "I speak my sentiments on this subject openly and candidly, and at the risk of giving you offence; but I do so both for your own sake and that of religion. The course you're pursuing will undoubtedly prove, in the end, to be an injudicious one — and you will only have the mortification of knowing, in your old days, if you persist in it, that the church of God has gained nothing by your advocacy."

Here the conversation was interrupted by the entrance of a servant, with Captain Petersham's compliments, and his request to see Father Brennan at the court house.

"Ah, I expected as much," said the latter. "This trial of young Barry has just commenced, I suppose. Will you accompany me, doctor?"

"No, I should rather not, just now," replied Henshaw. "I have some preparation to make before leaving to-morrow."

"What! going so soon!"

"Yes; I must return by to-morrow's packet."

"Why, we shan't have time to make up our quarrel, then. O, you mustn't think of it, doctor."

"To-morrow I shall positively start for Derry."

"Well, well, we must talk of that again. Come with me now, for an hour or so, to the court house, to hear this trial If you refuse, I shall say you parted with me in anger. Come, we are old friends, doctor, and must not get estranged for trifles — come;" and the priest, after several unsuccessful attempts, at length prevailed on his discomfited friend to accompany him to the court house.

CHAPTER XXVII.

Randall Barry's Trial. — Kate Petersham on Moll Pitcher. — She balks, but facing the Wall a second time, clears it. — The Negro on the Witness' Stand. — Else Curley comforts Robert Hardwrinkle.

WHEN Father Brennan, accompanied by his learned friend, arrived at the court house gate, he found the yard filled with people. At the door stood two or three policemen, with bayonets on their muskets, keeping out the crowd, now clam-orous for admission, and on the walls several groups of men and boys, peeping in through the windows. As the priest made his appearance, however, the noise ceased for a moment, and the usual whisper ran round, " *Ta shin saggarth, ta shin saggarth* " — There's the priest, there's the priest.

" Stand back," cried a voice in a tone of authority; " stand back, and let his reverence pass."

The priest glanced quickly in the direction of the speaker.

" Who is that?" inquired Henshaw.

" Lanty Hanlon, if he's alive."

" What! our quondam skipper?"

" The very man — what a fool-hardy crack-brain he is to come here after carrying off Miss Hardwrinkle. He hasn't got an ounce of sense, that fellow."

" Fall back," shouted the policemen; " fall back, and let the gentlemen into court. Make way, there."

As the latter gained the upper step at the court house door, a loud cheer suddenly broke from the crowd.

" Hurrah! there she comes, the darling!"

" So ho!" ejaculated Henshaw, turning on his step; " what now?"

" Kate Petersham! I declare it is."

" Hurrah!" shouted the same voice; " there she comes, on Moll Pitcher."

" Hold on," said Henshaw.

" What's the matter?"

" Look! look! sir; she faces that wall."

" Pooh! that's nothing."

" Good Heavens! sir, she'll break her neck."

" Not a bit of it — she learned to ride in Galway."

" It's sax feet high — there! — hold, her horse balks!"

" Balks! that's strange, eh! what can have happened; something she shied at, I suspect. Moll Pitcher was never known to balk in her life."

Whilst the priest was yet speaking, Kate rode her horse close up again to the wall, as if to show her the difficulty she had to encounter, and then wheeling round cantered back for another start.

"She'll balk again," said Henshaw, confidently.

"Wait a while — we'll see."

Every voice was now hushed, and every eye fixed on the rider, for the leap was dangerous, and the spectators, as might naturally be supposed, felt anxious for the safety of their favorite. The spot where she tried to cross was the only one in the wall accessible for a leap, on account of the large rocks which lay along either side for a distance of a quarter of a mile or more; and even there the ground rose so abruptly as to put the horse to a perilous disadvantage. Had the rider been aware of the danger before she approached the leap, very likely she had ridden round, and avoided the difficulty; but having once made the attempt, she determined to risk every thing rather than fail. Perhaps, too, the sight of so many spectators, and the cheers which reached her, had something to do with confirming her resolution.

As the fearless girl turned her horse's head to the wall, she let the reins drop for a moment, and leaning over on the saddle, tightened the girts a hole or two; then adjusting her cap, and patting the spirited animal on the neck, again cantered along at an easy gait.

"Now!" said the priest; "now for it!"

"The girl is decidedly mad, sir," said Henshaw.

"Hush! she raises the whip."

Moll Pitcher knew well what that sign meant, and with a snort and a toss of her saucy head, sprung forward with the fleetness of a greyhound.

"God assist her," muttered the priest to himself; "it's a frightful risk."

"Amen," replied Henshaw, catching the words; "amen — though she don't deserve it — her fool-hardiness is unpardonable."

"Now!" and the priest unconsciously seized his friend's arm — "now!"

As he spoke, Kate again raised the whip, and Moll Pitcher rose to the wall.

For a second or two stillness reigned as deep as death. If the animal touched the wall in crossing, horse and rider would both, in all probability, have been seriously injured, if not killed. If she did not, there was still danger from the broken, stony ground on the opposite side.

"Hold!" exclaimed Henshaw, "they're both down — good Heavens, sir, they're killed!"

The mare rose and stood in an almost perpendicular attitude for a second, as if to gather all her strength for the effort. It was an instant of painful anxiety to the spectators; but it was only an instant, for in the next she made the spring and crossed without touching a stone, the foam flying from her mouth, and the streamers from her rider's cap floating back in the breeze.

"Hurrah! hurrah! God bless her!" now broke in one loud burst from the crowd; but the exclamation was suddenly checked, for it was soon found that rider and horse had both fallen.

"The girl's killed," exclaimed Henshaw.

"God forbid!" replied the priest, straining his eyes as he spoke. "But she has certainly fallen."

Then a general rush was made towards the gate, each vying with his neighbor for the credit of being first to reach the ground.

"What means all this uproar?" demanded Captain Petersham, suddenly appearing at the court house door, accompanied by one of his brother magistrates — "eh, what has happened?"

"Miss Petersham has fallen, sir, crossing that stone wall," replied a policeman.

"Fallen — impossible. What! on Moll Pitcher?"

"I fear she's hurt, captain," said the priest.

"Ah! Father Brennan, you here, too? Hurt—nonsense!"

He had hardly uttered the last word, when another wild shout rose that made the very welkin ring again; and there, plain to every eye, came Kate, firmly seated in her saddle, bounding along the meadow, and waving her handkerchief in acknowledgment of the greeting.

As she jumped the last ditch, a man apparently in disguise —for his clothes seemed to accord little with his figure and gait—advanced and laid his hand on the reins.

"Well, Lanty, is the trial over?" demanded Kate, bending to her saddle-bow, and whispering the words.

"No, my lady, it didn't begin yet."

"Glad of it—I feared I should come late."

"Is your ladyship hurt?"

"Not in the least."

"Nor Moll Pitcher?"

"Not a particle."

"The darlin," exclaimed Lanty, laying his hand on the mare's neck; "she's as true as steel. O, my life on her for a million."

"The moment will soon come to try her," said Kate, as Lanty stretched out his arms and lifted her from the saddle. "Are you sure all's ready?"

"Ay, ay, never fear."

"Where is Miss Hardwrinkle?"

"In the mountains, safe and sound."

"And the police, how many here?"

"Not many," responded Lanty; "but don't stay, or the guard will suspect somethin."

The above conversation passed stealthily and rapidly, under cover of the cheers of the crowd.

"Fall back!" again bawled the police; "fall back there, and make way for the lady."

"Ho! Kate, my girl," cried the jolly captain, snatching his

sister up in his arms, and kissing her affectionately, as she ascended the steps. " The rascals here would have you hurt or killed; but they little know the metal you're made of, nor the gallant bit of flesh that carries you, Kate. A little out of sorts by the fall — bruised or stunned, eh?"

"Not a whit," responded Kate. " I could ride a steeple chase this moment with the best blood in the country. Ah, Father John, you here? I'm glad to see you;" and bending reverently, she kissed the priest's hand.

"My dear girl," responded the latter, " I'm delighted to see you unhurt, for I must confess I felt rather anxious."

" O, it was nothing — a mere stumble; the mare lighted on a round stone and fell, that's all. O, hoh! and Dr. Henshaw; I'm glad to see you too, sir," she continued, holding out her hand. " You must come up and see us to-morrow at Castle Gregory. Now don't say a word; I shall have no excuse. You must positively come, and you may cut up Swift, too, into mince meat, if you like. Father John, I lay my sovereign commands on you to present yourself and Dr. Henshaw at Castle Gregory to-morrow."

" And, Kate, you must put in a good word for me," said the captain, looking over good-humoredly at the doctor. " But never mind; we'll settle all that to-morrow; let us now proceed to business. Come in, gentlemen; we have some spare seats on the bench. Ho, there, police! make way, make way. Come in; there's quite an interesting case in court."

As the parties took their seats and looked round the room, the first object that arrested their attention was the negro. He was standing in the witness box, apparently awaiting the return of the presiding magistrate to resume his examination. On the right of the bench, and immediately below it, sat the cabin boy, wrapped in a thick, blue blouse, and looking pale and emaciated after his sickness. Beyond him, and near the dock in which Randall Barry stood, shackled and guarded by two constables, appeared the tall form of Else

Curley. She was seated on one of the steps leading up to the jury room, the hood of her cloak, as usual, drawn over her head, with the white elf locks visible beneath it. But the object which appeared to attract every eye, and challenge universal attention, was the noble, manly figure of the young outlaw, as he stood before his judges, awaiting his trial, his left arm still in a sling, and his right bound by a chain running round his waist, and fastened by a padlock in front.

Randall Barry was now in his twenty-fifth year; but misfortune and disappointment had cast a shade of melancholy on his countenance that made him look several years older. His face was eminently handsome, and his person tall and muscular. Though far from being robust, his limbs were well moulded, and evidently capable of great physical exertion. As he stood in the dock, his dark eye wandered slowly over the faces of the multitude, resting now and then for a moment on those he recognized. But when Kate Petersham appeared, and took the place assigned her by the clerk of the court, he glanced at her sharply for an instant, and then, as she raised her eyes to his, bent his head and blushed at the thought of his degradation. But to return to the negro.

"Your name is Sambo?" resumed Captain Petersham, addressing the witness.

"Ees, massa."

"Sambo what?"

"Nigger Sambo."

"You're a negro — that's pretty evident; but what's your surname?"

"Don't know, massa."

"What are you called, Sambo Smith, or Sambo Brown, or Sambo Robison? You've some family name, have you not?"

"Noting, massa," replied the African, "noting but Sambo."

"Why, you rascal, do you mean to tell me you've got no family name?"

"O sartin, massa, I'm got famly name."

"And what is it, then ?   Answer directly, sir.   I've been examining this stupid fellow a full half hour, and can get nothing out of him," added the captain, turning to the priest ; "he's the most provoking creature I ever met with.   Answer me, sir ; what is your family name ? "

"Famly name, massa ! "

"Yes, yes, yes ; you had a father, I suppose ? "

"Fader — well, supposin I'm had a fader."

"Supposing you had a father?   By George, this is absolutely intolerable.   Had your father a name ? "

"Sartin, massa."

"And what the fury was it ? "

"Sambo, massa — him was Nigger Sambo, too."

Here the whole assembly, magistrates and spectators, broke into a loud laugh at the discomfited captain, and the negro yah-yah'd, and shook his sides in true African fashion.

"Excuse me, captain," said Henshaw, "but these unfortunate creatures seldom or ever have a surname."

"Yes, yes, I was aware of that ; but I have an object in ascertaining what his second name is.   He must have a name, either from his father or master.   Silence in the court, there !   Tell me, sir," he continued, "what is that boy's name, sitting there before you ? " and he pointed to the individual in question.

"Dat boy? — Natty Nelson."

"Where was he born ? "

"Don't know, massa."

"Where did you first see him ? "

"I seed him in de baccy field — yah, yah ! "

"In what state ? "

"Ole Virginny."

"On whose plantation ? "

"Whose plantation?   Can't tell dat, massa, no how," replied the African.

"You must, sir ; I shall order you the bastinado this instant if you refuse."

"Yah, yah, massa; this am free country. Nigger here am good as white man."

At this stage of the proceedings a stir was seen in the crowd at the lower end of the room, and presently entered Mr. Ephraim C. B. Weeks, covered with jewelry, a gold-headed cane in his hand, and the silver card case protruding as usual from his pocket.

Sambo was so intent on evading such questions as might be likely to criminate his *protegé,* and so fearful, at the same time, of provoking the magistrate's anger, that · he neither heard nor saw any thing of Mr. Weeks, till that gentleman · attracted his notice by throwing his feet upon the very platform on which he was standing.

" Golly, Massa Charles, you dar?" he exclaimed, as his eye turned on the new comer. " Massa — I mean Massa Week," he added, endeavoring to correct the blunder.

Captain Petersham's quick eye saw the confusion this un-expected recognition caused the Yankee, and instantly writing a few words rapidly in pencil, dropped them on the clerk's desk, and again resumed.

" Witness, I again repeat the question — on whose plan-tation did you first see this boy?"

" Me no tell dat, massa," replied the negro, decidedly.

" Then I shall commit you. Clerk, make out his com-mittal. I'll send you presently where you can have plenty of time to determine whether you'll answer or not."

" Mr. Petersham," observed Hardwrinkle, leaning over on the bench, and speaking in low tones, but still sufficiently loud to be heard by his brother magistrates, " it does not appear to me that the name of the proprietor of the planta-tion is essential in this case."

" Certainly not, so far as we regard simply the ownership of the rosary; but there's a secret of some importance, I sus-pect, in connection with the case, which I'm anxious to dis-cover."

" But are you justified, nevertheless, in committing the witness for your own personal gratification ? "

" Perhaps not ; but at present I'm disposed to run the risk," replied the captain ; and turning abruptly from Hardwrinkle, he handed the committal to a constable, and ordered him to take the witness forthwith to the barrack, and keep him in close custody.

The negro, finding himself in the hands of an officer, looked beseechingly first at Weeks and then at the boy, but said nothing.

" You may depend on it, Sambo," said the captain, as the poor fellow left the witness box, " you shall never leave the lock-up till you tell who the owner of that tobacco field is, or was, when you first saw this boy — away with him."

" Massa, massa, I'm want to speak one word to Natty."

" Not a syllable."

" One leetle word."

" Not a letter of the alphabet."

The boy now rose, and in feeble accents begged permission to accompany the negro to prison. " He has been my friend," he said, " please your worships, my best friend ever since I was a child, and I would grieve to part with him."

" It cannot be," replied the captain ; " he must go alone."

During this conversation Weeks sat leaning back against a partition, with his feet stretched out before him, pointing a pencil with a penknife, and apparently quite indifferent to what was passing. He was cautiously deliberating, however, all the while, whether it were better to acknowledge he had taken the rosary from the lighthouse by mistake, or run the risk of the negro and the boy keeping the promise they had made him. If he admitted having taken it, he should produce it, and the existence of two rosaries would at once discover the whole secret. If he did not, and the boy, from his strong affection for the negro, should be driven at last to confess the truth, it might be worse still. The reader must here

29

observe, that up to the moment of the boy's arrest at Crohan
House, Mr. Weeks never dreamed of his having a rosary in
his possession; and even when the constables took him off, he
never imagined it could possibly involve him in any trouble.
Hardwrinkle was not so, however. The instant he saw the
rosary, he knew it, at once, to be a duplicate of that he had
seen with his sister Rebecca, and already aware of the boy's
connections in Virginia, thought it prudent to apprise his
cousin of the danger, and accordingly despatched a private
message to him to that effect; the latter, believing his presence at the trial might be the means of deterring the negro.
from divulging the name of his master, if he should happen
to be so inclined, made his appearance in court,'as we have
already described. Things, however, had taken rather a different turn from what he expected. The African was now
committed for contempt, and on the point of being separated
from his *protégé* — a separation he knew to be most painful
to both; and he began to feel somewhat apprehensive lest the
negro's promise of fidelity should give way to his love for the
boy. " Well, I swonnie," said he to himself, as he pointed
the pencil, or rather whittled it, (if one could judge by the
quantity of chips,) "I swonnie, I don't know. I guess it
might be just as well to make tracks from this here place as
soon as possible; things are beginning to tighten in so's to
make one feel sorter uncomfortable. There's that darned
note, though, of the light-keeper's — if I had that cashed, I
kinder think I'd bid the folks in this section good by for a
while. Well, the sheriff's after him, any how — that's a comfort — and O, crackie! if I don't make him pay for his in-
sults at Castle Gregory. If I don't screw him tight up —
well, if I don't, it's no matter; that's all." In this fashion
Mr. Weeks kept communing with his own thoughts, weighing
his chances of success and failure, till the boy rose and
begged the court to allow him the privilege of being confined in the same cell with the witness. " Ah," thought

Weeks, "I guess I'm about long enough here. I see the tears in his eyes — he'll never hold out ; and if he comes to blab, I might feel sorter unpleasant ; " and so thinking, he took his hat and turned to quit the court house.

"Excuse me, Mr. Weeks," said Captain Petersham, "we must detain you a little longer — you're summoned to give testimony in this case."

" Summoned ! "

"Yes, sir. Here, constable, hand this to the gentleman. Have the goodness to resume your seat, Mr. Duck — ah, Mr. Weeks, I should have said ; we shall want you presently. Clerk, call Else Curley."

"I'm here," responded Else, promptly, rising from the low step on which she had been sitting, and brushing back her gray hair under her hood with her brown, bony hand, — "I'm here."

"Take your place on the witness stand," said the clerk.

As Else advanced, every eye was upon her. Hundreds there who had come from a distance to hear the trial of the young rebel, and had never seen Else Curley, now pushed forward to get a glimpse of that far-famed fortune-teller and solitary of Benraven.

Having taken the usual oath, the old woman folded her arms in her gray cloak, and awaited the pleasure of the magistrates.

"Shall I examine her ? " said Hardwrinkle, addressing the captain.

"I thank you," replied the latter; "no, I should prefer to examine her myself."

"Your name is Else Curley, and you reside on Benraven Mountain ? " began the captain.

"Yes."

"Do you know Mr. Lee and his daughter, of Araheera lighthouse ? "

"I do."

" Have you ever seen a rosary of a peculiar description in Miss Lee's possession ? "

" I have."

" Can you describe it ? "

" It was a silver-baded rosary, with a crucifix set in diamonds."

" Look at this one, and tell me if you ever saw it before."

Else took the rosary, and after looking at it for a moment replied, " This is the very picthur of Mary Lee's, if it been't itself."

" Can you swear positively it is Miss Lee's ? "

" No," responded Else, " but it's as lake it as one thing can be lake another."

" Have you seen a rosary like that in Miss Lee's possession ? "

" A hundher times. I tuck one like it from her dead mother's neck among the rocks of Araheera, the mornin after the wrack of the Saldana, and put it on her own."

" On whose ? "

" Mary Lee's. The child was livin in her mother's arms when I found her."

" What ! " exclaimed the captain; " you must mistake. Do you mean to tell the bench that you found a living child in the arms of a dead woman on the morning after the wreck of the Saldana, and that that child is the same Mary Lee who now claims this rosary ? "

" I do," replied Else, confidently.

This declaration of the old woman, made so promptly and positively, took the whole audience by surprise. Even Hardwrinkle himself, who thought he knew more of Mary Lee's history than any other in court, looked confounded and astonished at the unexpected revelation. In a moment he foresaw the disclosure would eventually lead to the discovery of his cousin's matrimonial speculation, the boy's relationship with the proprietor of the Virginia plantation, and his own confusion and disgrace, unless he succeeded in damaging the witness's testimony.

"Captain Petersham," said he, turning to the presiding magistrate, and speaking in the gentlest possible accents, "may I take the liberty of putting a question or two to the witness? It really cannot be possible she speaks the truth in this matter."

"As you please," replied the captain; "but I don't see how it can affect the case whether she speaks the truth or not about the discovery of the child. She swears positively that the rosary is as like that which Miss Lee lost as one thing can be like another, and she had even described it, before she saw it, as consisting of silver beads and a gold crucifix set in diamonds. Now, for my part, I don't believe you could find another rosary through all Europe of the same description. But proceed, sir; satisfy yourself, by all means."

"Else Curley," said Hardwrinkle, addressing the witness, "of what religion are you?"

"I was once a Catholic," replied the old woman; "I'm nothin, now."

"Do you believe in a future state of rewards and punishments?"

"Humph!" she replied; "why shouldn't I? God surely'll punish the persecutor and the murdherer in the nixt world, if the law don't in this;" and as she uttered the words, she fixed her keen, deep-sunken eyes on her questioner.

"How long is it since you've been in a house of worship?"

"Well on to thirty years."

"You are commonly called the witch and fortune-teller of the Cairn, are you not?"

"Sometimes fortune-teller, and sometimes she-devil," replied Else; "just as the people fancy."

"Do you know what crime it is to take a false oath?"

"I do."

"What is it?"

" Parjury."

" And what is perjury ? "

" The crime yer father committed whin he swore agin my only sister, and sint her to an untimely grave."

Here a laugh came up from the crowd below ; but it was soon suppressed by the police, and Hardwrinkle proceeded.

" I repeat the question, witness ; what is perjury ? "

" The crime yer father committed whin he swore my brother to the hulk, and sint him to die in a forrin land, with irons on his limbs. The crime ye committed yerself whin ye sint me twice to the dark dungeons of Lefford jail, and when I come out, driv me to burrow lake the brock in the crags of Benraven."

" Woman, I shall send you to jail for the third time, if you persist in using such language in court."

" Scoundrel ! hypocrite ! murderer ! I defy you," cried Else, throwing back her hood, and raising her shrivelled arm as she spoke ; " yer villany's discovered at last. There," she ejaculated, pointing to Weeks, " there, tell the court who sent that man to me for spells and charms to make Mary Lee marry him ; who tould him of the witch and fortune-teller of Benraven ; who tould him she would sell her sowl to fill her pocket ? Ah, little ye thought, when ye made this greedy cousin buy up the light-keeper's notes, that ye might have the means of sending him to jail if he refused his niece, little ye thought the bedlam of the Cairn was watching ye —— "

" Hold ! hold, woman ! " exclaimed Captain Petersham. " What does all this mean ? "

" Mane ! " repeated Else. " It manes that this cousin of his, this man of trinkets, come here from America in search of the heiress of William Talbot, and that Robert Hardwrinkle conspired with him to take her off by fair manes or foul. It manes that at the instigation of that devil there in human shape, the Yankee here paid me eighty British pounds for spells and charms, and my good word besides, to make her marry him. It manes that, after watching for thirty years, I found at last evidence to prove to the world that the pious, God-fearing, saintly, smooth-spoken gentleman on the bench there beside ye, is a hypocrite and a villain."

" Police! take charge of this woman," commanded Hardwrinkle, his long, dark, sallow face pale with confusion and anger; "take her away."

" No, no; not yet, Mr. Hardwrinkle, not yet," interposed Captain Petersham; " we cannot permit her to leave after casting such aspersion on your character. As your brother magistrates, we feel concerned for your reputation, and must for your sake, and indeed for the honor of the bench, make further inquiries into this matter.

" Else Curley," said he, " you have just charged Mr. Hardwrinkle, a magistrate of the county, and a gentleman — up to this moment, at least — of unexceptionable character, with having conspired with Mr. Weeks to take off Miss Lee by fair means or foul. What proof of that fact can you offer?"

" That, on the third day afther Weeks arrived at Crohan House," promptly replied Else, " he came into my cabin on the Cairn, and paid me twenty pounds earnest for my sarvices to help him to secure Mary Lee, and *that* afore he iver seen a faiture of her face. How cud he know that I was acquent with Mary Lee, or how cud he tell that I'd take his money for sich a purpose, or how cud he know any thing about me, if Robert Hardwrinkle didn't tell him who and what I was?"

" Yes, but all this amounts only to mere suspicion. Have you proofs?"

" Weeks's bank notes, that I have still in my possession, clean and fresh out of the Bank of Dublin, is proof enough on his side, I'm thinkin; and the note in the sheriff's hands can spake for Robert Hardwrinkle's."

Here the deputy sheriff entered the court house, accompanied by the light-keeper and his afflicted niece, closely followed by her old, faithful domestic, Roger O'Shaughnessy, in the bottle-green livery with the faded lace.　As the constables drove back the crowd to make way, and Mary appeared, deeply veiled, leaning on her uncle's arm, Captain Petersham rose and saluted her with marked respect, and then a murmur of sympathy ran round the assembly; and as she advanced nearer to the bench, her dear friend Kate, her eyes suffused with tears, and regardless of the spectators, ran to meet her, and flinging her arms round her neck, embraced her with true sisterly affection.

CHAPTER XXVIII.

Trial continued. — Else charges Hardwrinkle with Conspiracy to carry off Mary Lee. — She proves William Talbot, Mary's Father, to be still living, by Means of the Rosary found on the Person of the Cabin Boy. — Mary's Feelings overpower her on hearing the Announcement. — The Rescue of the Rebel. — The Riot. — Hardwrinkle's Death.

The crowd outside the court house grew more and more clamorous for admission, as the trial proceeded.　Stones were several times thrown at the doors, and finally, the multitude grew so excited as to be on the point of rushing up the steps to disarm the constables, when suddenly the word "halt" was heard ringing clear and sharp from the direction of the street, and next moment a detachment of police, headed by a lieutenant, passed through the gate, and opening a passage with their bayonets, took their position on the court house steps.

This reënforcement, it is needless to observe, was ordered by Mr. Hardwrinkle himself, from the neighboring village, without the knowledge or consent of Captain Petersham. Hardwrinkle, in fact, saw from the beginning that the captain 

determined to throw every obstacle in the way of Barry's committal, and he, on the other hand, resolved to leave no means untried to thwart and disappoint him. Hence the moment he found the police had all been sent in search of Lanty Hanlon and his sister, with the exception of three or four to guard the prisoner, he despatched a messenger to the nearest officer in charge, and under pretence of an anticipated riot, commanded him to bring forthwith all the force he could muster, to sustain the magistrates in the execution of the law.

After the slight interruption occasioned by the entrance of the sheriff and his party, the chairman again resumed his examination of the witness.

"My good woman," said he, "you have made a very grave and serious charge here, in open court, against one of my brother magistrates; no less a charge, indeed, than of conspiring with another individual here present to entice, seduce, or carry off, by fair means or foul, a highly accomplished and respectable young lady, Miss Lee, of Araheera Head. I now call on you to substantiate that charge, or confess yourself guilty of a foul and malicious slander."

"Slander!" repeated Else, drawing herself up and looking round the audience. "I niver was guilty of slander in my life. I'm now fourscore years and more: thirty of them I spent in the wilds of Benraven, under the foul name of witch and devil's dam; but where's the man or woman here ever knew Else Curley to tell a lie or slander a neighbor? If there is, let them spake. What I am, that man there on the bench has made me. For these long and weary thirty years, he stud between the light of heaven and me; and yit though I niver expect to see God but in anger, I wudn't tell a lie to send him to the gallows."

As Else uttered these words, her look was calm and defiant, and she stood as erect as a statue, her arms folded on her brown bare breast, and her deep gray eyes fixed on Robert Hardwrinkle.

The spectators gazed on her in silent astonishment. Her mien, her attitude, but above all the dignity with which she spoke, struck them as extraordinary in a woman of her character and years.

"She has seen better days, that old creature," observed Henshaw, turning to the priest.

"Ay, so report says."

"But on what grounds," again demanded the captain, "have you made this charge against Mr. Hardwrinkle?"

"Humph! grounds enough, sir, grounds enough. First ask the sheriff there to produce the promissory note Mr. Lee's now arrested for."

"My jurisdiction don't extend so far, my good woman. If the gentleman, however, chooses —— "

"Certainly, sir," replied the latter, "certainly; I can see no objection."

"Well, I guess you might as well not mind it just now," drawled out Weeks, who had resumed his seat, and kept whittling his pencil.

"How so?"

"Well, I object to the production of the note — that's all."

"The objection don't hold, sir — the note being now in possession of the civil court," responded the sheriff, handing the document up to the bench.

"Hah!" exclaimed the chairman, as he read it over. "This note's drawn in favor of Steven C. Ingoldsby, and indorsed by Robert Hardwrinkle to Ephraim C. B. Weeks — with interest added up to 13th ——. Witness, how does this date correspond with Weeks's arrival at Crohan?"

"He was here two weeks to a day," promptly responded Else — "just time enough for his cousin there to go to Dublin, and ferret out Mr. Lee's creditors."

"You're of opinion, then," said the captain, "that Mr. Hardwrinkle bought up this note and indorsed it to Weeks, as a means of coercing Miss Lee to marry him through fear of her uncle's incarceration?"

"I am."

"And yet, my good woman, you have given us no proofs that Mr. Weeks ever proposed marriage to the young lady in question."

"Proofs!" repeated Else, running her hand into her bosom, and drawing out a pile of letters. "Proofs — there's proofs enough here."

"How came you by these letters?"

"Weeks gave them to me to deliver to Miss Lee."

"Ah — and you did not deliver them?"

"No; I kept them."

"Miss Lee, then, never saw these letters?"

"Saw them — humph! no; it'd ill become the daughter of William Talbot to touch the love-letters of such a scare-crow as that;" and her eye pointed to the Yankee as she spoke.

"Hand me these letters," said the captain; "we must see what they look like."

After glancing over the contents of one or two taken at random from the parcel, he turned to Weeks, and requested to know from that gentleman, whether he acknowledged the authorship, and if so, had he any objection to have them read in court.

Weeks hesitated for a moment, at a loss what reply to make. He felt a great temptation to disavow the letters altogether, if he could only do so with impunity; but he feared he could not, and to fail in the attempt would only cover him with greater shame and confusion than ever.

"You have heard the question, Mr. Weeks?"

"What! about writing these letters?"

"Yes!"

"O, I acknowledge the corn right straight off. I guess I hain't got nothing in them to be ashamed of — have I? Well, the hull amount of it is, I sorter liked the girl."

"Just so, sir."

" There's no treason in that, I reckon."

" Certainly not."

" As for the lady been of gentle blood, and all that sorter thing, why, it's right enough, I guess, over here, in this old country of yourn. And so, folks round here may think, perhaps, a Yankee merchant, like me, ain't good enough match for her; but I tell ye what, gents," he continued, rising to his feet, and thrusting his hands down, as usual, deep into his breeches pockets, — " I tell you what, I'm the son of an old revolutionist, and I've got a notion that the descendant of one of these same old heroes is about good enough for any Irish girl ever walked in shoe leather. I may be wrong, gents, but them's my sentiments notwithstanding."

" Witness," resumed the chairman, without appearing to notice this speech; " witness, since the gentleman acknowledges having written these letters and made honorable proposals therein, what can you show us disreputable in his conduct, or that of his cousin, Mr. Hardwrinkle, respecting the overture of marriage ? "

" Wasn't it the act of a mane, designin villain," responded Else, " to try to enthrap a girl of her years into a marriage to save her uncle from beggary or a jail, when he knew her to be the heiress of William Talbot, now livin in the United States ? "

Mary started as the sudden announcement fell upon her ear.

" Hush, hush ! " whispered Kate; " keep quiet for a moment."

" O, my God," she murmured — " what do I hear! my father still living ! "

The light-keeper glanced at the chairman, and then at the witness, as if he feared the old woman's wits were wandering; and the priest, turning to Dr. Henshaw, quietly observed that " things were beginning to assume a new complexion."

" Else Curley, be careful what words you utter here," said

the captain, anxiously looking down at the two young friends, now folded lovingly in each other's arms. " You may have excited hopes, perhaps, which never can be realized. On what authority do you make that assertion ? "

" What, that William Talbot is still livin ? "

" Yes."

" Plenty of authorities : first and foremost, that rosary there in the priest's hand ; then the draggin up of that poor cabin boy under a warrant, for fear he'd tell the secret when he'd recover; and last of all, the condemned look on that dark, dismal countenance there beside ye."

Hardwrinkle raised his head and smiled at the old woman, but it was a smile so ghastly that the spectators felt chilled by its death-like expression.

" Hah ! ye smile," said Else ; " ye smile, and well ye may, for you're the bloodsucker and I'm the victim. Ye hunted me long, and run me down at last. From crag to crag ye hunted me, and from peak to peak ; from the mountain to the glen ye hunted me, and from the glen to the prison. Ay, ye hunted me, and ye famished me, and ye robbed me of my sowl at last. Ah, well ye may smile at the rack and ruin ye've made ; but never mind ; bide yer time, bide yer time ; it's a long lane has no turn. That hellish smile can't last forever. May be yer time is shorter nor ye think for. The hand of God may reach ye yit afore death reaches me. Bide yer time ; wanst I thought I cud niver die till I seen yer corpse at my feet and my heel on its neck ; but Heaven, it seems, or fate, will have it otherways. There's but one bein livin cud save ye from my vengeance, and there she's now," cried the speaker, turning to Mary Lee ; " that very girl there, that spotless child, that ye tried to make the victim of yer cold-blooded villany, has three times saved yer life —— "

" Woman, woman," shouted the chairman, at the top of his voice, after several fruitless attempts to silence her, " woman, stop ! I shall commit you if you don't desist instantly."

"Pshaugh!" exclaimed Else; "what care I for yer committal? Hah, hah! commit me! But go on, go on, captain; put yer questions, and I'll answer them."

"You say this rosary is a proof that Mr. Talbot is still living; how do you explain that?"

"Aisy enough. That rosary is the property of William Talbot, and the boy here must have received or stolen it from its owner when he left Virginia three months ago. Call up Roger O'Shaughnessy; he can identify it."

"Is Roger O'Shaughnessy in court? Witness, you may remain as you are."

"Ahem! yes, please yer honor," responded Roger, rising, and making a profound obeisance to the bench.

"Have you any objection to be sworn in this case?"

"Not the laste in the world, yer honor."

"Clerk, swear him where he stands."

After the usual solemnity of taking the oath, Roger raised his hands, and smoothed down his few remaining white hairs over the collar of his old bottle-green coat, and then looked across at his young mistress, as if to say in as many words, "Don't be afraid, my child, don't be afraid; I'll say nothing to injure the credit of the family."

"Witness," began the chairman, "what is your name?"

"Roger O'Shaughnessy, sir."

"You have been a servant in Mr. Talbot's family — how long?"

"I was forty years steward and butler at Castle ——, the family seat of the Talbots, and my father before me for nearly as many more."

"Clerk, hand him that rosary."

Roger took the precious relic from the clerk's hand, and drawing out his spectacles, deliberately wiped them with his handkerchief, and then slowly adjusted them.

"Well, sir," demanded the chairman, after a long pause, "have you seen that article before?"

"I have, sir, a hundred times."

"In whose possession?"

"In Mr. William Talbot's, and in his father's, Edward Talbot's, of Castle ———."

"Have you ever seen another like it?"

"I have, sir; the fellow of it, in the possession of Edward Talbot's lady, and afterwards in that of her daughter-in-law, Miss Mary Lee's mother, from whose neck it was taken after the wreck of the Saldana, by the witness, Else Curley, and placed on the neck of her fosther child here present."

"Can you swear the rosary you now hold in your hand is not the rosary Miss Lee lost recently, but that which at one time belonged to her father?"

"I swear it."

"How can you swear it, when the two are so much alike?"

"Ahem! ahem!" ejaculated Roger; "they're like one another, to be sure, your honor. But I carried this rosary several times to the jeweller in Cork, with my own hands, to be mended, and can take my oath to the crack here yet under the arm of the crucifix."

"You swear that."

"I do, sir."

"Very well, that's sufficient; and now let me ask another question in connection with the rosary. Do you think, from what you have known of William Talbot's disposition, he would be likely to part with this rosary — give it as a present, for instance, to this boy?"

"Ahem! yer honor," responded Roger, "I didn't think so wanst, any way. I mane the night his father died, when he called Master William to his bedside, and throwin the rosary round his neck, cautioned him never to part with it as long as he lived, for there was a blessin in it, and he'd find it out some time before he died. 'I bequathe it to ye, my son,' siz he, 'as the best legacy I can lave ye. Since the Duchess of Orleans give it to me as an acknowledgment for saving her

life at the Virgin's Chapel at Aix, I niver yet went to sleep
without telling those beads. I hope, my dear boy, you'll follow your old father's example.' Ahem! I was present myself your honor, standin by when that happened, and if I
could judge by Master William's vows and promises that night,
I might safely say, he'd never be likely to part with it
willingly."

"From the Duchess of Orleans, did you say?"

"Ahem! yes, sir," responded Roger. "Her grace gave one
to Mr. Edward Talbot, and the fellow of it to his lady, at
Vairsells, with her own hands. I heerd the old master tell
the story to the lords and ladies many an evening at Castle
——. But, och! sure, yer honor, that's neither here or there,
now; no, no! these old times can never come back again.
Och, och! it's little I thought wanst, when I used to see as
many as seventeen lords and ladies of the best blood in the
land seated in the great dining hall at Castle ——"

"Well, well, Roger, we mustn't talk of these things now,"
interrupted the captain. "You must remember you're on
your oath."

"Ay, ay, true enough; I had almost forgot that. But I'm
ould, yer honor, ye know, and my memory's not just so good
as it used to be."

"It's now nearly twenty years since Mr. William Talbot
was last seen in England — is it not?"

"Ahem! ahem!" ejaculated Roger, pausing for a moment
to recollect himself; "ahem! no, sir, it's not so long as that;
no, it's just eighteen years ago come next Michaelmas since he
fought the duel; we niver seen him more after that night."

"Nor heard of him?"

"No, sir; not a word. Some thought he crossed over to
France, and some thought he went out to America — but no
one could ever tell. For a long time we expected he'd write
home, but no letter ever came; and then we began to think he
heerd of his wife been lost, with the rest of the passengers in

the Saldana, and made up his mind to bury himself in some distant country for the rest of his life."

"Gentlemen," said the chairman, addressing his brethren of the bench, "perhaps you wish to examine the witness further."

No one seemed inclined, however, to interfere; and then he turned to Father Brennan and his learned companion, and observed, somewhat quaintly, that the history of the rosary was a very interesting one, and likely to involve important consequences.

"Important, I trust, for your young friend here," said the priest, in reply. "Her tender devotion to the Mother of God, and her constant practice of saying the rosary, will soon find their reward, I hope, in the discovery of a long-lost parent."

"It's a very curious affair all through."

"Remarkably so; but you know, captain, I often told you how God Almighty makes use of strange means sometimes to accomplish his designs. The discovery of one rosary by the loss of the other, is clearly providential."

"By the Lord Harry, it looks very like it," exclaimed the captain. "To judge from the circumstances, one would suppose Providence had certainly some hand in it. But we must try to get through the business of the court a little faster, or we shall have to stay here all night. Witness," he continued, again resuming the examination, "I have another question to ask before I dismiss you. Can you remember what day it was Miss Lee first missed her rosary?"

"I cannot, sir, exactly; but I think it was on or about the time Mr. Weeks paid his first visit to the lighthouse."

"Yes; *about* that time, you think — you can't swear to the day?"

"No; I can't swear to that — but Miss Lee is here present; ye can ask her."

The captain hesitated a moment — at a loss whether to call on Mary for her testimony in presence of so many spectators, or suffer the circumstance to pass unnoticed, and come to some conclusion respecting the cabin boy without further delay.   His deliberation, however, was suddenly interrupted by the sheriff, who now rose and begged to be permitted to leave with his prisoner as soon as possible — it being late in the afternoon, and the distance to Lifford jail some six hours' travel.

"What's the amount of the debt?" demanded Else, interrupting the captain, who was about to reply to the sheriff. "Mr. Lee shan't leave here the night in your costidy if I can help it.   How much is the debt?"

The sheriff, looking for an instant at the execution, named the sum.

"Humph!" ejaculated Else, running her hand down into her pocket and drawing out her wallet — "humph! the sum's big, but I've enough here to pay it."

"You?"

"Ay, me.   Hah, hah!   Isn't a witch's money as good as a queen's, if it's current?   Mr. Weeks there will tell ye these notes came fresh from the bank; hah, hah!"

"Why, how's this?" demanded the captain; "how did you come by this large amount of money?"

"That's not a fair question, captain, and I'm not bound to answer it; but to plaze ye, I'll tell ye: I got eighty pounds of it from that gentleman there, Mr. Weeks, for sarvices rendered, an the rest here in goold I saved from my husband's earnins. Here, Misther Sheriff, count out yer money, and let the prisoner go."

The sheriff took the bills and gold, and laid them on the table; then counting over the amount marked on the back of the execution, he receipted for the same, and handed the document, with the balance of the money, over to the witness.

While this transaction was passing, the whole audience seemed in commotion; every one expressing his astonishment to his neighbor, that a woman of so infamous a character as the fortune-teller of the Cairn, should thus part with the gold she loved so much to save a comparative stranger from the hands of the law. Even the light-keeper himself was taken completely by surprise, and the magistrates looked at one another, and shook their heads, as if they suspected some mischief at the bottom of it. As the sheriff was about to consign the bills to his pocket-book, a sudden thought seemed to strike him, and drawing out a small bank detector, he laid it before him, and took up one of the notes to examine it.

"Humph!" he ejaculated, after a pause of considerable length; "I might have suspected as much. Witness, let me see that note of hand and execution for a moment — I fear I made a mistake."

"Too late, sheriff," responded the old woman — "too late; but if the fragments 'd be of any use to ye, they're here at my feet."

"Any thing wrong?" inquired the chairman.

"Yes, sir; these notes are counterfeits on the Bank of Dublin."

"Counterfeits!"

"Not a doubt of it, sir. The Dublin Bank, in its last circular, cautions the public against tens and twenties, counterfeits of its new plates; and here," he added, handing the detector and one of the notes up to the bench, "you can see in an instant the plate is a forgery."

The captain examined it for a moment, and then turning to the witness, demanded to know if she could affirm on oath these notes were given her by Mr. Weeks.

"I protest against putting that question to a woman of such disreputable character," cried Hardwrinkle, "and but this moment convicted of an attempt to pass counterfeit money. I object to the question."

Those of the spectators within hearing of this unexpected disclosure, who happened to have had any dealings with Weeks during his short stay in the neighborhood, now began to feel alarmed; and one of them, a dealer in dry goods, who had furnished him with fishing tackle, gaffs, landing nets, &c., stood up and begged to inform the bench he had now in his possession a bank note from Weeks in payment for goods delivered, and prayed the chairman to examine it.

The latter took the paper, and, after looking at it for a moment, pronounced it an impression from the same plate.

"Here's another, plase yer honor," cried a little tailor, who had mounted on the shoulders of his neighbors, and flourished a bill over the heads of the audience; "here's another I got from Mr. Hardwrinkle, and I'm afeerd it's of the same family."

"Send it up."

The tailor's note, like the haberdasher's, proved also to be a counterfeit.

"Clerk," said the captain, "make out a warrant instantly for the arrest of Ephraim C. B. Weeks, in the name of the state, on a charge of having uttered counterfeit money."

"And I," said the light-keeper, "as Mary Lee's guardian, charge Ephraim C. B. Weeks with having stolen that young lady's rosary from my house at Araheera Head."

"Clerk, when you have made out the warrant, take Mr. Lee's deposition.   Witness," he added, motioning to Else Curley, "you have done — you may retire."

"Ay, ay," muttered Else, drawing the hood of her old gray cloak over her head as she turned to leave the witness stand; "I'll retire now, but there's more work to be done yit afore the sun sets.   Let the wrong-doers luck to themselves."

"Stop, woman! for whom is that threat intended?" demanded Hardwrinkle.

"Ask yer own conscience," replied Else, halting on her step, and casting back a look of intense hatred at her persecutor; "ask yer own conscience, if ye have any.   All I say to ye now, Robert Hardwrinkle — luck to yerself, for God will soon call ye to yer reckonin;" and so saying, the old woman slowly descended the steps, and silently took her place

close by the dock where Randall Barry stood patiently awaiting his doom.

The reader, perhaps, may think it strange that such insulting language as Else Curley uttered during her examination should have been permitted in a court of justice; but it
must be remembered that Else bore the reputation of witch
and sorceress, and in that character claimed for herself priv-
ileges and immunities which no ordinary woman would dare
have aspired to. Besides, she was well aware that as long as
Captain Petersham presided in court, she had little reason to
fear Hardwrinkle's resentment. In addition to all this, however, Else Curley was naturally a bold, fearless woman. Her
look, her speech, her very gait proclaimed her such the mo
ment she appeared. Supercilious to her equals, she was as
arrogant in her intercourse with those above her; and very
likely had the judges of assize presided in that court house,
surrounded by all the pomp and circumstance of supreme
judicial power, instead of humble county magistrates, Else's
conduct towards Hardwrinkle would have undergone but
little change.

"Miss Lee," said the chairman, when Else had retired, "I
regret exceedingly to be obliged to call on you for testimony
in this case, or rather, that your uncle's deposition, just made,
requires it. But you will perceive it's a matter of grave
importance, and needs a thorough and patient investigation.
Have the goodness, if you please, to take the witness stand."

As Mary rose and advanced, leaning on Kate's arm, her
whole frame trembled, and her heart seemed to sink within
her at the thought of being exposed and questioned before so
many spectators. In passing the dock where Randall Barry
stood shackled, patiently awaiting his trial, she raised her
handkerchief to her face, under her veil, as if to hide it more
effectually from her lover's gaze, and timidly ascended the
platform.

The moment the audience saw the graceful figure of the young witness, and heard it whispered about she was the light-keeper's daughter, a general rush was made in the direction of the bench. Those in front forced their way along the passages either side the council table, and, despite the threats and efforts of both policemen and magistrates, succeeded in obtaining positions where they could behold the far-famed beauty of Araheera Head.

"Your name is Mary Lee — is it not?" began the captain, after silence was again restored.

"Yes, sir."

"Will the witness have the goodness to remove her veil?" said Hardwrinkle.

Mary trembled as she heard the words, but made no motion to comply with the order.

"I must insist upon it, however painful."

"Miss Lee, I fear you must gratify the gentleman in this little matter," said the captain. "According to the usage of the court, the witness should uncover the face during examination. I had hoped, indeed, Mr. Hardwrinkle, under the painful circumstances of the case, might have waived this point of court etiquette; but I find I have been mistaken."

Mary slowly raised her veil, and, with trembling hands, laid it gently over her shoulder. As she did so, a murmur of admiration broke from the crowd of spectators, like that we sometimes hear at public exhibitions, when the covering is removed from the face of a beautiful statue.

"God bless me! how lovely she is!" exclaimed one of the magistrates, unconscious of what he said, and gazing on her face as if it had been a vision.

And well he might gaze, for never saw he such a form and face before. And yet it was not so much in those features, so perfectly moulded by the plastic hand of Nature, that her beauty lay, as in the angelic blush and unaffected modesty with which her pure soul had so radiantly suffused them.

Dear reader, this lovely girl was a child of Mary — an humble, gentle servant of the Mother of Jesus. And there lay the great secret of her beauty. The perfection of her features nature gave her, but that which defies all the art of the sculptor or the painter — that inexpressible charm which animated them — was the gift of religion.

Looking at this exquisite being, as she stood there before the admiring multitude, her eyes cast down, and her cheeks covered with blushes, one could hardly help thinking of those fine lines of Williams's Sister of Charity : —

> Thy soothing how gentle ! thy pity how tender !
>   Choir-music thy voice is, thy step angel grace,
> And thy union with Deity shrines in a splendor
>   Subdued, but unearthly, thy spiritual face.

"Miss Lee, have the goodness to look at this, and see if you can recognize it," resumed the captain, handing her the rosary.

After a moment's examination, she replied in the negative.

"Any marks by which you can distinguish it from yours?"

"Mine, sir," she replied, "was much more worn than this."

"Ah! from constant use, I suppose," said the captain.

Mary kept her eyes cast down, but said nothing in reply.

"Don't blush, my child, don't blush; you love your religion, and practise it. I wish to Heaven we could all say as much for ourselves. As to the devotion of the rosary, though I'm far from being a Catholic myself, I look upon it as the most beautiful devotion in the world."

"Thank you, captain," said the priest; "thank you for your generous testimony. You'll find," he added, "before very long, there's a charm in the rosary you little suspected. The Immaculate Virgin, whom that spotless creature has so long served with such tender affection, will not suffer her love to go unrequited."

"I don't know, but by the Lord Harry," responded the burly captain, "I'm beginning to think there's *some* mysterious influence at work;" and he hitched his chair a little closer to the desk, as if he felt an increasing interest in the investigation.

"And now, Miss Lee, can you inform the bench when you missed the rosary?"

"On the 12th of —— "

"From what place?"

"From an old family Bible, in which I usually kept it."

"Did you make a thorough search for it?"

"Yes, sir."

"Did you see Mr. Weeks, here present, at the lighthouse on that day?"

"I did, sir."

"Where — in what part of the house?"

"In the parlor."

"Was it in that room you kept the Bible?"

"Yes, sir."

"Did any other person visit the lighthouse on that day?"

"A gentleman called, but did not enter the parlor."

"I have but one more question to ask, Miss Lee. Are you of opinion that some one not a member of your family took or stole the rosary?"

"I am, sir."

"Whom do you suspect?"

"I know of no one who could have taken it but the gentleman I saw in the parlor."

"That's enough, Miss Lee — you may retire," said the captain, leaning back in his chair. "Gentlemen," he continued, addressing his associates, "the testimony of the sick girl, Mr. Hardwrinkle's servant, who found the rosary on the floor of Weeks's room, the morning after his first visit to the lighthouse, and Miss Lee's corroborative evidence, make the case a pretty clear one against Weeks; and as it comes within our jurisdiction, being but a case of petty theft, we must commit him, and send the forgery affair up to a higher court."

"Hold on a minute," exclaimed the Yankee; "you ain't a-goin to commit me, I expect, without hearing me in my own defence?"

"Well, sir, go on," replied the chairman; "proceed, but don't be long about it, for we haven't much time to spare. This trial has taken up too much of our time already."

"Well," said Weeks, gathering in his legs and rising to his feet, "I can't say I know much of English law, though I do think I'm pretty well posted up in law of the States. But, gents, I've got a sorter notion — well, I may be mistaken, ye know — but still, I've got a sorter notion that there's no law to be found in any civilized country in the world to punish a man when he hain't committed no crime. I guess that's a point won't admit of much dispute, any how. Well, let's see now what injustice I have committed. There's Miss Lee to begin with; I hain't stolen her rosary. I took it, I allow — inadvertently put it in my pocket; but I had no intention of stealing it, not a mite. We Yankees ain't a given to hooking, as a general thing; it ain't our nature. We speklate once in a while beyond our capital, and come it over greenhorns now and then in the way of trade, but hooking ain't a Yankee trick, no how, specially such a tid-re-eye consarn as that. I acknowledge I took it, gents, and you may do what you've a mind to about it; but as for hooking the affair, I swonnie I never thought of it from the time I left the lighthouse till cousin Rebecca showed me the darned thing a day or two after, and called me a Papist in disguise for having it in my possession. Now, as to this old lady here, she hain't got nothing to complain of either, that I know of. The hull amount of the matter is, she did nothing for me, and I paid her nothing; ain't that so, gents?   Ha, ha! the old thing thought she was smart — and so she is a darn'd sight smarter than I took her for — but she forgot she had a Yankee to deal with;" and Weeks shut one eye as he spoke, and thrust his hands down into his breeches pockets — "she forgot she'd a Yankee to deal with, a live Yankee, with his eye peeled, and fresh from Connecticut."

Here the magistrates, after commanding silence several times, (for the audience got so tickled at Weeks's language and gestures they could no longer restrain themselves,) at length broke out into a loud laugh, the captain's fat sides shaking as he turned to and fro to say a merry word to the priest or his next neighbor on the bench.

"Silence, you rascals down below there," he cried, when he recovered himself.   "Can't a man speak without a brogue on his tongue, but you must laugh at him?   Silence, and let the man be heard."

"Stand him up, captain, jewel; stand him up on the table — we can't hear him," responded several voices in the crowd.

"Up with him! up with him!" now became the general cry, and Weeks, in the midst of the uproar, mounted the table, and trusting to his own resources to elicit sympathy from the audience, boldly resumed his defence.

"Well," said he, pulling up his shirt collar and pushing back his long sandy hair behind his ears, as he looked round the hall — "well, ladies and gents, I guess I hain't got a great deal more to say.   All of you know pretty much by this time that I'm a stranger in these parts, and I know, on the other hand, you're Irish to a man.   Well, I ain't a-goin to make the inference — no, I leave that to yourselves.   All I shall say is, the Irish at hum and abroad are famous for their hospitality to the stranger."

"Be aisy, avourneen," said somebody near the door; "be aisy now, and don't be tryin to soft soap us that way.   Don't ye remimber the weddin at Ballymagahy?"

"Well, there!" exclaimed Weeks, turning round to look.

"Who's that?" demanded the captain.

"By thunder! if it ain't the tarnal rascal again!"

"Who?"

"Lanty Hanlon, if he's alive."

"Impossible — the police are now in pursuit of him."

"Well, pursuit or not," replied Weeks, "if he's out of limbo, that's he, or I ain't Ephraim C. B. Weeks."

"Police, see who that fellow is," said the captain.

"Lanty Hanlon's the man, and no mistake," repeated Weeks. "I could swear to his voice on the top of Mount Tom."

"Ho there! at the door below! has the detachment from Milfred arrived?" demanded Hardwrinkle.

The answer came up in the affirmative.

"Then let search be made instantly for Lanty Hanlon. You, sergeant, hold a warrant for his arrest — see that he escape not, at your peril."

"What! how's this?" demanded Captain Petersham — "a reënforcement without my knowledge or consent?"

"I apprehended a riot and rescue of the prisoner," replied Hardwrinkle.

"Ha! a rescue!" and the captain turned to look at the young outlaw. "Rescue a man with a broken arm, under charge of constables! What, shackled, too! — good heavens! this is barbarous. Constable, remove those irons — off with them instantly. What! chained like a felon, even before he is found guilty!"

"He's a bold, daring fellow," pleaded Hardwrinkle.

"Psaugh! psaugh! sir, your explanation only makes the matter worse. Your conduct's a disgrace to this bench, sir, and an outrage on the feelings of your brother magistrates."

"Hush, hush! captain," remonstrated the priest, laying his hand on his friend's arm and speaking low. "You must take another time and place to rebuke Mr. Hardwrinkle."

"No, sir, I shall not," replied the indignant captain.   "This is the proper time and place to rebuke him; and I tell him now, here in open court, that his conduct throughout this whole affair has been both unchristian and ungentlemanly."

"Captain Petersham, you know I'm a man of peace," said Hardwrinkle, "or you would hardly dare to utter such language here."

"Dare!" and the captain turned on him such a look as might have withered him up.

"I shall quit the court under protest," said Hardwrinkle, rising, "since neither the law nor the feelings of a gentleman are respected here."

"Not an inch, sir. Move but one step from where you stand, and I commit you."

"What! commit me?"

"Ay, you, sir, for conspiring with your worthy cousin there to carry off by force and violence the person of Mary Lee, in an open boat from Araheera Head to Malinmore, in the event of her not consenting to the marriage. I have now, sir, in my possession due information to that effect, sworn by two of the very men you engaged to execute that damnable design."

"The charge is false," said Hardwrinkle, but in tones so low and husky that the very sounds spoke his guilt.

"And that no time might be lost," pursued the captain, without noticing the denial, — "that no time might be lost, the young lady was to have been carried off this very night, as soon as the sheriff had removed her uncle, and no one left to protect her, in that remote and desolate spot, but her old and feeble servant, Roger O'Shaughnessy."

Here a murmur of indignation ran through the audience, and every eye turned on Hardwrinkle. That gentleman made no reply, however, but after a moment's reflection quietly resumed his seat, as if he had made up his mind to bear his sufferings with the patience and humility of a martyr.

During the interruption, Weeks stood on the table, or plat-form, with his hands driven down into his breeches pockets, and apparently as little concerned at what was passing as if Hardwrinkle had not been "a drop's blood to him in the world." Even when the charge of conspiring to carry off Mary Lee was made against that respectable relation, he hitched up his shoulders, and jingled the silver as usual, but showed no sign of either surprise or resentment. At length, however, silence was restored, and, at a nod from the chair-man, Weeks again pulled up his shirt collar and resumed his defence.

"Well, ladies and gents, I ain't a-goin to detain you long. No; speech-making ain't in my line; but still, you know, every man should be able to tell his own story. Well, as to this darn'd old critter here, half devil, half catamount, I guess I have given a pretty considerable fair account of my trans-action with her — well, enough to show I hain't done her no wrong, any how. Then, as to the dry goods man, let him produce his bill, and if I hain't paid him the full value of his goods already in pure gold, independent of the fifty dollar note, why, I'm ready to suffer the consequences; that's all. I calklate, gents, to give every man his due, but dang a copper more; and if I find a man tryin to impose on me, I manage, some how or other, to pay him off in his own coin. I repeat it, gents, let this dry goods man, who supplied me with fishing tackle and all that sorter thing, let him stand up here and produce his bill. That's plain talk; ain't it, gents? Well, then, all that remains now, is to account for my transaction with Mr. Hardwrinkle here about that note. It goes agin me to do it, it does — that's a fact; but considering the fix I've got into, I feel bound to go through with it. Mr. Hardwrin-kle may feel a little put out about it, I guess, but he's here, you know, on his own soil, while I'm a stranger, and nothing to depend on but the bare truth. Besides, this is about the

31*

last day, I reckon, I can spend conveniently in this section of the country, and for the sake of New England, should like to leave it with a good name."

"And why wudn't ye, *asthore* — by the powers, ye earned it richly," said some one close by, in a stage whisper. "Faith, yer a credit to the country ye came from, *avourneen.*"

"Silence, there," commanded the chairman, hardly able to suppress a laugh; "silence, there, and respect the court."

"Go ahead," cried Weeks, "whoever you be; go ahead; I'll wait till you've got through. I ain't in no hurry."

"Proceed, Mr. Weeks, and don't mind the fellow."

"Well, the hull amount of the matter is, the note cost Mr. Hardwrinkle nothing, not the first brass cent; he got it from a Dublin attorney on commission, to make the most he could on't."

Hardwrinkle here attempted to interrupt him, but the captain interposed, and the speaker continued.

"I ain't surprised at Mr. Hardwrinkle's gettin riled, not a mite, for I swonnie it looks kinder mean in me to talk so after enjoying his hospitality; but I've got into a sorter snarl, gents, you see, about this here marriage concern, and I must tell the truth, for I don't see any other chance of getting out of it. Well, then, to be plain about it, we had an understanding — Mr. Hardwrinkle and I had — well, it was just like this: if we succeeded in getting rid of Lee by means of the note, and could then induce the young lady to marry right straight off, or, if she refused, to carry her off to the nearest place we could catch a vessel bound for the States — I say, if we succeeded in this, Mr. Hardwrinkle was to have ten thousand dollars cash, and I run the risk of the note, succeed or fail."

"Scoundrel!" ejaculated Hardwrinkle, hissing the words between his teeth. "Gentlemen, this is the most outrageous falsehood ——"

" Psaugh! hold on a bit — don't get riled, Cousin Robert."

" But what could I expect, when the fellow's ignorant of the very first principles of religion?"

" Do say! Well, I never made much pretension about it, you know, cousin, and so you couldn't expect much from me in that line; but for you, who's praying and reading the Bible most part the time through the week, and Sabbath especially, why, it was going it a leetle mite too strong to try to do me out that note — worn't it now, Cousin Robert? By crackie, Bob, for a pious, God-fearing man, you're about as smart a one as I've met since I left Connecticut; you are, I swow; no mistake about it. But, gents, I don't see no use now in talking over the matter further. I was a-goin to produce Mr. Hardwrinkle's letters to me before I left the States about this here marriage, to show you I ain't the only one to blame in the transaction; but I guess it's just as well to let the matter drop as it is. As regards the speculation I came here on, why, all can be said about it is, *I failed* — that's the amount of it. The fact is, gents, I always heard the Irish were an almighty green sort of folks, both at hum and abroad, and thought a Yankee, specially a Connecticut Yankee, had nothing to do but go right straight along soon's he got among them; but I find now I made a slight mistake in that respect. It ain't so, gents; the Irish at hum ain't so green by a long chalk as some I've met in Vermont."

" Nor all the Yankees so smart as they think," added the captain, smiling.

" Well, sometimes we get sniggled, you know, like the rest of folks. Well, it's just like this: we hain't got to our full growth yet, but give us fifty years more to get our eye teeth cut, and I tell you what, captain, should like to see the foreigner then could come the blind side of us; that man 'd be a caution, I tell ye. As for Mr. Hardwrinkle here, I don't wonder he's smart, for he belongs to a pretty considerable smart kinder family. Well, he's got a cousin in Ducksville, name of Weeks, said to be about as smart a man as you can scare up in that section of the country ; and still he hain't been a hundred miles from home, I guess, all his life time."

" Brother of yours, I suppose," said the captain.

" Well, no, he ain't."

" I thought, being a Ducksville man, and a cousin of Mr. Hardwrinkle's here, he might be your brother, or cousin, at least."

" No, not exactly ; he's much about the same, though, we've always been so intimate. It was he first told me of his relations here, the Hardwrinkles."

" First told you !   What, did you not know that already? "

" No ; can't say I did."

" Are you not Mr. Hardwrinkle's cousin? "

" Not that I know of."

" Not that you know of ! Why, how's this? Have you not passed for a cousin of Mr. Hardwrinkle's since you came to reside here? "

" Well, yes, pretty much, I guess."

" Pretty much !   Why, sir—— "

" Hold on," said Weeks, " hold on a moment, captain ; I can explain that, too, quite to your satisfaction, I reckon. The Weeks family, then, you must know, and ourn were terrible intimate, being next neighbors for a little more than twenty years — well, the fact is, we got to be so intimate we never made any difference with respect to relationship, or that sorter thing — not a mite."

" Stop ; you don't apprehend the question, I suspect ; I want you, sir, to tell us in plain terms, and briefly as possible, whether you are, or are not, a relative of Mr. Robert Hardwrinkle here present ; " and the captain motioned to the latter gentleman, who, to the infinite merriment of the beholders, kept gazing at the Yankee in undisguised astonishment.

" Well, come to think of it," replied Weeks, as if he had been trying hard to recollect himself, " come to think of it, I guess there is some relationship."

" You guess there is ! "

" Yes, I rather think so — by marriage."

" Mr. Weeks," said Hardwrinkle, " remember you are now in a court of justice."

" Allow me, Mr. Hardwrinkle," interposed the chairman; " I shall finish in a minute or two. Your turn comes next. You say you *guess* there is some relationship by marriage, Mr. Weeks."

" Yes; one of the Weeks married a Bigelow, if I don't greatly mistake, somewhere about the end of the revolutionary war or thereaway. I kinder think Uncle Nathan used to —— "

" Stop, stop, sir ! Confound you and Uncle Nathan. You can't speak a sentence, sir, but you have Uncle Nathan at the head and tail of it. Answer at once, sir; are you or are you not a cousin of Mr. Hardwrinkle's ? "

" Why, as to blood relationship, I guess there ain't much of that to speak of. But still it amounts to pretty much the same thing in the end. The Weeks and Bigelows were always in and out, you know, like one family. And then young Ephraim and I — or Eph, as we used to call him 'bout the doors — went to school together for eight or ten years, and never kept a secret from one another more than if we had been twin brothers."

" Well, by the Lord Harry," cried the captain, turning to his associates, " if this ain't the coolest fellow I've met in my day ! And so," he continued, looking at the imperturbable Yankee, " it turns out at last there's no relationship at all between you ! "

" No, guess not, except by marriage. Still, it's much about the same thing. The Weeks have always been as intimate with us as cousins could be. Well, in fact we were cousins in every thing but the near blood."

" Ha, ha ! " laughed the captain; " this is capital, eh ! Not only outwitted your friend here by passing counterfeit bills, but passed yourself off, too, as his American cousin, eating and drinking of the best in his house.   Ha, ha! by George, that beats Bannaher."—Here the audience, at length fully comprehending how matters stood, broke out into a general laugh, in the midst of which a curly-headed fellow, mounting on a window-sill, waved his hat and shouted at the top of his voice, "More power to ye, Weeks, more power to ye, *Ma bonchal.*"

"'Pon my conscience, captain, jewel, it's chaired he ought to be, instid of sint to jail," cried another.

The chairman now rose to command silence in the court, but was met with cheers for Weeks and groans for Hardwrinkle. "Hurrah for the bowld Yankee—down with the black sarpint."

"Order! police, keep order there below! Silence, you vagabonds, silence!" cried the captain; "this is pretty conduct in a court of justice."

"Send him out till we chair him, captain, send him out; he desarves it for puttin the ' Leek ' in Black Robert."

The police, after several efforts, at length succeeded in restoring silence, and the chairman was about to take up the charge against Randall Barry, when Weeks, who still coolly maintained his position in front of the bench, his hands, as usual, driven down into his pockets, begged leave to say a word or two before he left.

"I shan't keep you long," he said ; "no, a word or two is all I've got to say.   I came to this country, gents, as most of you know by this time, on a matrimonial speculation.   Well, I failed — I did — no mistake about that.   Now, then, gents, all I ask in return for my loss of time and money — not to speak of several mishaps in trying to put the thing through — is simply this: that you won't let the darned affair get into the newspapers.   I'm a Yankee, gents, a full-blooded Yankee, of the old Puritan stock, and should hate, of all things, to have it known that a New Englander — and a Connecticut man at that — could be taken in by the Irish.   I swonnie,

I'd rather put for Texas right straight off, than return to the States, and find it published all over the country; I would by a long chalk. Why, I should ever after be looked on as a disgrace to Yankee land. So, as I said before, I'm willing to put up with the hull of it if you only promise me this tarnal trial shan't get into the newspapers."

"Cool again," said the captain; "put up with it indeed! Any thing more to say?"

"No, I've got through, I guess."

"Very well, sir. Constable, take this man in charge."

"Hold on a minute," cried Weeks.

"Take him away."

"See here! Hold on! Hain't you made a mistake? What's the crime?"

"Passing counterfeit notes on the National Bank."

"But who's cheated, I should like to know?"

"Away with him," commanded the captain.

"Look here!"

"Silence, sir, and quit the stand instantly."

"Well, now, I swonnie, if this ain't going it a leetle *too* strong," muttered Weeks, as he stepped from the platform, in the hands of the constable. "I ain't gone to the county house yet, though! No, I sorter reckon not. By crackie, captain, you'd better look out, for I tell you what, my dear fellow, you'll find it no joking matter to incarcerate a citizen of the United States —— " The remainder of the sentence was lost in the murmurs of applause which greeted him from the audience.

And now the captain was about to call the witnesses in the case against Randall Barry, when the cabin boy rose, and, in feeble accents, begged to have the negro liberated.

"It can't be," replied the captain. "You or he must first acknowledge on what plantation you lived in Virginia, and from whom you got this rosary, found on your person."

"There's no longer cause for keeping the secret," said the boy, "as Mr. Bigelow is committed for forgery."

"Bigelow!   Soh, ho! then his real name is Bigelow."

"Yes; he was always called Bigelow on the plantation."

"Did you know him there?"

"He did so," exclaimed Weeks, again making his appearance before the bench, "he did so; no mistake about that; many a good lickin I gave him. I'll give you the whole history ———"

"Gag that fellow, constable, gag the rascal," cried the captain; "nothing else will stop his tongue."

"Hold on a minute."

"Silence, sir, and sit down."

"See here, captain; don't get put out with me. Natty there's sick, and I want to save him the trouble of talking. Besides, I should like to have the credit of telling the hull story myself.   Well, the amount of the matter is, the boy and the negro both belong to Mr. Talbot's plantation, in Virginia, and ran away. I was sent after them to hunt them up, and, as if all h— had a hand in it, here they come to this here place of all other spots in creation, to blow the hull secret."

"Heaven, you should have said, sir," observed the captain.

"Heaven or h—; call it what you've a mind to; but that tarnal, danged rosary has discovered all."

"Yes, sir; Heaven has made use of your villany to requite the very person you would have made its victim for her piety and devotion to the Mother of God. Your scoundrelism, and that of your associate here, have, under the direction of Providence, resulted in the restoration of a loving child to the arms of a long-lost parent. Miss Lee, I congratulate you most sincerely on the happy issue of this trial, and pray God you may live long—as you have lived ever since I had the happiness of knowing you — the pride and ornament of your sex."

" God bless her! God bless the dear girl!" now resounded from all parts of the court house, while the lovely object of congratulation was herself shedding tears of gratitude to the mother of orphans in the arms of Kate Petersham.

"And now to the prisoner in the dock — who demands his committal?" inquired the captain.

"I do," responded Hardwrinkle; "I demand it in the name of the state. Clerk, call Sergeant Joseph Muller. Swear him."

As the latter came up to the stand, Hardwrinkle pointed to the prisoner. "Have you seen that man before?"

"I have, sir."

"What is his name?"

"Randall Joseph Barry."

"Do you swear that?" said the captain.

"I do."

"What! did you see him baptized?"

"No; but I was brought up within a stone's throw of his father's house."

"Gentlemen," said the prisoner, interrupting the witness, "it's quite unnecessary to proceed further in this examination. My name is Randall Joseph Barry; I am a rebel to the British government, and the same individual for whose capture the reward of three hundred pounds is now offered by the crown. I have no defence to make, and I ask no favors. Proceed, if it so please you, to make out my committal."

"Fool!" ejaculated Else Curley.

"Young man, the court does not expect you to make admissions likely to criminate yourself," said the chairman, casting a reproachful look at the prisoner.

"He has avowed himself a rebel," said Hardwrinkle; "he is therefore unbailable, and now I demand he be committed forthwith to Lifford jail."

"Have you any thing to say in your vindication," said the captain; "if you have, we shall hear you patiently."

"Nothing," promptly responded the young outlaw. "I have deliberately done that which British law declares to be a crime, and am now willing to suffer the consequences. Had I effected my escape to a foreign land, as was my purpose," (and whilst he uttered the words, his eyes involuntarily turned

32

in the direction of Mary Lee, the sole cause of his detention,)
" had I effected my escape, I should have been *there* no less an
enemy and a rebel to the British government than I am here
on my native soil, nor cease for one single day of my life to
compass its overthrow."

" Lost! lost!" exclaimed some one under the bench, in
tones so heart-rending that every eye turned in the direction
of the voice. It was poor Mary Lee — she had fainted in
the arms of Kate Petersham.

At a single bound the prisoner cleared the dock, and stood
beside her breathless form, as it reclined against that of her
affectionate companion.

Instantly the uproar and confusion became so great that
Hardwrinkle rose and commanded the police to advance and
arrest the prisoner.

" Back!" cried Randall; his dark eye flashing under the
excitement of the scene — " back, slaves; I have no intention
to escape;" and he waved his hand at the police, as they
rushed forward to secure him.

" Forward, fellows! What stops you, when I give the
order?" repeated Hardwrinkle.

" Hold!" said Captain Petersham. " Not an inch further.
I command here.   Constables, keep your places."

" Mary," whispered Randall, stooping over her — " one
word — speak to me but one word, and then we part."

" Part!" murmured the gentle girl, opening her eyes, and
looking lovingly into his; "O Randall! Randall! has it
come to this?"

" Hush, dear Mary; hush!" whispered Kate; "it may all
be well yet — hush — you have a friend coming you little
dreamed of."

" Good by, Mary; good by! We shall never meet again,"
said Randall, his face quivering with emotion, as he uttered
the words. "You have at length found a father, who will
love and protect you as I would have done."

"O, stay! do not leave me," said Mary; "the queen will pardon you. She is so good. O, no, no; you shall not leave me — never."

"It cannot be," said Randall — "my doom is the gallows — for pardon I shall never ask."

"Back with ye! back with ye! hell hounds, give way," now came ringing out in tones as clear as a trumpet, from a stout, curly-headed fellow, at the head of some dozen others, cleaving their way through the crowd, and smashing heads and bayonets with their blackthorns in their stormy passage. "Give way, ye dogs, give way. To the rescue — *corp au dhoul*, to the rescue."

"By the Lord Harry," exclaimed the captain, jumping to his feet, "there comes Lanty Hanlon. I vow to Heaven it is. Well done, my gallant fellow, well done!"

"O Lanty, you never failed me yet," said Kate, proudly. "My life on you for a million."

"Now comes the tug o' war," said the captain, whispering to the priest.

"Police, do your duty," cried Hardwrinkle; his face no longer wearing its demure aspect, but fired with passion at the danger of losing his victim, after whose blood he had thirsted so long. "Do your duty! I command you."

For a moment the outlaw looked round the court, as if to calculate his chances of escape — in the next, he was driven forward in the centre of a group towards the door.

"Shoot them down!" vociferated Hardwrinkle, gesticulating furiously — "shoot down the rebel and his rescuers."

"Hold! hold!" commanded the chairman, in a voice of thunder. "The first man that fires dies; he's not yet committed — hold your fire."

By this time Lanty and his men had gained the side of the dock where Else Curley stood, her arms folded as usual, and her keen, deep-sunken eye fixed on Hardwrinkle. As they did, the whole detachment of police rushed from the door,

despite the captain's orders, and charged the rioters with fixed
bayonets.

"Surrender the prisoner, or we fire," cried the lieutenant.
"I order you to surrender, in the queen's name, instantly."

"Cudn't ye wait till th' morrow?" said Lanty, sneeringly.

"I again command you to surrender the prisoner," repeated
the officer.

But hardly had the words escaped his lips when a blow
from behind felled him to the ground, and then the riot commenced in good earnest.

"Down with the Sassenach dogs!" shouted Lanty, making
his staff play round him in true Celtic fashion. "Down with
them — *corp au dhoul* — drive them before ye."

Else Curley, at this moment, by some chance or other,
succeeded in forcing her way in amongst the combatants, and
thrusting the silver-mounted pistol she carried into Randall's
breast, drew forth, herself, the old Spanish dagger, which the
reader saw once before at her cabin on the Cairn, and waved
it in her brown skeleton hand high over the heads of the
rioters. "Come on!" she cried; "the young lion is now with
his dam, and see who'll dar injure a hair of his head. Come
on! let the enemy of my house and home come on, and see
how soon this good steel 'll drink his heart's blood. Away
with him to the door, there, and balk the tiger of his prey —
away with him, my hearties!"

Hardwrinkle now jumped from the bench, and calling on
the police to stab the prisoner and his rescuers, forced his way
also in amongst the rioters, his eyes flashing fire and his face
flushed with intense passion. At this moment Randall Barry,
after breaking bayonet after bayonet with the pistol which he
held still undischarged in his hand, turned to defend himself
from those in the rear, and met Hardwrinkle face to face.

"Rebel!" cried the latter, snatching a carabine from the
next constable — "rebel, traitor, enemy of your religion and
your country, take now the punishment you deserve;" and as

he spoke he attempted to pull the trigger, but his hands trembled so in the fury of his passion that he missed the spring. Next instant Else Curley's long bony fingers had grasped him by the throat, and he fell backwards on the flags of the court house, the musket exploding as it reached the floor.

Lanty and his comrades had now fought their way bravely on, step by step, Randall defending himself with his single arm against the repeated assaults of the constables, and still reserving his fire, as if for a last emergency.   It soon came.

They had succeeded, indeed, in driving the police before them out through the court house door; but here the danger and difficulty increased, from the fact that once beyond the threshold, Captain Petersham's authority ceased, as presiding magistrate, and Hardwrinkle was at liberty to give what orders he pleased, if he only assumed the responsibility. How he extricated himself from the hands of Else Curley 'twould be impossible to say ; but certain it is, that, much to the surprise of the beholders, he was suddenly seen jumping from a window of the building down on the low wall enclosing the yard, like one demented.

" Fire ! " he cried, as he alighted and glanced at the preparations made for Barry's escape — his quick eye detecting in an instant the reason of Moll Pitcher being kept there standing at the gate.   " Fire ! " he repeated ; " on your lives let not the prisoner escape — fire ! "

But he had come too late : Randall had already gained the outside of the yard, borne on by his trusty defenders, foremost amongst whom fought Lanty, his head and arms bleeding profusely from bayonet wounds, whilst Randall's own were hardly in a better condition.

Hardwrinkle saw there was but one chance remaining, namely, to intercept the fugitive and detain him till the police could come up and arrest him ; and making all possible speed to where his horse stood in the hands of his groom, he mounted and dashed past the gate in order to head the prisoner off.

32 *

Randall, however, was already in the saddle. He had sprung to it by the strength of his single arm, and instantly gathering up the reins, gave Moll the word. The splendid creature, knowing well that something more than usual was expected of her, reared for an instant, and then shot forward like an arrow, making the fire fly from the pavement.

"Glorious!" cried Lanty; "now for it! If horseflesh can save ye, Randall Barry, it's Moll Pitcher."

"Shoot him down! shoot him down!" vociferated Hardwrinkle, as he rode on before the fugitive with the intention of wheeling round and intercepting him in his flight.

The words were hardly spoken, when three or four shots came in quick succession. They did no mischief, however, — one of them slightly grazing Barry's cheek, while the others went wide of their mark.

The crowd now rushed through the gate and over the wall in wild confusion; some throwing stones at the police, and others venting curses loud and deep against Hardwrinkle and his *Sassenach* crew.

Randall saw, as Hardwrinkle wheeled his horse to intercept him, that if he happened to be detained but a second, he should, in all probability, fall by a bullet from the police, before he could get out of musket range, and so, drawing the pistol from his breast, he let the reins drop on his horse's neck, and prepared himself for the worst. He had hardly done so when Hardwrinkle was up within ten yards of him. "Keep off! keep off!" cried Randall, " or I fire."

But his antagonist took no notice of the warning, and as he rushed on in the blindness of his fury, Randall dropped the muzzle of his pistol, and shot his horse through the head. "There, take your life," he cried; "I shall never have a dastard's blood on *my* hands."

The horse dropped instantly, the ball passing through his brain.

And then rose a cheer wild and loud, that made the very

heavens ring again, as Randall was seen flying up the hill on Moll Pitcher, clear of all danger, his long black hair floating on the breeze, and his broken arm still visible in the sling.

Whilst the crowd stood cheering and gazing after the young outlaw, Else Curley, followed by several of the constables, hurried to the spot where Hardwrinkle had fallen. Else was first on the ground. "Hah!" she cried, as if about to utter some malediction, but suddenly stopped, and bent down to gaze on the face of the fallen man.

"What's the matter? — is he hurt?" demanded the constables.

"Ay, he's hurt," responded Else, dryly.

"He don't move — how's that?"

"He's dead!"

"The horse, you mean."

"Horse and rider — they're both dead."

———————•———————

CHAPTER XXIX.

Weeks escapes in the Riot. — Is pursued by a Constable. — Climbs over a Wall, leaving his Coat-tail behind him in the Constable's Hands, and finally disappears. — Else takes her Leave, and retires to Benraven Mountain, there to pass the Remainder of her Life. — Lanty Hanlon, in the Dress of an old Woman, winds up the Story. — Postscript, which is Characteristic of the Author of the Preface, terminates the Story in manner similar to that in which it began.

ON examination, it was found that the unfortunate man had carried a small dirk or stiletto in the breast pocket of his coat, which, having been displaced by the fall, was driven by the crushing weight of the horse fairly through his heart —

the animal dropping so suddenly as to leave him no time to extricate his feet from the stirrups.

Captain Petersham and his friends, on hearing the melancholy intelligence, hastened to the scene of the disaster, and there found the body stretched on the road, and surrounded by a gaping and wondering crowd.

"Dead?" inquired the captain.

"Yes, your honor," replied a policeman, touching his cap; "he's dead — this dagger passed straight through his heart; I drew it out this moment."

"Shocking!" exclaimed the priest, stooping and laying his hand on the forehead of the corpse; "most shocking! Gone to meet his God without a moment's preparation."

"And in the very flush of his guilt," added the captain, gazing at the dead body. "The victim of his own inveterate prejudices and his love of gold, for I'm very much inclined to think the fear of losing his share of the reward had more to do in driving him to this last act of desperation than his hatred of the young man. Hand me the dagger. Kate, you and Mary had better leave here at once," he continued, turning to his sister; "we shall call for you at Greenmount."

"And bring Father Brennan with you," said Kate; "don't forget that."

"No — but look you here, madcap; take care not to present Mary suddenly to Mr. Guirkie, as he may lose his senses altogether; be prudent."

As the captain took the dagger in his hand to examine it, Roger O'Shaughnessy, who was standing by, touched him on the arm, and whispered in his ear, "That's Else Curley's, yer honor."

"This dagger!"

"Yes, sir."

"Else Curley's! — you must make a mistake, Roger."

"No, sir, that's her old Spanish dagger. I'd know it amongst a thousand."

"But how could it come into Mr. Hardwrinkle's possession?"

"Ahem! I don't know that, yer honor; unless, whin he was strugglin with her on the floor of the court house, he might have wrested it from her hands."

"That accounts for it, then," said the priest. "I saw Else waving a dagger after the riot commenced."

"Humph! then he died by his enemy's weapon, though not by his enemy's hand — curious enough, eh!"

"Yes; and I'm very happy to think the poor old woman, after her long thirty years of deadly enmity to the unfortunate man, is still guiltless of his death."

"She's a desperate woman, Father Brennan — desperate."

"True, she was always of a wild, ungovernable temper; but yet not half so bad as she seemed. Her care and love of Mary Lee, the once houseless and homeless orphan, and her fidelity to Randall Barry, in requital for his uncle's kindness at the siege of Madeira, are enough to redeem worse women than Else Curley."

"But where is she?" inquired the captain, looking round.

"Where is she, indeed! — now that I think of it."

"There she is," replied some one in the crowd. "There, beyont, yer honor, settin on that stone, by the ditch, with the ould goat beside her."

As the captain, followed by the priest and Dr. Henshaw, approached the old woman, she seemed absorbed in deep thought; her head bent, and her folded arms resting on her knees.

"Else!" said the captain, touching her shoulder, to make her aware of his presence. "Else Curley!"

"Humph!" ejaculated the old woman, looking up slowly. "What's the matter?"

"Come — you must go with us to Castle Gregory."

"For what?"

"We want to see you there."

" Who wants to see me — you ? "

" All of us.   Mary Lee, in particular, before she leaves. Besides, I should like to make some better provision for your old days, than the cabin on the Cairn affords."

" No, no," said Else, rising and folding her gray cloak round her emaciated shoulders, — " no — I'll go to see my foster-child afore she leaves Fanid; but I'll niver quit the cabin till my bones are carried up to be laid with my sister's, in Mass-mount churchyard.   And that won't be long, either; for now, since the one I loved best has found a father, and him I hated most a grave, I have nothing in this world to live for.   In regard to the ould cabin, it's but a dissolit spot to look at, captain, but it's all the world to me.   I lived in it so long, and ivry rock and blade of heather about it got so familiar to my eyes, that if ye put me in a palace, I'd steal back to it again."

" But, Else, remember you're old," remonstrated the cap-tain, " and will need some one to take care of you."

" Ay, ay, take care of me ! " she said, with a melancholy smile.   " Care 'd kill me afore my time, captain, I'm so un-used to it.   No, no; as I lived alone, I'll die alone."

" But what of your soul, Else ? " said the priest.

" Ah ! " she replied, " the weight that lay upon it for thirty years is at last removed — and now I begin to feel life in it again."

" Thank God, you're guiltless of the death by which that heavy load was removed, at all events."

" Amen," said Else; " amen.   Three times did Mary Lee stand atween him and my vengeance, and now, for the fourth, the thought of her kneelin to me at the lighthouse with tears in her eyes, to persuade me against his murder, held back my hand as I raised it to plunge the dagger in his heart.   But he's dead now, and so is my anger — fare ye well ! fare ye well ! " and the old solitary turned her steps in the direction of Araheera Head, followed closely by her faithful companion, bleating and trotting after her, to her mountain home.

"There she goes, poor old soul," said the captain, gazing after her, and leaning his hand on the priest's shoulder as he spoke; "I fear her death, like her life, will be miserable."

"No, no; don't fear," said the priest; "I'll take care of her."

"God bless you! and for her temporal comfort I'll look to that myself."

"Humph! I see you begin to take an interest in the old woman."

"Why not? who could help it, after those proofs of fidelity and attachment to Mary Lee?"

"O, poor Else! the creature's as true as steel. You saw how she clung by Randall Barry, too, and protected him even at the imminent hazard of her life. But, by the by, where is Lanty all this time — eh?"

"Lanty! O, never mind him; he'll take care of himself."

"The police may have got hold of him — the unfortunate fellow!"

"Of Lanty Hanlon! — no, sir; there's but little danger of that. He'll turn up somewhere, depend on it, before the week's out. Come, we must follow the ladies to Greenmount, and see how Uncle Jerry behaves after his discovery of Mary Lee."

"He'll go crazy, I fear, when he sees her."

"Shouldn't wonder in the least. I told Kate, however, to prepare him for the meeting. But come — I have already given directions for the removal of the body;" and the speaker, taking Father John's arm, turned towards Greenmount, leaving Dr. Henshaw and the light-keeper to follow after.

They had gone but a short distance, however, when they overtook a woman in a blue cloak and ruffled cap, (both looking rather worse for the wear,) and to judge from the stoop of her shoulders and a distressing cough, evidently very old and sickly.

"Hilloa!" cried the captain, in a bantering tone, as he passed her. "What the mischief brings such an old hag as you here among blood and bullets?"

"Me!" replied the crone. "Ugh, hugh, captain, dear, it's no wondher ye say it, for this cough's killing me. I'm — ugh!—ugh!—I'm racked to death's doore with it!"

"Then why didn't you stay at home?"

"Ay, ay, dear; true enough, captain; but—ugh, ugh— it's an ould sayin, and a true one—The ould fool's the greatest of all fools."

"Did you see Lanty Hanlon any where about here, lately?" inquired the priest.

"Is it me—ugh! ugh!"

"Ay, you," repeated the captain, half provoked at the delay.

"Ugh, ugh! O dear, I can't spake a word with this terrible cough; and captain, dear, it's always wuss about sunset."

"Confound you and your cough together! Come, Father John, let us hasten on to Greenmount."

"If it's Lanty Hanlon ye mane," said the old woman, at last, "I didn't see him since ye seen him yourself, captain;" and the speaker uttered a sort of low chuckle, as if she saw something amusing in the inquiry.

"What's the matter, now, old dame? what do you laugh at?"

"To hear ye inquirin for Lanty Hanlon;" and the speaker's voice changed all of a sudden.

"What! hilloa! whom have we got here, eh!" and the captain drew back the hood of her cloak. "Lanty himself! by George, it is! Why, you unfortunate vagabond, don't you ——"

"Whist, whist! the constable's beside ye, there. Don't mintion my name for yer life. Remimber the warrint ye sent afther me for taking the loan of Miss Hardwrinkle."

"I do—and I tell you now, Lanty, what you may rest assured of."

" Well, sir ? "

" That you'll be hung if you stay here — you will, sir. By the Lord Harry you will."

" Me ! "

" Ay, you, sir ! "

" Hung ! "

" Yes, sir ; hung by the neck."

" That rope's not made yit, captain, dear. No, no, my pride niver carried me that high."

" Quit the country, sir ; quit the country — that's my advice to you — and quit it immediately, too, for I can save you no longer."

" Cudn't ye hould out for another year, captain ? "

" No, sir ; nor for another week, either. Are you not aware that the abduction of Miss Hardwrinkle is a transportable offence ? But why another year, pray ? "

" Well, there's a sort of a sacret in that," responded Lanty, wiping the blood from his face.

" And what's the secret ? "

" Why, then, it isn't much to spake of, captain, only in regard of a bit of a girl up here, that I had a kind of a notion of, and she tells me she's not just to say ready, yit."

" Ho, ho ! that's it — well, never mind, I'll make her ready.   Who is she ? "

" A girl of the Kellys of Minadreen, sir."

" A daughter of one of my tenants — very well ; send her up to Castle Gregory to-morrow or next day — I'll give her her outfit. Send her up, and prepare yourself to leave, for you're not safe here an hour."

" Captain," said a policeman, touching his cap, " Lanty Hanlon, I fear, has escaped."

" What ? fled ! "

" Yes, sir. We have searched every where, and can't find him."

" Shouldn't doubt it, sir, in the least," replied the captain.

33

" By the Lord Harry, sir, you should — every man of you — be drummed out for a set of poltroons. Ten constables; and couldn't make a single arrest! I shall see to it, sir. You have the Yankee still in custody, I trust."

" No, sir; he has escaped also."

" Escaped!"

" Yes, sir; he jumped the wall, and fled in the confusion of the moment."

" And could nobody catch him, sir?"

" Not on foot, sir, for he ran like a greyhound, his long hair floating back on the breeze. I pursued him myself for nearly a mile, but found it was of no use, and gave it up as a bad job. Once I thought I had him, as he scrambled up a stone fence. I seized him by his coat tail, but he left the tail behind him, and disappeared."

" So that's all that remains of him," said the captain, looking at the piece of gray broadcloth in the policeman's hand.

" That's all, sir," replied the constable, holding up the skirt for inspection.

" Well, it's of no consequence; let him go. He has seen enough of Ireland, I suspect, Father Brennan, without visiting our jails — eh? don't you think so?"

" He's not the only one," said Dr. Henshaw, coming up behind, " has seen enough of Ireland. My own expaireance of the country is vary short, but I think I've seen plenty to know it's rather a hard place for strangers who are fond of their comforts."

" You must matriculate, doctor," said Father John, good-humoredly."

" Matriculate!"

" Certainly. And after that you'll feel quite at home."

" Humph!" ejaculated the doctor. " My matriculation then — as you call it — is ended, for I leave to-morrow."

" To-morrow!" repeated the captain; " nonsense! By the Lord Harry, my dear fellow, you'll do no such thing."

"To-morrow, sir, at daybreak; you may rest assured of it."

"What! and Mary Lee to be married to-night, and Uncle Jerry to dance at the wedding! you mustn't think of it."

"I've made up my mind, captain."

"But Kate—you know Kate has an apology to make about that quarrel you've had. She'll never forgive you if you don't come with us to Castle Gregory."

"No, sir, I've been once at Castle Gregory, and that I think is quite enough for me. I thank you, captain, however, for your proffered hospeetality."

"But, my dear sir," urged the captain, "I should feel very sorry to have you leave with bad impressions of the country."

"Humph!" said the doctor, in reply, "I'm vary much inclined to think, if I remained longer, they would grow worse."

"Worse!"

"Ay, sir, worse. Here's abduction, robbery, forgery, riot, and murder, all in a single week. Good Heavens! Sir, there's not such another country on the face of the globe, and what makes its condition the more deplorable is, that its religion is no longer able to redeem it."

"Its religion!" said the priest.

"Yes, sir; there's not even the ghost of your old Katholeecity remaining. No, sir; what's left is but syllabub and water gruel."

"I'm sorry you think so."

"And so am I too, sir. But so it is—between your deeviltry and your Katholeecity, I have had enough of Ireland. Good by, gentlemen, good by!" and the doctor, having taken his leave of the party, thrust his thumbs into the armholes of his waistcoat, and wended his way slowly to the village inn.

POSTSCRIPT.

DEAR READER: We have carried you through a long, and perhaps, in the main, a weary, tedious narration. At length, however, it has come to a close, and such as it is, you have it; or, to borrow the words of Lord Byron, —

> What is writ is writ;
> Would it were worthier! but I am not now
> What I have been — and my visions flit
> Less palpably before me — and the glow
> Which in my spirit dwelt is fluttering, faint, and low.

—

SECOND POSTSCRIPT.

THE above is the story of MARY LEE, as it came into our hands.

Mr. Pinkie, it seems, had not finished it when he left Ireland, and was never afterwards able, on account of the rheumatism, to finish it here. We suppose this must have been the way of it. Whether he actually intended to make the end of Childe Harold the end of Mary Lee also, it's of course now very difficult to tell — though, indeed, for ourselves, we must confess we have a strong inclination to think in the affirmative, especially as, being brought up together, we remember well many personal proofs of his short and snappy disposition. But be that as it may, 'tis evident the tale wants another joint; and so, being appointed his legatee, we have considered it no more than our duty to make up for the deficiency the best way we can. With that end in view, we wrote to a faithful correspondent at Rosnakill for information respecting the fate of some of the principal actors in the drama, and the following is the result: —

"In reply to your favor of recent date, I have the pleasure to acquaint you with the following facts. They have been obtained after very considerable trouble and inquiry, and therefore I shall expect you to put them to my credit in the old account.

"First, then, it seems the meeting between Mr. Guirkie and Mary Lee was very affecting — so much so, indeed, that the captain, stout-hearted as he is, after rubbing up his grizzly hair two or three times in quick succession, and plucking down his waistcoat as many more, was finally obliged to turn his face to the window and whistle against the glass. Uncle Jerry's joy knew no bounds; he sat her on his knee, and smoothed down her hair, and looked up in her face, and wept, and vowed she was the very picture of her that was gone. Mrs. Motherly, poor woman, is said to have entered the parlor just at that time with her master's leggings, to button them on, but seeing what she did see, turned short on her step, and drawing the door after her with a bang, quit the house instantly, and was never heard of since. For the last fact I cannot vouch exactly, my own impression being that she did return once more, and even had a pension granted her by Mr. Guirkie for her faithful and matronly services.

"As you are already aware, the captain entertained the party that night at Castle Gregory, and, so far as I can learn, a merry night they had of it. Mary Lee and Randall Barry were married, of course, by the good Father Brennan; and Uncle Jerry, curious enough, is reported to have given away the bride. It is further asserted, and on excellent authority, too, that the same gentleman, after slipping a check on the Bank of Londonderry for two thousand pounds into Mary's hand as a marriage portion, instantly called on Kate to play the 'Sailor's Hornpipe,' and danced with his hands on his sides till he fell back on the sofa, and there actually went to sleep from sheer exhaustion.

"Ten days after the wedding, the captain's yacht was seen

weighing anchor at Ballymastocker, and slowly moving up to the landing place under the castle. Presently a party of ladies and gentlemen issued from the vestibule of the old mansion, and crossing the lawn, descended the bank of the rabbit warren, and stepped aboard. The party consisted of the captain and Kate, Randall and Mrs. Barry, Mr. Lee, Mr. Guirkie, and Father Brennan. After a few minutes' absence, the latter came ashore, and waving his hat in adieu, the little Water Hen moved off gently from the wharf. She had not cleared it a cable's length, however, when a brown water spaniel, followed by a tall old gray-haired man, in a long-skirted coat, was seen running down to the beach. The old man kept waving his hand as he hobbled along; but the dog, who had reached the shore before him, sprang into the water and made for the little vessel, howling most piteously as he buffeted the waves. The yacht hove to for a moment, the dog was lifted aboard, and then the old man, apparently satisfied with what had taken place, fell on his knees, and, with uplifted hands, seemed to pray fervently for a happy voyage.

"Next day the Water Hen returned, but none of the party was seen to step ashore but Kate and the captain. Where the others went to, no one here can tell. It is generally surmised, however, that the United States was their destination, and that Lanty Hanlon and his winsome wife, Mary Kelly of the black hair, went out with them, having been snugly ensconced under the Water Hen's hatches before she weighed anchor on the evening of her departure from Castle Gregory.

"Roger O'Shaughnessy, now too infirm to venture on so long a voyage, remains at the castle at his old occupation. Once or twice a week he burnishes up the old silver salver as usual, and tells how often it has served wine to the lords and ladies at Castle Talbot.

"And Kate Petersham too — I mustn't forget her. She is now, I am happy to tell you, a fervent Catholic, devoted to her religion, and a model of piety to the whole parish. But you must not conclude from all this, that she has changed in other respects. Not at all. She practises her religion faithfully at the altar and in the closet; but beyond this, she is the same reckless, light-hearted being she ever was, and ready at any moment to cruise in the Water Hen, or ride a steeple chase on Moll Pitcher, with the best blood in the county. She has been trying hard to bring the captain over to the church too, people say. But I'm afraid she'll hardly succeed —at least for the present. Indeed, the captain said as much to myself, swearing at the same time he liked the religion well enough, but by his Lord Harry, he never could get over the confession. 'I offered to compromise the matter,' he added, 'but Father John wouldn't listen to it. He insisted on the confession as a necessary condition, and I insisted, on the other side, to have that clause left out. So there rests the whole difficulty.'

"With respect to Ephraim C. B. Weeks, he made his way to Rathmelton bareheaded, and with the remaining skirt of his coat tucked under, to give it the appearance of a jacket. Once more only was he seen, and then at the Liverpool packet office in Derry. A friend of mine, who happened to be present at the time, assures me he did nothing but curse Ireland and all the darned Irish in it, from the time he entered the office till he left it. He swore you couldn't find such 'a tarnation set of varmints in all almighty creation,' and when he 'got t'other side the big pond, if he wornt a-goin to give them "jessie" in the newspapers.' And so, lighting a cigar," added my friend, "he took up his valise and umbrella, and started furiously for the New York packet.

THE END.

www.ingramcontent.com/pod-product-compliance
Lightning Source LLC
Chambersburg PA
CBHW032159110726
47902CB00003B/762